DAMN IT
WAKE ME UP

E. G. LANDER

This is a work of fiction. Names, characters, places, and incidents are products of the author's imagination or are used fictitiously and are not to be construed as real. Any resemblance to actual events, locations, organizations, or person, living or dead, is entirely coincidental.

World Castle Publishing, LLC
Pensacola, Florida
Copyright © E. G. Lander 2015
Print ISBN: 9781629892306
eBook ISBN: 9781629892313
First Edition World Castle Publishing, LLC April 15, 2015
http://www.worldcastlepublishing.com

Cover: Karen Fuller
Editor: Maxine Bringenberg

Table of Contents

DEDICATION

This modest work is dedicated to two incredibly special people, my wife and my daughter. My wife Nancy made no secret about the love and patience she had for her often overbearing and thoughtless husband. Every day she displayed a total concern for me, no matter how much I didn't always return that truly remarkable loyalty. It is amazing how much she encouraged my efforts to tell stories, while that telling often taking so much time away from her. God must be very happy she is with Him. She must light up His heaven like few have ever done. She was incredible. I miss her so. Every minute of every day.

To our daughter Jennifer Marie, who left us in her thirty-first year, taking her wonderfully sparkling blue eyes and unmatchable smile to heaven, along with a heart so big it mocks the generosity of anyone I have ever known. She taught us that the most important things in life are not what we have, but how much we share. Nothing demonstrated that more than her efforts to proof my simple writings, as she lay in her hospital bed, dying.

My tears for both of these angels could fill an ocean.

Acknowledgements

To my amazing wife Nancy, who taught me to believe first, then to question. Her loyalty and beautiful patience was always incredible. She was the world's best listener, even to all my ramblings. How could any woman be so perfect? I praise God for letting me have her in my life for so long. I miss her every second. Every second. Every second.

To my precious daughter, little Jenny, who took so much of my wife's and my heart to heaven with her. Her fire and spice, mixed with a softness and an incredible compassion, showed all of us an unbelievable source of unlimited love. Much of her fire is in Mary Calley. No one could ever match her tenderness and her kindness. We will always miss Jenny. ALWAYS!!

To my son Chris, who has brought me back to reality on so many occasions. He was a nice contrast to his sister, allowing us to enjoy a colorful mixture in life. He, too, looks forward to seeing Jenny again one day, in a very special place. I admire his toughness while his heart is broken.

To my wonderful grandchildren. Mattie and Mary remind me of the beauty of a family and the little joys in life. I am the guardian of the other two—Connor and Kaylee. Connor is a little boy with a man's mind and love. I wish everyone I know could know Connor. He is a special, special friend who helps keep me in the right lane on life's sometimes awful highway. Kaylee shows me every day that love can overcome anything-anything. Those two are really the "sails on my sinking life raft".

To my siblings who were there during the darkest, most painful hours. Their love for me was more than just a family duty, it was from their hearts. They hurt with me.

To the great people at Willowbrook Elementary School in Oak Ridge, Tennessee, who helped me through the lowest times in my life. People like Karen Aldridge, Rebecca Mullins, Betty McKinney, and Jo Bruce. You all are special to your school, your kids and to me!

To Anthony Gunderson, who helped so much in his little spare time to proofread this story.

Chapter 1
What's With Connor?

Tony Calley trotted down the stairs, spotting Mary in the kitchen. "Sorry baby, but I don't have time for breakfast. I've got a meeting with Ron and Chester at seven-thirty." He finished the knot on his necktie and folded his shirt collar down as he glanced at himself in the hallway mirror. "Just a glass of juice is fine. I'll grab a donut at the office."

Mary turned aside, away from the stove, drying her hands on a red and white dish towel. She opened the refrigerator, grabbed a carton of Mickey Mouse orange juice, poured it into his insulated cup, then opened the cabinet door over the sink, moving a few prescriptions aside until she found his vitamins. After knocking the bottle on her hand, she took the one pill that decided to come out and handed it to him along with the juice. "Here, take this. What are you worried about, anyway? You're the boss; you run the biggest investment business in Rymont, probably the biggest one in all of Tennessee. So what if you're five minutes late? Who cares?"

He took the pill and drank the juice with one gulp, wiping his lips with a shirt sleeve, then grabbed his suit coat off a chair next to the kitchen table. "No, not the biggest firm in Tennessee, at least not yet, but I bet you we'll take over the number one spot in the whole Nashville area real soon, baby." He shook his head. "Hey Mary, I couldn't get Connor up. What's with that boy, anyway?"

"I have no idea. He used to be so excited about going to school, now he acts like he hates it. I wish I knew what was going on. Oh, don't forget, I've got that appointment with his principal this morning. Maybe he can tell us why Connor's rebelling all of a sudden."

Tony put his empty cup in the sink then leaned on the edge of the counter, looking out the kitchen window. "Maybe he's just not getting enough sleep. He didn't stay up late again last night, did he?"

Mary walked over to her husband, putting her hand on his back. "I don't think so. I know he was still working on his computer after you went to bed. But when I walked by his room about ten, his computer was off and his lights were out."

Tony turned around, putting a hand on each of her cheeks. He kissed her on the ear, then on the lips. "How about calling me when you get done at Connor's school?"

Mary wrapped her arms around him, feeling the back of his shirt hanging out. She pushed the rest of his shirt tail into his pants and patted his rear end. "You went to bed so early last night we didn't have time for any fun, Tony. How about me using up that rain check tonight?"

"Sure, baby, you've got a date." He looked at the time on the microwave. "I really got to go; I'll see you tonight." He kissed her as he was moving and went out the back door.

She smiled, thinking about Tony. He was a beautiful man with wide muscular shoulders fitting perfectly into his six-foot-two frame. Everything about him was what a woman would call a "hunk," from his baby blue eyes to that wonderfully soft looking dark brown hair. She smiled again as she heard him pull away. The smile didn't last long as she walked up the stairs to her son's room. "Okay, Connor, it's time to get up. The third grade is waiting for you," she said, looking at her watch. "Now, don't give me any grief. You've got to clean up your room, get dressed, and have some breakfast, all within twenty minutes." She pulled the blanket off of his head and he still didn't move; then she noticed a paperback book on his bedside table entitled The Incredible Bucky Berrot. She picked it up, scanning the first few pages. "Pretty heavy reading for a nine-year-old," she whispered as she put it back on his table. "Come on, Connor, let's go. You can't miss any more school; let's hit it, young man."

Connor rolled over, turning away from his mother. "Oh, Mom, I don't want to go to school. Why can't I just stay home? I hate school. Why can't you give me a ten minute extension, please?"

She pulled the covers down, lying next to him. "Hey, you already got an extra twenty minutes because I'm taking you in this morning. At least you don't have to ride the bus." She started rubbing his eyebrows. He brushed his forehead like a fly was bothering him. "Time to get up, my sweet Connor. We don't want to be late, do we?"

"Okay, okay. I can't wait until Saturday so I can sleep in," he said, sitting on the side of his bed, rubbing his eyes, purposely not looking at his mother.

Mary got up, walked back into her bedroom, and noticed her husband's BlackBerry on his bedside table. "Oh, my God, he'll go nuts when he finds out he left it." She picked up the bedroom phone and dialed his cell number.

"Hey, what's up, Mary?"

"You left your BlackBerry. I found it in the bedroom."

"I'm almost at the office. I can't come home now, my meeting can't wait. Do you think you can bring it over?"

"Sure, after I get done at Connor's school. The only problem is I don't have any idea how long that will take. His teacher didn't tell me, she just said the principal wanted to see me this morning."

"Hold on, I got a cramp in my... damn it, I hate these Charley horses."

"Tony, pull over. You can't drive in pain."

"It's okay, it went away. Don't forget my BlackBerry...oh shit, here comes another one. Son of a bitch...bye. Call me."

Mary hung up, leaning back on the bed with her arms spread apart. She looked out the window, thinking about Tony. She still loved him even with their problems, especially his gambling habit. But she was developing that "wife sense" about him. Either there was another woman or he was going nuts betting again. It was different and was starting to eat away at her. No, he couldn't be cheating after nine years of a wild sexy marriage. It had to be the money. She'd been noticing the credit card bills...not that he was over-using them, but now he was only paying them the minimum. Something was wrong. She knew it. That "sense" was shouting at her.

Ten minutes later Connor joined his mother in the kitchen. He was carrying his backpack, then dropped it on the floor next to the chair he plopped into. "Why do you make me go to school every day? It's not fair. I'm ahead of all the other kids and they get to miss school once in a while."

Mary sat next to her son and watched him pour milk on his cereal. "Connor, why don't you like school anymore? You used to love it. What's happening?"

"I just hate it, Mom. The only thing I like about it is Mrs. Howard. She makes it fun. If they were all like her, I'd still love school. She makes me think about the world outside her class. All my other classes are boring and easy."

"Well, at least you've got Joelle Howard to look forward to every day, huh?"

"Yeah, but she's only one hour out of the whole day, Mom."

She shook her head, putting a hand on Connor's head as she stood up. "I wasn't going to tell you, but I've got an appointment to see her this morning, along with your principal."

He stopped drinking his fruit juice and turned towards his mother. "What? Did I do something wrong?"

"Oh no. I just want to see how you're doing, that's all. Now you just finish your breakfast and we'll go." She took a minute to look into the mirror before she left. Her long black hair wasn't perfect, but it was okay. She really liked her new dark red lipstick; it brought out the sparkle in her green eyes. She still liked seeing the few freckles she had left; they made her feel younger. "Not bad for a thirty-year-old," she whispered, knowing no one was listening as she bounced a few hairs with her hands. Fifteen minutes later, they got into her Mustang and rode to his school without talking. She was worrying about what the principal and his teacher wanted, and Connor was wondering what he might have done wrong.

When they pulled in to Lindenbrook Elementary's entrance, Mary looked for a parking space in the main lot by the front door. There wasn't one. As they went by the main entrance, Connor asked her to drop him off. It was embarrassing for a nine year old to walk into school with his mom. She backed up so he could get out. He threw his backpack over his shoulder, slammed the car door, and walked into the school, still bothered that she was there.

Mary drove around the parking lot one more time. There was still no place to park, so she drove down the hill to the secondary parking area, which used to be an outside basketball playground, finally finding a spot between two buses. Grabbing her purse, she started to walk up the hill. Less than thirty feet from her car she twisted an ankle, breaking the heel off her left shoe. She cursed silently and took off her other shoe, carrying both of them up to the school. When she finally got to the front door of the school, Mary walked in, watching a mob of little people going in all directions. A few of the munchkins stared at her as she was barefoot, holding her shoes. She found the office and pulled on the heavy door, wondering why it was so hard to open. "Must be it's that way to keep the kids out," she mumbled.

Suzie Harriman, the school's longtime secretary, was going through some papers in a tall black filing cabinet next to her desk when she saw the shoeless Mary walk in. Suzie always had that special smile, with almost a teasing look. She had a slight New England accent, always intermingling words like "yeah" or "eh" in her sentences. She was probably the most efficient and well-liked woman working at the school. She was very popular amongst the male teachers, with her dark shimmering hair and beaming eyes. She turned and noticed Mary. "Do you need any help, Mrs. Calley?"

"No, I'm okay. I just need to sit down for a minute, that's all." She found a soft-looking red cushioned chair near the long desk in front of

Suzie. "I sure hope this shit is worth it, that's all I got to say," she muttered at half-volume.

"Excuse me, did you say something?" Suzie asked.

"That was just me talking to myself. That hill of yours about wore me out. I had to park at the bottom of the hill, then a heel came off my shoe, and now I'm tired. I've got to catch my breath for a minute."

"I'm sorry about that…I've had to park down there a few times. You're right, that's not a fun walk up here from that parking lot."

"I'm just glad it wasn't a gravel road, that's all, Suzie." She took a deep breath to compose herself. "I've got an appointment with Mr. Jinks. Would you see if he's ready for me?"

The secretary walked into the principal's office, then returned less than a minute later. "You can go in now, Mrs. Calley," Suzie said, opening Jinks's door.

Mary walked into his office. Stacks of papers were everywhere. The wall over his desk was loaded with three rows of plaques, lined up so unevenly, one would think a drunk had put them up. The room smelled like old clothes mixed with body odor.

Joelle Howard, Connor's teacher, was sitting in a chair to the left of the big brown desk that took over the room. She was a very young teacher with shoulder length blonde hair surrounding a cute face loaded with freckles.

Jinks stood up, giving Mary his usual sickening smile. He was about fifty, with jet black hair sticking out from each side of his head, combed over in an obvious attempt to disguise his bald top, dye and all. He had the ugliest brown mole, which was surrounded by long black hairs, on his neck. Every time he saw Mary, he tried to flirt with her. Today he was wearing what looked like a new suit, although his pants were two or three sizes too small, leaving his gut hanging out. If he was trying to look his best for her, his best was still very weak.

"Well hello, Mrs. Calley…or can I call you Mary?"

Mary shook his hand, feeling its cold sweat. It reminded her of touching a gutted fish at the grocery store. "Sure, Mary's fine, Mr. Jinks. It's nice to see you again."

Jinks motioned for Mary to sit down in front of his desk on an old wooden chair, so worn it was amazing anyone could sit on it without breaking it.

The principal sat behind his desk, smiling at Mary. "You know Miss Howard, I assume?" (With an emphasis on Miss, like he was delighted she wasn't married).

Mary looked at Connor's teacher, nodding.

15

Jinks smiled at Mary again, this time showing the holes where two side teeth used to be. "So, Mary, what happened? I see you're carrying your shoes?"

"I broke a heel coming up the hill. There weren't any parking spots open up here near the front entrance in your tiny parking lot, so I had to park down in the fenced-in area. When I started walking up a heel broke off, so I had no choice but to carry both of my shoes."

"You could have called Suzie and I would have been happy to come get you. My car is always up here," Jinks said with a wink.

"That's okay; I can use the exercise, anyway. So, tell me, Mr. Jinks, why did you want to see me? Connor's not in any trouble, is he?"

Miss Howard giggled. "No, not at all. Connor's probably the sharpest student I've ever had. We just want to talk to you a little bit about how he's doing, that's all."

Jinks opened a file that was sitting by itself on his desk. "Mary, Miss Howard is right. Connor is exceptional. I'm sure you've heard from each one of his teachers that he's like a sponge, soaking up everything they throw at him."

"Yeah, they say that, but why do you want to see me? I know he's a smart boy," Mary said, wiggling in her chair.

"Well Mary, Miss Howard and I are concerned about Connor. His learning ability and IQ are in the genius category, but we think he's getting bored because the subject material is just too easy for him. He needs a challenge, so here's what we propose to do; we would like to move him into the fourth grade immediately, with him taking advanced classes there, too."

"Wow," Mary chuckled. "I thought you wanted to see me because either Connor did something wrong or because someone's been bullying him. I had no idea you would want to do this. I didn't think kids skipped grades anymore."

The principal leaned forward, getting closer to Mary. "Oh yeah, we still do that, but it's rare. But I think this is a case where it's justified. I mean, we've got a bright kid wasting time in the third grade."

"You said advanced classes. Won't that be like going from third to fifth grade? I mean, taking advanced classes in the fourth grade?" Mary asked, looking at Jinks, then Miss Howard.

"I guess you could say that, but he'd still officially be in the fourth grade," Jinks said as he looked down at Connor's file.

"What about the other kids? Connor's not real big now…he'd be so much smaller than the fourth graders. Don't you think, Mr. Jinks?"

"I don't think that's such a big deal," he answered. "If he would have been born four months earlier, he'd be the fourth grade anyway. Now, we

16

can't do this without your blessing, so why don't you sleep on it? Talk to your husband and talk to Connor—he's smart enough to understand—then please get back to me tomorrow if you can. Do you have any questions?"

"I can't think of any…you kind of blew me away."

"Well if you do, here's my card," Jinks responded. "I even wrote my cell number and my home number on the back if you need them." He gave her a big grin, showing his teeth holes again. "Oh, Miss Howard has something for you, don't you Miss Howard?"

The teacher held up a big green book. "Mrs. Calley, this is the fourth grade advanced history book. Why don't you let Connor look at it? I'm confident it won't be over his head. In fact, I bet he'll get excited once he starts glancing through it."

Mary got up, grabbing the book. "I'll give you a ring tomorrow, Mr. Jinks." She turned towards Connor's teacher, shaking her hand, and couldn't resist temptation. "And it was nice seeing you again, Miss Howard."

Jinks stood up, giving Mary a small wink. "Do you need a ride down to your car?"

"No thanks, I'd rather walk. It's got to be a lot easier going down than it was coming up. Besides, it's such a beautiful day, and it'll give me some time to think about everything. Thanks, anyway." She shook his hand and left his office.

Mary called Tony's cell phone the second she got outside. There was no answer, so she punched in the office number.

"Burns and Calley investments. This is Michelle Archdale, how can I help you?"

"Michelle, is my husband busy?"

"Well hello, Mrs. Calley. Your husband is in a meeting. Do you want me to ring him in the conference room?"

"If you don't mind; I need to talk to him."

"Sure, hold on and I'll connect you." Mary waited a few seconds, then her husband picked up. "Hey Mary, what's up? Is everything okay?"

"Tony, can you talk?"

"I sure can. We're just shooting the bull waiting for some faxes to come in, so what's going on?"

Mary got to her car and unlocked it. "Tony, I met with Connor's teacher and his principal. They said he's bored and needs a new challenge because he's so much smarter than the rest of the kids in his class. They want him to go into fourth grade next week…I mean, with advanced classes, too. I told them I had to talk to you." She sat in the Mustang, grabbing the bottle of water between the seats in order to a throw down a couple of Tylenol capsules.

"I didn't think they did that anymore."

"That's exactly what I asked Jinks. He said it still happens sometimes. Tony, maybe they're right. Maybe he'd like school again if he wasn't so bored with it. I got a copy of the history book he'd get. I really think he can handle it."

"Mary, let's do this; let's just think on it today. We can talk about it more tonight. I have to run, Ron's bringing in the faxes. We're working on a big deal. Oh, are you bringing me my BlackBerry?"

"I sure am. I'll be there in about fifteen minutes. I'll leave it with Michelle. Bye."

CHAPTER 2
A Prize For Connor

Mary stopped by the house to grab some different shoes on her way to her husband's office. She couldn't go into that grand building barefooted. She was so proud of the red and white bricked office that gave her a kick every time she pulled into the parking lot, looking up to see the big gold sign over the door that read Burns and Calley.

She pulled open the thick glass front door, heading towards her husband's private suite, just as Michelle came out of the restroom. Michelle had been Tony's secretary for over eight years, and had become an icon in the office, training all the new girls and keeping everyone on track. She had also become part of the Calley family since her husband died two months earlier. Michelle took it hard, having been married to Bob for over thirty years. Now she was alone, so the Calleys had kind of adopted her. Michelle was a very small woman. She could pass for anyone's perfect grandma, with her tiny wire-rimmed glasses on the tip of her nose and her golden hair always tucked back in a little bun. She wore a sweater every day, even in the heat of the summer, and that sweater always had to have a tiny fresh flower pinned to it.

Mary smiled as she closed the front door behind her. "Michelle, how are you doing? Is Tony treating you okay?"

"Good morning, Mrs. Calley," Michelle answered from behind her desk. "Yes, he's treating me just fine…he's always nice to me." She turned to the side and sneezed. "Excuse me."

"God bless you, Michelle. So tell me, how are those grandkids of yours doing up in Louisville?"

They both looked at the little photos pinned to the small tan bulletin board on the wall behind her. "Oh, I miss them so much I can hardly stand it. Little Mattie and Kaylee mean everything to me, especially with Bob being gone. It's so hard being away from them, they're so special. You know, I only get up to see them about every three to four months. My son keeps offering to fly me up there, but it just costs too much. Besides, it's just awful saying goodbye to them when I have to come home."

Mary sat on the green and white striped chair next to Michelle's desk. "I bet you're right…leaving those babies has to be tough. I always heard that grandkids are special; some people say they're better than your own kids."

"You'll find out one day, Mrs. Calley…it's just different. You keep hearing jokes about how great it is having grandkids because you can send them home whenever you want. Well, that's just B. S. I'd like to be with both of my grandbabies every day." A tear was forming in her right eye. "Now listen to me run my mouth. You're here to see your husband, I bet. He's in a meeting, but I can get him if you want."

"No, that's okay. I just wanted him to get his BlackBerry. You know how men are! He forgot it this morning. Would you make sure he gets it right away?" She pulled the little device out of her purse, laying it on Michelle's desk as she stood up.

"I sure will. He ought to be done with his meeting before long. I'll give it to him the minute he comes out."

Mary bent over and kissed Michelle on the cheek. "You're a doll, you know that? I'll see you later." She turned, walking towards the front door.

"Goodbye, Mrs. Calley," Michelle said, in a soft, sad voice.

"That was a little strange, that goodbye," Mary said as she opened the car door.

****

That afternoon Tony got home from work early. He walked into the kitchen, finding Mary reading the fourth grade history book at the kitchen table. After picking up a banana from the wooden fruit bowl at the center of the table, he started to peel it as he sat down next to her. "So, my little princess is back in school nowadays?"

"No, I was just glancing at the history book Connor's teacher gave me. It doesn't seem that hard to me. I'll bet Connor won't have any trouble with it." She continued flipping pages, then closed it, sliding it over to Tony.

He opened the textbook to a chapter about the Great Depression. Tony lowered his eyebrows and wiped his lips with his right hand. "I don't know, Mary, there's some big words in here…but maybe that's good. This whole deal might be exactly what Connor needs. Where is he anyway?"

"He's upstairs on his computer. He did his homework in about five minutes, then he told me he was going to play some computer games. I think Hunter's coming over."

Tony glanced at the stairs. "So, when do you want to talk to Connor about what Jinks said?"

"Let's tell him after dinner that the school thinks he needs more of a challenge, and this is what they came up with. How does that sound, Tony?"

"That sounds good to me." He twisted his neck, rubbing the back of his head. "Man, I'm really tired tonight. It was a strange day."

"Why do you say that?"

"Well, I've got some good news and some bad news. The good news is that I think we got that big account today. It will mean thousands coming in real soon. The bad news is that I've got to find a new secretary."

"What? I just saw Michelle this morning when I brought you your BlackBerry. She didn't say anything to me about quitting. You didn't fire her?"

"Oh no…she wants to move in with her son up in Louisville. Honey, she needs to be with her family, especially those grandkids. I didn't try to talk her out of it. I feel so sorry for her." He finished the banana, throwing the peel into the waste can in the corner.

Mary bit down on her lower lip. "I wonder why she didn't say anything to me about all that?" She shook her head. "Do you know, when I left your office she said goodbye to me in a weird way. I guess she really did mean goodbye."

He nodded. "Michelle told me the times she is the happiest and she doesn't think about her husband's death is when she is holding her grandbabies. I really think moving up there will make her happy."

"Tony, she's been with you so long; what are you going to do about replacing her?"

He lowered his head, almost touching his chest. "Well, she gave me two weeks' notice. That should be enough time to find someone good. She called one of those placement companies, and I've already got six girls to interview tomorrow. That's a start."

Mary put a hand on his arm. "Honey, I've got an idea. How about if I try to help you for a while? I'd love to help you. I don't eat much and I'll try not to get in the way." She shook her head. "Why did I say that? I think I saw it in a movie somewhere…I think maybe it was The Wizard of Oz. Why that came to me, I don't know. But really, what if I get a quick course from Michelle and fill in some?"

Tony chuckled, giving her a faint smirk. "Nah, we'll have someone in training in a day or two. It sure would be nice to have you around, but I don't think I'd be able to concentrate with you there. I'd want to close my office door and love on you. No, we'll get a new girl this week." He stood up, bent over, and kissed her on her cheek, almost like he was kissing his sister. "Now, I'm going to check out Connor. Connor, where are you, son?" Tony hollered, walking up the stairs.

"Up here, Dad, on my computer."

Tony walked into his son's room and sat down on the edge of his bed. "Hey, Bud, how are you doing? How was school today?"

Connor raised his shoulders. "Oh, the same as yesterday, and the day before that. Every day's the same. No big deal."

"Well, that's not good. Maybe you'll get into some new subjects you like before the school year ends and make it more fun; who knows? So, what are you doing on the computer?" He leaned over Connor's shoulder, looking at a chess game going on.

"Just playing chess against the computer. My record is eleven wins in a row. If I win this one, it'll be twelve. And it doesn't look good for the computer right now. He just lost his queen. Do you want to play?"

"Maybe after dinner. Right now I've got to get changed and get something to eat...I'm starving." He patted Connor on the shoulder, heading out the door to his bedroom.

****

Before dinner, Mary told Connor she had a prize for him and she would give it to him after he ate everything on his plate, including his carrots. After he finished emptying his plate, he asked for his reward. She reached behind her, grabbing the history book off a shelf on the china hutch. "What's this, Mom? My prize is a school book?" He glanced at a few pages. "I thought you said I'd get a prize. A book is not a real prize, not like a new toy or video game...that's a real prize."

"That book is a special prize, better than any toy. It's a fourth grade history book. Your dad and I were wondering if you might want to go into the fourth grade. Your teacher said you could handle it. Even your principal said it was the best thing for you."

Connor thought for a second. "I think that would be cool. First off, Hunter's in the fourth grade and he's my best friend. And you know what else that means? It means I can get into college one year sooner. That would be sooo great!"

Tony stood up, taking his dishes to the sink. "Connor, it's not going to be as easy as you think. You'll be going into a new class, with new teachers and new books, and you've got your Christmas break in what, four weeks? You'll have to really push yourself to catch up with your other classmates by then."

"I'm not worried about that, Dad. I think it will be fun trying to see how long it takes for me to pass everyone else in my class. That part sounds neat. And guess what? I'm glad I ate my carrots tonight. So, when does it start?"

Mary got up, rubbing Connor's red hair on the way to the refrigerator. "It looks like it may happen Monday. Mr. Jinks said I need to let him know something tomorrow, and if we're okay with it, he'll move you into the fourth grade right away."

Connor started reading his new book after dinner. By the time Mary came in to tuck him in, he had read about a fourth of it. She reached over and pulled the textbook out of his hand. "You need to go to sleep now, honey. Besides, if you get to go into the fourth grade, it won't be until at least next week, not tomorrow."

"I know, Mom, I'm just anxious."

"Good night, son." She reached across him to turn off his lamp, then kissed him on the forehead.

CHAPTER 3
The Interviews

Tony woke up the next morning to the sounds of his nine year old son singing in the shower. That hadn't happened in months; maybe their plan was going to work after all. He glanced at his little black alarm clock on the bedside table and saw that it was just a little after six, so he rolled over, putting a pillow over his head. Mary walked over to his side of the bed and pulled the pillow away. She was naked. He couldn't believe how great she looked. Her body was as beautiful as the first time he'd seen it in high school. She was incredible, as usual. It just wasn't the same, after nine years. He liked sex with her, but it had lost some of the excitement.

She bent over, kissing him on his ear. "It's time to use up that rain check," she whispered.

"What about Connor? He's up."

"I locked our door; he won't bother us. Now scoot over; let's have some fun, Tony."

They finished in less than thirty minutes. Tony struggled to get up after his bride wore him out. He forced himself to move, knowing he had a full day of interviews planned. He shaved and showered as fast as he could, then ran downstairs, dressing as he went.

Mary was in the kitchen, stirring something in a big silver pan. She looked very fresh, wearing a pink jogging suit with a white apron. Her incredible dark black hair was laying neatly on her shoulders and down her back. When she heard him come into the kitchen, she turned and smiled. "Good morning, Tony. How about some breakfast?"

Tony shook his head. "Nothing for me. Oh, maybe just some coffee. I'm a little late getting started this morning, if you know what I mean."

She looked at him with a sly smile. "That's okay, baby, I'm a little behind schedule, too. Sometimes it's fun not getting up too fast, huh?"

He walked over and kissed her just as Connor walked in.

"Oh, gross," the little boy said. "That's gross."

Tony grabbed his coffee, rubbed his son's head as he went by, and headed out the back door to get to his car. "See you later, Connor. I love you, Mary. Bye."

****

Fifteen minutes later Tony pulled into the office parking lot, noticing Michelle's car along with a car he didn't recognize. He walked in and found his secretary filling the coffee pot. "Good morning, Miss Archdale; how are you this morning?"

"I'm doing fine. How about you, Mr. Calley?"

"I've already had a pretty good day. So, tell me, when do we start the interviews?"

"I've got them lined up from nine to three, Mr. Calley. Each interview is an hour max, and I saved an hour for your lunch. Here's a list of the girls coming in, with their appointment times." She handed him a typed schedule. "Oh, Mr. Calley, I cancelled all your appointments for today. I just told everyone you were sick."

He put his back up against the door frame, scratching himself. "I'm going to miss you, Michelle. You sure know how to take care of me. Say, did you tell the other secretaries what was going on?"

"I sure did. I was really surprised how nice everyone was about it. Rudi Gall started to cry. I'm going to miss how wonderful she is…she cares so much about all of us, like a family. Rudi always brings sunshine into the office with her sweet little smile and those cute glasses. Melanie Baer was kind of broken up. She's like a sister to me. Even Beckie Knott seemed disappointed I was leaving. She's been so kind to me. They all seem to like me a lot."

"I'm not surprised; everyone's going to miss you. Now, it looks like I've got about twenty minutes before you send the first one in."

"You can start early if you want. The first girl is already here. Her name is Trudy Cole. How soon do you want to see her?"

He grabbed a donut out of the Dunkin Donuts box on her desk. "Give me five minutes, then bring her in." He walked towards his office, then turned back. "And, don't forget to tell whoever we hire about bringing in donuts every morning." Tony went into his office, put his suit coat in the closet, and cleared all the papers off his desk. After opening up his laptop, he noticed he still had some white donut sugar on his pants, so he brushed it off just as Michelle knocked on his door.

"Yeah, come on in."

Michelle walked in, followed by Trudy, who looked very nervous. He motioned for her to sit in the chair in front of the desk, and they talked for almost the full hour. Trudy was about thirty with short red hair and a very friendly smile. He was impressed with how professional she was. She seemed like the perfect fit until he noticed she was pregnant. Then he quickly ended the interview, telling her he'd get back to her if she was selected.

The next two girls Michelle brought in didn't impress Tony at all. They certainly didn't measure up to Trudy.

He looked at his watch. It was after eleven. Now he had an hour and a half break before the next applicant, so he called Mary.

"Hey, sweetheart, have you talked to the school yet?"

"I got off the phone with Mr. Jinks about an hour ago. I told him it was fine with us. It's all set up for Connor to go into the fourth grade Monday. Jinks said he'll have Miss Howard bring over the papers we've got to sign and some books for Connor after school tonight. To tell you the truth, I'm glad it's her bringing the stuff and not Jinks...he gives me the creeps. I feel like wearing a sign that says 'I'm married' every time I see him."

"You might as well face it, Mary, men are naturally attracted to you. You're a ten."

"Yeah, right. I don't feel like a ten if I'm attracting losers like Jinks...hold on, there's someone at the door. I wonder who that is. Are you still there, Tony? I'm talking as I'm walking. Hey, come on in."

"Don't tell me that's Jinks?"

"Funny. No, it's Bobbie. I'll call you back in a little bit; bye."

****

Bobbie walked right by Mary, heading towards the kitchen. Bobbie was Mary's best friend, other than Tony. She only lived three houses down, so she was also a great babysitter. She was about ten years older than Mary, but she looked like she might be her mother. Bobbie was twice Mary's size, and always wore giant moo moos loaded with big yellow and red flowers or colorful animals. Mary thought she must think they made her look skinnier. Her hair was always stringy and dirty-looking. If Mary was a ten, then Bobbie was a two.

When Mary got to the kitchen, Bobbie was already sitting at the table, sobbing, her head on her arms.

"Bobbie, what's wrong. Did anything happen? Don't tell me it's one of the kids."

The big woman lifted her head up, showing streaming tears heading down her freckled face. "No, Mary, it's not the kids. No one died. But I might as well be dead. Jerry left me. I found his note after I got home from the store." She started crying again, letting out loud sobs. She carried on for a few minutes, then blew her nose, stopping long enough for Mary to talk.

"I'm so sorry, Bobbie. What'd his note say?"

"It said he was sick of me and he wanted someone to love he could be proud of. He even said he didn't want to see me or the kids again, that he wanted to start his life over. Mary, we've been married over fifteen years. I don't look like a model like you do, I know that. But I think I've always been a good wife and a good mother. Why would he leave me? Why?"

Mary's cell phone rang, giving her a break from listening to Bobbie moan about how much she loved Jerry and how her world was crushed.

"Mary, I've got a big break from my interviews so I'm taking Michelle to lunch; do you want to join us? We're going over to Bitellios…Michelle loves Italian. Do you think you can meet us there in about twenty minutes?"

"I'm sorry, honey, but Bobbie's got some major problems. She needs me right now."

"Oh, okay. Listen, Michelle's ready to go. It's okay, we'll have a chance to take her to lunch or dinner before she goes. Hey, give me a call after Bobbie goes home. It sounds to me like you've got your hands full. I'd like to hear about it. Bye."

Chapter 4

She's the One

Tony and Michelle drove to Bitellios, with most of the conversation centering on her grandbabies. She was so excited about her upcoming move to Louisville and all the things she was going to do with both of her granddaughters, as well as with the other grandmother up there. It was strange how it all worked out. Betty McKinney was one of Michelle's best friends in high school and college, and their kids married each other. And oh, how Michelle loved Betty. She used to say that Betty was "an angel from heaven, sent here for her kids and her friends." They were like sisters, sisters anyone would love to call "family." They talked and laughed about all their years together until they had to head back for his interviews. When they got to the office, they were told the next girl was waiting in the lounge to talk to Mr. Calley. He told Michelle to give him five minutes, then bring her in. After he put the papers from the earlier interviews into his bottom desk drawer, Michelle walked in, followed by the most incredibly sexy woman Tony had ever seen. He'd always thought his wife was the sexiest woman in the world, but this one even had Mary beat. She was a little under six feet tall, with soft, bouncing long red hair laying on her shoulders…she was a true knockout. She almost made him nervous as he stood up to shake her hand. Her figure was absolutely perfect. He thought to himself that Mary would not approve of this one, but he decided to be polite and talk to her anyway, just as he had done for the others.

She sat down and crossed her legs, giving him an easy view halfway up her skirt. She pulled a resume out of a flat brown notebook and handed it to him, giving him something else to look at besides her.

Tony looked at the resume. "So, you list your first name as Brenda and your middle name as Jean. Which do you prefer?"

"To tell you the truth, Mr. Calley, I prefer both. I like it when people call me Brenda Jean, Brenda Jean Sanders," she responded, giving him a wonderfully sexy smile.

"Uh, okay, Brenda Jean, why don't you tell me about yourself as I'm glancing over your resume?" "Well, I'm twenty-seven years old, I'm single, and I love working with clients. I think I'm a very loyal employee who wants to find a firm that I can grow with. I have a BA from the University of Kentucky with double majors, one in communication and one in business administration. I can type over seventy words a minute and I don't think I ever missed a day of work. My family lives here in Rymont, and I'm so happy being back home. That about covers it, Mr. Calley."

"So, what are your career goals, Brenda Jean?"

"I want to learn everything I can about the investment business. I've worked in this business for a while, and I'm ready to move up. I think I'd be good at being an analyst. Then who knows? Maybe one day I can own my business like you do."

She crossed her legs again, flipping them by putting the left leg on top. It was very distracting for Tony. He cleared his throat, looking at the paperwork again. "You have a very impressive...uh...resume. I would think you should be able to find a job a lot better than being a secretary."

"I know, but the way the market is right now, it's hard to find anyone hiring. So, I figured I'd start with a secretary's job and prove I can handle more with a good firm like yours."

Tony took a big breath, then continued. "I see you worked for Blakely and Blakely in Knoxville for....let's see....almost three years. I know the Blakely's some. Tell me about working there."

She smiled. "I loved working for them. They taught me so much about investing. It's a very good company to work for, but I just couldn't see much of a future with them. I tried real hard to get promoted there, but it never happened. Besides, I missed my folks. They live right here in Rymont, so I decided to move back here and see what kind of job I could get."

"So, is that why you left them, because of your parents?"

"That and some personal reasons. It was no big deal; let's just say someone working there wanted me to become more than a fellow employee, if you know what I mean." She raised her shoulders, giving him her best little girl look. "Anyway, I'm here now. Instead of beating the concrete looking for a job, I decided to sign on with a 'temp' agency, and that's how I got this interview."

"Brenda Jean, you put Blakely and Blakely's phone number on your resume. What do you think they would say about you if I called them?"

He looked up at her, noticing for the first time how much sparkle was in those baby blue eyes. How could any woman look more perfect?

"I think they would say I did my job and I was good with their customers. Both Blakely's asked me not to leave. They even offered me a big raise to stay, but by then I had made up my mind to come home."

He spent the next twenty minutes giving her different scenarios that might happen, asking what she would do for each one of them. She amazed him with her answers. Brenda Jean really understood the investment business.

Finally, he had run out of things to ask her. "Okay, Brenda Jean, you present yourself very well, but I need to check your references. I might ask you to come in for a second interview if I have any more questions; that is, unless you find another position elsewhere. So, why don't we leave it like this…if I want to hire you, or talk to you again, you'll get a call by Friday. If not, then we filled the position with someone else; that way I don't leave you wondering about what we think. Is that fair?"

She stood up, extending her arm. "That's more than fair, Mr. Calley." They shook hands. "I just want you to know that if you take a chance and hire me, you won't be sorry. I'll be the best employee you've ever had, I promise you that. Thanks for talking to me."

She let go of his hand, turned, and walked out. Tony noticed she looked just as good from the back as she did from the front.

Tony interviewed the last two girls on the schedule, neither of whom interested him. He kept thinking about Brenda Jean. He picked up her resume, started to study it again, and then decided to call John Blakely in Knoxville.

"Hey, John, this is Tony Calley over in Rymont. Do you got a minute?"

"Well, if it isn't my old golfing buddy from Nashville…I mean Rymont…and what are they, ten miles apart?"

"About that, John. So tell me, how's business?" Tony asked, doodling on Brenda Jean's resume.

"Oh, same as everywhere I bet, with this piss-poor stock market right now. But we're still holding our own, making a few bucks here and there. I still get out on the course every Thursday. Say, how's your golf game these days? It looked to me at that tournament out in Vegas you'd be damn good with some practice."

"I don't have time for golf anymore, John. I'm just trying to scratch out a living. Maybe one day I'll make enough to spend a day on the golf course once a week."

"So, what I can do for you, Tony?"

"John, I was wondering if you could tell me anything about Brenda Jean Sanders. I just interviewed her and she put on her resume that she worked for you for three years. What can you tell me about her?"

"Tony, she was great. She worked for Connor Shelander, one of our junior partners. I still don't know why she left. She said she wanted to move closer to her family, but I think it was more than that. But, I'd take her back in a minute. Hire her, she knows her stuff, and she was tremendous with our clientele. She's got that southern charm you can't buy anywhere. Our older male customers sure ate it up, if you get my drift?"

"Yeah, I know what you mean. She just left my office. Only thing is, she sure makes it hard to concentrate."

"I wouldn't worry too much about that, Tony. She's very professional. But you're right, she can be distracting. She didn't disrupt us here, but I can see a young colleague getting a hard on around her. God sure was good to that girl."

"Hey, thanks a lot, John. If you ever get over here, let me know and we'll play a round together."

"You got it, partner; see ya."

Tony hung up the phone thinking about his problem. He needed a secretary. Michelle was leaving in less than two weeks, and Brenda Jean seemed perfect as her replacement. But she brought some baggage with her. How could anyone concentrate on their job with her around? He had to sleep on it. After all, he could still get some more girls from that placement service. He picked up her resume, looking at the clock on his desk. It was almost five, so he decided to head home.

Mary was sleeping on the couch in the family room when he got home. He kneeled down in front of her, kissing that beautiful forehead. She smiled, opened her eyes, and reached out to hug him, but she couldn't do it. She fell back, instantly going back to sleep. "Mary, oh Mary, I'm home. Wake up." He shook her and she tried to reach out to him again. This time she was able to sit up.

"Hi, baby, how was…how was…you know…how was worrrrrk?"

Tony grabbed her face with both hands, shaking her head. "Now you're starting to scare me, Mary. Have you been drinking? Wake up, wake up." He leaned down to smell her breath. There was no alcohol smell. She fell back on the couch again. Tony stood up, looking towards the stairs. "Connor, come here. Get down here NOW."

Connor ran into the family room, knowing there was a problem. "What's wrong, Dad?"

"I don't know. I can't wake your mother up. Was she sleeping when you got home?"

"No, but she was acting kind of groggy. Is she okay?"

"I don't know. Grab her purse, it should be in the kitchen. We're taking her to the emergency room. Hurry."

They got in his Mercedes and raced towards the hospital. When they pulled up in front of the emergency room, Tony carried his wife through the sliding glass doors, where two nurses put her on a gurney. In an instant she was in a small examining room, with a Dr. Karen Aldridge taking charge quickly, checking Mary's heartbeat and oxygen level.

"I need some blood drawn here, stat," she hollered, then looked at Tony. "Is she on any medications?"

"She takes pills for a bad thyroid and a sleeping pill at night. That's all I know of except some vitamins."

"What kind of sleeping pills?"

"It's more of a relaxer than a sleeping pill, I think. It's called Activan or Ativan, or something like that."

"Okay, we're taking her upstairs. You and your son can sit out in the waiting room. I think I know the problem," Dr. Aldridge responded as she pulled Mary's bed towards the elevator.

Tony and Connor went back to the waiting room next to the entrance. Tony held his son, waiting for someone to tell them something. Finally, two hours later, Alridge found them in the waiting room. She walked up to the two worried Calleys, as she was pulling off her blue rubber gloves. "Mr. Calley, your wife is going to be fine. I'm sure you already know she has a condition called hypothyroidism. That's when her thyroid gland doesn't produce enough hormones. After you told me about her medications, that's the first thing I checked, and sure enough, that was it. We gave her an IV of levothyroxine and it only took about thirty minutes for her to come around. When I talked to her, she said she hadn't taken her medicine in two or three days because she feels better and her menstrual cramps are much lighter without her medicine. Let me tell you, she is playing a dangerous game with her thyroid."

"Oh, thank God. You mean it was just because she didn't take a pill on time?"

"Mr. Calley, I don't know if you understand. She has a serious condition with that thyroid gland. She's probably had it most of her life. You may have saved her life getting here as fast as you did. I've seen women go into shock because of a bad thyroid. If your wife would have gone, let's say, another twenty four or forty eight hours without her meds, she probably would have gone into what is called a myxedema coma, and that could be fatal. So, I suggest you make sure she takes her prescriptions exactly as they are labeled."

"Wow, I didn't realize all that. You don't need to worry about her taking her pills on time anymore, I'll see that she does. Can we go see her now?"

"Not for a little while. Why don't you go over to a registration desk and get the paperwork done? We'll bring her down in about an hour, then you can take her home. I just want to watch her a little bit more and get some nourishment into her. But it looks like she'll be fine. Oh, don't let her exert herself tonight…just baby her. You wouldn't want her to overdo it."

"You bet. Thank you so much for all you did for her. God bless you," Tony said, as the caring and capable doctor turned back towards the emergency room. The whole thing was amazing.

When they finally brought Mary downstairs, she acted normal, but the men folk didn't act normal. Connor cried when he saw her, while Tony hugged her. It was amazing. They had gone from a panic mode to one of pure relief, now knowing she was going to be okay. Connor cried when he saw her, while Tony hugged her.

"Wow," Mary said, as she went from a gurney to a wheel chair. "It looks like you all really missed me. I guess I was a bad girl, not taking my medicine right. Well, everything is fine now, let's go home."

They helped her get into the car and started to go home, when Tony stopped at a Walgreens drug store. He said he had something important to get, then disappeared into their favorite store. Five minutes later he returned, carrying a small shopping bag. He pulled the receipt off the bag and opened it up, handing his wife a surprise. He'd given her a pill reminder, a pink one that was labeled for all seven days of the week, both AM and PM, with flip up plastic lids.

"Mary, I want you to use that. Every Sunday load it with your pills for each day. Do you see the AM and PM holes? Just put your pills in there and take them out on the right day at the right time. And don't ignore any pill because of your monthly, or anything else. Did the doctor tell you how serious your condition is?"

"Yes, she told me, Mister Boss Man. I got it. Now I know better." She scooted over next to Tony, kissing on his ear. "Thank you for helping me tonight, darling. That sweet Dr. Aldridge said you may have saved my life. I had no idea it was so serious. I've been taking those thyroid pills for a long time and I never had anything like this happen before. I promise, Daddy, I'll be good from now on. That coma thing scares me. I can't imagine something that terrible. No, I'll be good, you'll see."

She looked back at Connor. He was watching all the cars go by. "Connor, I haven't had a chance to talk to you. How do you like those books you got for fourth grade?"

"They seem pretty easy to me, Mommy. I don't think I'll need until Christmas break to catch up."

"I bet you won't either." She looked back at her husband. "So, Tony, how was your day? Did you find a secretary?"

"Well, let's see. I interviewed six girls today. There was only one that I might consider hiring. She was very qualified, maybe even overly qualified, but she has some baggage that comes with her."

"What do you mean?"

"I guess you could say I have some concerns if I hire her. First off, she just sounds too good to be true. I mean she really knows the business, she a great typist, and I think she'd be good with our clientele. But you know, when someone is too perfect for a job, they usually end up going elsewhere for more money. That's the first hang up. The second one will blow your mind. She looks like a model, just like you do. She might be too distracting for the office."

"Did you check out her references?"

"I called a guy I met in Vegas last year at that investment convention, somebody I played golf with. He lives over in Knoxville. She worked for him for three years. He said she was great and to hire her, but I don't know. You'd have to see her. Maybe the other girls will resent her or something."

They pulled into the garage. "Tony, Michelle's leaving, what, at the end of next week? You know what, if all this girl's references say she's good, I wouldn't be afraid to hire her. So what if she's pretty? It's her work that matters. Maybe Michelle should be involved more. Why doesn't she interview her? Call it a second interview…why not? I would think she would want you to have a good secretary, wouldn't you?"

"You are something, Mary; you are really something. I think that's a great idea. Michelle's going to like doing that, I'll bet. Well, let's get you inside. The doctor told me to make sure you rest tonight, and that's exactly what you're going to do."

Chapter 5
What Happened to Our Account?

When Tony got to the office the next day, he stopped in front of Michelle's desk. "Do me a favor…call Brenda Sanders and ask her to come in this morning for a second interview."

"You got it, Mr. Calley." She opened up his appointment book. "It looks like you don't have any appointments after eleven until two thirty. What do you think, eleven sound good?"

"As usual, you're right, make it eleven," he said, grabbing a chocolate covered donut and heading toward his office. He turned around, looking at his girl Friday. "I'm so glad you're on top of things today. I'm just not myself; I was up all night at the hospital with Mary."

"Oh, my God. Is she all right? What happened?"

"She's fine now, but she was in bad shape last night. She's got a bad thyroid gland and she didn't take her pills for a few days. She was passed out when I got home last night, so we rushed her to the emergency room. They gave her an IV at the hospital, and we were even able to take her home last night."

"Thank God." Tony got into his office, then remembered he wanted to tell Michelle about her doing the interview with Brenda. He pushed the call button on his phone, asking her to come into his office. A minute later she was standing in front of him.

"When Brenda gets here, I'm going to talk to her for a couple of minutes, then I want you to interview her. Ask her whatever you want, but when you're done, I want you to tell me if I should hire her or not. Be thorough and dig some…I value your opinion. Here, take this," he said, handing Michelle a copy of the application Brenda had filled out. "Make a copy so you can plan on your questions. How does that sound?"

"That sounds like fun, Mr. Calley. Thanks for trusting me; I won't let you down."

Brenda got to the office a little before eleven, and after talking to Michelle for a minute, she followed her into Tony's office. She sat in the same chair she'd used the day before. She was dressed more professionally this time, wearing a blue blazer over a white blouse, with a white skirt that was a little too short for her long legs, but Tony didn't mind that at all. Once again, she crossed and recrossed her legs, making it hard for Calley to concentrate. For the first time, he noticed her perfume. It was a wonderful scent, combining flowers and spices, seeming to be perfect for Brenda Jean.

"Brenda, I appreciate you coming in on such short notice. I wanted to ask you a few more questions, then Michelle, the lady who brought you in here, will be talking to you when I'm done. She's my secretary and she's leaving me next week, and I value her opinion a lot. So, I want her to ask the bulk of the questions today, but I still have a couple of things to ask you."

"Sure, Mr. Calley, fire away," she answered, wiggling in her chair as she leaned closer.

"Okay, I talked to John Blakely. He said you left on good terms and he would rehire you in a minute. He said you were great with his customers. That's what I wanted to talk to you about. We built this business from the ground up. We take pride in our standards and professionalism here. Now, I don't need to tell you that you're a very attractive lady. But we need everyone here at Burns and Calley to concentrate on our investors. Do you think you could wear clothing that is a little less revealing on a daily basis, kind of the way Michelle looks today?"

"Sure, I've got a ton of business suits at home. You know, I dress differently for an interview than I do when I'm working. Most of the time I wear my hair up in a bun at the office, and I never wear dresses or skirts that are too short. All that's not a problem for me."

"Good, that's what I was hoping you'd say. I didn't offend you by asking that, did I?" He looked down at her resume again, scratching his head with a pen.

"No sir, I guess I would have asked the same question if I were you."

"Okay, I've just got a couple more things to ask you." He scanned her resume again. "I see here that you worked for a law firm right out of college. What did you do there, and why did you leave them?"

"My parents always wanted me to go to law school, so I told them I would work in a law office after I graduated college, to test the waters. But by then I was sick of school, so I knew I wouldn't be going to law school for a while, if ever. I tried it like I promised them, and I hated it. It was just too boring. I like to stay busy and stay excited, if you know what I mean."

"Uh huh, I guess. So how did you get into the investment business?"

"My best friend in college was a year ahead of me. She was in my sorority and she got a job working for a stock broker. She loved it and bragged about how much money she was making, so I went to work with her at the same firm."

"And why did you leave them; that's Bolter and Sims, right?" he asked, studying her resume.

"That's them. They were fine, but it wasn't a good fit for me."

"Why not?"

"They just seemed too rigid for me. I loved working with their customers, but the bosses seemed so boring, like there was no room to do anything but look at a computer screen."

"So, tell me, what do you like most about this business?"

"For me, it's really fun helping people make money instead of figuring out ways to get all of their money." She raised her eyebrows, smiling at Calley.

"That was a great answer, Brenda Jean. Now, let's see, after Bolter and Sims, you didn't list any employer for about three years. Did you forget to put something down?"

"Can I see that, Mr. Calley?"He handed her the resume. "Oh yeah, that, uh…that was…uh…when my dad got real sick. He owns a coin operated laundromat and he needed help, so I managed it while he recuperated. I didn't put it on my resume because I wasn't really officially working, it was more like helping." She handed the paper back to Tony.

He felt uncomfortable with her answer, but decided not to pursue it. "Is there anything else you want to tell me or ask me before I get Michelle?"

"Just one thing, Mr. Calley. I can promise you that I will end up being your best employee if you hire me. I want to learn this business from you. I respect you already because you own something like this and we're about the same age. That's the reason I want to work for you; I want to learn how you were able to become a partner so maybe I can be one someday too."

"That's a good goal. Who knows? Maybe you'll own your own investment company one day, Brenda Jean. You sure have the smarts and the enthusiasm to do whatever you want. Now, you just wait here, I'm going to get my secretary. I would think this will be your last interview with us." He left but returned shortly, bringing Michelle back with him.

"Michelle, I would like you to interview Brenda again. You can use my office. I'll be in with Mr. Burns. Just come get me when you're done."

Tony headed to Ron Burns's suite. Ron was his partner, and one of the best salesmen Tony had ever seen. Ron's clientele portfolio was at least three times that of Tony's. He was a natural salesman. People used to joke that Burns could sell ice cubes to penguins in Alaska.

"Ron, I need a favor," Tony said as he sat in the cherry-colored oversized wooden chair in front of Ron's desk. "Do you have a couple of minutes?"

"Sure, what's up?"

"Well, you've probably seen some of the girls I've been interviewing to replace Michelle." He raised his lower row of teeth, rubbing it on his top lip.

"I haven't really noticed them too much, except the one you're talking to today. She is one incredibly beautiful young lady."

"She kind of stands out, doesn't she?"

Ron leaned back in his chair. "Well, she sure doesn't look like the other secretaries around here. But who cares? What's important is if she's any good."

"She's got very good references, but I'm a little concerned about hiring her."

"Why's that?"

"Do you think everyone will keep their minds on their work with her here? I mean, with the way she looks and everything?" Tony asked, scratching the side of his face.

Ron took off his wire-framed glasses and rubbed both of his eyes. He thought for a minute, tightening the deep wrinkles on the top of his forehead till they almost touched his white hair. "What's the problem? You and me are happily married, Chester's engaged, and Bobby...who knows about Bobby and who he wants as a partner, if you know what I mean? So, who would be distracted? The way I see it, the only problem you could have with her is if she's lazy or a troublemaker."

"You're right, Ron. I guess I'm worrying about nothing. Michelle's interviewing her now and we'll see what happens. Maybe it's not so bad having someone nice to look at anyway."

"That's pretty clever, Tony, having your secretary interview her replacement. I'm sure Michelle will want you to have the best. Yeah, that's smart, I'll try that if I ever need to replace anyone."

Forty minutes later, Michelle walked into Ron's office. "Mr. Calley, I'm done talking to Brenda Jean. Do you want me to tell you what happened now, or do you want to go to your office?"

"Sure, go ahead. I'm not worried about Ron hearing anything. So, what do you think, should we hire her?"

"Mr. Calley, she knows her stuff. It won't take a week to train her. I asked her a lot of questions about investing. She answered every one of them. I doubt if you'll miss me at all after next week. She'll do great for you. Plus, she's a cutie. I think she'll fit in fine here. I can think of at least a dozen male investors who will like coming to the office because of her. She must think she has to overdress around me…she kept saying that she likes to wear business suits."

"Why do you think she told you that?" Ron asked.

"I got a feeling she wants to tone down how she looks. I bet that's because men probably bother her a lot. She wants to please without being a distraction. I don't see how you can lose by hiring her."

"Thanks. Tell her I'll call her this afternoon."

"You got it, boss," Michelle said, slowly closing Ron's office door.

"Well, Ron, that was the best reference yet. I'll go ahead and hire her."

Two hours later, Tony called Brenda Jean, telling her he wanted her to be his secretary. She accepted, excitedly telling him he wouldn't be sorry and she'd make him proud, then asking when she could start. He told her to be at the office at eight the next morning. After the conversation, Tony leaned back in his chair, sighing. He knew he'd done well. He now had a great secretary ready to replace another great secretary. He looked over at his wife's picture on his credenza, then looked at his watch. "She should be done with the doctor by now," he said, picking up his phone and dialing.

"Hi, Mary, how you feeling?"

"I'm fine, except I'm very tired. I've been tired all day."

"What did your doctor say?"

"He said I'm a very lucky lady. I heard the same thing the doctor at the hospital said last night. Well, anyway, you don't have to worry about it again. Dr. Dickenson said I shouldn't have an issue with anything as long as I stay on my medicine. I heard enough from everybody how close I came to a coma last night. I guarantee you that I won't miss a pill again, let alone skip them for a couple of days."

"Did you ask Dickenson about being so tired?"

"He said my body went through some shock yesterday and it will take a day or two to get back to normal. Anyway, I'm going to be fine. So, tell me about your day."

"Well, I hired the girl I told you about last night. Her name is Brenda Jean Sanders. I told her, in my own way, she needed to dress more conservatively. She was fine with that. I think she'll be okay…she's starting tomorrow. I had Michelle do what you suggested; she did most of the interview today. She said I should hire her. I want you to meet Brenda as soon as you can, I think you'll like her."

"I will. But, no matter what, you're going to miss Michelle a lot."

"That reminds me, I invited her to go to dinner with us, including Connor, on Sunday. It's kind of a goodbye dinner. I knew you wouldn't mind."

"Of course not, Tony, that's the least we can do."

"She cried like a baby when I asked her about Sunday. I think she's going to miss us as much as we'll miss her."

"Oh, Tony, I forgot to tell you; Ken Reynolds at the bank called me this afternoon. He wants me to come see him today. He didn't say what it was about, he just said it was important. I'm heading over there now."

"I'll take care of it, honey. You just get some rest. I can stop over there on the way home." He could feel sweat beginning to pop out on his forehead.

"That's all right, Tony, I'm almost there."

"I wonder what's up at the bank? How about if I meet you there? I'm done with all my appointments anyway."

"Tony, I'm a big girl. I'll see what he wants and call you when I'm done. It's no big deal."

"Okay, just don't overdo it, honey."

"I won't. I promise. Bye."

Mary pulled into the Eastshore Nations Bank parking lot, found a door with Reynolds's name on it, and told his secretary that he had called her. Reynolds came out of his office and guided Mary to an overstuffed chair next to his desk.

Reynolds was a very skinny man, decked out with Elvis-like sideburns and wearing a pair of glasses so thick they made his eyeballs look twice their size. He was very hard to look at.

"Thanks for coming in on such short notice, Mrs. Calley. I only have your home number on file or else I would have called your husband. I don't know why we don't have all your cell numbers. Maybe you can give them to us when we're done today?"

"Is everything all right?" Mary asked, laying her purse on the floor next to her chair.

"Not exactly, Mrs. Calley. We have a problem with your accounts."

"What do you mean, a problem?"

"Well, as you know, your checking and your savings accounts interact with each other, so if you run short in your checking account, we just automatically pull from your savings account."

"So, I already knew that. Why are you telling me how our accounts work?"

Reynolds took a deep breath. "Mary, you and your husband have been important customers with us for a long time. That's why I wanted to talk to you in person. We certainly value your accounts…your personal ones and your husband's business account. To us, you're not just bank customers, you're our friends."

"Thank you, we like your bank, too. But can you get to the bottom line?"

"We've got some problems," he answered, opening a thick file that was laying on his desk.

"You already said that once. Please stop beating around the bush, what is it?"

"We have to get some help from you all covering your balances. We have done all we can for quite a while, but we can't keep overlooking your shortages."

"You lost me. What do you mean, overlooking our shortages?" She lowered her eyebrows, squinting her eyes. "What are you talking about?"

"Mrs. Calley, your checking account is now eight thousand dollars overdrawn, and since your savings account is empty, we need you to get some money into checking real soon." He cleared his throat, biting his upper lip. "You know you have an executive account here. That means if you write a check and you can't cover it, we first move money from your savings to make it right, and then if your savings account can't handle that…well, then we try to help you all we can. But we can't help anymore. You surely must know your funds are not there, Mary."

She leaned back in her chair, crossing her arms. "This can't be. Are you sure you're talking about us, the Calleys?"

"Yes, I'm talking about you."

"Tony takes care of all the banking. He wouldn't let this happen." She pulled her billfold out of her purse. "Let me check the account number you're looking at. You must be talking about somebody else."

Reynolds lifted the file, showing her Tony's name and the account number. "I'm sure, Mrs. Calley. I'm sorry about all this, but you really are eight thousand dollars short in your accounts, and we can't cover it any longer."

"That's impossible. What is this, a bad dream? My husband has a very successful business, there's no way we can be short in our account." She leaned forward, putting her elbows on his desk, trying to look more at the file.

Reynolds turned the file around so she could see it easier. "I can print it out for you, Mrs. Calley, if you want." He pointed to the left page of the file. "Look, see here? These are all the transfers from your savings to your checking account. It's all right here."

"There has to be some kind of mistake, Mr. Reynolds...there has to be. Go ahead and print that for me and I'll get with my husband and find your mistake. You all really screwed up this time."

"I really wish you were right, that there was an error on our part, but unfortunately, there's no error. But I'll go ahead and make you copies of everything." He stood up, pulling pages out of the file, and walked over to his copy machine. "I can give you forty eight hours to straighten out your account, or we might have to take legal action, and we don't want to do that. I'm very sorry, Mrs. Calley."

"I cannot believe what I am hearing. This is crazy. Son of a bitch, this reminds me of something in a Twilight Zone movie. How can eight thousand dollars disappear?"

"I hope you find the answer, Mrs. Calley. I sure hope you can straighten all this out."

Mary jerked the copied pages from his hand, starting to fold them. "You bet your ass we'll straighten this out. And when we do, you won't need to worry about us anymore. There are a ton of banks out there that would love to have our business, especially Tony's office account." She stood up and turned away from the weird looking banker, and slammed his office door behind her.

Mary was dialing Tony's number even before she left the bank. "Tony, can you come home?"

"I'm on my way now. Where are you? Is everything okay?"

Mary was shaking, trying to answer her husband. "I just left the bank, and no, everything it not okay. It's a mess. How soon will you get home?"

"I'll be there in twenty minutes. What is it?"

"Tony, we're short in our account. I mean real short, like eight thousand dollars. How does that sound to you? You haven't been gambling again, have you?"

"What are you talking about?"

"Just get home, and I'll show you." She threw the phone on the passenger seat, put her face into her hands, and cried. A minute later she laid back, staring at her picture of Tony and Connor that was wedged in an air vent. "That son of a bitch. Why would he do this to us?" After she wiped her eyes with a tissue, she squealed the tires on her way out of the bank's parking lot.

When she got home, Tony's car was in the driveway. She walked in the front door, wiping the last of her tears off her cheeks.

Tony was sitting in his recliner with his tie off. Just as she opened the front door, he stood up to greet her. It was like he was waiting for her to come home. He walked over and put his arms around her waist. "Baby, what were you talking about on the phone? How can we be so short in our account? If we're low in checking, they just move money from our savings account."

She sat down on the couch, pulling him to sit next to her as she opened the bank papers on the coffee table. "Look, Tony, just look. Look at all the transfers from savings to checking. They add up to over eight thousand dollars, all in the last six months. And that's on top of your paycheck that goes into checking. What happened?" she asked, glaring into his eyes. Tony picked up the papers, shaking his head. "Let me study this, honey, there must be some kind of mistake."

"You gambled away all our money, didn't you? How could you do that?"

Sweat was beading on his forehead as he flipped the pages. "Don't worry, sweetheart, I'll figure this out and fix it."

"Fix it? Fix it? How the hell are you going to fix it? It's all right there in black and white. You drained our savings account; look Tony, look at the numbers. Six months ago there was over fifty three thousand in savings. You spent all that, including what was in checking, and guess what? You even spent eight thousand we didn't have. That was our future…that was the start of Connor's college fund. How could you do that?"

"I make all the money, I guess I can spend it. What's the big deal?"

"What did you say? You son of a bitch. That's not just your money, that's our money, yours, mine, and Connor's. You son of a bitch. What is wrong with you?"

He was quiet for a few seconds, collecting his thoughts. "Honey, you know I've got a problem. I've been working so hard to stop, I never thought it added up to this much." He looked at the bank's papers again. "I'm so sorry, honey," he said as he reached out his arms towards her. "Come here baby."

She brushed his arms away. "You're an asshole, you know that? How can you do this to us, to Connor? Now we're short eight thousand in our checking and our savings is empty. Do you know Reynolds said he's giving us forty eight hours to fix this or he's going to take legal action? How does that sound, Tony? Well, I'll tell you one thing, you did it, and now how are you going to fix it?"

Tony raised his shoulders, letting out a giant sigh as he looked out the front window. "I'll straighten this out, I will. Just let me do some thinking on it. I can get the money. I'll get it tomorrow somehow, then I'll never gamble again, I promise."

She turned away, heading to the kitchen, then stopped and looked back at him. "Just where do you plan on getting all that money tomorrow? Do you plan on robbing a bank? It looks like you just tried that and it didn't work. Oh my God, I feel like such a fool. I basically told Reynolds to go to hell, and he was right the whole time. I sure never imagined my husband would do something like this. Why? Why did you do that, and how did you do it? How did you lose our life's savings in six months?"

Tony lifted his shoulders, like a ten year old who couldn't answer his teacher's questions. "I kept thinking the next race would be mine. The more I lost, the more I wanted to win just to get ahead. I figured our savings would always take care of everything, then I'd win the big one and replace everything and no one would know anything. I guess it got out of hand. I'm so sorry, Mary." He put his face in his hands.

"So, how are you going to get that eight thousand dollars tomorrow? Are you going to bet on something? You got a lead on a sure bet at the track? I couldn't gamble away that much money if I tried. How big of bets were you making?"

"I made some big bets."

"I think a normal person goes to the track and bets like two dollars to win, or something like that. No, not my Tony. I'll bet—wait a second, let me rephrase that—I assume you were laying hundreds or maybe even the thousands on a race, huh, Tony...huh?" Tears were rolling down her cheeks.

"I know I messed up. You don't have to be a smart ass about it. I'll just go to the bank and get Reynolds to lend me enough to clear everything up. I've got a lot of money in the business account to use as collateral. I'll talk to him and take care of it in the morning."

"What, do you think I'm a fool? Even I know you can't take any money out of your partnership account without Burns's okay. I'm sure that would be illegal...maybe not as illegal as defrauding a bank of eight thousand dollars, but it's still got to be illegal. Don't you bullshit me. I still can't believe you did this." She made a fist as if she was going to hit him, then pulled back, starting to cry again.

He reluctantly walked up to his wife and grabbed both of her arms, trying to get her to put her head on his shoulder. She turned her head to the side, not wanting to look at him. He put a hand on each of her cheeks. "I'm not going to take money from the office account, Mary. I'm just going to use it as collateral, and get a small loan."

"Can you do that without Ron's approval? I mean, use your office account to back up a personal loan? He does own half of that money."

Tony nodded. "He did that a couple of times, using that account to borrow money. Remember when he put that pool in? I signed off on that for him. I'll just tell him we need to get something, that's all I've got to do."

Mary took a deep breath. "Tony, I'll tell you what you're going to do. You're going to cover the shortage, and then you're going to call Gambler's Anonymous and get some help, do you hear me?" She turned back towards the kitchen, shaking her head.

He followed her and opened the refrigerator door. "You've got my word, Mary. I'll take care of everything tomorrow, but I don't need to call anyone. I'll just stop gambling on my own."

She grabbed his arm as he reached for a glass out of the cupboard. "No sir, you're going to call them. I am not going to live like this. How can you look your nine-year-old son in the eyes and pretend nothing's wrong? You just blew a couple of years of his college on what, the horses? How could you do that?" She pointed a finger in his face, not more than three inches from his nose. "This is going to stop, do you hear me? You're going to stop blowing all our money right now, or I'm out of here, and so is Connor. I've overlooked your gambling for years and years; I'm not going to do that anymore."

He slammed the glass on the counter. "Mary, I can't undo anything, but I can fix it. I'm going to fix it for you tomorrow. Now quit nagging me, will you? I'm going upstairs to see my son."

She threw a towel across the kitchen at him. "You better straighten everything out fast, and I mean real fast. In fact, I'll lay a hundred to one odds you're going to be sorry if you don't make things right. Got that? A hundred to one."

Tony stopped on the bottom step and started to turn around, but changed his mind. He just shook his head, continuing on his journey to see his son.

Chapter 6
No More Gambling for Me

Connor was lying face down on his bed playing Nintendo when Tony walked in. "You still haven't freed the princess from the castle?" Tony asked, sitting on the desk chair next to his son's computer.

Connor put his game on pause, looking at his father. "I've already done that. I'm just trying to do it again. I saw online that there are still some secret stars I missed. Hey, what was all that screaming about a couple of minutes ago?"

"Oh, me and your mom just had a little argument, it was nothing. I came up here expecting to see you pounding away at those fourth grade books."

"I'm just taking a break. I read five chapters in my social studies book when I got home, so I decided to play some."

"Watch out for that bomb thrower, he's going to get you," Tony said, leaning his body to the right as if he was dodging the fireball heading at Mario on Connor's game.

"I know what I'm doing, Dad. I'll see you later."

"I guess that's a big hint, huh, son? You want to be left alone, right?"

"Sorry, but this is an important part of the game."

"Okay, but you better get to a stopping point pretty soon. Mom's getting dinner ready. I'll see you downstairs, son."

Tony went into his bedroom and put on a tee shirt and a pair of shorts, then went downstairs to see Mary, who was on the phone in the kitchen. He only heard the end of the conversation, but he could tell Mary was talking to Bobbie about a plan to fix his gambling problem. He cleared his throat, sending his wife a signal he was about to come around the corner. She looked at Tony coming into the kitchen, then said goodbye to her best friend.

"Who was that, Mary?"

"That was just Bobbie. She's still going nuts about Jerry. She said she's going on a big diet and getting her hair done to get her husband back. She was wondering if we could watch her kids if she finds him. I told her that would be fine. But I don't think he's coming back…it's already been three days. I feel sorry for her…she wants him back so bad. It's so sad."

"No offense, but she's no keeper. I don't blame Jerry at all. Five years ago she was a beautiful woman, but she let herself go and now look at her. It will take a hell of a lot more than a diet to fix her up. See, Mary, you don't have it so bad. At least I haven't left you."

"Yeah, but at least Jerry didn't blow all their money at the track. I guess that means he's not so bad, either."

Tony picked up an apple from the tan bowl on the table. "I see you're still ragging on me. I'll be in the living room. Just call me when dinner's ready."

She didn't respond, just went back to setting the table.

Fifteen minutes later they all sat down to eat. Connor looked at his dad. "Why's everybody so quiet?"

Mary looked at Tony. "Your dad just had a bad day at work, that's all."

"It couldn't be any worse than my day. Mrs. Jeffers decided to tell everyone in my class that I'm going into the fourth grade Monday. A bunch of kids made fun of me all day. But I'm not going to let it bother me, I just remind myself that one day they will all be seniors in high school and I'll be in college."

Mary started crying, then threw her plate in the sink, sending pieces of china and food all over the kitchen. "What about his college?" she asked Tony as she went out the back door.

Tony brushed a couple of plate pieces off the table with his napkin. "You just eat, Connor; I'll check on your mother."

He found her on the wooden bench by the garage. She looked up, hearing him get closer. "I don't know if I can ever forgive you for gambling away all our money. What else have you done? Do we have a second mortgage on our house now? How about a third?"

He sat next to her, staring at her small rose garden. "No, Mary, we don't have a second mortgage. What's the big deal? So, I screwed up. I'm going to make everything right in the morning. Besides, we just got that big account; a ton of money's going to be pouring in, you'll see." He ran his fingers through his hair, sighed hard, then turned to her, lifting up her face. "I promise, Mary, I'll make up for this. Don't worry."

Mary wiped the tears off her cheeks. "Let me ask you something. How can I ever trust you again? Were you ever going to tell me about our accounts?"

"I thought I'd replace it with what I won. I'll tell you what, I promise…I promise I'll stop gambling. You can check the bank every day. I'll tell Reynolds to call you if he ever has to transfer money again. I want him to call you, not me. How does that sound?"

"Will you call Gambler's Anonymous?" Mary asked, giving him a pleading look.

"I'll do that tonight. No more gambling for me. You can even listen when I talk to them. Come on, let's go back in. I think we scared Connor. I'll straighten out everything in the morning," he said, pulling on her arm to lift her up.

Mary pushed his arm aside, wanting to be sure he understood her forgiveness still had not arrived. She walked into the kitchen, looking at her son. "Mommy's sorry she got mad. Your dad and I just had a misunderstanding. Everything's okay now." She sat down next to Connor, handing him a basket full of muffins. "Why don't you tell me about all those fourth grade books you got?"

Connor put his fork on his plate, taking a quick drink of milk. "Well, my plan is to read over half of each one of them by the time we get back from Christmas break. By then, I figure I will have not only caught up with the rest of the kids, but I'll pass them. Do you think I can do that?"

Mary swallowed a big gulp of ice tea, looking at Connor. "Of course I think you can. You've never come up short before once you set your mind to do something."

They finished dinner quietly. Connor went upstairs to read while Tony made the call to Gambler's Anonymous. Mary finished the kitchen then took a long bubble bath, trying to avoid her husband. They both went to bed early, not talking to each other all night.

****

The next morning Tony got to work at seven thirty. Brenda was getting out of her little Volkswagen when he got there. She looked different, wearing a custard-colored pants suit with a pink blouse. She was trying to look like a grandma, but she failed. There was no way to hide that fabulous figure.

"Good morning, Mr. Calley."

"Good morning, Brenda Jean. Welcome aboard. Today, you'll be spending all day with Michelle, learning the ropes."

They walked into the office together, finding Michelle at her desk. She was ready for Brenda Jean, and handed her a steno pad that was already full of information. Tony walked into his office, closing the door

51

behind him. At nine thirty, he called Ken Reynolds at the bank. "Ken, my wife told me about yesterday. Let me ask you, why didn't you let me know about the problem with our accounts? With one phone call I could have straightened everything out. But no, you had to get my wife involved. Did you know she just got out of the hospital?"

"No, I didn't. But your account was so—"

Tony interrupted him. "What about my account? Mary said you didn't have my cell number so you had to call her. Why is that? My business is in the white pages and the yellow pages. Now, you've got everyone upset. So, here's what you're going to do. I'm going to send over by courier an okay from Mr. Burns to use our business account as collateral. I know we have over two hundred thousand in our investment accounts most of the time. So put twelve thousand into my personal account, you got it?"

"I sure do. I'm sorry, Mr. Calley, I was just doing my job."

"Well, you weren't doing it very well. Do you want to make me happy?"

"Yes sir."

"Then call Mary—you've obviously got her number—and you tell her that everything is fine now, and you over-reacted yesterday. Will you do that?"

"Consider it done. And Mr. Calley, after thinking about it, I don't need any collateral for the twelve thousand for your account. Don't worry about anything, I'll just work up the contract on the loan. You can stop by anytime to sign it."

"Thank you. Now, do you see how simple everything can be if you just work with me?"

"You're right, Mr. Calley. I went about this all wrong. I'm sorry. I'll take care of everything. Bye now."

Tony found a little grin as he hung up the phone, leaning back in his chair and staring at the ceiling.

"Mr. Calley, you've got a call on line two. It's a Parker Hayes," came over his phone's intercom.

"Is that you, Brenda Jean?"

"Yes sir, it's me."

"You did that very well."

"Well, thank you, Mr. Calley." He picked up line two. "Hey, Parker, what's happening?"

"Do you want any action today? I've got a lead on the fourth at Hialeah. It's a twelve to one that can't miss. It's a three year old named Lucky Punch. This one is like taking candy from a baby. How much do you want me to put down for you?"

"Oh, lay two thousand to win, Parker."

"You've got it."

Tony was feeling better. He was going to get money from the bank to please Mary, and now he had a lead on picking up another twenty four thousand on Lucky Punch. It was like he was walking on air as he left the office to go to the bank. He drove over to see Reynolds at the bank, signed the loan papers, then called Mary. "Honey, I took care of the bank deal. Everything is fine now. Reynolds told me he would call you anytime we run short in our checking. See, I kept my word. Besides, it's only three days until I can put my paycheck in the bank. We'll be in good shape then, just like I said. So what you doing today, baby cakes?"

"I'm going to head over to the mall and find a new dress. I want to look good for the dinner we're having with Michelle Sunday."

"That sounds great, Mary. I'll catch up with you later on the way home. Bye."

"Bye, Tony."

When he got back to the office, he spotted Michelle and Brenda Jean decorating the lounge for Christmas, including putting up a Christmas tree. He leaned against the door frame. "I can see you're teaching her all the important stuff on her first day, huh Michelle?"

"Yeah, she might as well see all the things we do around here. Besides, it looks like she'll know everything I know in a couple of days. She's catching on real fast."

"It's kind of early to pull out the Christmas tree, isn't it?" he asked, handing Michelle a box of ornaments laying on the floor. "Not really, Mr. Calley; if I was staying here, my tree would be up at home. How about you, Brenda Jean?"

"I just go with the flow," Brenda Jean said, smiling at both of them.

"That's a great answer," Tony said. He watched her for a minute. She bent over to pick up a small box of icicles, and he could see down the top of her blouse...and what a sight it was. She was wearing a blue half bra and her breasts were huge. Even her conservative outfit couldn't hold them back. She looked up at him, noticing him gawking at her. She smiled, almost telling him with a glance that it was all right to look. He smiled back and went into his office. Opening his laptop, he shook his head. "Damn, she's hot," he whispered.

Just before four, he pulled up the results of the Hialeah race. Lucky Punch had come in third. "Shit," he hollered, slamming his fist on the desk.

All he could think of while driving home was the two thousand dollars. Maybe Mary was right; it was time to quit gambling. But he could make up for the money he'd just lost with one small bet tomorrow. He started to wonder how much he owed Parker now; he'd been on such a bad streak.

****

When he got home, Connor was watching people building robots on the Discovery Channel. He loved that channel, and watched it almost every day. "Connor, can't find anyone to play with, huh?" Tony pulled off his tie and unbuttoned the top of his shirt.

"No, not really," the little red-headed boy answered. "Besides, I'd rather just relax for a while. I've got a lot of reading to do tonight."

"Save some time for fun, Connor. There's more to life than reading and the Discovery Channel."

Tony walked by Connor into the kitchen. Mary was bent over loading the dishwasher. He snuck up behind her, grabbing her by the waist and lifting her up. "I've got you, and I'm never letting you go."

"Come on, Tony, I've got a lot to do. Now let me down, will you please?"

"You're no fun anymore, baby," he said as he lowered her onto a kitchen chair, then opened the refrigerator.

Mary turned to her husband with a cute little girl look. "Why don't you go upstairs and take a shower, Tony, and I'll take a bath. Who knows what will happen after that?" Her hints were very clear to Tony.

"Okay, I'll meet you up there."

Tony went up into the master bathroom, undressing as he turned on the shower. He picked out clothes to wear from his giant walk-in closet. Mary walked in wearing nothing but a towel. She closed and locked the bedroom door, walked up to him, and let the towel fall to the floor.

CHAPTER 7
Where Do I Get That Kind of Money?

Monday morning, Tony woke up with a pounding headache, undoubtedly the result of drinking five Long Island ice teas at Michelle's special goodbye dinner the night before. Grabbing his bathrobe out of the closet, he started down the stairs. Mary was sitting at the kitchen table glancing through one of Connor's fourth grade textbooks. The newspaper was still in a plastic bag in front of her.

"Good morning. Where's Connor?"

"He's in the bathroom. Do you know he got up before five? I heard him in the shower so I got up. He's so excited about school now. I can't wait until he gets home tonight and tells us all about fourth grade. It's like he's a different little boy now, Tony."

Tony opened the refrigerator, grabbed a bottle of cherry cranberry juice, took a long drink right out of the bottle, and then put it back. "That was just what I needed. I'm so damn thirsty." He let out an elongated belch, then wiped his lips with his bathrobe.

"That's a sign of a hangover." Mary gave him a smirk as she took a drink of her coffee. He sat down next to her.

"You're right. I still don't feel so good. But that was a fun dinner last night, wasn't it? You sure seemed like you had a good time." Tony picked up the newspaper, searching for the sports page. "Yeah, it was nice to let loose some. Now I'm looking at a new girl at the office. Hope that goes well. Brenda seems to have caught on. All she needs is one or two more training days."

Mary leaned back in her chair, crossing her arms. "I'm really anxious to meet this Brenda."

"Okay, why don't you stop by and introduce yourself today? She mentioned to me last Friday she'd like to meet you too."

"I just might do that, sometime...whoa, there he is, the new fourth grader," Mary said, watching Connor walk in the kitchen. He didn't acknowledge her at all as he sat down to pour milk over his cereal. Mary tried again. "What do you think, Bud? Do you think they're ready for the top student to finally arrive in the fourth grade?"

Connor raised his eyebrows, turning his head from side to side as he grabbed a spoonful of Sugar Pops. "I don't know about that, but it's kind of neat, just like going to the first day of school; but I'm kind of nervous."

Mary handed Connor a plate of toast and poured him a glass of fruit punch. "Just take good notes today. It's going to seem like a whole new world for you. And Connor, don't get flustered if they talk about stuff you don't know. It will be a while until you catch up."

Connor lifted both arms up. "Huh, I don't think it will take that long. I've already read a lot from the books I've got. I bet you I'm not so far behind anyone right now."

She stacked his books, sliding them over to Connor. "If you don't care, I'd like to take you to school today."

Tony put down the sports section. "Why would you do that? You know the boy doesn't want either one of us to walk into his school with him."

She smiled at her son. "I would just feel better about everything if I take him in."

Connor stopped chewing. "Just do me a favor, Mom. Don't go into my classroom and meet my first period teacher. That would really embarrass me with all the other kids."

"Okay, I won't, mister fourth grader." After breakfast, Mary put Connor's lunch bag into his backpack and got him into her car, then they followed Tony out the driveway.

****

Tony got to his office a little after eight, finding Michelle sitting in the lounge. "So tell me, how are you doing today?"

"I'm fine, Mr. Calley. I'm gonna miss this place. At least I know I'm leaving you in good hands with Brenda Jean. Plus Rudi will help her a lot. They really like each other, and if I needed a good trainer, it'd be Rudi Gall, that's for sure. But Brenda Jean will do great here with all the girls."

"She'll never replace you...no one can." He reached down and patted her on her arm.

Twenty minutes later Ron Burns walked into Tony's office. He had a tired and sad look on his face as he closed Tony's door, sitting in front of his partner. "Tony, I need a favor. We got a call yesterday from Vickie Anne's mom. D.J. had a real bad heart attack last night. They're not sure how long he'll live. Vickie Anne is taking the kids and flying up there today. I need to get up there right away, but I had to come in this morning to wrap some things up. Can you cover my accounts for me? Right now I have no idea how long I'll be in Duluth."

"Ron, I'm so sorry. But don't you worry about a thing here. You need to be with your wife and your in-laws. Just download all your accounts to a disk, and I'll take it from there. Do you have anything urgent going on with any client?"

Ron nodded. "Just one, the O'Donnell account. He's got over four hundred thousand in escrow now. I just talked to him Friday, and he wants to put half of it into money market accounts. He'll be calling here at the end of the week, so you've got some time to get prepared."

"Don't worry about anything. You just get up to Duluth with Vickie Anne. I'll call you if I need help with any of your customers, but I doubt if anything will come up that I can't handle. Just get me that disk."

Burns stood up, looking at Tony for a few seconds before he shook his hand. "Thanks, buddy. I'll be in touch," he said, walking towards the office door.

Tony followed him, patting him on the back. "Please give our best to Vickie Anne. Be sure to tell her Mary and I are here if she needs anything, and we'll be praying for her and her father."

An hour later, Brenda called him on the phone intercom. "Mr. Calley, Parker Hayes is on line two. Do you want to talk to him?"

"I'll take it, Brenda Jean."

"Tony, this is Parker. I'm starting to get some heat from the big money guys about how much you owe us. By my records, you're up to over sixty two thousand dollars. I've got to get some of it back from you real fast."

"Parker, you know I'm good for it. All I need is about ten days and you'll have your money. I just hit a bad streak, that's all."

"Okay, but I have to cut you off as far as betting goes. The powers to be want this resolved, without adding to it. That means I need the dough by a week from Wednesday. After you get caught up, then we can talk about more bets."

"What? I've been in the hole a lot more than sixty two grand before. How do you expect me to come up with that kind of money if I can't bet?"

"You've had a dry spell and don't get me wrong, I know you're good for it, but I got costs, too. Plus, I don't back the funds. There are some very, very powerful people behind the scenes that wouldn't like you reneging on your debts, and they wouldn't appreciate me not collecting it. So, Tony, just get the money and we'll all be happy."

"Parker, how about giving me another twenty thousand credit line? That would give me a fighting chance. My luck is fixing to change, I know it."

"I'm sorry, Tony, I can't do it. Just get me what you owe. I've got to go. I'll see you in ten days."

Tony sat there, scratching his head with a pen, wondering what to do about Parker. Where could he come up with all that money? And if he did, how could he do that without either the company or his wife finding out? It was really Parker's fault. He was the one with all the leads. Why wouldn't he give him an extension to win it all back? He felt like his head was going to explode, but he knew he would figure something out. He needed to get away and think for a while. He decided to go to lunch early, and began looking for a place to sort everything out. He spotted a Wendy's, and debated whether to go in or use the drive-thru. Glancing in the front windows, he could see a lot of people in line in the dining room. He decided to use the drive-thru, ordering a burger and a Coke.

After paying for his lunch, he pulled out and his Coke fell off the passenger seat. When he reached to catch it he felt a big thud. Looking up, he saw the back of a red truck. A fat older man wearing blue suspenders and a red and white t-shirt got out of the truck and walked back to Tony's car, throwing a cigarette across the pavement. "What the hell? I just bought this truck two weeks ago, and now look at it, you asshole. What's wrong with you? Didn't you see me in front of you? I mean, this is not a Japanese fake fucking plastic truck; it's easy to see." He followed Tony after he exited his car, showing him the damage on the truck.

"I'm sorry," Tony responded, sighing. "I bent over to pick up my drink that spilled, and I didn't know anyone was in front of me. I'll take care of everything, starting with getting your truck fixed, don't worry."

Tony leaned down, looking at the front of his own car. The front grill was in pieces on the pavement, and the left bumper was pushed tight into the tire, which was already flat. "You bet your ass you're going to take care of it, mister big shot. And the cops are going to take care of you." The old man went to his truck, pulled out his cell phone, and dialed 911. "You just wait here, they're on the way, you rich fucking asshole!" he hollered back at Tony.

"Fine." Tony called the office, and Brenda Jean answered. "Brenda Jean, call AAA. I'm in the parking lot of a Wendy's on Galeberry Avenue…I was just in an accident."

"Oh, my God, Mr. Calley, are you okay?"

Tony walked behind his car. "I'm fine, but I sure can't drive my car. I need a tow in a hurry. I'm blocking the drive-thru lane here and everyone is screaming at me. I'll probably be here a while…the other guy called the cops."

"Do you want me to come and get you?"

"Somebody needs to, once I get everything wrapped up here. I'll call you, but please get AAA out here fast. Bye."

He dialed Mary's number, but got no answer. He left her a short message, telling her he was in an accident, but he was okay. The redneck in the suspenders walked to the back of Tony's car. "I hope you got some good insurance, Bud. You look like you don't give a shit; all you care about is your fancy ass Mercedes. Now how the hell am I going to get back and forth to work?"

"I told you I'll take care of everything. That's what insurance is for. I'll make sure you get a rental car while your truck is getting fixed." Tony pulled out his wallet, looking for his insurance card. When he found it, he handed it to the old man. "I guess I need to look at your insurance papers, too."

"What the hell for? This wasn't my fault. You just wait until the cops get here." He gave Tony back his card, turned, and walked to the front of his truck, where he leaned up on the hood with his arms crossed, waiting for the police.

Finally, a police car pulled up next to Tony's dented Mercedes. The cop listened to their stories, then wrote out a ticket charging Tony with failing to stop to avoid an accident. The old man tied his hanging tailgate to his truck and drove off, leaving Tony to wait for his tow. Flipping open his cell phone, he called the office again.

"Brenda Jean, did you call AAA?"

"I sure did, Mr. Calley. They should be there any minute. Are you sure you're all right?"

"I didn't feel a thing. Just come and get me. The tow truck just pulled in, I've got to go."

"I'm on my way, Mr. Calley. I should be there in about five minutes."

Brenda drove around the Wendy's parking lot when she got there, looking for her boss. She found him inside, drinking a cup of coffee. "Mr. Calley, did they take your car away?"

"Yeah. Remind me to call the insurance company with I get back to the office." He got in her little car, looking around. "Do you know I've never ridden in a Volkswagen before? This is going to be quite an experience for me."

"Are you talking about just the ride, Mr. Calley?"

"Of course. There's an engine in the back, right?"

Brenda Jean pulled out onto Galeberry Avenue. "Yep, and the trunk's in the front. But the best thing is that I get over forty miles a gallon. I sure need that with my budget."

"What smells so good, Brenda Jean?"

"It must be my perfume. You probably can smell it because it's so tight in here."

"Well, I sure like it. Do me a favor, keep wearing it."

She pulled into the office parking lot, pulled her key out of the ignition, then turned to Tony. "I'm so glad you didn't get hurt." Brenda put a hand on his left knee. He pretended he didn't feel it as he exited the little red car.

Tony got into his private office and found Ron's disc on his desk. He slid it into his computer and started to scan it. Ron was right, O'Donnell was a big player. He'd made over a hundred thousand dollars in the market over the last six months. No wonder he trusted Ron with the four hundred thousand. Tony pulled up the numbers for all the money market accounts, found a couple of plans to recommend to him, and noticed how many times O'Donnell called Ron. O'Donnell called on Fridays. "That's a lot of money sitting in escrow waiting for a Friday," he mumbled.

There was a light knock on his office door, and Mary walked in. "Hey, honey, how's the stock market today?" She walked over and kissed him. "I came by to see if you wanted to buy me lunch, but you don't look all that happy to see me. What's going on? And where's your car?"

"I haven't had a good day. I just got into a fender bender at lunch. Nobody got hurt. I tried to call you but you didn't pick up."

"What happened?" she asked, sitting in front of him.

Tony shook his head as he raised his shoulders. "I went through Wendy's drive thru and my drink fell off the front seat. I tried to catch it, but there was a truck stopped in front of me. I didn't see it, so I hit it hard in the rear end. I got a ticket and had to have my car towed. You ought to see the front of my car, it's a real mess. I'll probably need a rental car for a few days."

"Do you think you'll need me to pick you up after work?"

"Nah, I'll just get one of the girls to take me home. Oh, did you hear about Ron's father-in-law?"

"No, what happened?"

"D.J. had a heart attack yesterday...I think it's a bad one. Vickie Anne and the kids went up to Duluth last night and Ron left this morning. I'll be taking care of his accounts for a while."

Mary sat back down in her chair, leaning towards her husband. "Tony, that's awful. How's Vickie Anne, did he say?"

"Ron said she's devastated. I'm thinking he'll call us tonight."

Mary put her hands on her knees. "I'll try to talk to her when I get home. Oh, I finally met Miss Brenda. She seems like a nice girl...a very beautiful nice girl. It's a good thing I trust you, with her around. But I think you're going to have a big problem with her," Mary said with a straight face.

"How's that?"

"You won't know what do with all the male investors that are going to start flooding your office. She's a real beauty. I really like her, and she sure seems to know what she's doing. Maybe you lucked out."

"I hope so. Listen, I'm sorry about lunch. I wish I would have gone with you instead of going to Wendy's."

Mary got up, leaning over the desk to give him a cold kiss. "I'll see you tonight. If you change your mind and want me to pick you up, give me a call. I'm not picking up Connor, so it's no problem. He really likes riding the bus all of a sudden." She twisted her lips to the side, nodding. "I'll bet you see a new Connor tonight. Bye Tony," she said, heading back out to her car.

Just before they closed up the office, Tony called Brenda. "Brenda Jean, I need a ride home tonight. Do me a favor and check with Michelle, see if she can give me a lift."

"I can take you home, Mr. Calley. That will give you another chance to ride in my fancy car."

"Okay, I'll be ready about four thirty."

Tony and Brenda were the last ones to leave the office. After locking up, he got into her little VW. Her perfume was driving him crazy again, as it seemed even stronger; or maybe he was looking for it this time? He glanced over at Brenda Jean, noticing a small smile. "You seem happy, Brenda. I guess you had a better day than I did."

"It's just nice having someone riding with me. Do you see those apartments over there?" she asked, leaning her head towards the right. "That's where I live, over there in Ridgewood Arms. That's really a neat place. They've got an indoor pool, a great exercise room, and a very neat tennis court. It's a super place, plus it's so close to the office."

"It looks like a nice place. Turn left at the next light," Tony told her.

"You've got it, boss."

CHAPTER 8
I Went Shopping

Thursday morning all the office employees, except Ron Burns, had a going away party for Michelle. The office lounge was decorated with posters wishing her luck, along with some old and new pictures of her sitting at her desk. Crepe paper was draped from the Christmas tree to the center table that was loaded with presents and a big white "good luck" cake.

Tony walked into the lounge just as Beckie Knott, Ron's personal secretary, told him Ron was on the phone. He went into his office. "Ron, how are things going up there?"

"Not so good, Tony. D.J. is fighting hard, but the doctors say it's day to day. I don't have any idea how long we'll be up here. Please tell me everything is okay down there."

"We're fine. There haven't been any problems all week. We're just having a going away party for Michelle this morning. She's leaving us right after the party."

"The new girl must have caught on quick, huh? She's only been there, what, a little over a week?"

"Yeah, she's a quick learner, that's for sure. Say, Ron, how's Vickie Anne doing?"

"Tony, she's a basket case. She loves her father so much. She's right next to his bed every minute. She won't leave him even to get a bite to eat. Vickie Anne sleeps right there in his room. I guess she doesn't want him to die alone. I can't blame her for that."

"Ron, please tell her we're praying for her. And don't worry about us. You need to hang in there for her."

"I just wanted to give you an update. I don't have any idea how long I'll be here. I'll fill you in as soon as anything happens. Oh, Tony, be sure to give my best to Michelle. Tell her I think she's great and I will really miss her."

"I sure will, Ron. You take care, you hear?"

"Thanks, Tony, I'll be in touch."

Tony went back to the party, giving Michelle a big hug. "We're going to miss you, Michelle."

She wiped her eyes and looked around the room. "Decorations and a cake, my goodness…and look at all the gifts. I wish you wouldn't have done all this. Oh, who am I trying to bullshit? I love it. But listen, I'm not going to the moon or anything, I'll bug you all every week, you'll see. Oh yeah, Rudi and Beckie and Melanie, you're going to hear from me." Tony stood up, looking at Michelle. "I just got done talking to Mr. Burns. As you know, he's going through some tough times right now. He asked me to wish you the very best, and said he's sorry he couldn't be here to say goodbye. He told me to tell you he thinks you're great, and he'll miss you a lot."

They all sat in the lounge with Michelle, watching her open her presents. They laughed and cried with her until she gathered everything up, hugged everyone goodbye, and left, going out to her car with Tony. He helped her load everything then kissed her goodbye, just as Mary pulled into the parking lot.

"You leaving now?" Mary asked as she leaned on Michelle's car door.

"Yep, I'm heading north. I should be with my grandkids sometime tonight. I can't wait to see them."

Mary wrapped her arms around Michelle while looking into her watery eyes. "There's no way I can tell how much you mean to us. I'm really going to miss you."

"And I'm going to miss you, and this place." Michelle looked at the sign over the front door and started crying. "God, I'm sure going to miss my office." She turned and hugged Tony. "Thank you so much for being the best boss in the whole world." She was sobbing when she got in her car and pulled away, with Tony and Mary watching her drive off.

****

Mary looked up at her husband, seeing a tear forming in his left eye. "You're really going to miss her, aren't you?"

"I miss her already. We need to stay in touch with her. So, Mary, how about some lunch?"

"I wish I could, but I've a few errands to run with Bobbie. Then we're going out to the famous Rymont Mall. Bobbie needs some attention right now. She's still trying to figure out where Jerry went and why he left her." She gave him another quick cold kiss as she opened her car door.

"Fine, it's your loss. I'll call you," Tony said, closing her car door and heading back to the office.

He walked by the lounge and noticed that the girls were cleaning it up. He pulled up the market numbers when he got back to his desk and Brenda Jean walked in.

"That was nice, don't you think, Mr. Calley?"

"It sure was. Who did all the decorating?"

"I did most of it. I owed her that much. She really helped me get started here, and she made me feel so comfortable from day one. She's a very special lady."

"Well, Brenda Jean, you did a nice job, with the party and the Christmas stuff, too."

"That's one of my specialties, decorating. I've got a lot more specialties. I guess you'll eventually get to see all of them. One, thing, though…there's still something that we have to do for Christmas." She sat on the chair in front of his desk.

Tony leaned back, locking both hands behind his head. "What's that, Brenda Jean?"

She leaned forward, putting her hands on her knees. "Every place I've worked we've had some mistletoe in the lounge for Christmas."

"Mistletoe? What for? We don't want employees kissing on each other around here." He scrunched his eyebrows together. "Mr. Burns and I want to keep this office very professional. No, we don't need any mistletoe."

Brenda Jean smiled at Tony. "It's just part of Christmas, Mr. Calley; it makes people feel good. It's not inviting affairs or anything, it's just a way for friends to kiss each other for the holidays. Heck, people in some countries kiss when they meet someone. I talked to Beckie and Rudi and they said it was okay with them. Why don't you let me bring some in?"

"There's no place for that in a business setting, as far as I'm concerned, but if you want to put some up, I don't care. I know I won't get near it, that's for sure. But I'll hold you responsible if it causes any kind of trouble."

She stood up, giving him a sexy smile. "I'll get one tonight and put it up tomorrow." There was a bounce in her step as she turned away from Tony and walked out the door.

For the first time, he felt excited about Brenda Jean. She'd been giving him a lot of reasons to think she was interested in him, and now she was talking about putting up mistletoe. She was so beautiful and so alive. But she still was an employee. He tried hard to get her out of his mind, but she kept creeping back into his head. The drive home seemed like it took only five minutes, as he was sorting through all the flirting thrown his way.

****

Connor was sitting on the floor in the living room, hidden behind a stack of books, when Tony got home. "Hey Bud, how's it going? Tell me, how was day four in the fourth grade? Do you still like it?"

"It's a snap, Dad."

"You're something else, Connor. Where's your mother?"

"She's over at Bobbie's. They got home from shopping about the same time I got home from school. They left about ten minutes ago. She's already called me once to see if you were home. She told me your dinner is in the microwave."

Tony took off his coat and tie, threw them on a kitchen chair, then looked in the microwave. He grabbed the roast beef sandwich he found there, and reached into the refrigerator to pull out a beer. "I wonder what's going to happen tomorrow?" he asked under his breath.

"What'd you say?" Connor asked as he walked into the kitchen.

Tony put the beer down, turning to his son. "Oh, uh, I just said I wondered how you will like school tomorrow, that's all."

Connor walked over to the refrigerator and pulled out a fruit punch. "Tomorrow is going to be great, Dad. We go to the science lab on Fridays. That's when I get to play with a microscope. That's so cool." He started up the stairs just as his mother came in the back door.

"Hey, Tony, I see you found your dinner. Sorry, but it's the best I could do. I was kind of short on time, shopping and all. I hope you don't mind." She put her bags on the counter, bending down to kiss him.

Tony patted her on her butt as she walked by. "Just so you had a great time, that's all that matters."

"We had a ball. For the first time in a week, Bobbie wasn't crying about losing Jerry. She was her old self. In fact, let me tell you what she did. A guy about twenty-five or so started following us. I could tell he wanted to talk to me. He finally got in front of us and looked back, telling me I was his lifelong dreamboat. I laughed, thinking he would go away, but he didn't. He kept telling me how beautiful I was and asked me to give him my phone number. I think it made Bobbie mad, because even though she's looking better these days, no one ever comes on to her. Anyway, this man wouldn't leave us alone. It got old real quick. I get so sick of guys trying to hit on me; it's been like that all my life. Sometimes, I wish I looked more like Bobbie so I would be left alone."

"No, you don't. If you looked like Bobbie, I would have never chased you. We wouldn't even know each other now if you looked like her."

"I suppose you're right. Anyway, when we went by that fountain in the middle of the mall, Bobbie pushed him right into the water...she sure did. I guess he met his match with her."

He picked up his sandwich, not caring about her story. After taking a big bite, he drank some beer, then looked over at her shopping bags. "It looks like you didn't leave much at the mall."

"Do you want to see what I bought?"

"Sure. What'd you buy me?"

"Sorry, Charlie, I went shopping for me this time, and for Bobbie. She helped me pick out some neat blouses, and I bought her a super outfit to go man hunting." She laid all her new clothes out on the table next to where he was eating.

Tony picked up a price tag on a blue and white blouse. "Wow, I'll bet all this cost us a fortune."

She put the clothes back in the bags without looking at him. "Probably less than one bet at the track."

He slammed his beer on the table. "What the hell does that mean?"

"It means I went by the bank today and checked our accounts. You've made over three thousand dollars in withdrawals since that loan was deposited." She jerked her shopping bags off the table, glaring at her husband. "You promised me you were going to stop your gambling. And what about the Gamblers Anonymous meetings? You haven't gone to one of them. So I decided that if you want to piss away all our money, I'll help you do just that."

He got up, grabbing her arm. "I told you I wasn't going to gamble anymore, and I didn't. I took out some money for your Christmas presents. What do you think of that, smart ass?"

She turned her head to the side, hiding the tears running down her cheeks. "Three thousand dollars for Christmas presents…do you expect me to believe that? You always buy my Christmas presents a day or two before Christmas, when you can't put it off any longer, and you never spend that much on me; it's usually some God awful set of pajamas from Walmart, not any three thousand dollar present. Do you swear you didn't play the horses at all this week?"

He sat back down in his chair, picking up his precious roast beef sandwich. "I swear. The only thing I did was bet a little on the lotto, that's all. That's not gambling, that's the lotto."

Mary leaned in, getting about six inches from his face. "You make me sick, you know that? You just make me sick." She glared at him until she got to the doorway to the stairs.

Tony got up, throwing his empty beer can into the sink, breaking plates and glasses on its voyage. "What are you trying to say? I told you I wasn't going to gamble anymore, and I haven't. Give me a little credit, will you? What's three thousand dollars, anyway? You've never had to worry about money before, and you don't now. I'll be sure we've always got money."

She continued her trip up the stairs, with her shopping bags hitting each step on the way up. "Sure, sure, don't give me that shit. I am not that stupid. Just leave me alone."

Tony plopped back down on his kitchen chair. He felt like his head was going to explode. How could she go so nuts over three thousand dollars? If she knew he only had a few more days to come up with sixty-two thousand, she'd really go psycho.

He sighed, then started to get up when he heard a knock on the back door. He reached over and pulled the door open, only to find Bobbie standing there with her hands on her hips.

"You better not be hurting her, Tony, or I'll call the cops. Where is she?"

Tony sat back down, grabbing the rest of his sandwich. "She's upstairs."

****

She walked by him heading up the stairs, not seeing him sticking out his middle finger in her direction. She found Mary lying face down on her bed, crying, with her new clothes scattered all over the room.

Mary turned over, hearing Bobbie come in. "Bobbie, close the door. That son of a bitch. He acts like he's perfect, like he's never done anything wrong."

"Did you tell him you went to the bank?"

"You bet your ass I did. Do you know what he said after I told him that? He said he took out the money to buy me Christmas presents. Is that crazy or what? He's still gambling, Bobbie. I thought I could trust him, but I can't. We're going to lose everything because of his gambling."

Bobbie put her arm around Mary's shoulders. "Do you still love him?"

"I think so, but it's getting harder. I'm not so sure anymore. Bobbie, what would you do?"

Bobbie turned her head to the side, looking at the rocking chair in the corner. "Well, since you think you might still love him, I'd try to get him to stop his gambling somehow, or I'd have to take my son and leave him before it's too late."

"But…." Mary walked over and opened the door. Tony was standing there. "What, now you're listening to my conversations, huh? Can't I have any privacy?"

"I got to go," Bobbie said, walking by them and heading downstairs.

Tony sat on the edge of the bed. "Yes, I was listening. Why the hell do you have to tell her about our personal business? Can't we discuss our problems without getting that fat ass slob involved?"

Mary sat down next to her husband, interlocking her hands between her knees. "Who else can I talk to? You're always so worried our fancy-dancy friends will learn about our dirty laundry, who else do I have to talk to? You don't want to talk about it. All you do is lie. You know you're still gambling, and you know I know it."

Tony shook his head, falling back on the bed. "What do you want me to say? Do you want me to say I'm sorry? Okay, I'm sorry. But I'll tell you one thing, you haven't had to work since the day we got married."

She laughed. "So, what the hell does that have to do with anything? Are you saying that since you're the bread winner, you can blow everything at the track?"

"Of course not. What I am saying is that I've always taken care of you. You've never wanted for anything. You'll see, we'll be all right. I'm not worried about money at all. We've had tougher times than this, and we'll get through this together."

"No, we haven't. We haven't had tougher times than this. Sure, we had a lot less coming in right after we got married, but we had a lot less going out. Can't you see? Everything we've worked for is going out the window, one bet at a time. It worries me. I mean, how we can afford this mortgage, our cars, and most importantly Connor's college bills, if you bet it all away?"

"I'm not going to talk about it anymore, Mary. I told you not to worry, now quit nagging me about money. Just leave me alone." He went downstairs to sleep on the couch, leaving her crying in their bedroom.

They didn't see each other or talk the rest of the night. She was worrying about money, and he was thinking about Brenda Jean. She wondered if he would bet again the next day, while he was hoping there would be mistletoe in the employee's lounge.

E. G. Lander

Chapter 9
Mr. O'Donnell Is On Line Two

The next morning Tony took a long sudsy shower. He wasn't sure what the day would bring, but he knew he wanted to look good and smell good. A couple of extra doses of after shave were needed. He didn't care what Mary thought of how he looked or smelled, he had other things to think about. He left the house without speaking to her anyway, as she was asleep in their bed; or at least she looked like she was asleep.

He got to the office at the same time as Brenda Jean. He opened his door and walked over to her VW. She grabbed her purse off the passenger seat without looking at him. "Good morning, Mr. Calley."

"Good morning, how are you doing?" he asked, closing her car door.

"I'm fine, I guess, and you?"

"I'm doing great." He unlocked the office door and followed her in. He noticed she didn't seem to be as upbeat as normal.

"You sure you're okay, Brenda Jean? Is there something wrong?"

She laid her purse on her desk, then turned around to look at him. "I'm sorry, Mr. Calley, I've just got a lot on my mind right now. It hasn't been a good day for me so far, that's all."

"Is there anything I can help you with?" Calley asked as he turned on the office lights.

"No, not really. I've just got to work through some personal problems, but thanks for asking. You're so sweet."

Tony walked into his office, thinking the day was not going the way he'd expected. He turned on his computer and pulled up the O'Donnell file. It was Friday and O'Donnell always called on Friday. He wanted to be ready for that call.

An hour later Brenda Jean called him on his intercom. "Mr. Calley, there's a Bill O'Donnell on line two."

Tony took a deep breath, then picked up the call. "Hello, Mr. O'Donnell, this is Tony Calley. I'm taking all of Ron Burns's calls this week." He moved his chair closer to his desk as he brought up the O'Donnell account on his laptop.

"I know that. Ron called me a couple of days ago about his father-in-law. He told me you were his partner and you would handle my account while he's gone."

"That's right, Mr. O'Donnell. I'll do the best I can to help you."

"What's with this mister stuff? Call me Bill."

"Okay, Bill. Ron told me that you're his favorite client and I needed to be sure you're treated right, and that's exactly what I'm going to do."

"Great. Did he also tell you how I invest?"

"He sure did. He said you were looking to move some of your funds into a money market account. I've been studying all the markets this week, and I've got some ideas for you." He pulled a paperclip out of his desk drawer, starting to wrap it around his pen. Tony was nervous…this was a very important telephone call.

"I'll tell you what, Tony; I'm taking the wife on a three week European cruise, so you won't be able to reach me about anything for a good while. Just put two hundred thousand in a hot market account, and the other two hundred thousand into something that will make me the most money. I don't want to worry about any of it. The only thing is when I get back next month, I want to see a nice return on all of it, got it?"

"I sure do. That shows you've got a lot of trust in our firm, and we appreciate it."

"You all haven't let me down yet. I expect to be surprised how much money I've made when I get back."

"You've got it, Bill. Burns and Calley will take care of everything."

"I hope so. I've got to go. Good luck, Tony."

"Have a great cruise. I'll talk to you in a few weeks."

Tony hung up, spreading his arms apart, hollering "yes." Nodding, he hit Brenda Jean's intercom line. "Brenda Jean, please bring me all the current market data."

"Will do, Mr. Calley."

A couple of minutes later she brought in the reports. He noticed she was back to her old self. "You look like you're feeling better, Brenda Jean."

"Yes sir, I took care of everything that was bugging me this morning. I'm sorry if I came across as grumpy when you got here. That's not me, I was just preoccupied."

"Hey, don't worry about it…I'm not." He flashed his best smile.

Tony spent the rest of the day developing a plan to invest O'Donnell's money. It was kind of neat having no restrictions on what he could do with that much money. "Just think of what I could turn this into at the track. Nah, what if I lost? That could be jail time. But it sure is tempting," he muttered, looking at the four hundred thousand number on his computer.

A little after five, Tony picked up his briefcase, put on his coat, and headed out to the front door. He thought he was the only one in the office until Brenda Jean came out of the lounge. She was drying her hands on a paper towel.

"Brenda Jean, are you going to lock up, or do you want me to wait for you?"

"I'm almost ready to go." She picked up her purse off the desk. "Oh, Mr. Calley, did you see the lounge?"

"No, I didn't; what's with the lounge?"

She motioned to him with her head to look in the lounge. "Take a look."

He followed her into the lounge, looking around. Everything seemed normal. Then he noticed what she wanted him to see; a small mistletoe bush was dangling from the ceiling over the side door. "Now I see it; you got some mistletoe after all."

"I sure did. Christmas is in the air. That means it's time for everyone to be happy. Now we've got some mistletoe, do you want to try it out?"

"I don't think so, Brenda Jean. I'm a happily married man with a beautiful wife...I don't think I want to start kissing employees and hurt her in any way."

"That's okay, I wouldn't want to hurt her or anyone else. It's just a little Christmas kiss. That's what mistletoe is for...for friends to enjoy the holidays, nothing else. Come here and I'll show you." She took a couple of steps, looking up, making sure she was under the kissing plant.

"All right, just a small kiss between friends, Brenda Jean." He walked over to her, planting a quick kiss on her cheek.

"Not that way, like this," she said as she wrapped her arms around his neck, pulling him to her. Her mouth was open. She wanted his tongue, and he gave it to her. He could smell that wonderful perfume. She pulled him closer to her, rubbing up against her boss. His right arm went around her back, under her arm, and found a breast. He didn't intend for that to happen, it just did. Tony slid a hand down touching the top of her pants. The top button was undone; she was obviously expecting him to reach down there and she was ready for him. He slid his hand under her pants, feeling her silky underwear. She squeezed his neck even harder, then pulled away.

"Not here...it's too dangerous here. How about my apartment? It's only a minute or two from here. Let's go over there."

He pulled back, grabbing both of her arms. "This isn't right, I've got an incredibly beautiful wife...not that you're not beautiful, you really are, but I don't want to jeopardize my life with my wife and my son over this. We can't do this."

She whispered in his ear. "You wanted me a minute ago. What happened?"

"I don't know. All I know is that this isn't right. Damn, it's tempting, but it isn't right. Let's just pretend this didn't happen, okay?" He started running his fingers through his hair, shaking his head. He knew he would regret saying "no" later, but everything was happening too fast.

"If that's what you want. But I'll be here or in my apartment, if you want to get together. I like you, Mr. Calley, a lot." She stepped back from Tony, brushing off her pants suit. "But I respect you, and I'll respect your wishes. I promise this never happened, and it won't happen again, ever, unless you want it to. We can still work together, right?"

"As long as this is the end of it. I got carried away, and shouldn't have." He pointed to the mistletoe over his head. "And get rid of that, will you?"

She pulled down the dried plant and went to her desk to pick up her purse. "I'm ready to go if you are."

He followed her out to their cars after locking the office. They didn't say goodbye, or even make eye contact. Tony headed home, constantly thinking about what almost happened. He was proud it didn't go further with Brenda, but also wished it would have.

****

As he walked in the back door he smelled pot roast. Mary walked up to him wearing an apron.

"Now Tony, you just get comfortable and get ready for your favorite meal." She pulled off his coat and removed his tie.

He sat down on a chair closest to the back door. He was confused. Just a few hours ago she wouldn't even talk to him, now she was acting like Donna Reed in *It's A Wonderful Life*. "So, what's the special occasion?"

She bent over and kissed him, hard. "There's no special occasion, sweetheart. Connor's over at Hunter's, so we're alone for a while. I just wanted to make you a nice supper and spend some time with you, that's all."

Tony smiled, looking up at her and shaking his head. "Wow, if I knew I would be getting this kind of treatment, I probably would have come home hours ago."

She grabbed a stick of butter off the top shelf of the refrigerator. "Maybe you ought to try it more often...I mean coming home early."

Tony ran his fingers through his hair as if they were a comb. "Really, what's going on, Mary? What's this all about?"

Mary walked behind him, putting her hands on his shoulders. "Honey, we've had some problems lately. I was hoping we could forget about all that and be friends again; what do you say?"

"That sounds good to me. What else do you have planned?"

"You'll see." She leaned down and kissed him again, an incredibly soft kiss.

Her kiss didn't come close to matching Brenda's, but he tried to make Mary think he liked what she was doing. "I guess things really are getting back to normal around here."

She patted him on the shoulder. "Now you just go upstairs and take a shower while I finish dinner. Connor won't be home until around nine, so we've got a lot of time to have some fun."

Tony followed orders as he kept thinking about his day, especially Brenda Jean. After getting into his pajamas, he walked quietly down the stairs to sneak up behind Mary, but heard her talking on the phone.

"He's upstairs, taking a shower. I don't know if it will work, Bobbie. I really think he thinks everything is fine, and he doesn't have a gambling problem. But he's ruining us. Are you sure this is the way to go? I hate to say this, but it's not easy. I mean, I don't have the same feelings for him I used to have, and do you know what? I kind of feel he's lost some love for me, too. I suppose it's worth a try, saving our family. I've got to go, he'll be downstairs anytime. Thanks for your help, Bobbie, bye."

Tony coughed to let her know he was coming. She hung up the phone, turned, and watched him come down the stairs. "Well, don't you look comfy? Dinner's almost ready. I think you'll love it, and I know you'll like the dessert." Mary smiled, bending over to pull the roast out of the oven. "I put a USA Today paper on your chair. Why don't you just relax and watch some TV?"

"You got it." He kissed her on the cheek and moved to the living room. Tony found the paper, as well as a beer sitting in a bowl of ice. "This is quite a setup," he said under his breath. He opened the newspaper, pulling out the business and sport sections. A few minutes later she brought him another beer, putting it in the bowl of ice. "You make me feel like a king, princess," he said as she turned around to head to the kitchen. He grabbed her leg as she left, moving his hand up her legs, finding her special spot. She was still a remarkably sexy-looking woman, a woman that most men would die for, and he wanted her no matter what, but he was still thinking about Brenda Jean.

Mary softly pushed his hand away, smiling. "Not yet, Tony, after dinner…it's almost ready. Why don't you go ahead and sit at the table?"

He followed her out into the kitchen, constantly slapping her rear end. "Stop it, Tony. That's starting to hurt. I like it when you're gentle; you know what I mean."

Tony sat on a chair, noticing tall white candles burning on the table. "If I didn't know better, I'd think you're trying to seduce me, or it's an anniversary or something...I mean, candles and all. When's the last time we had a candlelight dinner?"

Mary opened the oven door. He could see she wasn't wearing any underwear as she bent over far enough to show him everything. "Oh, I don't know, Tony, it's been a while." She stood up and leaned her head around. "Wait until you see this roast, it's perfect."

"I just saw something perfect; who needs a roast?"

She sliced the meat, adding carrots and potatoes to a plate she pulled off the table. "Here you go, baby. Oh, I made your favorite rolls, too. You know, the ones that are hard on the outside? They should be done now." She turned back to the oven, giving him another show. No one but his wife was on his mind now. How could he concentrate on eating? She was teasing him and he loved it, even knowing it was all planned between her and that fat ass Bobbie. But he didn't care, she was incredible. He quickly finished his dinner. "Now that was a supper; so what's for dessert?"

She picked up his plate and put it in the sink. "Tony, you just go back to the living room and get relaxed. Remember, Connor won't be here for another hour and a half, so I'll bring you your dessert out there."

Tony sat back down on his recliner in the living room and started to watch a basketball game. Fifteen minutes later she walked in, wearing only a see-through blouse. Sitting on the arm of his chair, she started kissing his ear as she pushed a hand under his pajama bottoms. She kneeled between his legs, pulled down his pajama bottoms, and watched him roll his eyes and smile. They made love on the living room floor for over forty minutes.

When they finished, she laid her head on his shoulder, looking up at him. "I told you you'd like dessert."

"I sure did, I loved it. You were wonderful, you know that?" He kissed her forehead, thinking for the first time in months that she was the hottest woman he'd ever known, even if it was all fake. Mary sat up, lightly scratching his stomach, starting to arouse him again. "Honey, can we talk?"

"Sure, what's on your mind?"

She started rubbing his ears. "We've got something special. I don't want to lose it. Just think how nice it would be if we didn't have any problems, and every night could be special just like tonight?"

"We don't have any problems, Mary."

She tilted her head to the side, still looking at him. "I mean the gambling and the money problems; all that stresses me out."

"Now I get it. You make love to me so you can nag at me about my gambling." He sat up, pushing her arm away.

"No, I made love to you because I love you, nothing else. But I'm concerned about our future together. We've only got one thing to fix, and that's your gambling."

He sucked his cheeks in and out, then sighed. "I heard you talking to Bobbie. Let me ask you, Mary, how much of tonight was real and how much was pretend?"

She stood up, picking up her blouse. "You son of a bitch," she screamed, as she started to cry. "Why the hell are you so defensive? Don't you know all I want is to save our marriage? I give up, I just give up." She ran to the stairs, throwing her transparent blouse back towards him. Tony put his pajamas back on and pulled a beer out of the ice bowl that was now a water bowl. He downed it without taking a breath. What should he do? Should he go upstairs and try to make peace? But tonight was just a sham. She'd done everything because of his gambling, nothing else. He sat back in his chair, scratching his jaw as he grabbed another beer.

Twenty minutes later Connor walked in, carrying his book bag. "Dad, you got your jamas on. Are you going to bed this early?"

Tony put his empty beer can on the coffee table, making it a four pack of finished beer cans sitting there. "No, I just thought I'd get comfortable. I had a tough day at work, that's all. So, Connor, how's school going?"

"It's fun. It's even easier than the third grade." He put his book bag on the sofa next to his father, then sat on the floor in front of him. "Hey, Dad, I'm thinking about taking golf lessons. Hunter's dad is teaching him how to play. Do you think I could get some lessons and play with him?"

Tony leaned back, folding his arms in front of him. "I've got an idea. Why don't we play some this weekend? I'm not very good, but maybe I can teach you some stuff."

"That would be great, but I don't have any clubs. Do you think we can buy some?"

"I bet we can rent them at the course. Let's not worry about lessons or buying clubs until you try it a little bit, okay, like at a driving range?"

They played golf Saturday and Sunday. Connor was a natural. Tony told him to do just two things—keep his head down and try to hit the ball on its back side—and it worked. It gave Tony a reason to get out of the house and spend some quality time with his son. Mary wasn't talking to him again, and he didn't care. When he was playing golf with Connor, he wasn't thinking about either Mary or Brenda Jean. But Sunday night his mind started thinking about his new secretary, wondering what the next day, the next week, would bring. It was an exciting time for Tony Calley. He knew he had a lot of feelings for Brenda Jean, probably more now than for his wife. And for the first time in a long time, he was looking forward to going to work, just to see what would happen or what would be said. He was feeling like a teenager, making sure he looked good every morning, enjoying those old time butterfly gymnastics going on in his stomach.

Chapter 10
Chad's Late Model

After a night thinking about his secretary, Tony woke up Monday morning anxious to get to work. When he pulled into the office parking lot, her car was not there, but as he pulled the front door open he could smell the wonderful scent of her perfume. It almost filled the office. His laptop computer was on, with a spreadsheet lying next to it on his desk. "She must be here," he mumbled, feeling that excitement again.

Ten minutes later, he decided to go out and find her. As he stood up, he heard her voice over the intercom. "Mr. Calley, Mr. Hayes is on line three."

"Thanks, Brenda Jean."

"Tony, this is Parker. Your ten days are up tomorrow. Have you got that sixty two grand ready for me?"

Tony leaned back in his chair, running his hand through his blond hair. "Yeah, I've got it. I'll have it ready for you about four this afternoon. Just come by the office."

"I knew you'd come through. As soon as I get it, I'll let you know about a 'can't miss' at Calder, okay?"

"We'll see, Parker. I've got to go."

Tony hung up, realizing he had to do what he had been thinking about all weekend. He called Brenda Jean into his office. She knocked on the door, waltzed in wearing a dress, then sat down in front of him in her "hello, it's showtime" chair.

"Good morning, Mr. Calley, what can I do for you?"

"Good morning, Brenda Jean. Say, I didn't see your car when I got here this morning. What'd you do, walk to work?" Tony asked with a tiny giggle.

She shook her head. "No, I had some brake problems this weekend. My car's over at Goodyear right now. They said they'd bring it over here when they were done."

79

"How did you get them to do that?"

"Let's just say a little flirting can work wonders."

Tony leaned back, cupping his hands behind his head. "Uh huh. Well, I need you to do me a favor."

She raised her eyebrows. "Sure, Mr. Calley, anything you want."

"I want you to go to the bank, as soon as your car gets back, and get a check ready for sixty-two thousand dollars, made out to Parker Hayes, coming from this escrow account." He handed her a piece of paper with O'Donnell's account number as he was looking at his computer screen.

She stood up to grab the paper, then sat back down in the chair.

"Is there anything else I can do for you?"

Tony looked back at her, seeing her dress now a few inches above her knees, with her legs slightly spread apart. It was obvious she was teasing him. He looked back at his computer, clearing his throat. "No, that's all for right now, Brenda Jean. Just get me that check as soon as you can."

After she left, he shook his head. He really wanted her, but was it worth it? His head was spinning, thinking about Mary, Connor, Brenda Jean, Bill O'Donnell, and even his partner. He'd just paid off a gambling bet with a client's escrow fund. And he couldn't get his secretary off his mind. Tony started to feel sick, so he went outside to get some fresh air. He sat on the bench on the side of the building with his head lowered onto his chest. "How can it get any more confusing?" he mumbled.

Ten minutes later, Brenda Jean came around the corner. "There you are. I've been looking for you all over. Your wife is on the phone. She says it's important. She's on line two."

He stood up and tightened his tie. "Did she say what it was about?"

"No, she just said to get you as soon as possible. It sounded like she might have been crying."

He took a deep breath, letting the air out slowly, then walked in and grabbed the first phone he could find, the white lounge wall phone. As he punched in line one, he noticed the string still dangling that had held the mistletoe. "Mary, what's wrong?"

"Tony, Mom just had a bad car accident. She's in the emergency room at the hospital. I've got to get over there." She started crying.

"Oh my God, what happened?"

"Dad said she got hit by a school bus and it was bad. It took them over forty minutes to even get her out of her car." She cried louder. "Tony, what about Connor?"

"Did you call Bobbie?"

"No, but I will." She sniffled as the sobbing stopped. "I'm sure she'll watch him until you get home. I'm going to call and book a flight now.

But I don't know what to do about getting back. What do you think I should do?"

"Don't worry about it; just get a return flight a week or so from now. You can always change it if you need to. You know I can drive you there if you want. It's only a little over what, two and a half hours to Athens?"

"No, I've got to fly. There's a flight in forty five minutes. What if something happens in the next three hours? I'd never forgive myself."

"You're right, you just go. But call Bobbie and let me know what we're doing about Connor."

"I'll call you back."

He hung up, rubbing his forehead. What else could happen? Now he had to batch it for a while. Mary might be gone for a while, but that wasn't all that bad, with the way he was feeling about his new secretary.

Brenda Jean leaned her head into the lounge. "Is everything okay, Mr. Calley?"

"Not really. Mary's mom was just in a bad car wreck. Mary's flying out this afternoon. It looks like I'll be both Dad and Mom at home for a little bit."

She put her hand on his arm. "I'm so sorry. Please tell her I'll be praying for her. And Mr. Calley, if I can help in any way, just let me know. Oh, my car's back. I'm going to the bank to get your check."

"Good. Don't forget to get me a receipt."

Fifteen minutes later Mary called, telling him she was at the airport and Bobbie would be taking care of Connor after school.

Just after Brenda Jean got back, she called Tony, telling him Parker Hayes was in the waiting room. He asked her to send him in.

Parker strolled in and sat in "Brenda's chair." He was wearing a black T-shirt, with white words spread across his chest, saying, Give Me Some Space, Asshole. Tony shook his hand, then sat back in his chair. "That's some shirt, Parker. I wish I could be as carefree as you are."

"Hey, I do my business by telephone. So, do you have my check, Tony?"

Tony picked up a white envelope off his desk and pulled out Parker's check. "Here, Parker, just like you said, sixty two thousand."

"You're a gentleman and a scholar, Tony. I was confident you'd find it. Now that your account is paid up, do you want the tip of the year?"

Tony twisted his lips, wiping his upper lip with his tongue. "What you got?"

"This is a once in a lifetime tip. It's the closest thing to a sure bet I've ever had. It's like taking candy from a baby. Are you interested?"

"I'm listening."

"Okay, in the fifth tonight at Irving Meadows, there's a twenty to one shot that's been programmed to win, if you know what I mean. No lie, Tony, I'm even laying some of my own money on it. That should tell you how sure I am about this one."

Tony rubbed the side of his face. "What's the name of the horse, and how can you be sure it's programmed to win?"

"The horse is Chad's Late Model, and you don't need to know why I'm so sure, I can't tell you. Just trust me, it's a gimmee. Do you want some action?"

"You say it's twenty to one?"

"That's where it's at right now, but that will probably change by race time."

Tony thought for a second, thinking about the O'Donnell account. "I'll tell you what, lay four grand on him to win."

"You got it, Tony." Parker stood up, walking towards the door, then looked back at Tony. "I'll give you a call tonight with the results."

"That'd be fine. About what time?"

"Oh, I'll probably know about eight or so. See you later, Bud."

He pulled up the O'Donnell account again, hoping to figure out how to cover the transfer that already showed up. He leaned closer to his laptop, hoping to see an answer, when his cell phone rang.

"Tony, I've got to get on the plane, but I wanted to say goodbye."

"Please be careful, Mary, and call me when you land, will you?"

She didn't answer. She was crying again. Finally, she spoke up. "I got to go, Tony. I love you."

He tried to answer her, but she was already gone. He looked at his watch, realizing he had over five hours to wait for that horse race. He really needed Chad's Late Model to come through. Tony called Brenda Jean back to his office, hoping just seeing her would let his swirling brain settle down and concentrate on one thing. While he was waiting, he was trying to think of something to tell her to do so it wasn't so obvious all he wanted to do was to look at her. She walked in and sat in the "show chair."

"Brenda Jean, I know it's getting late, but I want you to bring me everything you can find about Bill O'Donnell. Start by Googling him. Find out how he made all his money, what his background is, everything you can find out. That may take some time, so if you have to stay late tonight, I'll get you some time off to make up for it whenever you want."

She wrote everything in her notebook, this time giving him even more of a show. She reversed how her legs were crossed in slow motion. He could see almost everything under that dress, enough to know she wasn't wearing any panties. He was going crazy. There was nothing in the world he wanted more than to grab her and throw her down on his desk. He couldn't; he wanted to, but he couldn't. His mind was too cluttered with the money he took from a client's account and Mary's problems to do anything. Besides, the other two secretaries were still in the office. "Goddamn it," he said, looking away from her.

"I'm sorry, what'd you say, Mr. Calley?"

"I said damn, there's something I want to do, but I can't just yet."

She looked puzzled, then realized what he was saying. "Well, maybe you can do whatever it is later, when everything is right for you?"

"I hope so, I really do. Anyway, go ahead and get that info for me, okay?"

"You got it."

****

Tony turned onto his driveway, wondering what he was going to do about dinner for Connor. When he opened the front door he saw Bobbie and Connor playing cards on the kitchen table. "Hey, guys, it looks like you're staying busy."

Connor turned towards his dad. "We've been playing war. I won the first two games, and I'm way ahead on this one, too."

"I know, you beat everybody in everything; but I'll bet she's a good match for you." He looked over at Bobbie. "Hi, Bobbie, thanks for helping out."

She grabbed the cards, putting the stack back on the table. "I'm doing it for Mary. She told me to ask you about dinner. Do you want me to fix something?"

He could feel the tension in her voice. "No, that's okay, Connor and I will be fine. We might even go out to Chubby's Roadhouse; that's his favorite restaurant." He put his briefcase on the kitchen counter, then threw his coat on a chair. "Right, Connor?"

The boy lowered his eyebrows in deep thought. "Dad, I've got a lot of reading to do; how about just making me pancakes? That sounds so good to me."

Bobbie turned back, looking at Tony without looking into his eyes. "Do you want me to make them for you boys?"

Tony opened the refrigerator, grabbing a beer. He snapped the top of the can, then responded without even glancing at his overweight neighbor. "Nah, I can handle it. Pancakes are one of the few things I can make without screwing it up, especially the ones that come from a box in the freezer. Thanks, anyway."

"Suit yourself. Bye, Connor, I'll see you tomorrow after school." She opened the back door and walked out.

83

Connor stood up, picked up the deck of cards, and put them in the kitchen drawer. "She sure doesn't like you much, huh Dad?"

"Oh, I don't know. I think she's just worried about your mother. Now, what do you want with your pancakes?"

"How about some sausages? I saw some in the freezer when I got a Popsicle."

"That sounds like a plan. Why don't you get cleaned up and I'll get supper going. We'll show em, won't we, Connor? We're just two guys getting along by ourselves. Yep, we'll show 'em, and we'll have fun doing it."

"You bet, Dad," Connor answered, heading towards the bathroom.

Tony opened the pantry door next to the sink, looking for the maple syrup. He pushed aside a big box of chocolate chip cookies and a bag of potato chips. There were two bottles behind them, both pints. One was a bottle of vodka and the other was Kahlua. "I wonder what this means?"

"Did you say something to me, Daddy?" Connor asked as he sat down at the table. "No, I was just mad because I couldn't find the stuff for your pancakes. But I've got it now."

After their big pancake dinner, Connor headed upstairs to read.

"You're just trying to get out of cleaning up this mess," Tony said, looking around the kitchen.

"No I'm not. I'll help you if you want, but I really do have a lot of reading to do. I'm almost there, Dad…I mean, caught up in all my classes. Now I want to get ahead of everyone."

"That's all right, I'll take care of it. You go ahead and read."

Just as Tony finished filling the dishwasher, his cell phone rang.

"Hey, Tony, I'm at the hospital. Mom is at least stable now."

"That's great. So it's not serious after all?"

"Well, I didn't say that. She's fifty seven and she's got a broken leg and a cracked rib. The doctors say they have to watch her for a few days in case there's any internal bleeding. It looks like I'll be here three or four days. Dad's real scared…he needs me now. Is everything all right with you and Connor?"

"We're doing fine. I made pancakes tonight for supper. He loved them. I'm just lucky he picked an easy meal for me to make. Bobbie was here when I got home and she said she'd cover every day between when he gets off the bus until I get home. But I got to say, she's got a real burr up her ass about me."

"Oh, don't pay any attention to her. She's one of a kind. Listen, Dad's waiting for me to go to dinner with him. How about if I call you later, say about ten?"

"I'll be here. Give my best to your parents. I'll talk to you later. I love you."

He finished cleaning the kitchen, then plopped on his recliner, finding a basketball game to watch. He didn't realize he'd fallen asleep until his ringing phone woke him up.

"Tony, this is Parker. Are you sitting down?"

"I'm sitting down, Buddy, what's up?"

"Well, you know that little bet you...no, we made today? It came in. It sure did. Chad's Late Model won in a photo finish."

Tony slammed in the bottom of his recliner, standing up. "Are you kidding me? You mean we won? Oh, my God, Parker, I needed that." He raised his arm in the air, making a fist. "Yes sir, we won. He went off at nineteen to one. Let's see, you put down four grand on him to win. That means you won seventy six thousand, less my cut. Let's see, that leaves you with seventy two and change. Not bad for one day's work, huh Tony?"

"You got that right. Thank you, thank you, thank you."

"Hey, I made some dough on that three-year-old, too. I put down a grand and I'm getting back nineteen big ones. We both did good today."

Tony sat down on the sofa, taking a long, deep breath. "I can't believe this, Parker. So when do I get my money?"

"I can bring your check by your office in the morning if you want."

"That would be great; and thanks again, Parker."

Tony hung up the phone, threw it on his recliner, then put his arms in the air. "Hallelujah," he screamed at the top of his lungs.

Connor came running down the stairs. "Are you okay, Daddy?"

"I couldn't be better, son. Uh, your mom called. Your grandma's going to be fine."

"I knew she would be. I prayed for her. See, Daddy, I told you God listens."

"He sure does. Yes sir, He sure does. Now you run upstairs and finish your reading."

Tony walked out on the front porch. He didn't care that it was cold. He felt the weight of the world being lifted off his shoulders. Now the O'Donnell account could be fixed, leaving him with over ten grand to put into his pocket. He could relax now. It was as if his mind had a lot of items needing to be checked off, and he was on his way to doing just that. The O'Donnell problem, checked off. Mary's mom, checked off. Connor's school issue—checked off. His bank account shortage—checked off. His feelings for Brenda Jean...oh God, what was he going to do about that?

CHAPTER 11
I'm So Glad You Called

After getting Connor on the school bus, Tony drove to his office thinking it was going to be a great day. It was collection day. To a big-time gambler, the thrill of winning surpassed almost anything else in life. And Tony surely was that, a big time gambler. Parker Hayes was going to pay him enough to cover the money he'd pulled from the O'Donnell account, and still leave him with some extra to play with.

His mind was tunneling in on straightening out all the books until he pulled into his parking lot, noticing Brenda Jean's car. Her VW was the only car in the parking lot. He parked next to it, noticing the inside ceiling light was on. After reaching in to turn the light off, he walked into the office, hearing her on the phone in the small conference room.

"Listen, you asshole, for the very last time, I don't care who you tell about me. Besides, no one would believe you anyway. You'd better quit calling me here. I'm warning you, you'd better stop. You know I can stop you if I want to. It's over, you just go to hell." She slammed down the phone as hard as she could.

Tony reopened and closed the front door, giving her a signal of his arrival. He walked by the conference room, pretending he didn't see her, then took two steps backwards to look at her. "Well, good morning, Miss Brenda Jean, how are you?"

She stood up, wiped a tear off her face, then brushed her pants suit off. When she finally looked up, her admiring boss was leaning against the door frame. "Oh, I'll be all right. I've just had a rough start for the day, that's all."

"Is there anything I can do to help you?"

She shook her head. "I wish you could, but I don't want to get you involved. It's kind of complicated. Besides, I'm sure you've got enough problems of your own, you don't need any from me."

He grabbed her by her arm. "Listen, I'm here to help. Why don't you come into my office and we'll talk?"

"Can you give me a minute or two, Mr. Calley? I need some time to catch my breath before we talk." She wiped more tears off of her cheeks.

"How about in ten minutes?"

"That will be fine. I'll be in my office."

Brenda Jean knocked on his door exactly ten minutes later. She sat down in front of him, raised her shoulders, and let out a long sigh. "Thanks for wanting to listen, Mr. Calley. I can really use a shoulder right now. I'm not sure where to begin with all this, but I'll try."

"That's okay, you just take your time. Let's see if I can help."

She took a deep breath, putting her hands on her knees. Tears were still sliding down her face. "I hope this doesn't cost me my job, and I hope I can trust you. All my problems started after I left my job at that lawyer's office. I met someone that I thought loved me. We were even going to get married, but he started using drugs. I don't mean marijuana, I mean heavy drugs like heroin and cocaine." She wiped the corners of her eyes with a lacey pink handkerchief. "One night he went crazy. He needed some cocaine, and neither of us had any money.

"He begged me to drive him to meet someone in a very bad part of town, so I did. He told me to park next to this run-down barbershop and wait. About a half hour later, a car pulled up. My boyfriend got out of the car and started arguing with someone. I couldn't tell who it was because the other guy was wearing a big hat and it was dark. Mr. Calley, are you sure you want to hear all this?"

"You bet. I'm only here to help. Go ahead, keep going."

"Okay, well, about two or three minutes later, my boyfriend got back in the car, screaming at me to get going. Then a couple of blocks later, a cop turns on his lights behind us. I was scared to death. We lost control of the car, sliding alongside a big concrete divider-type wall that goes between the lanes; you know what I mean?"

Tony moved his chair closer to his desk and to his secretary, putting his head into his right palm. "Sure, you mean lane dividers. So what happened next?"

She turned, looking outside his window at the parking lot, with tears glistening in the early morning sunlight. "This is where you have to believe in me. All my life I've been looking for someone special to believe in me, and I'm hoping I found that someone in you."

"Don't worry, I believe in you. So, tell me the rest of the story."

"I need this job, and I really care about you. So, promise me you won't fire me no matter what I tell you."

"I promise."

"Okay, my boyfriend stabbed the guy in the other car we'd met. All over drugs. I didn't even know about it until we were arrested. He was charged with attempted murder and I was charged with being an accessory to attempted murder. That one night ruined my whole life, Mr. Calley; it ruined my life." She started sobbing. "I don't know what happened. I couldn't believe it when they put handcuffs on me. That's why I didn't put anything on my application about working there; I mean I had a record and I even went to prison. I spent two years in a penitentiary in Terre Haute, Indiana. Please don't hate me, Mr. Calley, please. I didn't know Frank stabbed that guy, I really didn't. Now I've got a guy stalking me because of all that."

Tony sat stunned for a few seconds. Brenda Jean was crying as he was trying to figure out the right words to comfort her. "I'm so sorry. That must have been awful. It sounds like you were just in the wrong place at the wrong time. Don't you worry, it doesn't change anything for you here…you still have a job. And no one needs to know what you just told me. You are still very important to me. But tell me, who's been stalking you?"

Brenda Jean raised her shoulders, putting her head back. "The guy that's bothering me is the husband of a woman I met in prison. She's still there, but he's been following me around. I told him to leave me alone and he won't. He said he's going to ruin my job here and tell you about everything unless I go out with him. He's so nasty, I just want him to go away. All my life jerks like that have been bothering me."

Tony stood up, walked around his desk, and stopped in front of her. "Here, give me a hug." He grabbed both of her hands, pulling her up. She wrapped her arms around his neck, starting to sob again. He carefully wiped her tears away. "Brenda Jean, your secret is safe with me, and I won't get involved unless you ask me to. I'll make sure you're okay, you'll see. Now you just go back to work, Brenda Jean. I've got some things I need you to do today. Why don't you go into the restroom and put some water on your face? We don't want the other girls to see you this upset. Then come back and see me in an hour or so, okay?"

She turned, walked towards the door, then stopped, looking back at Tony. "Thank you," she whispered, giving him one of the prettiest smiles ever thrown his way.

Thirty minutes later, Brenda Jean called him on the intercom. "Mr. Calley, I'm fine now. Thanks for listening and thanks for caring. Oh, there's a Parker Hayes out here. Do you want me to send him in?"

"Please do."

Parker strolled into Tony's office without knocking. "I'll bet you are glad to see me, huh Tony? I've got something for you." He sat in Brenda's chair, pulling a yellow envelope out of his back jeans pocket. "This ought to make your day go a little bit better." He opened the envelope, handing Tony his check for seventy-two thousand, two hundred dollars. "Parker, you have no idea how great this is. I've won more than this before, but the timing on this is just super. Do you know I promised my wife last week I wouldn't gamble anymore? And look what happened this week."

Hayes snickered. "I know somebody who's glad he broke a promise, don't I? Say, do you want some action on a 'can't miss' greyhound in Tampa tonight that's at thirty to one?"

"No, not right now. I'm going to enjoy this check for a while, if you know what I mean."

"I sure do, Tony. Just give me a call when you want some action, I'll be around." He left the fancy office, not seeming to have any doubts that it was just a matter of days until Tony was back betting on the horses.

Tony looked at the check. Yep, it was made out to him for over seventy-two thousand big ones. He nodded and smiled, calling Brenda Jean. "Can you come in here for a minute?"

She was there in less than a minute. "What can I do for you, Mr. Calley?"He was looking at his computer screen. "Just sit down, give me a second, then I've got something you need to do." He grabbed a piece of paper, writing down numbers he was retrieving from whatever he was looking at. He handed her the paper. "Brenda Jean, do you see that account number? I want you to take this check over to the bank and deposit sixty-two thousand of it into that account. The account is listed as the escrow account of Bill O'Donnell. I need it in the bank right away, and make sure it gets posted today."

"What do you want me to do with the other ten thousand?"

"Oh yeah, the rest. Here's my personal account number." He handed her another piece of paper. "Now, Brenda, don't get them mixed up, got it?"

"I won't; I'll head over there now, then I'll bring you back the deposit slips."

Twenty minutes later, she returned with the deposit slips. He checked his computer accounts constantly for two hours until he saw the transactions get posted, then deleted the original withdrawal. Now everything was back the way it had started; the only difference was the extra money that was now in his checking account. He spent the rest of the afternoon working on Bill O'Donnell's escrow account, trying to put his money where it could get the quickest return. He looked at his watch, shaking his head. "Oh my God, where did the day go? I've got to get home to get Connor."

Tony closed his briefcase and left his office, finding Brenda Jean's purse on her desk. After turning to look out at the parking lot, he realized they were the only ones left in the office. "Brenda Jean, where are you?"

Brenda Jean walked out of the lounge. "I'm here. I was fixing to leave, Mr. Calley...everyone else is gone." She picked up her purse, putting a pen and a small notebook in it, then grabbed Tony's left hand, pulling him into the almost dark lounge. "Mr. Calley, thank you for today. Just talking about everything made me feel so much better, I owe you." She put her arms around his neck and kissed him.

Tony pushed her away. "Brenda Jean, you don't owe me, I'm just glad I was able to help. Now, remember what we promised, no more of this stuff. I know you're emotional from this morning, but this really has to stop." He looked into her begging eyes, realizing how badly he wanted her, but he held back, even though he knew he couldn't hold back much longer.

"I understand, Mr. Calley, I really do. I know your wife is gone, so maybe you'll need someone to talk to. Here, take this." She put a folded piece of paper into his shirt pocket. "That's my cell number. If you ever want to talk, or whatever, give me a ring."

They went out to their cars without talking, knowing that they were close to doing what they both wanted. Tony pulled her little note out of his shirt pocket four or five times on the way home. It was loaded with the wonderful scent of her perfume, and it was driving him crazy. Just before he saw his house, he put his new souvenir into his billfold. After opening the front door, he found Connor and Bobbie huddled on the couch, looking at Connor's Nintendo game. "There they are; who's winning?"

"Nobody's winning, Dad. She's just helping me get the thousand stars I need to kill the monster dragon and rescue the princess. I never knew a girl could be so good at Nintendo. Aunt Bobbie's helped me a lot. I think she's gotten over a hundred stars herself."

Tony put his coat on the rocking chair next to the door. "Congratulations, Bobbie, that's quite a compliment."

Bobbie got to her feet, looking down at Connor, ignoring what Tony said. "Now, Connor, be sure to save all those stars. We wouldn't want to start over again. I'll see you tomorrow after school, honey."

She turned towards Tony, looking at him with an obvious desire not to. "I ordered a pizza from Pizza Hut...it should be here in about fifteen minutes. Connor said you like Italian sausage, so that's the kind I got. I'll see you tomorrow night." She walked out the front door with her head down, heading for the sidewalk and home.

Connor ran back to the couch, picking up his Nintendo game just as Tony's cell phone rang.

"Hi Tony. I'm sure missing you and Connor," Mary said. "This has been an awful trip for me."

"You sound funny, Mary. Have you been taking your medicine right?"

"Yes, I've been good about that. I'm following the little pill kit you bought me. I just don't feel good. I went to dinner with Dad last night and had a couple of drinks. I think I might have a little hangover."

"What do you mean? What did you drink?"

"Oh, just a couple of white Russians. No big deal."

"It is a big deal. You can't drink while on that thyroid medication. Didn't you see that on the bottle?"

"What bottle? All I've got is that pink plastic thing full of pills."

"Honey, I know you like to drink, but please don't do that again."

"What do you mean I like to drink? Are you saying I'm an alcoholic? That's bullshit. Now, let me talk to Connor."

He handed the phone to his son, disgusted with what he'd just heard. He was trying to manage things at home, and she was out drinking white Russians and messing with her new medicine.

After Connor and Tony finished their pizza, Connor went upstairs, leaving his dad to clean up the whole downstairs. When he finally got upstairs to check on his son, he set his billfold on his bedside table. "Should I or shouldn't I?" he mumbled. It wouldn't hurt to just talk to Brenda Jean for a minute. He walked over, quietly closed his door, then sat back on his bed, grabbing her number out of his billfold and smelling the note one more time.

"Hello," Brenda Jean answered.

He didn't respond at once. Finally, he cleared his throat. "Hi, Brenda Jean, this is Mr. Calley. I just wanted to call and see how you are doing tonight, with everything that happened at the office this morning."

"I'm so glad you called. I'm real sorry about today. You made me promise to cool it with you, and I tried to, but it was such an emotional roller coaster all day, I kind of lost it."

"Listen, I understand. I'm just glad I was there to help you, that's all. I like you a lot…I mean a lot, and I want you to be happy."

"Do you know what would make me happy, Mr. Calley?"

"No, what?"

"What would make me happy is being around you more. You make me feel like a teenager again. You may want to fire me, but I'm going to be honest with you. I'm falling in love with you. There, I said it, I just want to be with you all the time."

He took a deep breath. "Brenda Jean, you're putting me in a tough spot. I don't know how to respond to that."

"I think I've got you figured out too, Mr. Calley. You want to be with me as much as I want to be with you. And we both know it has to be on the QT. That is, as long as you're married. But that doesn't mean we can't be together as long as we keep it quiet."

"You're right, Brenda Jean, you do know me pretty well. I do want to be with you more."

"So, why don't we just do what we both want? I know I'll keep it quiet, and you better believe I won't let anyone in the office know how I feel. Mr. Calley, I want to see you tonight, just for an hour or so. Do you think you can get away?"

"Sorry, but I'm fixing to put Connor to bed. Maybe we can get together somehow tomorrow." He smelled the white paper again, inhaling her wonderful scent. "Brenda Jean, I have to ask you something; what's the name of the perfume you wear?"

"It's called Jontue…it's an old Revlon fragrance. I've worn it since college."

"Just keep wearing it, it drives me crazy. Oh, one other thing; feel free to wear dresses more at the office. They kind of lift my spirits, if you know what I mean."

"I know what you mean. What would you think about me coming over there after your son goes to sleep? I'll be real quiet, I promise. I really want to see you tonight, I really do."

"What time is it now?"

"It's a little after nine. What time is good for you?" she asked.

He was so excited he could hardly talk. "Connor's usually out after ten. Ten thirty would be good. Do you remember where I live?"

"I sure do. I'll be there at ten thirty. Do you want me to come to the front door or what?"

"I'll be waiting for you on the front porch with the outside lights out. Just park a couple of houses down the street and I'll let you in when you get here. Oh, call me on the way in case Connor's still up. I'll give him some Benadryl. That should get him to sleep, but call me anyway. I can't wait to see you too, baby."

E. G. LANDER

Chapter 12
Did You Recognize Her?

Mary didn't get home for four days, giving Tony and Brenda Jean three more nights to get Connor to sleep early with that great cough syrup. It was becoming a ritual for them, with Brenda Jean walking up the steps to his darkened home around ten thirty. But now it had to change. After his wife got home, his time in private with his mistress was limited to a couple of days a week, when he'd meet her at her apartment for lunch…or at least they called it lunch. He didn't dare do more than that; it had to be discreet. Ron Burns was still with his wife in Minnesota, watching over a dead man who was still breathing. Tony was working hard to make O'Donnell a good return, hoping to eliminate any possible discovery of what he'd borrowed from him without his approval. He was lucky with the picks he made, increasing his escrow account by over five per cent in less than one week. But he wasn't so lucky with his bets at the track, already wiping out the ten thousand he'd put in his account, plus creating an additional nine thousand debt to Parker Hayes. Once again, his world was collapsing around him. He didn't dare do the same thing to cover his gambling losses…using the O'Donnell account. So far, he was very fortunate no one knew anything about what he'd done; that could get him jail time. He could cover everything for a week or two by releasing his salary to his account early, but he really needed to pick a winner with Hayes fast. Brenda Jean called Tony on the intercom. "Mr. Calley, can I come see you?"

"Sure, come on in." His heart was beating fast again. He was now madly in love with her, and his body reminded him of that every time he saw her.

She lightly knocked on his door, then walked in, finding him waiting for her just a few feet from the closing door. He grabbed her, kissing her hard while his hand was finding the bottom of her dress so he could move it up to caress what he really wanted.

Brenda Jean pulled his hand away, pushing him towards his desk. "Tony, I didn't come in here for that. I need to talk to you about something very important."

"Okay, doll baby, let's do it your way. Go ahead and sit down and we'll talk. But let's make it a quick talk; I'm burning up all over for you right now."

She looked over at the closed blinds covering the window. "Tony, I love you. I've never loved anyone like I love you. You are my whole life now. But I can't keep going on this way. I feel cheap. We're trying to be so careful, we hardly hold each other anymore. I don't want to be just your mistress...I love you too much for that." Tears were starting to cascade down her cheeks, landing like sparkling snowflakes on her enormous breasts. "I don't want to keep doing this. I feel like I'm just your whore. I don't know what the answer is, but it hurts me too much to be around you and have to pretend you're just my boss."

"I know, Brenda Jean. I hate this, too. I wish I could tell you I can fix it all real fast, but I can't."

"I don't have any answers either, Tony. But I don't want to work here anymore seeing you every day and having to ignore my feelings; that part I hate. I came in here hoping you could help me, but I didn't think you could. You've got a wife and a son...you know, the perfect All-American family. All I can offer you is me. I think I'm just going to have to quit. The way it is now is torture for me."

"Now hold on a second, Brenda Jean. I want you to stay here with me. I know it's not great this way, but I've been thinking a lot about us, and how we can get together without hiding. I'm trying to work some things out. You've just got to trust me. It may take a little time, but I promise I will figure it out." He walked up to her, pulling her chin up. "Please don't cry anymore. I'll fix it somehow, you'll see."

"You promise?"

"I promise." He crossed her heart with his right hand, giving her nipples an extra second or two as he could see them pushing against her blouse. "I want to be with you every minute I can while I'm working this out, because I love you more than life itself; I really do."

"Okay, I trust you. But please remember I can't wait forever."

"I know, it won't be forever." He kissed her on her cheek as she rose to leave his office. "Now, why don't you go get some fresh air? I don't want the other girls to think I'm beating you up or anything."

Tony sat back in his chair, looking at the ceiling. He really did love Brenda Jean, and he had lost almost all of his feelings for Mary. After thinking about his dilemma, a dilemma that had bugged him almost every minute over the last ten days, he decided to put a plan in action. He spun his Rolodex until he found the right name, then dialed that number.

"Hello, this is James and Foster, can I help you?"

"Hi, Kaylee, is Bo there?"

"Is that you, Mr. Calley?"

"The one and only."

"Hold on."

"Well, hello Tony. How are you doing? Don't tell me there's a problem with your office building?"

"No, everything is fine here. You've got us covered just fine. Ron and I are both happy with how you handle our office insurance."

"Say, Tony, I heard about his father-in-law; how's he doing?"

"He's still holding on, Bo. Listen, I called to talk to you about my personal insurance, the life policies for me and Mary."

"How can I help you, Tony?"

"Well, first off, what kind of life coverage do we have?"

"Hold on, let me pull you up." He clicked away on his keyboard...it sounded like it was one finger at a time. "Okay, Tony, you have a one million dollar term policy on you, with Mary being the beneficiary, and it carries a triple indemnity for an accident. So, heaven forbid you die accidentally, Mary gets three million dollars. Now, let's see...she's got the same thing, identical in every way, with you being the beneficiary, of course."

"So, Bo, can you define what the word accident means?"

"Sure, it's any non-suicidal death that is not natural. That's the company's textbook definition. You kids are what, about thirty years old? I'd say unless you get a deadly medical issue like a heart attack, or cancer, or stuff like that, and it's not an obvious suicide, it must be an accident. So, what are you wanting? Do you want a bigger policy?"

"Maybe. I've been thinking about doubling the benefits on both our policies. I mean, they're good now, but you know, with what's happening with Ron and his wife, I want to be sure the little woman is taken care of if anything happens to me, that's all. What would it involve to make the death benefit two million dollars and keep the triple indemnity on both of us as well?"

"Let me see, Tony. You all took this out a little less than two years ago, so you're just under the wire there, meaning you don't need to take any more physical exams. You just need to get me an update on any new health issues, then all we've got to do is sign the paperwork. Your premiums will almost double. If that's okay, I'll drop all the forms by your office tomorrow."

"That's fine. Just give them to my secretary, her name is Brenda Jean."

"One other thing about changing your policies, Tony; your new benefits will not take effect for thirty days with this plan. But the coverage you've got now will still be in effect until then."

"Oh... that's okay, Bo. We're only thirty years old; neither one of us plans on dying in the next thirty days, that's for sure."

"Well, I should hope not. Now, Tony, I still wouldn't mind getting the coverage on that mansion of yours. I can make you a great deal."

"Bo, I'll tell you what...when you drop those papers off, tell my secretary I told you to come see me next week and she'll get you an appointment. Maybe I can put all my insurance coverage in one basket, even for our cars and maybe the house. The only thing I wouldn't want to change is my major medical plan that gets paid for by the office."

"You've got a date, Tony. I'll see you sometime next week, and I'll bring everything by in the morning on your new life coverage. Anyway, thanks for calling and thanks for the appointment."

"You bet, Bo. Take care of yourself, bye."

He picked up his phone again, calling Brenda Jean back into his office.

She walked in, looking much fresher. She didn't sit on her usual chair; she walked behind him, rubbing his shoulders while she kissed and blew in his ears. "So, boss man, what can I do for you now?"

"I can think of a lot of things, but I really...oh my God, that feels good...I really just wanted to tell you that I have already taken step one in solving what we talked about a little bit ago. See, I told you to trust me."

"I will, my darling, I'll trust you," she whispered, as she lightly rubbed the bulge covered by his pants. "But I better get back to my desk or I'll rip all your clothes off you and rape the shit out of you right here." She glided towards his closed office door, giving him a sweet smile on her way out.

When he got home and opened the front door, he saw Mary and Bobbie sitting on the couch. When Bobbie saw him she looked away, but Mary got up and gave him a fast kiss on the lips, like one would give to a sister. She was obviously cold for some reason.

"Wow, what kind of a welcome was that, Mary? Are you okay?"

"Yeah, I'm okay. I just don't know if you are."

Bobbie got up, moving towards the back door as fast as she could.

Tony shook his head. "What's going on, Mary? What did I do now?"

"Well, let's see. How about some woman coming to see you late at night when I was with my mother in Athens? What's that all about? Did you really think you could get away with that? I heard it was at least two times. Do you want to tell me about that, or are you going to try to lie your way out of it like you do with your gambling?"

"What are you talking about? You can ask Connor. I let him stay up late a lot while you were gone. He'd know if anyone was here. Where in the world did you get that crazy story?"

"Bobbie saw it, Tony. She said she noticed a young woman walking by the Stantons then going up our steps two times last week around ten thirty. She couldn't tell if you let the bitch in, but she said she never saw her walk back. You son of a bitch. What has happened to you? You don't want to touch me anymore, but you get someone to come see you late at night when I'm gone. Who is it, a hooker? You can't even wait a couple of days for your wife to get home, you have to get a hooker? You are something, you know that?"

"Mary, I don't have any idea what you're talking about. It doesn't make any sense. I have the most gorgeous wife in the world, someone any man would want. Why would I throw all that away with a hooker? To tell you the truth, I wouldn't know how to even find a hooker. Besides, I'm not a nympho…I can wait for you more than a few days. Get serious, Mary." He took his tie off, sat in his recliner, and grabbed the remote.

"No Tony, you're not going to twist my mind on this one. I believe Bobbie, and I don't believe you." She grabbed the remote. "No, no TV. We're going to iron this out before we do anything else, you got it?"

He shrugged his shoulders. "Mary, this is silly. I told you I don't want any hooker. I don't want anyone but you. Are you going to believe the loser down the street more than your husband who loves you? Let me ask you a question…if that fat bitch saw a woman come here, when did that person leave? Oh, did she stay all night, with Connor right down the hall? Did the elephant woman tell you about that, huh? Maybe Bobbie doesn't want to be the only one around here who is miserable, did you ever think of that?"

"Oh yeah, how about this?" Mary pulled an empty Benadryl bottle out of her apron pocket. "Do you want to tell me about this? I bet Connor will. This was a full bottle when I left, and now it's empty. Don't tell me you drugged your son so he'd sleep and you could screw some bitch while I was gone. When he gets home, let's ask him if you gave him any of this; what do you say?"

"Go ahead, ask him, I don't give a rat's ass. You are going to be so embarrassed when you ask Connor. Go ahead."

They both heard the school bus stop in front of their house. Mary walked to the window to watch her boy-genius head towards the house, then she went into the kitchen, talking to Tony on the way. "I'm going to ask him about the Benadryl and let him go upstairs. I don't want him to hear any of this. I want to talk to you in private, in your car."

"Hey, Buddy," Tony said, as Connor opened the door. "How was school today?"

"Oh hi, Dad. It was great. I was the only kid in the entire fourth grade who memorized the Declaration of Independence. They couldn't believe it. Where's Mom? I want to tell her, too."

"I think she's in the kitchen. Tell her what you just told me." He watched Connor put his backpack on the floor as he left to find his mother. Tony picked up the remote again, starting to surf for anything to catch his interest. His head felt like it was going to explode. A couple of minutes later, Mary came back out into the living room. "Connor told me you didn't give him any cough syrup while I was gone."

"See, I told you. You're something, you know that?"

"You didn't let me finish. He did say you let him have a Coke every night. Is that how you gave it to him, in a Coke? Look at this bottle, you asshole; just look at it. Let's go out and check out your car, Tony."

He didn't respond. She had caught him. They both went outside and got into his car.

"Tony, we need to…what's that smell? That's not my perfume. Who has been in this car wearing that perfume?"

"Oh my God, Mary, you are getting paranoid. That's not perfume, that's this new aftershave I bought at the convenience store. You were with me when I bought it. I use it when I forget to put some aftershave on in the morning. Here, smell it." He handed her the small bottle from the little pouch on his door.

Mary sprayed it on her wrist, then sniffed it. "That's not the same scent, Tony. Good try, but now I really think you're messing around on me. How do you explain a woman coming to our home late at night two different times?"

"I can't explain anything that crazy fat woman tells you. She's a pathological liar. I guess it boils down to you either believe me, someone who has always loved you and worshiped you, or you believe Miss Bobbie Fatso Loser. Why do you think Jerry left her?"

She shook her head. "I don't know, I just don't know. Tony, I want to believe you, I really do. I can't prove anything, but I'll tell you one thing…something weird is happening. You act so differently towards me. I can't explain it…call it woman's intuition. You just aren't the same man I married. You used to be so tender and horny around me, now you act like we've been married thirty years." She looked out the side window, trying to hide her tears.

"We can work this out, Mary. Just love me. And trust me, trust me more than that three hundred pound loser who tries to control you. I'll make everything better, you'll see."

He knew he may have talked his way out of a nuclear war. He followed her back into the house, awaiting some hint about what was on her mind. After a family steak dinner, he got his answer when she threw him a pillow and a blanket when he was sitting on the couch watching TV. An hour later, he went into the kitchen to grab a Coke. Both Mary and Connor were upstairs so he decided to check something out. Pushing aside the boxes and bottles in the cupboard, he looked for the two pints of liquor he'd found the night he made pancakes for Connor. They were gone, replaced with a twenty four pack of vodka miniatures and about ten to twelve loose minis of Kahlua.

"She's an alcoholic…sure she is, she's an alcoholic," he mumbled as he straightened up everything to make it look like no one had disturbed anything. "That's incredible. With that medicine, she's going to kill herself. Huh."

CHAPTER 13
A Wild Lunch Break

Tony was in a real hole. Parker Hayes had cut him off again, giving him another ten day demand for payment. Now he owed Parker over nine thousand dollars. Tony could cover that with one stroke on his computer, by advancing his January salary four weeks early, but that would leave him with very little in his account for two months. The noose was tightening. Where was he going to get what he needed now?

It was a slow drive to his office. It was raining so hard he could only see about twenty feet in front of his Mercedes. His mind wasn't on the weather; he was looking forward to his lunch break at Brenda Jean's apartment. Tony had to pull his car off the road as the storm got worse, coasting into a parking lot full of potholes. He could see red taillights in front of him on the side of the road. It looked like everyone else was getting off the highway.

Tony looked to his right, watching the lights come on in a pawn shop that also lent people money for their car titles. He looked at the shop's entrance for a few minutes, waiting for the rain to let up, then he decided to check it out. Tony pulled the front door open to the sleazy-looking operation and saw a short, fat man in the back wearing a sleeveless undershirt chewing on an oversized bagel.

"Can I help you?" the round man asked.

"Maybe. I saw your sign after I pulled over when the monsoon hit. Maybe we can do some business together? I've got a brand new Mercedes and I've got the title. I was wondering what the title's worth, how much time I would have to pay it back, and what kind of interest rate I'm looking at?"

The owner walked to the front door, looking outside. "Are you talking about that black one right in front?"

"That's the one."

"Can you leave it here for me to check out for say, an hour?"

E. G. LANDER

"I can do that if you can give me a lift to my office."

"Let's go. Barney, where are you?" he screamed.

A tall greasy-looking teenager with tattoos all over his arms came out from the back. The short man told him to cover the store while he took Tony to his office. Tony grabbed his briefcase out of his car and jumped in the passenger seat of an old Ford truck, getting a bumpy ride to work. "Give me your business card and I'll call you after I check out your car. Are you sure you've got the title?"

"Yeah, it's in my safe at home. I can get it to you tomorrow morning."

"That's really a nice Mercedes. I'll get you a figure as soon as I can. Here, take my number." He handed Tony a dirty, slightly torn small piece of paper.

Tony jumped out of the truck when they got to his office, running towards the front door as the rain picked up again. He couldn't tell whose car was parked in front of the building. He opened the door, finding no one in the office, but all the lights were on. When he got to his suite, he brushed himself off and plopped into his fancy chair, just trying to catch his breath.

Almost immediately his intercom lit up. It was Brenda Jean. "Mr. Calley, can I talk to you?"

"Sure, what do you need?"

"You."

"Brenda Jean, can anyone out there hear you?"

"No, no one's here but me."

"Well then, did you miss me as much as I missed you this weekend?"

"I'm sure I missed you more, Mr. Calley. I was wondering if I could go home? I'm so tired. I didn't sleep much last night thinking about you."

"I don't see why not. You're entitled to six sick days a year. What about lunch?"

"Oh, I'm sure I'll be better by then. How about around eleven? It doesn't hurt anyone to have an early lunch once in a while."

"You've got a date. Just tell one of the girls I said it was okay for you to go home if you're sick, and that they need to cover for you."

Tony looked at his watch, figuring in less than three hours he would be holding his new sweetheart. The minutes took forever to go by. An hour later, he still had two hours to go. He was visualizing Brenda Jean answering her door when he got there. What would she be wearing, just a towel or maybe a nightgown...or how about nothing? He was getting aroused imagining what it would be. When he was within forty minutes of hopefully seeing Brenda Jean, his intercom light lit up from Brenda's desk.

"Mr. Calley, your wife is on line three."

He shook his head, swallowing hard, wanting to sound normal. "Hi, Mary, what's up?"

"Not our checking account, that's for sure. I just left the bank. I got a print out of the last thirty days. Let's see, I can see where we were eight thousand short, then you got a loan for twelve thousand. The bank took their eight thousand, leaving us four thousand. Then you got your November paycheck of fourteen thousand. Now, let's see, if you add four and fourteen, you should get eighteen thousand. So, I looked at your withdrawals, trying to see how you spent the eighteen thousand."

"Get to the point, Mary."

"The point is you paid seven thousand in bills this month. That should leave us about eleven thousand in our checking account, and of course we don't even have a dime in checking or in savings. Now, I'm trying to be calm about all this; my doctor told me I had to stay calm with my new medicine."

He felt little beads of sweat rolling down his back, not even sticking to his shirt on their slow journey. "I meant to tell you about some withdrawals I…uh…made. Mary, I bought some stock. Not a lot, but I had a chance to get in on the ground floor with an exciting new company. I bought it in chunks, and I'm selling most of it short as we speak. I expect I'll be able to put more than the ten thousand back into our account by the end of the week, I promise."

"Why do I find it hard to believe you? Can you prove what you just told me?"

"Not now, the stock certificates are gone. But, uh…I can bring you home the transaction log showing the selling of the stock I bought. I'll do that tonight."

She sighed. "Once again, I think you're covering your tracks. Okay, show me tonight. You know, Tony, this is getting old. I just don't trust you anymore. You don't go to Gambler's Anonymous meetings, and I have no idea what our finances are. What kind of a marriage is this, anyway?"

"I'll tell you what, why don't you do the bills? I'll give you the checkbook, Mary. You can check on every cent we spend. How does that sound?" She hung up on him.

Tony took a deep breath, wondering if his strategy had worked. If it did, she'd call back almost instantly. He looked at the phone. Sure enough, the red light under Rudi Gall's name lit up. "Mr. Calley, while you were talking to your wife, a Mister Leo Harter called. He said it was personal and that you had talked to him this morning while the storm was real bad. Do you want me to get him back on the phone?"

"No, that's okay, Rudi. I'll call him back in a minute, I've got his number." He looked up at the clock on his desk. It was twenty minutes to eleven. He had to wrap things up fast and he didn't even have a car to take him to his wonderful lunch date.

It took four agonizing rings before anyone picked up at the number on the tattered paper Leo had given Tony that morning. "Fast Buck Pawn and Title, Barney speaking."

"Barney, is Leo there? This is Tony Calley."

"Leo, phone call," Barney hollered, loud enough to wake the dead.

"Leo Harter here."

"Hey Leo, this is Tony Calley. I'm the guy you took to work this morning. Do you have the figures worked up on my Mercedes?"

"Yeah, wait a second. Let's see, I can lend you nineteen thousand, five hundred on your car. It's blue book is right at fifty thousand, and the most I ever go is forty percent. It would be at thirty-two percent interest in twelve equal payments of about twenty two hundred a month. What do you want to do?"

"That sounds fine. So when do I get the money?"

"Bring me your title tomorrow and you'll get your money after you sign all the papers. By the way, whose name is on the title?"

"It's in my name."

"Great; do you got someone to pick your car up today?"

"I was wondering if you could get it here real fast. I've got to take a very good customer to lunch."

"Look, Buddy, I took you to work and now you want your car hand delivered? I run a legit company, not a shuttle service."

"I'll give you a hundred dollars if you can get it to me in less than ten minutes."

"Now that's different. I don't mind anyone calling us Leo's Shuttle Company. I'll be there in five minutes." Tony hung up the phone, smiling. Once again, he'd diverted an emergency. Now he would get almost twenty thousand, give Parker the eight he owed him, and put the other twelve in the bank. All he had to do was two things; he had to create some paperwork showing when he bought and sold some stock to show Mary. She should buy that when she called the bank and found out there was twelve grand in their account.

Brenda Jean's light came on again. "Mr. Calley, this is weird. This time when you were talking to that Leo, your wife called again. I told her you were on the phone. She said she'd call back."

"I'm meeting a client for lunch, so if she calls back, tell her that. I'll be leaving here in a couple of minutes, but I'll take my cell phone with me."

He walked outside to wait for Leo. A couple of minutes later, Leo parked the Mercedes alongside the curb, followed by Barney driving Leo's old Ford pickup. "Here's your car, Mr. Calley," Leo said as he opened the door and handed Tony his car keys. Tony gave him a hundred dollar bill.

Tony started his car, looking into the mirror and combing his hair with his fingers before he piled on some after shave from the little bottle in his door pocket. It was fun time. He drove to Brenda's apartment and started to knock. She opened the door before his knuckles hit the door. He walked in, realizing she was standing behind the door. After she closed it, she stood in front of him wearing only a half-open fuzzy pink bathrobe. Within minutes, he was laying with her in her bed, forgetting about everything else in his world but enjoying the short time he had with his sexy secretary.

After they finished, she ran her fingertips over his chest. "Tony, what are we going to do? I want to be with you every day, not just at lunch time at my apartment. Last week you said you'd already starting solving our problems about your wife. What were you talking about?"

"Oh, it was nothing, but it was a start. I really don't want to talk to you about it in case there's a problem; I don't want you involved yet."

"What are you talking about? You can trust me, I'm in love with you."

"Well, do you remember when Mary got real sick?"

"No, I wasn't your secretary yet, but Michelle told me about it. Wasn't it something to do with her thyroid?"

"Yeah, she almost went into a coma that could have killed her. She didn't take her pills for a couple of days and her thyroid almost shut down. So, last week, I called our insurance guy just to check on her life insurance policies in case her thyroid does eventually shut down."

"Are you saying that you expect her to die?" She continued to lightly scratch his chest and stomach. He was getting excited again.

"I didn't say that, but Brenda Jean, I don't want to talk about any of that stuff now. I'm running out of time; let's have some more fun." He rolled over and they did.

After he got out of her shower, she pulled a sheet over her body, laying with her head on her right palm. "Tony, will you call me after you get back to the office? I really want to know more about what we were talking about."

"What do you mean?"

"You know, that insurance stuff and why you call it a start to solving our problems."

"There's nothing else to add to that," he said, pulling up his pants. "If something does happen to Mary, I wanted to be sure I had good insurance on her."

"So, how much is the policy for?"

"It was a million dollar benefit, but I doubled that last week with that phone call."

"Are you shitting me?"

"No, but it's only life insurance. She's only thirty, she might live another forty or fifty years. Maybe I was just dreaming when I told you I took the first step. Sometimes I say stuff that I don't necessarily mean. I don't know, I'm thinking of some things, but I haven't worked everything out. Just trust me, baby."

"I understand Tony, I think. Anyway, call me if you can. I love you so much." She stood up, seeing that he was ready to go. She rubbed her naked body against him as she kissed him goodbye. He'd given her a great lunch break and some wild things to think about.

CHAPTER 14
Triple Indemnity

Tony got back to the office and pulled up the O'Donnell account. He had made that man a little over a seven percent return on his "use it anywhere, but make me some money" two hundred grand investment in less than ten days. Ron would be real proud. He turned his attention to the money market accounts for the rest of his money, finding them flat, making O'Donnell just four hundred dollars profit to date. Oh, well, the whole picture was great, and he was probably heading towards a nice bonus.

He took a deep breath, knowing what his next job was. He had to perform a secret mission, manufacturing all the paperwork on a fictitious set of transactions that matched the withdrawals he'd made from his checking account. After calling the automated service at his bank, he wrote down all the dates and amounts of his recent withdrawals. Tony started scanning his laptop, quickly finding a company that had at least a twelve percent jump in their stock price.

It was easy to fix the withdrawal problem. He found a customer who bought that stock, then copied and pasted transactions that matched up with his withdrawal dates and amounts. All Tony had to do was put his name on the top of the ledger pages, replacing the customer's name. He printed a copy of everything and it really looked legit. Mary had to believe him now, especially if she matched her bank records to what he'd just created. "Oh yeah, who's the man?" he asked himself under his breath.

Tony laid back in his chair, staring at the ceiling. He knew he could take care of any problem. So what if he added a twelve thousand dollar loan to his bills, or over a two thousand dollar monthly payment for his car title, or he emptied his savings account? Who cared? He was due to hit a big one at the track. His time was coming. Yep, he was going to make a killing, and no one would ever know he ever had a run of bad luck. It was kind of a challenge to him, staying ahead of Mary. But she was no match for him. He was too smart to ever get caught, he thought.

"Mr. Calley," Susie said over his phone. "There's a Bo Foster from Foster and James Insurance here dropping off some papers. He wanted to know if you needed to see him."

"Go ahead and send him back, Susie."

Bo walked in, bringing his usual insurance salesman smile. "Well, howdy, Mr. Tony. It's been a while. Here's the papers for the change in yours and Mary's term life policies." He plopped into the overstuffed burgundy chair next to the desk, stretching out his legs and displaying the snakeskin cowboy boots he bragged about all the time. "You and your gorgeous wife can sign them anytime, as long as you have a witness."

"Thanks, Bo. Did you get an appointment for next week?"

"No, I guess your secretary is out sick. The girl out there told me to call a Brenda Jean tomorrow. I got to tell you, Tony, I'm anxious to discuss what we can save you, especially on that house of yours."

"Great. I've been meaning to consolidate all my insurance coverage. I guess now is as good of time as any to look at it. Say, Bo, I have one more question about our life insurance. You said there's a triple indemnity clause for an accident. I know that makes the new benefit six million, but I need to ask you something about that, just so I can be clear when I talk it over with Mary."

"Fire away, old buddy."

"Well, we're both always worried about our medicine. I would think if one of us forgets and take too much medicine, that wouldn't be an accident because some could construe that as bordering on a suicide. But what if we undertake our medicine and it screws us up?"

"Under that scenario, are you describing a medical death that is created by not taking the medicine to keep a problem under control?"

"Exactly."

"That wouldn't be an accident either. That would be defined as a medical death not caused by an external accident, but one that was brought about by not getting the proper treatment or medication. That would only pay the beneficiary two million dollars with your new policy, with, heaven forbid, your death or Mary's."

"That's what I thought. That was Mary's question, not mine. Anyway, I'll have these all signed and witnessed and I'll send them over to you. Oh, when you come back next week, bring me info on your homeowners and auto insurance. We're with Johnson Battles now, and our home is valued at a little over nine hundred thousand. I'll get the car stuff together for you before your appointment."

Bo stood up, extending a hand to Tony. "Thanks so much for thinking of me. I'm really looking forward to seeing you again next week."

"Take care, Bo," Tony said as he shook his hand, then watched him leave. He picked up his cell phone, calling Brenda Jean. "Hey, baby doll, I just wanted to see how you were doing."

"I'm fine. I'm just sitting here watching TV, eating a banana, and thinking about you."

"That sounds a little kinky."

"I didn't mean it that way, silly. But I do miss you. How about stopping over here on the way home? What do they call that at the track, a daily double? That's right, a daily double. That's what I need today, a daily double."

"I wish I could, but I've got to go see Connor's new teacher tonight. It's parents' conference night at his school."

"Oh, okay; maybe you can call me sometime tonight when you get a minute. Just tell your wife you've got to go the bathroom, and duck out the door and give me a ring, will you?"

"I'll try. I love you, darling. Bye."

It was almost four, and he had to get home to make his appointment at Connor's school. He put the manufactured stock purchase/sale summary into his briefcase and headed out the door.

****

The second he opened his car door, his cell phone rang. It was his partner Ron Burns.

"Tony, B.J. died this afternoon."

"Oh, Ron, I'm so sorry. I was hoping he'd pull through. Is there anything we can do?"

"No, not that I can think of, except one thing; why don't you ask Mary to call Vickie Anne tomorrow? I think that would be good for Vicki. By the way, B.J. didn't want a funeral, he wanted to be cremated. There's going to be a small family service tomorrow night, so you don't even have to worry about coming up here. I just wanted to let you know what was happening. Say, is there anything new at the office?"

"Not really, except I've made your Mr. O'Donnell a ton of money so far on his investments. Other than that, it's been real quiet."

"Don't get any ideas of stealing Bill away from me, Mr. Calley," Ron responded with a laugh. "Listen, Tony, he's very generous with bonuses. Good luck. Keep sucking up to him like I know you are."

"I will. Now you call us if we can help, and how about emailing me where tomorrow night's service is going to be? I'll let everyone know down here."

"Will do. See you, Tony."

Tony sat in his car for a few moments, looking at nothing. He opened his door, walked back into the office to tell the girls about Mr. Burns's father-in-law, then headed home, constantly thinking about Brenda Jean…that is, until he drove by his favorite pawn shop and title company. "Yes," he hollered out his open window, raising his fist into the air.

As he approached his house, he noticed Mary's car was parked almost sideways in the garage, forcing him to park in the driveway by the back door. When he walked in, there was a bad smell coming from the kitchen, the smell of something burning. He looked in the oven, seeing what looked like a very black meatloaf. When he opened the oven door, smoke filled the kitchen at once, igniting the fire alarm above the table. Tony grabbed a dish towel that was wrapped around the handle on the refrigerator and fanned the alarm, like a bullfighter would fan a charging bull.

He quickly grabbed the meatloaf pan, throwing it into the sink. After he turned the faucet on, the meatloaf let out even more smoke, once again turning on the alarm. "Mary, Mary, where are you? I need some help here."

There was no response. After he got the kitchen settled down, he started looking for his wife. He walked upstairs, constantly calling her name. Tony found Connor in his room, bouncing his head to whatever he was listening to on his headphones.

"Where's your mom?" Connor didn't move.

Tony reached over and tapped Connor's shoulder. Connor took the loud speakers off his head. "Hey, Pops, what's up?"

"Do you know where your mother is?"

Connor rolled halfway over, looking at Tony. "She was downstairs a little while ago, but she sure was acting funny."

"What do you mean, acting funny?"

"She was singing some song I'd never heard of, and she was talking kind of weird."

Tony turned around, walking into the hall. "Mary, where are you?"

He checked every room upstairs, then picked up his search downstairs, finally finding his wife on the laundry room floor. She was singing as she continually picked up different pieces of clothing, throwing each one of them at the ceiling. Mary was drunk. He picked her up with one arm and she slid back down. "Well, if it isn't my favorite husband. Are you ready to go to work? Oh, wait, you might be going to the track." She started laughing uncontrollably, then put her index finger on her chin. "No, wait, he's got a date at the bank. There must be a few cents still in our accounts; he'd better go get 'em."

"Mary, what are you doing? You're crocked. We've got that conference with Connor's teacher in an hour. You got to get up, sweetheart."

"Fuck his teacher, fuck everyone! The only one who cares is Bobbie…not my husband, my cool and debonair husband. No, all he cares about is betting. Betting on anything, he doesn't care…." Her head fell on her chest as if she were asleep.

He shook her again. "Mary, wake up. You're not supposed to drink with your medicine. Come on, let's get you into the shower and get some coffee in you. Please get up."

"Your dinner is in the oven. I hope you enjoy it." She started giggling. "Not much of a wife, am I? Oh, you want to make love? I think it's been weeks since you enjoyed it, at least with me. Oh, and I love your new perfume—I mean aftershave—on your shirts lately. I know you must accidentally run into whores at the track…sure, that's it. Just leave me alone, will you? This is my second home, the laundry room. While you're out partying, I'll be here pouring bleach and fabric fucking softener over all your bouquet smelling clothes."

"You are not only drunk, you're crazy," he said as he pulled her up. Tony got her undressed and into the shower. She stood there, leaning up against the side wall with a constant stream of cold water cascading over her. He stared at her, thinking how beautiful she still was despite how he felt about Brenda Jean. At that moment, though, he realized how much he loved his secretary, not his wife. Now he just felt sorry for Mary.

He found her medicine bottles and checked all the little labels on the sides, one of which warned against drinking alcohol with those pills. He pulled his cell phone out of his pocket and punched in the predial for her doctor. He got an answering service.

"This is Tony Calley. Dr. Hunnington sees my wife Mary. I need to talk to him right away. She's taking a new thyroid medicine that has a warning on the bottle not to drink, and she's very drunk. I don't know what to do."

"I'll call Dr. Hunnington, sir, and he should be getting back with you momentarily."

Tony was panicking. "Should I take her to the hospital?"

"Just give the doctor a few minutes. I'll tell him it looks like an emergency."

"It doesn't look like anything, it is an emergency."

Five minutes later, the doctor called him. "Tony, I got your message. So Mary's been drinking, huh? I'd just put her to bed and let her rest, but be sure she takes her meds in the morning."

"But, but…the label on the bottle says not to drink alcohol. I think she drank a hell of a lot, based on how she's acting. What about that?"

"The label is appropriate. What it means is that alcohol really makes her medicine useless. It won't hurt her to drink, except it makes it like she never took her pill. It negates it. The ingredients in her pill are very good, but it can be dangerous if she stops taking it for more than two or three days. With her drinking, you might as well say she missed one day; just don't let her miss any more, okay?"

"I got it, Doc. Thanks for calling back."

"No problem, Mr. Calley. Do me a favor and tell her to stop in my office tomorrow morning. I don't care what time, I'll work her in."

Tony turned around to see Connor leaning up against the door frame. "Dad, what's wrong with Mom? Why were you talking to her doctor?"

"She just had something to drink today that hit her wrong. She'll be fine, all she needs is some sleep. Listen, Bud, what are we going to do about your teacher conference tonight?"

"That's okay, Dad. Mrs. Moore told us if we can't make our appointment, tell our parents to email her tomorrow and we can still meet up with her after school one day this week. I don't know her email address, but I know her first name…it's Holly, and I think her middle initial is 'A.' You know what? I'd rather stay home with Mom, anyway."

Tony pulled his wife out of the shower, dried her off, and put her in a pair of pajamas, then slid her into their bed. She didn't wake up as he pulled the covers over her. She was still mumbling something about the bank. He cleaned up the kitchen and the laundry room, then ordered a pizza for dinner. An hour later Tony and Connor finished eating.

"Dad, do you mind if I go lay with Mom for a while? I promise I won't wake her up, but I'm worried about her. Would that be okay?"

Tony nodded. "Sure, go ahead. In fact, I'll just sleep down here if you want to stay in our room all night. Let me know if she wakes up, will you?"

Connor went upstairs, leaving his dad on the family room couch. Tony got up to grab a beer, then looked for those miniatures. He pushed all the food aside on that shelf, finding no vodka or Kahlua. "How can she drink so much? She's got a problem, that's for sure," he whispered.

He put his feet on the coffee table and surfed the TV, looking for something interesting on the sports channels. All he could find was an old bowling show that looked like it was at least forty years old. The bowlers were wearing checkered pants with white shirts that had their names on the back. He turned the TV off and moved to the front porch, wishing it was ten thirty and Brenda Jean was sneaking over. He decided to call her.

"Hey, Tony, are you at school?"

"No, we didn't go."

"Why not?"

"Well, my wife decided to get drunk tonight. You should see her, she's embarrassing. She's got a big problem. And catch this, she knows if she drinks it could be dangerous because of the medicine she's taking."

"Wow. Is she going to be all right?"

"Oh yeah, she's sleeping it off right now. I called her doctor and he said when she drinks, it's like she hasn't taken her pill, and if she goes more than a day or two without them, she's in trouble."

"Remind me to bring her some beer after work every day."

"Brenda Jean, that's not funny. You were joking, right?"

"Of course, Tony. But you did tell me about her life insurance this morning, didn't you? Sorry, just joking again."

It was silent for a few seconds until Tony spoke up. "You know, she sure disgusted me tonight. It's getting so I don't even like looking at her. That's a shame after all our years together, but that's what it's turning into."

"Hey, sweet stuff, how about me coming over tonight? She'll probably sleep through everything, anyway. I can do my ten thirty delivery thing."

"We can't do that anymore. I've got a very nosy neighbor who saw you come over when Mary was gone. It's like she constantly checks on me."

"Oh, my God, did she tell your wife?"

"She sure did, but I convinced her nobody came by."

"Good. So, there's no way I can see you tonight, huh?"

"I guess not, Brenda Jean."

"Well…okay…maybe we can coincidentally go to lunch at the same time tomorrow?"

CHAPTER 15
The Beginning of a Plan

Tony woke up the next morning to the sound of Connor's bus stopping in front of their house. "Oh, my God, he's going to miss the bus," he said as he tried to get up off their couch too fast and fell to the floor.

Conner streaked by him, dragging his backpack. "Bye, Dad, I'll see you tonight."

"How did you get…?" Tony started to say, but only watched through the open front door as his son climbed up the little black stairs into the bus.

Tony walked out into the kitchen and found an empty cereal bowl with a few drops of milk in the bottom of it next to a half full box of Trix. As he turned around he noticed a little note taped to the refrigerator. He pulled it off, recognizing Connor's printed writing. "Dad, I tried to get Mom to make me breakfast, but she won't wake up. So I decided to take care of it myself. Sorry for the mess. I love you, Connor. P.S. I let you sleep because I figured you probably had a bad night on the sofa."

Tony ran his fingers through his hair. "That's some kid. Oh my God, he said Mary wouldn't wake up. Oh my God," he said under his breath, with the words getting louder. He ran up the stairs, skipping every other step. "No, I can't be this lucky," he said, trying to catch his breath as he ran into their bedroom.

She was breathing okay. He shook her, getting only a rambling "Hey, what's going on?" out of her. She turned her head towards him, letting out a sickening liquor smell as she yawned and fell back on her pillow.

Tony lay down on the foot of the bed and glanced at the clock on the table next to her. Noticing that it was almost eight, he got up, took his shower, and got dressed. Glancing at her as he stepped towards the stairs, he could see she hadn't moved since he'd tried to wake her up, but she was still breathing. He found her pill reminder and put it next to her on the bedside table, along with a glass of water. Then he scribbled her a note he leaned against the water, saying, "Take your pills. Don't forget. Love, Tony."

When he got downstairs, he remembered he needed the title on the Mercedes, so he opened the safe in his office and ruffled through the papers until he found it. He put it in his briefcase and pulled out the fake stock sheet, looked it over with a smile, and taped it to the refrigerator next to Connor's note. Pulling a pen out of his shirt pocket, he wrote on it, "Wish me luck on how much we get back on this. I should know by tomorrow. T." He hurried out the back door, hoping to avoid his wife.

When Tony walked into the office all the girls were already there, and they were giggling. He saw Brenda Jean walk by. "Hey, what's so funny?"

"It's just us silly secretaries. We had a funny thing happen this morning, that's all," Brenda answered as she sat behind her desk.

"Okay; is it a girls only joke, or can you tell me about it?"

"Here's what happened," Beckie said. "I had a headache this morning, so I went to the medicine cabinet in the lounge and grabbed what I thought was my aspirin bottle. Well, I opened it and took three pills, only it wasn't the aspirin bottle...it was the ex-lax bottle. I swear I wasn't thinking, but those pills look exactly like my aspirin. Now my headache is going away," she laughed. "But I think I'll be visiting the toilet a few more times today."

Tony and the secretaries broke out in laughter, looking at poor Beckie, who was shaking her head.

"I know I'm dumb sometimes," Beckie laughed. "But anyone could make the same mistake just because of how those pills looked. I swear, they're identical. Anyway, Mr. Calley, that's how we got started this morning." She looked at her two buddies. "Just so they don't make fun of me all day as I take my bathroom breaks."

"I'm sure they won't, Beckie. That could happen to anybody...I just never heard of it happening to anyone I know before," Tony said, giggling as he walked towards his office.

Tony had a busy morning. He took his car title to Leo's pawn shop, got his check, and got a certified check for Parker Hayes. That left him with a little less than eleven thousand in his account. Now let Mary bug him; he'd be ready for that fight.

After getting back to his office, he called Brenda Jean into his office. She sat in her usual chair, putting her hands on her knees. "What can I do for you, boss man?"

"Is that a new dress?"

"Yes, sir. I knew you'd like it. Green isn't my color, but it's comfortable." She leaned back, giving him the best show yet, leaving nothing for his imagination. Even someone walking into his office would have no idea what she was showing him with her back facing his door.

Tony wasn't sure what to do. He was so aroused, but it was dangerous to do much at the office. "Brenda Jean, I'm sure you know what you're doing to me. But just for now, how about pulling your dress down and covering up some? I need to talk to you about something important, and you've got me so hot I can't think."

She did as he asked, but not without a little pouting look going his way. "Okay, I can wait. What do you want to talk to me about?"

"First off, do I have any appointments around lunchtime today?"

"No, sir. I'm trying to keep you open every day between twelve and two. That way if you ever want to join me for lunch at my place, we can do that."

"Don't say that so loud, someone may be using the copy machine. Okay, that was my next question. How about you leaving for lunch at twelve and I'll leave a quarter after, and we'll have a relaxing lunch together?"

"I can't wait." She looked at her watch. "That means I only have a little over one hour to go." She mouthed to him that she loved him.

"Now, I've got to go back to work. Here, take this; this is O'Donnell's file. Take out all the pages and copy them for me. Then put the originals back in the file in chronological order, and do the same with the copies, then bring both sets back to me, will you?"

She uncrossed her legs in slow motion again, giving him one last look before lunchtime. "Say, how's your wife?"

"She's probably still sleeping it off. I haven't heard from her, so she's either still out or she's still pissed. I don't know, and honestly I don't care. She is really starting to disgust me, I feel more like her babysitter and less like her husband."

"So, Tony, what are you going to do? You're obviously not happy living with her, and both of us are unhappy living apart."

"I don't know. I can't divorce her."

"Why not?"

"In this state, she'd probably get almost everything, including my business. Plus, she'd make sure I didn't get Connor, or at least didn't get to see him much. That would be terrible." He took in a deep breath, exhaling it slowly as he looked at his son's picture on his desk.

"What other option do you have, Tony? I mean, besides divorce, have you thought about separating?"

"No, that wouldn't work. That would just give her more fodder for a divorce. In Tennessee, the wife gets preferential treatment with everything, anyway. I wouldn't want to give a judge even more reason to be on her side."

"Honey, I'm not an expert on these things, so let me ask you a question. Can you buy her off?"

Tony sat straight up. "Not right now. I don't have the assets to make her a good offer. Besides, she'd want to wait for the divorce to get half of everything."

"Tony, I'll wait for you, as long as it takes." She lowered her voice. "I love you so much, I'll wait. I hate to say this, sweet stuff, but I was thinking that there's one way all this could be fixed."

"What's that?"

She raised her eyebrows, then looked at the wall to her left. "If she had another thyroid attack."

"Do you mean if she died?"

"Well...."

"Brenda Jean, I'm going to pretend I didn't hear that. She's still my wife and I know I don't love her anymore, but Mary and I have been through a lot, and I don't think I'd ever want to see anything bad happen to her." He said that even though he realized he'd been thinking the same thoughts as his secretary at the same time.

"I wouldn't either. Don't get me wrong, I'm not saying we should do anything to hurt her, I'm just saying if she did have another serious attack, who knows? I think we got to be prepared for anything, especially if she keeps drinking. Anyway, like I said, I'll wait. You're worth it." She got up, walked around his desk, and put her hands on his shoulder. She slid one hand down his front, finding what she was looking for. "Is there anything else you need, Mr. Calley?"

He rolled his eyes a little. "Not for now," he said, almost whispering. "But there will be in about an hour."

"See you then," Brenda Jean replied, leaving his office.

She barely had time to get back to her desk when she called him on the intercom. "Mr. Calley, your wife is on line one."

"Thanks, Brenda Jean."

"Tony, why didn't you wake me up before you left this morning?"

"I tried, Mary, I really did."

"I don't believe that for a minute. You didn't even sleep upstairs."

"But I was up there. I put you to bed and left a note about your pill reminder thing. You were totally drunk when I got home from work yesterday. We couldn't even go to Connor's parents and teacher thing because you were so wasted."

"So, what happened after I went to bed? Did your girlfriend call you, or did she sneak in the front door again?"

He sighed as he got madder and madder. "Listen, Mary, we've already gone over this once. I don't have a girlfriend, and even though your water buffalo friend down the street says she saw a woman there late at night, she is totally nuts. What is going on with you, Mary? Why are you so jealous of nothing, and why are you so miserable?"

"I'm not jealous of nothing…just your girlfriend. I started smelling perfume on your clothes about two weeks ago. I scrub your shirts over and over to get that stinking smell out of them, then the next day they smell again. You're not fooling me. I'm going to find out who she is, and then you and her both have got some big problems."

"I think you've lost it. Yep, you're going crazy. I've told you a thousand times how proud I am being married to one of the finest woman I've ever seen. You're imagining things, and I don't know why."

"Oh, I got your homemade stock purchase paper that was taped on the refrigerator. All I have to do is call the bank the stocks were issued on and see if they have your name on them. Do you really want me to do that? I'll bet you that you weren't involved with any of that, and you blew all that money from our account gambling on some 'can't miss' horses at the track."

"You'll see when you call the bank, your eleven thousand is back in there. There'd be more, but I had to pay a lot of taxes on such a short sale. But really Mary, I don't give a shit what you do. You aren't ever going to believe me anyway, so do what you want. I've got work to do, and looking at our house this morning, so do you; that is, if you can stay sober enough to do it. Be a good wife and a good mother for a change." He hung up on her.

His intercom light lit up all most instantly. "Mr. Calley, your wife is on line one again."

"Tell her I'm tied up."

Tony felt like his life was a box of fireworks, getting way too complicated and ready to explode. He walked out of the office, leaving his cell phone on his desk. He sat on the concrete bench on the side of the building, built for any smokers that might work there. All he wanted was some peace. He sat there for over a half hour. When he stood up to return to his office, he noticed a car that looked a lot like Mary's Mustang pulling into the parking lot. After it was out of sight, Tony peeked around the corner, watching his wife and Bobbie walking together towards the front door.

Tony walked towards them. "Well, look who came to see me."

Mary shook her head. "We didn't come to see you, but we did come to see who's in your office."

"Please don't make a scene, Mary, this is a professional business," Tony begged. "We don't need to bring our problems to my office, we really don't."

"Don't worry, I'm not going to make a scene. I just want to see who's working here today, that's all." She looked at Bobbie. "Come on, Bobbie, I want you to meet the girls."

Mary and Bobbie walked into the office, followed closely by Tony. Mary was very nice to everyone, introducing each one of them to her oversized neighbor. It only took about five minutes, then they drove off.

When Tony got back into his office, Brenda Jean called him. "What was that all about?"

"I don't have any idea. She's never acted like that before, coming and going so quickly. I bet I'll find out tonight when I get home what the hell she wanted. Say, it's almost twelve, I think it's lunchtime for someone special."

"You're right. Bye."

He waited until twenty after twelve, then he left his office and asked Rudi where Brenda Jean was. Rudi told him she'd gone to lunch a few minutes ago, and might be a little late getting back because she had some errands to run.

Tony looked at his watch. "By God, it is lunch time. I think I'll go get a burger. Does anyone else want one?" he asked, raising his voice so all the girls could hear. No one wanted anything, so he got into his car and headed out on the highway towards all the fast food joints, then made a U-turn to head back to Brenda Jean's apartment. She opened the door, once again standing behind it as he walked in. She was only wearing a big orange beach towel, which very quickly fell to the floor.

CHAPTER 16
I Guess We Have No Choice

Tony took his time driving home after work, not knowing what to expect from his wife. Why had she brought Bobbie to the office, introduced her to all the secretaries, and then left in less than five minutes? What was that all about? He knew he would find out when he got to the house, but what could it be? Maybe he could avoid her somehow.

He parked his Mercedes on the street so she couldn't hear him get out of the car. He quietly walked in the front door. "Shit," he whispered as he spotted Mary laying on the couch with a red washcloth over her forehead.

She took the wet wrap off and took a deep breath when she heard him open the door. "Hello, sweetheart, welcome home."

He didn't know what to say. He was expecting her to throw something at him or start screaming, but certainly not give him a friendly greeting, based on her attitude at his office. The emotional ups and downs between the two of them were driving him crazy. "Hi, honey, how are you feeling?"

"I think you can guess. I've had one hell of a headache all day. That was some ride...I mean the last twenty-four hours. I ain't never drinking again, I'll tell you that." She patted the couch next to her. "Come over here, baby, and sit down. We really need to talk."

Tony loosened the knot on his necktie, then pulled it out of his shirt, throwing it on a chair that was already holding his suitcoat. He looked at the spot where she wanted him to sit, then sat there without saying a word.

"Tony, can I talk to you?"

"Sure, but before you do, I need to tell you something I tried to tell you last night. Vicki Burns's father died yesterday. This is the first chance I've had to talk to you. I mean, you weren't in any shape to talk last night or this morning."

She shook her head. "Oh no, poor Vicki. I need to call her."

"That's what Ron said, that it would be nice if you called her; but you can't, at least not tonight."

"Why not? Do I still sound drunk?"

"No, it's not that. The service is tonight. He meant for you to call her earlier today."

She shook her head. "Well, I guess I screwed that up, huh?" Tears were building in her eyes. "Tony, I know you're not very proud of me today, but I really think we need to try to sort some things out."

"Okay, what things?"

"First of all, what is happening to us? We used to be so happy; now it seems like we live on different planets. I really want to rewind the clock and go back about two or three months. Remember when we could talk to each other and trust each other and enjoy each other? Do you remember those days? And now look at us. I've been doing a lot of thinking, Tony. Our marriage is on the ropes, we both know that. It seems to me we have three choices." She started counting on her fingers. "Number one, we can separate and see if we miss each other so much we get back together, but I don't see that happening. Number two, we can get a divorce and split everything up, but that will probably devastate Connor. Number three is to work things out, forgive each other, and hold each other and have fun like we used to." Tears were rolling down her cheeks. "I like that one; what do you think?"

"Let's get back to something you just said. You said we needed to forgive each other. What do you have to forgive me for, gambling with money I earn?"

"Tony, I'm trying to be a grown-up here. I know some things about you that most wives would never forgive, but I'm willing to forgive you."

He pulled back, like he was expecting a punch. "Okay, let's get it out in the open...why do you need to forgive me?"

"I really think you know what I'm talking about. It's the woman. I even know who she is," Mary said with a scowl.

"You're not going there again, Mary. Don't do this."

"Do I have to tell you what I know to convince you to be honest with me?"

Tony nodded. "Go ahead, I'm listening."

"Well, do you know why Bobbie and I went to your office today? Do you think we just went there to say hello to all the secretaries and then leave, all within two or three minutes?"

"I have no idea why you came to my office, so why don't you tell me?"

"Okay. I've been suspicious of your secretary, Miss Brenda Jean. I brought Bobbie with me to see if she thinks Brenda is the woman who came to our house those nights I was with my mom and dad at the hospital in Athens. And I wanted to see if I could pick up a scent from her—you know, like her perfume—just to see if it smelled like what's been on your shirts."

"Okay, I'll bite. So what did Miss Hippo say, and what did you smell?"

"Bobbie said she could have been the girl she saw those two nights. She said she was seventy-five percent sure of it, and I didn't get close enough to your secretary to smell what kind of perfume she was wearing."

Tony fell back on the sofa, rubbing his forehead. "Oh my God. Now a lonely, rejected tub of goo—from what, four houses down the street?—is filling your head with garbage. I'm surprised she said seventy-five percent and not a hundred percent. I don't know what else to tell you. If you believe her over me about this silly, stupid stuff, go ahead. It doesn't look like I can convince you of my innocence, so go ahead and shoot me."

"I'm sorry, Tony, but I believe her. It explains everything. Do you know your shirts all have the same perfume on them every morning when I do the laundry? It's not one of my perfumes, it's somebody else's. I've also noticed that both of you are gone about the same time for lunch almost every day. Here's something else…I found a little white piece of paper under our bed. It had a phone number on it, and it smelled just like your shirts smell."

"I think you've gone totally crazy, Mary. I have no idea what you're talking about." His voice started getting louder. "I can explain everything you just accused me of. That perfume smell, do you remember we talked about that before? When I'm running late, I forget to put on aftershave, so I use the little bottle in the car almost every morning."

"That's not aftershave, that's a flowery perfume. Prove it to me, Tony; go get that bottle from your car. Let me smell that next to the note I found."

He shook his head, stopped, then shook it again. "I can't; I used the last of it yesterday and threw the bottle out."

"That's so convenient. Okay, how about your lunch breaks with Brenda?"

"She's my secretary, Mary. I took her to lunch a couple of times to thank her for doing a good job on something or saving an unhappy customer. Besides, I've had lunch with the other girls in the office. Don't you remember I took Beckie and Rudi to lunch about a month ago? Does that mean I'm having an affair with all of them?"

"What about the phone number on that piece of paper?"

"I have no idea what you're talking about. I put phone numbers on whatever I can write on, especially when I'm driving. That doesn't mean anything."

"I called that number and got a message from Brenda." She started to cry again.

"So, let me tell you about that so you can feel silly. When you were gone, she stopped me at my car after work one day, offering her cell number in case I need someone to take care of Connor if I had to leave because of your mother. And as far as the same smell on the note as on my clothes, remember after I spray myself with aftershave in the car, it gets on my shirt pocket, the exact place I put that note. So, there's another one of your big ass theories that I disproved."

Mary wiped her eyes, then blew her nose with a very wet tissue she had tucked away in her left hand. "I don't know what to believe, Tony. All of these things add up to why you are so cold to me. I don't know what to believe." She looked out the front window. "You promised me you stopped gambling, but yet you pulled all that money out of our account this month, and I still think you didn't buy any stock."

"You know, Mary, this is getting very sickening." He pointed his finger in her face. "It's not a one way street here. You've been pushing me away, too. I mean with all the accusations and stuff. You've been very quick to be my judge, jury, and executioner without finding out the truth. And now you're drinking again. I mean, you know with this new medicine, you may be killing yourself, but you're still doing it. I'd say if you look at the big picture, you've been the one who's been messing up, not me."

She looked directly into his lying eyes. "So, you're saying it's all my fault? Everything is my fault? You should have been a politician…you think you can talk anyone into believing anything. Well, this time you can't. I'm keeping a record of everything in my diary. There's a lot of stuff in there already, and don't even think about finding it, you won't. It's my security blanket." He looked puzzled.

"What the hell does that mean?"

She stood up, looking down at her pathetic husband. "It's there if my lawyer wants it, but it's in a very secret place, a place you'll never find. And Tony, I thought I'd let you know that since your wife doesn't work, and her best friend doesn't work, you just might have someone spying on you all day long, maybe taking pictures; what do you think of that?"

He got up, trying to stare through her. "You don't scare me, because I haven't done anything wrong. So good luck spying on me…it's going to be very boring for you."

"I hope you're right. Do you know the sad thing?" she asked, looking at his open shirt collar. "The sad thing is that I thought all day about us getting back together by being honest, trying to forgive each other. But there's no way to save our marriage now, because you don't know how to tell the truth and you don't care enough to start over. And to think all I was going to ask you to do was to fire Brenda Jean. That was nothing but wishful thinking on my part. You're a loser." She turned, walking away from him.

He decided to try one more dramatic act. He found her in the kitchen with her head down on the table, crying. "Mary, I'm leaving. I'm trying to sort out everything you said. I realize now that you deserve someone a lot better than me. I've been a terrible husband, we both know that. I can't live anymore knowing how I ruined everything, and I don't want to live anymore without you. Don't look for me, you won't find me, and tell Connor I love him more than he'll ever know. Mary, thanks for all the good years. I hope I see you in a better place one day. Goodbye." She didn't look up or say anything. She just lifted an arm over her head, shaking it as if to say goodbye.

****

Tony got in his Mercedes and squealed out the driveway. As soon as he was out of sight of his house, he called Brenda Jean.

"Brenda Jean, we've got problems. My wife knows everything. That's why she came to the office with that fat woman. Her name is Bobbie, she's our neighbor. Bobbie told her she saw you coming over after ten when Mary was in Athens. Listen to me, Mary's putting it all together. She's even talking about keeping notes on everything for the divorce. We need to meet and talk, she's got me so paranoid about everything, I bet she knows you drive a VW, so why don't I pick you up?"

"Okay, where?"

"Let's see, go to the McDonalds on Third Street, park there, then walk to the pizza joint behind it; you know, the one next to the beauty parlor. After that, just look for my car. I'll be waiting for you there in about ten minutes, okay?"

"I'll see you there, sweetheart. I love you."

Tony got to their meeting spot early, constantly looking around for anyone who might be staring at him. Finally, Brenda Jean opened the passenger door and jumped in. He told her to lay down so she wouldn't be seen with him, then they left the giant parking lot.

When he was five miles out of town, he told her she could sit up. "I'm sorry about that, Brenda Jean, but I want to be sure we don't give her any more ammo to clean my clock with in a divorce."

She sat up, pulling down the visor mirror so she could straighten out her hair. "That's all right. So tell me, what are we going to do about your wife?"

Tony shook his head. "Hold on, let's park over there." He pulled into a bus station parking lot in Towley, a small town eight miles from Rymont. "Brenda Jean, we have to get rid of her."

"What do you mean, get rid of her?"

"Do you remember when we talked about her drinking and her medicine, and that I was trying to increase her life insurance?"

"Yeah, of course I remember," Brenda Jean said, looking out her window, watching an old man walk by with a sliding gait. "I didn't think you were serious."

"Well, I'm serious now. Don't get shocked at what I'm about to tell you, Brenda Jean. When I say get rid of her, I mean we have to kill her. That's the only way out of this. And don't forget I just upped the ante on her insurance. It's worth two million now, but there's a catch."

She put an arm around him, kissing his ear. "Not now, Brenda Jean, I need your help. Now, listen, I haven't even got the papers signed yet for the new policies. And she's got to sign hers, with a witness."

"What's the problem? Just sign it for her; I'm sure you can find something that's got her signature on it and fake it, or trace it, or whatever. Then get one of the girls in the office to witness it, just not me. We do that all the time for you all; we just cover up the paper except the witness line and anyone can sign it."

"There's one more thing; the new policy requires a thirty day waiting period to take effect."

"Tony, I think we can be extra careful for a month. We can still see each other in the office. I can wait thirty days for you. But what are you going to do to keep her from filing for a divorce before then?"

"I just have to warm up to her some, and ask for her forgiveness. She was ready to forgive me tonight until I got mad."

"Does that mean making love to her?"

"I may have to; I mean, it's only thirty days. If I don't treat her right, we probably won't get to see each other until after a nasty divorce, and you can kiss the two million goodbye."

"That makes me sick to my stomach, thinking about you loving on her. I guess we have no choice. Thirty days doesn't scare me, it's the thought of all those nights you make love to her that I hate." She started kissing his ear again. "Tony, please tell me you won't decide you love her more than me."

He turned to her, giving her one of his patented "going for a homerun" kisses. When he was done, she just laid there with her mouth open, wearing a smile. "Brenda Jean, one more thing; if something happens to her, it can't be on the thirtieth day. We may have to wait a couple of weeks or so after that to fix everything. We can't make it look too obvious. "

Brenda Jean looked out her window. "I hate to say it, Tony, but you're right. You're going to have to go back to her and beg her to take you back."

He pulled her to him. "That's why I love you so much; you not only look great, but you think great, too." He gave her another kiss, then started his car back up. She wanted more from him than a kiss, but he was planning his strategy. "I'm going to do what you said. I'll take you back to your car and go home and make peace with the bitch. But remember, we have to be extra, extra careful now. We can make everything work out if we're smart. It's only a few weeks, then we'll have a lifetime together."

"Tony, have you had any thoughts of how we're going to do it? I mean kill her?"

He nodded as he bit his upper lip. "I'm still working on it, but I'm getting close to figuring it out. I'll let you know."

"Is there anything I can do?"

"Yes, there is, Brenda Jean. I want you to be extra professional in the office for a while. Don't give anyone there any reason to support her in case it does come down to a divorce. In fact, why don't you start talking about your fiancé that's coming to town? Just make up a name and find a picture somewhere to put on your desk. Do you have a brother?"

"Yeah, he's in Iraq. I know I can get a good picture of him from my folks, or even one of my cousins, if I need to. Sure, I can be a good actor. Now, don't you get jealous of my fake fiancé, you hear?" she said with a giggle.

"Yeah, right. You just said you can be a good actor. How about starting up a conversation with Mary whenever she calls in. Talk to her about how much you like your job and how much your life is settling down because your fiancé is coming to town. See if you can convince her how much you are in love with him. Try to become her friend, then maybe she'll think Bobbie is nuts."

"I can do that. Let me know what she says about me. I bet it will be good," Brenda Jean said, as they pulled up to the beauty parlor, where she got back in her car and left.

When Tony got back home, Mary was sleeping on the couch until he walked in. She looked at Tony for a few seconds, then shook her head. "So, you're back. This is my lucky day. When you left, you wanted to kill yourself. What's the problem, you didn't have the balls to do it?" She sat up, wiping the sleep out of her eyes. "Why did you come back, anyway?

You made your point that you don't owe me an explanation on anything, that you never did anything wrong. I mean, according to you, you are the world's most perfect husband."

He sat next to her. "Mary, I've been driving around thinking about what you said. All you wanted was to start over and be honest with each other. I decided that wasn't too much to ask to save our marriage. Honey, I'm ready to talk about everything again, if you'll let me. I guess I was in denial. Maybe I've even convinced myself I didn't do anything wrong." He grabbed her hand.

She pushed his hand away. "So you want me to believe that you got hit by a big bolt of lightning and now you see the light, is that it? Well, Tony, I don't know if I'll ever be able to believe you again. But I'm willing to listen to you, just for Connor's sake. What do you want to say?"

He looked at the pictures on the fireplace mantel. "To begin with, I want to tell you that I've not been one hundred percent honest with you on everything."

She laughed. "Now, there's a scoop. Wow, I never could have imagined that."

"I'm serious, Mary. Please give me a chance to get some things off my chest."

She took a drink of water from a glass sitting on the coffee table. "Okay, fire away. I'm anxious to hear your bullshit."

"You're reading me wrong. I just said I lied to you some. I'm no saint, and I don't claim to be." He ran his hands through his hair. "Where do I begin? Well, I do have a gambling problem, and you were right, I didn't buy and sell stock. I took that money out of our account to bet on the horses, like I've done hundreds of times since we've been married. I think that trip to Vegas when I won all that money hooked me on gambling. Anyway, I knew you'd find out how short our account was, so I had to bet just to get you off my back and put some money in the bank. Friday I put my last six hundred on a twenty to one horse and he won, so I put the winnings back into our checking account. Now, that's the truth."

"That sounds believable, but how about your secretary coming here when I was gone?"

"I've been thinking about that a lot. First off, Bobbie can't see our house from her place unless she goes out into the street. I checked that out tonight. You ought to check it out, too. I swear no one came to see me while you were in Athens…no hooker and certainly not my secretary. Do you know she's engaged? Her fiancé is supposed to get here sometime this month. I don't have any interest in her, and she doesn't have any in me."

Mary took in a deep breath, then let it out in spurts. "Tony, I want to believe you, I really do, but how can Bobbie be so wrong? I mean, she

130

recognized Brenda as soon as she walked in the office today. How do you explain that?"

"I have no idea, but I know she hates me as much as I hate her. Maybe she did see a woman head to a house around here, and deep down, she wanted to believe that woman was coming in here. I'm sorry, but that's only a guess. Oh, by the way, I did tell you the truth about the note with Brenda's phone number; she just wanted to help us when your mother got in that accident. She's really a nice girl, but she's not my girlfriend." He grabbed her hand again. "You are."

"I don't know, Tony, I just don't know. So, what other lies have you told me?"

"Well, it's not exactly a lie because I never told you about it, but one time I took a lot of money out of one of my client's escrow to pay off some gambling bets. Mary, I broke the law, big time. But right after that, I won a big race at the Meadowlands and put it all back." He knew she couldn't end up using that against him, because he fixed it so it was untraceable.

"Let me go through this again, Tony. You say all of your lies are about gambling or the result of gambling, is that right?"

He nodded. "That's about the size of it. No other woman, no other stealing, no other anything, just my gambling problem. There's only one other lie I remember, that's when one night I told you I had to work late. Well, I didn't work late, I went over to Ron's place for some poker. In fact, when you see Ron, go ahead and ask him about it. I bet if you asked good old Bobbie about that, she'd say she saw me at a strip joint or something like that, or even cruising the streets looking for hookers."

"Tony, is that it, is that all? Wait a minute, tell me about the smell on your shirts and the incredible coincidence of you running out of your little after shave bottle the day before I asked you about it?"

He cleared his throat. "I told you the truth. I sprayed that on my hand and rubbed it over my face when I didn't remember to use aftershave in the morning. Sometimes it got all over me. Yes, I did run out and yes, I threw the bottle away."(He didn't tell her he'd thrown it out only two hours earlier). "Why don't I try to find out what gas station I bought it at and find another one so you can see it matches the smell on my shirts?"

"I don't know. At least we're talking about everything. I hope you're being honest with me now, you've lied to me so much. If you're going to bare your soul to me, tell me why you've been so cold lately. I mean, for over a month?"

"Okay, but don't get mad at me. A few weeks ago, I was looking for something in the cupboard and I found a couple of pints of booze there; one was vodka and the other was some Kahlua."

She looked over his head at the ceiling. "Uh huh, go on."

"You know, since my dad died from alcoholism and we almost lost my brother, I hate it when people I care about drink hard liquor. I know I like a beer once in a while, but that doesn't pickle a liver like the vodka and Kahlua. I've got to tell you the truth, Mary, I don't like drinkers and you know that. I saw the bottles and I knew you were hiding them from me. Oh, and later I found a lot of miniatures in the same place."

"So, that's why you don't want to be nice to me now?"

"It's not that I don't want to be nice to you, it's just that I don't like drinking, plus you know you can't drink with the medicine you're taking. I hate the smell of alcohol on anyone's breath. You know you have to admit to your problem, just like I did about my gambling."

"Tony, I don't have a problem. Yes, I like to drink, and yes, I know you hate me drinking, but when I worry about stuff like money, or Connor, or even you, booze just seems to help." She raised her shoulders, taking in a lot of air. "I'm glad you found my hiding place. Now it's out in the open. I'll make a deal with you, right here and now, Tony; you start going to Gamblers Anonymous and I'll start going to Alcoholics Anonymous."

"That sounds fair, Mary. Let me ask you, do you forgive me for everything? I forgive you for your problems, I really do."

"I can't say I forgive you, but I can say I'll try to forgive you, okay?"

He stood up, kissing her on her right cheek. "That sounds great to me. Man, I'm tired; I'm going to tuck Connor in and go to bed." He smiled as he left her, knowing he'd just finished an incredible acting job. It looked like he was close to being back in control. He now knew he had lost all his feelings for Mary. All he wanted was Brenda Jean, but he could keep putting on a show for a few weeks.

CHAPTER 17
Pill Shopping

When Tony got to his office the next morning, he noticed Brenda Jean's car was the only one in the parking lot. He unlocked the front door and went directly into his office. The life insurance paperwork was the only thing on his desk, folded open to the signature pages. He knew that was a signal from his secretary to get going on their plans to get rid of Mary.

He hung his suit coat up in the closet, then turned to see Brenda Jean staring at him. She looked so different compared to the last couple of weeks. Her hair was up in a small bun on the back of her head, she had on very little makeup, and she was wearing the most grandmotherly business suit he had ever seen. It was obvious she was on track to do her part.

"Wow, you look different; still sexy, but different," Tony said as he sat behind his desk. "Just trying to be a good little girl for a while," she said, closing the door. "Tony, when do you think we can have our normal lunch break together again?"

"Not for a while, but I've been thinking of ways to get together. Maybe some nights I'll work late, and since you live so close, you can walk back here from your apartment, then I'll let you in the back door. That way if somebody's spying on us, they can't watch the front and back door at the same time. But you know what? If you warm up to Mary and she thinks you're engaged to someone, maybe we can get together more, and she'll call the bloodhounds off."

She gave him a silly military salute. "Aye, aye, Captain, I'm up to the challenge. Come here, I want to show you something."

He followed her out of his office to her desk. There was a new eight by ten picture frame on the front of her desk, holding a photo of a man in a uniform.

Brenda Jean pointed to the photo. "Tony, I want you to meet my fiancé. His name is Tommy, and we're getting married in February. Doesn't he look handsome?"

"He sure does. I hope you all will be very happy," Tony answered with a smile. "You'll have to tell the other girls the good news. So, how long have you known this Tommy?"

"Oh, I guess I've known him for...what do you think? How about three years?"

"That sounds perfect. I see he's wearing a uniform. Is he in the service?"

"No, he just got discharged. He lives in Knoxville."

"I think you can pull this off. In fact, if I didn't know better, I'd be jealous of good old Tommy. Now listen, if Mary calls here and you talk to her, don't say anything about Tommy. It will look like a set up with the fight we had last night. Let someone else tell her. In fact, don't tell anyone about him at all. Let them discover his picture, then you can tell them all about him."

She looked at it as he put it back on her desk. "That really makes it look a whole lot better. I think everyone will believe I'm engaged now."

"I hope so. Listen, I'm going back to my office and sign those insurance papers. I've got a copy of Mary's signature, so I should be able to take care of that." He looked at her cousin's picture again. "Just come get the papers in a few minutes, and have one of the other secretaries sign all the spots for a witness. Once all that's done, you can drive them over to Bo at his office."

"Tony, after you sign them, can I look at them?"

"Sure, darling. Oh, and after you get back from Bo's, I need to talk to you in my office. I stayed awake last night working something out that you need to help me with. Let's call it our thirty to forty day plan."

"Now you've got me excited. Hurry up, go sign those papers, Tony."

Tony looked at Mary's signatures carefully. Each one got better and better as he wrote them out; no one could possibly think it wasn't her doing the signing. He copied all the pages, then called Brenda Jean into his office, telling her to get the witness's signatures and take the whole package over to Bo. While Brenda Jean was gone, Rudi called him on the intercom. "Mr. Calley, your wife is on line one."

"Hey, Mary, how are you doing?"

"I'm fine, but I just had it out with Bobbie. Tony, I'm still shaking."

"Catch your breath, sweetheart; what happened?"

"Well, she came over this morning for a cup of coffee. Then she told me she was having a tough time since Jerry left. She wanted to borrow some money and she didn't want me to tell you about it. I told her we were a little tight right now and that I would have to talk to you before I could help her. She didn't believe me; she said I had my head up your ass and you were screwing your secretary. I told her from now on to mind her own business, that she had enough issues in her house."

"Good for you, but I hope you told her Brenda Jean is engaged to someone else. I don't want that big witch spreading lies about me or anyone else. Did anything else happen?"

"Oh, yeah. When I told her to mind her own business she threw a half-full coffee cup at the dishwasher. You should see it; it's got a big scratch on it...I mean the dishwasher. I told her to leave and she did, screaming at me all the way down the sidewalk. I'm so mad I could spit, Tony. And to think all this time I listened to her tell me about how bad you were, and now it looks like she filled my head with lies. I'm sorry, Tony, I really am."

"That's all right, Mary. Like I said last night, we need to just get along and believe in each other. Let's not pay any attention to what anyone says, let's just worry about us."

"You're right, Tony. Say, sweet stuff, how about me buying you lunch today? I've got nothing going on."

"That sounds like fun. How about if I meet you at Nightboilers, say around one? I've got a few things to wrap up here, but I can get there by one."

"Better yet honey, I'll pick you up there at your office around a quarter to one, okay?"

"I'll see you then. Bye, honey."

After Tony hung up, he scratched his head. Can this really be happening? Or is she playing games or drinking again? That phone call was vintage six months ago. He laid back in his chair, looking at the dots on the ceiling tiles above him. It was just getting too easy. All he needed now was a long shot to come in at the track to get his car out of hock.

He grabbed his cell phone off his desk, dialing Parker Hayes. "Hey, Parker, what's up? You got any hot tips for today's races?"

"You bet. I got a lead on the seventh at Calder. I haven't told anyone yet because I don't want to bring the odds down, 'cause I'm getting some action on this one myself. It's a big horse...I mean a Secretariat-size stud. It's only had four races, finishing first or second in everyone one of them. But for some reason it's starting out at thirty to one this afternoon."

"What's his name?"

"It's 'Fun at Lunchtime.'"

"That's wild," Tony said with a laugh.

"How's that, Tony?"

"Oh, nothing, it's just a private joke I have with someone."

"So, how do you want to play it?"

"I'll tell you what, put three grand on it to win, will you, Parker?"

"Will do, Tony. That sounds like the perfect bet. It's not like it affects the odds much, and you might be looking at around ninety grand if it comes in. That's a brilliant move, Buddy. I'll talk to you later and I'll keep my fingers crossed."

His eleven o'clock appointment cancelled out, so he opened up his laptop to see what was happening in the markets. Brenda Jean knocked on his door.

"Come on in."

She walked in, sitting on the chair in front of him again as he motioned for her to shut the door. She nodded, smiled, and walked back to quietly close it, then sat back down in her special chair.

"Brenda Jean, did you find Bo okay?" She nodded.

"I just gave the papers to his secretary."

"Great. You're not going to believe what just happened while you were gone."

"Let me guess…your wife got drunk again and she's in a coma?"

"No, but she did call. I think she's starting to believe our stories. In fact, she's coming over here to pick me up for lunch just before one."

"Oh no. Is she going to go nuts when she sees me?"

"No, that won't happen. I don't want you to be here. Listen, I've got it all worked out. You go to lunch about twelve thirty, and when she gets here, I'll tell her I'm running a little late for our lunch date and to go out and talk to the girls."

"What will that do, Tony?"

"Listen, it's brilliant. While she's waiting for me, I guarantee she'll snoop around your desk. That way she'll see your fiancé's picture. Let's see what happens…my guess is she'll start believing our story."

"Shit, I was hoping we could have some fun for lunch, Mr. Boss Man."

"Remember our plan; we need to cool it so we don't raise any red flags if something does happen to Mary. Now, listen, I told you about me staying awake last night. I promised you a good plan and I've got one." He reached into his pants pocket and pulled out two tiny pink pills, which he laid on his desk. "Do you see these, Brenda? These are my wife's thyroid pills. I took them out of her bottle this morning before she woke up."

Brenda Jean leaned in closer to look at them. "But won't she miss them?"

"Not at all. She fills up her weekly pill reminder on Sundays, and never touches the prescription bottle after that until the next Sunday."

"So, what do we do with those two pills?"

"Listen, it's pure genius. Here's what we're going to do...we're going to find some pills that look exactly like these. I mean, nothing pills like aspirins or cold pills or something you don't need a prescription for."

"Okay, but why are we doing that?"

"Do you remember last week when Beckie took the wrong pills because they looked like her aspirin? Remember the joke about all the ex-lax she took? Well, that gave me an idea. If Mary took some aspirin from her pill reminder that looked like her thyroid pills, she'd think she took the right medicine but she'd end up taking no medicine." He laid back in his chair, raising his shoulders, awaiting a comeback from his secretary.

She lowered her eyebrows, looking mixed up. "I'm not sure I follow all that. Are you saying we need to find some pills that look like those two, and you'll put them in her weekly thing and her thyroid would go out of whack again?"

"Exactly. She almost died when she didn't take her thyroid medicine for three days. Just think of what will happen if she goes seven days just taking an aspirin or a vitamin or something simple."

"So, what are you waiting for? Give me one of those pills. I'll start my pill shopping tonight."

Tony shook his head. "You can start now if you want, but remember, I'm not doing anything until at least thirty or forty days down the road when the new insurance takes effect. They did date everything today at Bo's office, didn't they?"

"They sure did. Here's your receipt." She handed him a paper from out of her pants pocket, then she put the pill he gave her into that same pocket. "I'll find you the right pills, Tony, but let me ask you...after something happens to her, how are you going to explain the missing pills from her bottle with no medicine in her?"

He turned his head to the side, grimacing. "That was the hardest thing in this whole plan for me, trying to figure that out. Here's what I came up with. I'm going to wait until the week we want to do this, then after she fills up her pill holder on Sunday, I'm going to take all seven of her thyroid pills out of it, and I'll put them in a safe spot and replace them with the aspirin or whatever we find that looks right." He nodded. "Then, after a week, she'll be in trouble. That's when I'll put the pills back in her reminder box. That way, everyone will think she didn't take them, just like before."

Brenda Jean smiled. "Tony, you are incredible. How did you think of all that? This whole thing sounds foolproof. Everybody will think she didn't take them because they'll still be in her box, and then the prescription bottle will have the right amount in it…minus these two, of course."

"No, including those two," Tony said, almost in a whisper. "I need the one you just put in your pocket back when all this goes down, plus the one I've got. But listen, we have to be very careful around each other and not talk about any of this, all right?"

Brenda Jean nodded. "You can count on me, sweetheart."

"Good. Have any of the girls said anything about the picture on your desk?"

"Not a word, but they will."

"Brenda Jean, I can't wait until this is all over with and we can be together every day. Hell, with the insurance money, we'll go somewhere where no one knows us and have fun the rest of our lives."

"That sounds wonderful, Tony. But what about your son?"

"He'll be with us, of course. It will take him a while to get over his mother dying, but I know you'll be a great fill-in. He'll learn to love you, too, just like I do."

She walked over to him, grabbing each side of his face and kissing him as gently as she could, then slid her tongue into his mouth just before she turned and walked out, giving him her famous smile as she left.

****

At twelve-thirty Brenda Jean went to lunch. Fifteen minutes later, Mary walked into the office. She looked around, noticing Tony's secretary was gone. After greeting the other girls, she asked them where Brenda was. Rudi told her she'd gone to lunch about twenty minutes earlier. Everything was going according to plan.

Mary waltzed into Tony's office without knocking and found him with his head stuck in his laptop. She was relieved he was there, knowing Brenda Jean was at lunch. "Hey, lover boy, what are you doing?"

"Well, hello honey. I'm just wrapping up some stock research for a client. I should be ready in about fifteen minutes or so. I'm starving, but I've got to finish this up. Why don't you go out and see the girls while I finish here?"

"Okay, just come get me when you're ready to go. I'm looking forward to our lunch together. It's been quite a while since we've done that."

Mary wandered around the lobby for a few minutes, taking in all the sights and chit- chatting with the two girls. She started reading the investment flyers that were on a big bulletin board next to the front door, constantly checking to see if Tony was ready to go. She casually walked by Brenda Jean's desk on her way to the woman's restroom, noticing the picture of a very handsome man next to the telephone. Mary tried to read what was written on it, but the words were too small for her make out. Finally, she picked up the photo, studying the message written across it. She set it back down gently, nodding with a smile. "I guess he was telling the truth after all," she said under her breath.

****

So far, everything was happening exactly the way Tony had planned it.

CHAPTER 18
Who Sent the Flowers?

By the time Tony Calley got home, the seventh race at Calder should have finished. No call from Parker must mean bad news. "Oh, well, I'll call him anyway," Tony said as he opened his car door. He dialed his bookie's number as he started walking towards the back of his house. "Parker, this is Tony. Tell me, how did we do?"

"Sorry Tony, Fun At Lunchtime finished third. He was leading all the way until he was about fifty yards from the finish line, then he just pulled back. I think he hurt one of his legs somehow. That's one thing no one can predict, if a horse is going to pull up lame. I mean, you can set up everything perfectly, if you know what I mean, but you can't predict if a horse is going get hurt. Do you want to put something on a hot tip I got from the Jacksonville dog track?"

"No, that's okay, I'm home now. But let's see how good you are. If I wanted to bet, what dog would I have bet on?"

"Hold on...uh...here it is. In the third race tonight, I was going to tell you to put a bundle on number seven; let's see, he's called Mama's Gonna Be Mad. He should come off around ten to one, and my sources tell me he's even better than a sure thing."

"Okay, but I'm playing it very conservative; just put five hundred on him to win."

"Will do, Tony. Have a nice night."

He got in the back door just as Mary was putting on a pink and white apron. She walked up to him without saying a word and gave him a very wet and sexy kiss. Mary held both of his arms and leaned back like she was examining him. "Good, I don't smell any of that stupid after shave now." She kissed him again.

This time he sensed she wanted more than a kiss. But it was hard to look at her and not think of Brenda Jean. "What a wonderful hello. You really enjoyed your lunch today, huh? Listen, I've got plans for you tonight Mary, but right now I just want to relax in front of the TV with a beer. I'm pooped." He leaned around her, opened the refrigerator, and grabbed a Bud Light from the second shelf. He popped it open as he walked past her into the living room, taking off his coat and tie and watching them fly onto her rocking chair, and then removed his shoes. When they sat down for dinner, Mary smiled at her husband. "Oh, I forgot to tell you thank you for the flowers."

"Yeah, Dad, you did good this time," Connor said as he cut into his pork chop. "They're real pretty."

Tony swallowed a mouthful of water, looking at his wife. "I'd love to take the credit, but I don't have any idea what you all are talking about."

"Go look at them. They're in the front entry room. Come on Tony, who would send me flowers but you?" Mary asked.

Tony stood up. "I've got to see these flowers. I'll be right back." He walked towards the front door, finding a big bouquet of red and yellow roses. "What the hell? Okay, I give…what's going on?" Tony asked his wife as he rejoined her at the kitchen table.

"Quit kidding me, Tony, I know how sweet you can be. Besides, that's probably over a hundred dollars' worth of roses. No one but you would have done that." She pulled a little tan card out of her pocket. "Here, look at the note that came with them," she said, handing him the evidence.

Tony read it, shaking his head. It said, "I know we haven't been together much lately, not like I want us to be, but we'll fix that. My love for you will never end because you are a beautiful angel." It didn't have anyone's name on it. He looked at his wife, then his son, quickly deciding to take credit for the flowers even though he had no idea who'd sent them. That was the safe way out, avoiding any more problems with her when Connor was around. "I'm glad you like them. They say a lot, a lot about how I feel about you."

Tony smiled, then went back to eating. "So, Mary, what time did the flowers come?"

"Oh, I have no idea. They were on the front porch when I got home. I wouldn't have even seen them if it wasn't for all the green cellophane all over them."

He picked up the card again. It didn't have a florist's name on it. It looked like it could have been something made on a home computer. He wondered if the flowers could have been from a lover he didn't know about. But why would anyone be so ballsy to send her flowers to her home when she had a husband?

It was more likely she'd sent them to herself, or even put them on the porch to shake him up a little, to get him to want her more. He still had thirty or forty more days to go trying to keep her calm, and the flowers were a good start. "Now you owe me, sweetheart, and I aim to collect tonight," Tony said.

She put her index finger over her mouth, then looked at Connor. "Guess what? Now your father wants me to let him have the remote tonight after we go to bed so he can watch sports."

Connor laughed. "Good job, Dad. I'd trade some old flowers for a good basketball game any day."

After Tony finished his dinner, he tilted his chair back, rubbing his stomach. "Mary, that was some meal. I'm bursting at the seams."

"Well, I was going to ask you if you want any dessert, but that can wait. I'll get you your dessert later," she said with a twinkle in her eyes. He could read her mind. She was still kind of cute, but he knew it was going to take some acting to convince her he still was her lover. "You're right, I can't handle any dessert right now. I'll take a rain check, and you better believe I'll collect on it later. Right now, I think I'm going to get on the computer for a little bit. I'm going to play a little poker." He looked at Mary, noticing a scared look. "You know, the play money games. You can't find any real money games online anymore."

She sighed, starting to pick up the dishes. "Go ahead. Do you want to help me, Connor?"

"Okay," Connor answered reluctantly.

Tony walked by the flowers on his way to his office just as the house phone rang. Connor answered it.

"What? Of course I do. Huh?" Connor said to the caller, then listened for a minute and hung up.

"Who was that?" Tony asked his son.

Mary came out of the kitchen, wiping her hands on a dish towel. "Answer your dad, who just called?"

"Some weirdo. First he asked me if I loved my mother. Then he said he loved her more. After that, he wanted to know if she got the flowers. He was scary; that's why I hung up on him."

"Mary, do you have a boyfriend?" Tony asked, giggling. "If you do, he sounds like a real winner. All you have to do is look at the phone to see the last number called, then we can see who he was."

Tony grabbed the phone out of his son's hands, looking for a listing of the last few phone calls. The phone showed the last call as a private number. He looked at Mary, this time without any giggles. "What is going on, Mary?"

"You got me, honey. I must have an admirer somewhere I don't know about, that's all I can figure. Listen, there is no one in my life but you, Tony. If I was carrying on a flaming love affair with someone, I sure wouldn't want him to send flowers to my house or call me after dinner when my husband was home, would I? And another thing, why did you say you sent them? You were right the first time, it wasn't you."

"I know, Mary. I have no idea who sent them, but I can always use some credit. It sounds to me like you must have said hello to some social misfit somewhere who got your address and phone number so he can show you how much he loves you. What do you think, have you been overly friendly to a mentally challenged guy lately?"

"Of course not; but Tony, I can't control who likes the way I look. You know sometimes when I'm wearing the right outfits, some guys stare a lot, but I have no idea how anyone would get my phone number or know where I live." Now Tony wasn't sure what to think. He didn't want Mary any more, but he kind of didn't want anyone else to have her either. Because of what the guy said to Connor, Tony knew she didn't put the flowers on the front porch. He had no way to find out who her new boyfriend was, as long as the phone calls and flowers kept coming in such untraceable ways. It kind of made him sick to his stomach and he didn't know why.

He looked at his watch. It was almost nine. The third race at Jacksonville must be over by now. He Googled the race track and discovered that Mama's Gonna Be Mad did win, paying him eleven to one. "Yes," Tony said under his breath, loud enough for only him to hear. He'd just won fifty-five hundred dollars, less Parker's cut, leaving him with a little over five grand; not enough to help with his car title situation, but enough to get caught up with Parker. One more big hit and he could get his title back, then start working on the twelve thousand dollar loan from the bank. He decided to watch the news, so he found his favorite recliner in the living room.

Mary joined him, wearing her reading glasses as she brought a stack of mail and sat down beside her husband. "Tony, darling, can you turn the light up just a hair? I want to go through all this mail; it's two days' worth. I forgot to get it yesterday."

"Uh, huh," he replied as he surfed through some channels and turned up the brown floor lamp next to his recliner.

"Why do we get so many companies wanting us to refinance our house? Every day there's three or four of them," she said, starting a stack of mail she didn't even want to take the time to open. "Look at this, now we're even getting mail from pawn shops." She tore open the envelope from Fast Buck Pawn and Title Company. "Tony, what's this? Some pawn shop says you owe them twenty-two hundred and fifty dollars as payment one of twelve. Huh? Here, look at this." She handed him the bill.

144

"I have no idea who this is and why they think I owe them anything," he said as he crumpled up the letter. "It's just some junk mail. They want to loan me twenty-two hundred; I don't owe them anything." Tony threw the balled up pawn shop mail on top of her stack of trash.

She picked it back up, trying to straighten out the letter. "I don't think that's what it said, Tony. I want to look at it again."

He reached over and grabbed it out of her hands. "I told you it's just junk mail; don't you believe me?"

"I believe you, I just want to be sure no one is trying to rip us off." She stuck her arm out. "Please give it back to me."

He knew he was in trouble, but he didn't want to give in. He ripped up the letter into thirty to forty pieces, then gave them back to her. "That's how people steal your identity, stealing your junk mail, didn't you know that? That's how you handle shit like that. Here, take all this to the waste basket, will you?"

She picked up the stray pieces off the floor and put all the trash together. As she was forcing the trash into the kitchen trash can, she spotted the envelope that had enclosed the now torn-up pawn shop bill. "Tony, I'm going to take a bath. Don't forget to lock up. I checked the back door, but will you check the rest and turn the alarm on?"

"I will, baby doll," he said. He flipped the channels, looking for a basketball game, but couldn't find one, so he checked out the HBO channels, finding a movie just about ready to begin. It was a two hour comedy about a family vacation.

"That looks perfect," he said under his breath. She should be asleep long before it ended, and once he was sure she was out, he was going to call Brenda Jean. But it didn't work.

A few minutes later his phone rang and he answered. "Mary, what are you doing, calling me when you're right upstairs?" Tony asked.

"I just wanted to tell you that I'm taking a hot, hot bubble bath, and I'm going to be sure I'm super clean all over. Why don't you come up and see me when I'm done? You'll be glad you did."

"Honey, I'm in the middle of a movie; can you wait a while?"

"I'll tell you what…you can watch it up here, and then I'll give you a show, and you can decide which one you really want to watch. How about that?"

He had no choice. "Sure, and I'll bet you can give me something a lot better to look at than this movie. I'll be right up."

Tony lay in bed watching the same show he'd had on downstairs as she came out of the bathroom, wearing a light yellow see-through nightgown. He pretended that he was asleep. She turned off all the lights in the bedroom, leaving only the dim bathroom to shimmer its softness across their bed. She pulled back the sheets and laid down next to her husband, using her normal ways to get him excited. He enjoyed being with Brenda Jean more, but this wasn't half bad.

The next morning Tony woke up a little after eight. Connor was gone, and so was Mary. He walked to the window to see if he could spot her car, but it wasn't there. Maybe she took Connor to school for some reason?

He'd turned to go to the bathroom when he heard a car pulling up out front. He looked back out the window, expecting to see his wife, but instead he watched an older man run up to their porch, carrying a single flower. The visitor left the rose on a white rocking chair next to the front door. It was Mr. Jinks, Connor's principal.

Tony leaned over to the right, hiding his face behind the curtain as he laughed. So, this was the guy who was chasing after Mary? No wonder he knew their address and phone number...it was the weird-ass principal. Sure, that was the guy who'd called. He didn't care who was around, he was on a woman hunt, with Mary being the prey.

After grabbing a robe, Tony walked downstairs to the front door. He stepped outside, looked both ways, then picked up the bright red rose that was taped to a little note that read, "Mary, I lay awake all night thinking about you. I hope and pray that one day we can be alone together." There was no signature on the little love letter. Tony decided to put everything back on the rocking chair, giggling as he wondered if she would tell him about her secret admirer when he got home.

After dressing as fast as he could, Tony headed out to his car, anxious to see Brenda Jean at the office. When he drove by the Fast Buck Pawn and Title, he spotted Mary walking to her car, which was parked in front of the slimy business. He couldn't help but slow down, but as he got closer he hit the gas, passing a truck that was in the right lane. That gave him cover and hope that she hadn't seen him. What had she found out? It must have been the bill that caused her to go see Leo. "Oh, my God, it's all going to break loose now," he said under his breath. He had to talk to Brenda Jean.

Chapter 19
Maybe We Can't Wait 30 Days?

Now what was Tony going to do? He sat in his car next to his office, watching the traffic whizzing by, knowing he had to come up with something fast. Mary must have found out about the loan from the pawn shop guy. Why else would she be there? "That bitch must have taped together all the torn up pieces of the bill that came in the mail," he mumbled, pounding his fist into the dashboard.

He tried to think of a good lie to explain everything to his wife, but he was drawing blanks. How do you explain away a loan at over thirty percent interest on a new Mercedes? It was obvious Mary had figured out it was gambling losses. Tony knew he could find some way to buy his title back, but the problem was she had to know about the loan by now. He leaned his head against the window, trying to come up with something, when he heard a tapping on the passenger window. He rolled it down after seeing that the tapper was Mary.

"Tony, unlock the door." After he hit the unlock button, she opened the passenger door and slid into the thin, tan leather seat. "Let's go; I want to go for a ride, Tony." She didn't look at him once, focusing only on what was ahead.

"Okay," Tony responded in a submissive tone. He started driving, waiting for her to give him a hint of where she wanted to go.

"Pull over there. We need to talk," she said, pointing at a huge parking lot in front of an old closed-down grocery store over four miles from his office. "Let's not play any more games, Tony. I know you saw me at the Fast Buck Pawn Shop; I know about the twenty thousand you borrowed against the title of this car. In the last two weeks you've taken out a twelve thousand dollar loan from the bank, and now you've borrowed another twenty thousand from the pawn shop, of all places. By my count, that's thirty two thousand dollars going into our account, an account that was eight thousand dollars short to begin with. What is going on? Do you want to tell me how much is left in our checking account now, or do I have to call the bank and find out? I wouldn't be surprised if there's nothing left in any of our bank accounts."

Tony shook his head three times. "Mary, I'm not going to bullshit you. About three months ago, I was gambling every day...I mean every day. And I was losing my ass. Sure, I'd win a few races here and there, but I couldn't keep up." He took in a deep breath, letting it out slowly. "I started betting heavier and heavier to get my money back, which meant I lost bigger bets. I didn't know it, but the guy I was getting tips from and betting with was backed by some real bad people."

"Okay, how much did you lose?"

Somehow he was able to grab a couple of fake tears for this acting job. "Almost eighty thousand dollars."

"Oh, my God. Eighty thousand dollars in what, two months? That's impossible. If you owed your racetrack buddies eighty thousand, how come you borrowed only what, thirty two thousand? Don't tell me you still owe them fifty thousand dollars?" She looked bewildered. "I can't even keep these kind of numbers straight in my head."

He looked over at her. "Mary, I swear I've been paying them everything I can. I haven't been betting in weeks. I've made some great stock buys lately and the profits went into the business account, so I'd pay them out of that."

"That sounds funny to me, Tony, like it's illegal or something. Don't tell me you could go to jail over all this, all this betting?"

"I didn't break any laws. I have the right to buy and sell stock in my own name as long as there's no insider trading, like knowing inside dope of profits and stuff before the companies announce them. I've been so careful with our money just to get them paid. Then last week when I got down to owing them only twenty thousand, I couldn't figure out any other angle to pay them, and that's when they started threatening me."

She started to cry. "Tony, I'm sorry, but I don't believe you. You just lie and lie about everything. I wouldn't be surprised if you bet on something last night. It's in your blood now, in your DNA; you can't help yourself. Do you understand me? I've had enough."

"What are you saying, sweet stuff?"

"First off, don't call me sweet stuff; and secondly, I need some time to think about what I'm going to do, so take me back to my car. I'm not going to listen to your lies anymore. You are destroying our family, and I'm not going to stand around and watch you do that, you got that?"

"I could understand that if I was still gambling. I told you I don't owe anyone a cent, and all I've got to do is find thirty two grand to be even. I'll do that in thirty days, then we won't have any more problems."

He pulled up next to her car in front of his office. She got out without saying a word, slammed the door, and got into her Mustang. As she pulled away, the tires squealed enough to send blue billowing smoke skyward.

****

Tony walked into his office, trying to get to his suite without seeing anyone, as they all must have heard Mary leave. He pushed open his office door just as Brenda Jean pulled it from the inside, causing Tony to almost fall down. "Whoa," he said, grabbing his secretary to make sure she didn't fall.

"Hey, what happened out there? I was starting up your computer when I couldn't help but hear someone's car squeal out of here. I opened the blinds and all I could see was smoke and your wife tearing out of the parking lot like a teenager. Is everything okay?"

"Close the door," Tony said. He kissed her, hoping that kiss would take some of the tension out of his body. But it didn't work…he was still too shook up. He sat behind his desk, motioning for her to sit in her usual place. "Brenda Jean, it's coming to a head. Maybe we can't wait thirty days. I wouldn't be surprised if she's looking for a divorce attorney right now. I told you, I'm not going to lose everything to her. She's got dollar signs in her eyes and she's coming after me, that's for sure. We've got to move fast. Have you been looking for some pills? Oh, by the way, I should have told you that you look wonderful this morning."

"Well, thank you, sweet pea. To answer your question, no, I haven't been looking for the pills. But I will, I swear I'll find them. I think I'll start with Walgreens. They've got everything in their vitamin department. I mean, it's huge."

"I've got an idea, Brenda Jean."

"Let me guess; you want to come over to my place for lunch, huh?"

"No, that's not what I was thinking of, but that doesn't sound bad. What I was thinking of is you taking your pill to a drug store and asking the pharmacist if he can tell what it is. Tell him you found that pill on the floor and you have a baby that crawls around and it scared you when you spotted it. See if he can at least tell you what other medicines look like that."

She had a puzzled look. "How will that help?"

"Just think; if the pharmacist says that looks like a cold pill, for instance, then you can start your search on the aisle that has the cold stuff. Do you see what I mean?"

"That's pretty smart, Tony. How about if I leave a little early today and find a drug store to try out your theory?"

"Sure, go ahead; just ask one of the girls to cover for you. I'm going to see what I can find online. Who knows what I'll find just by Googling 'little pink pills'? No, I don't think that would be very smart. I don't need any proof on my laptop that I was searching for pink pills."

Rudi was on the intercom. "Mr. Calley, your wife is on line one."

Tony put his head down so low it almost touched his chest, then punched in the loudspeaker button. "Hello, Mary."

"Tony, I thought I'd let you know I'm going down to see my folks for a couple of days. Mom isn't a hundred percent yet and I need to get away and think about what is happening to us. I'm taking Connor with me."

"What about school?"

"There's no school Friday—it's a teacher's conference day—so all he'll miss is tomorrow. I'll just call him in sick for that."

"When do you think you'll be back?" Tony looked up at Brenda Jean, who was smiling while she faked clapping her hands together. "Oh, I don't know, maybe Saturday, maybe Sunday, who knows? I'll try to get back in time for Connor to go to school Monday. I need some quiet time to think, so I'm going over to Athens and figure out how to fix what's happening in our lives, whatever it takes."

"What do you mean, whatever it takes?"

"Whatever. Bye."

Calley looked at his girlfriend. "See, I told you it wouldn't be long before she comes after me with a lawyer." He leaned in, whispering to her. "We've got to work fast. I want to take care of this as soon as she gets back from her little trip to see her asshole parents. Besides, I bet her mom and dad fill her head with how terrible I am, you can count on that. That will make her even meaner. Let's get this done next week."

"But it won't be long enough for the new insurance policy you signed, Tony."

"Hey, losing a million is a lot better than her getting everything. We can't wait for thirty days now, Brenda Jean, we just can't."

She stood up. "You'll let me know when she leaves?"

"I'll deliver that message in person, sweetheart. So listen, go ahead and take the afternoon off, so you can find those pills."

"Okay." She leaned down and kissed him. "I love you, Tony."

"I love you too, Brenda Jean, with all my heart."

She went back to her desk, looking at her new make believe boyfriend's picture, even holding it up. None of the other girls had said a word about it. Maybe it was the right time to introduce good old Tommy to the troops.

She looked over at Rudi, who was going through some files. "Hey, Rudi, can you cover for me this afternoon? Mr. Calley told me I could take off at lunchtime because my fiancé is coming over to see me. I think he'll get here about one or so."

"Brenda Jean, I didn't know you had a fiancé," Rudi said.

"What do you mean? I told you about him when I started here. Haven't you seen his picture on my desk? It's been here for weeks." Brenda Jean held up the photo.

"You want to know something, Brenda Jean? I think that's the first time I've ever seen that picture. What's his name?"

"Tommy; we're going to get married next spring." She raised her head, proud of her future husband even if he was a fictional lover. She put his photo back on her desk.

Rudi raised up, trying to see the photo better. "Brenda Jean, if you get a chance, why don't you bring him by sometime? He looks hot in that picture...I'd love to see him."

"I'll do that, but I don't know if we'll have time this week. He lives in Knoxville and he has to be back to work Sunday. But I promise you'll get to meet him real soon." She felt like she was ten feet tall, even though all of it was made up.

Brenda Jean picked up her purse on her way out of the office. She peeked into Tony's office. "I'll see you later, bye."

"Have a good time this afternoon, and good luck," Tony said as she closed his door.

She put the single pill in her purse, as she started her car looking for a drug store a few miles away, finally spotting Greenwalls Drugs. It was seven miles from town, the perfect store. Brenda Jean walked to the back of the store and found a window that had a big Drop Off sign over it. A very young looking girl, wearing a yellow sweater that complemented her red hair, leaned over the counter and asked Brenda Jean if she needed any help.

Brenda noticed her name badge that read Tess Howley, Certified Pharmacy Technician. "Yes, I do; is there any way I can talk to your pharmacist?"

"Sure, just hold on a second," the freckled clerk answered. "Mr. Walker, can you help this lady?"

A white-haired pudgy man walked over, giving her a smile that displayed a wide space between his two front teeth. "How can I help you?"

She pulled the plastic bag holding Mary's thyroid pill out of her purse. "I found this pill on my kitchen floor this morning, and I have a nine month old who is starting to crawl. It scared me; I mean, I don't know if there are any more of these he might pick up or already has picked up." She gave him a pleading mother look, a look that also had a sexy mini-smile. "Is there any way you can tell me what this pill is for, and if it's dangerous for a baby if he puts it in his mouth?"

"I'll try, but let me ask you a couple of questions. How is the baby now? Is he displaying any kind of symptoms, like getting cranky, or sweating a lot, or drooling?"

"He seems okay for now."

"Did he put this pill in his mouth?" Walker asked, looking at her plastic bag.

"No, I just saw it sitting on the floor. I'm not sure he put any pill in his mouth. Maybe I'm just overreacting, but I want to be safe in case he finds another one like this one and swallows it."

"Well, if you see him acting funny in any way, you need to get him to a hospital and have his stomach pumped. In the meantime, let me look at your pill. I've put it on our scanner. That should help identify it…just give me a minute or two." He grabbed the bag holding the pill and headed to the back wall behind all the loaded shelves. Five minutes later he was back.

"This could be a prescription drug. Do you know if anyone in your house takes anything for asthma?"

"No, no one."

"Okay, how about a bad thyroid? Does anyone take anything for that?"

Brenda Jean shook her head. "No, sir. What else could it be?"

"How about blood thinners? Anyone you know taking pills for that?"

"Heavens no."

The pharmacist sighed. "That's about it for prescription medicines, but there's probably hundreds of OTC items that can look like this pill. There's no way we can check on those." He handed her pill back after putting it back in the plastic bag.

"What does OTC mean?"

"Oh, that just stands for over the counter drugs. And if I were a betting man, I'd say you could start by looking in the diet department over on aisle seven; some of them even show what the pill looks like on the front of the package. It could also be a pain pill, like an off-brand of aspirin; you know, like a generic Advil, or something like that. But I don't think it's a prescribed drug, based on our scanner."

"Thanks, you've been a lot of help."

"You're welcome. Good luck."

She looked up at the aisle markers, spotting aisle seven. As she walked away from the pharmacy, she could hear the pharmacist talking to a male clerk.

"Now, that was one hell of a great looking woman. God sure was good to her. When I see a young lady that looks like that one, I wish I was about twenty years younger and thirty pounds lighter." They both laughed, and Brenda Jean smiled. She started looking for any diet pill that could pass as Mary's thyroid pill. It was hard to see the shape or color of a lot of them. Most of the pills were in bottles that were sealed on the top. She didn't know if it was illegal to open the bottles. Looking up, she could see small cameras on the ceiling, and something told her to forget about breaking into all those bottles. She walked around, looking for pink pills on other aisles. It seemed like an impossible task until she noticed a stack of pink boxes in the laxative department that were labelled as containing Greenwalls' brand of stool softener for women. She opened the end of the top box, finding two blister packs of pink pills. She put Mary's thyroid pill next to one of the pills in the blister pack. They looked exactly alike. Just seeing the pills took her breath away. Brenda Jean couldn't believe it.

After buying a box of the stool softener, she walked out of the drugstore feeling like all her cares had gone away. Tony would be so proud of her. She called him the second she sat down in her VW. "Tony, you're not going to believe this, but I think I found the right pills already. I went to Greenwalls and bought a box of a generic women's stool softener, and I swear it's an exact match to the thyroid pill. I mean an exact match."

"Brenda Jean, you're incredible. How did you find the right pill so fast?"

"I started by doing what you said. I talked to the pharmacist and I played up what my little boy picked up off the floor. He scanned the pill I gave him and told me that there were only three or four prescription pills that matched. He even said it could be a thyroid medicine, how about that? He told me there were probably hundreds of over the counter drugs that might look the same as the pill I had. So, I went on a treasure hunt all over that store, and it was like this big stack of pink boxes was calling me to pick one up. And there it was, a perfect match."

"I'll tell you what, just hold on to everything. It sounds like Mary is leaving after Connor gets home from school. When I'm sure she's gone, let's meet somewhere for dinner. We've got a big weekend ahead of us and a lot to talk about. Remember, she said she'd be back Sunday. That's also the day she loads her pill reminder. Now darling, don't say a word to anyone. I'll call you as soon as I can...I love you."

"I love you too, Tony."

Chapter 20
We Have To Be Careful

Tony looked at his watch. Connor should be getting off the bus about now. Mary probably had their suitcases packed, already in the car. That's the way she was. If they were going anywhere, she'd start packing the car at least four hours before they left. He was so anxious to see Brenda Jean with no one looking over his shoulder, he decided to drive home and sneak a look at what was going on just to verify that his wife was gone.

As he turned onto their street, he saw Mary's Mustang pull out of the driveway, heading away from him towards the interstate. He could tell it was her, as he spotted Connor's red head sticking above the back seat. So far, everything looked like it was happening exactly like he wanted. He followed her from a distance until she pulled onto the interstate heading east. He immediately called Brenda Jean. "Hello, baby."

"Is she gone?"

"She's gone. Can I buy you some dinner?"

"That would be a good start to the evening, Tony, that's for sure."

"How about meeting at Copione's on Fourth Street, say in about twenty minutes?"

"What if somebody sees us?" Brenda Jean asked. "I mean, I think you know almost everyone in town."

"Hey, there's nothing wrong with me taking my secretary out to dinner. We've just got to act real professional, that's all."

Brenda Jean didn't say anything for a couple of seconds. "Tony, I don't want to act professional. Besides, I don't think we should take any chances, with what we have to do."

"You're right, sweet stuff. It's not worth one dinner to ruin our plans or have anyone get suspicious. Let's do it this way; let's meet somewhere and drive an hour or so heading west. I mean, I don't want to go one mile in the same direction Mary went. Maybe we can find a decent restaurant on the freeway, hopefully one close to a nice hotel. How does that sound?"

"That sounds perfect, Tony. Can you give me an hour? I need to go home and change my clothes...I'm still wearing work clothes. Plus, I need to put together stuff for tomorrow. I want to look beautiful for you."

"I don't care what you wear, you always look beautiful to me. Let's meet at Walmart. I'll park way out near the road right in front of the grocery entrance in exactly one hour. It's open twenty four hours, so no one will notice your car there overnight."

"Super. I'll see you there."

Tony drove home to take a fast shower and grab everything he needed for work the next morning. When he walked into his bathroom, he saw a folded note on the counter top. He opened it up and read, "Tony, what happened to us? We were so happy, but we've drifted apart so fast. I'm not sure if you still love me, and to tell you the truth, I'm not sure if I still want you, either. I guess I've hung in there because Connor loves you so much and I really want to get our family back together. You can call me anytime if you want to talk about saving our marriage. I'll leave that up to you. Don't worry about us, Connor and I will be fine. Mary."

Tony shook his head as he put her note back down on the counter. "She's a fruitcake," he said. He opened his sock drawer, then noticed the single rose and note from Mr. Jinks on the top of their dresser. He chuckled, wondering if Mary was thinking there was someone out there to turn to. She still looked good enough to get almost anyone, but even she would laugh when she found out who her secret admirer was.

After a sudsy shower, he put together everything he needed to meet up with Brenda Jean. Glancing at his bedside table clock, he knew he still had thirty minutes before he had to be at Walmart. He walked out the front door carrying a small black leather overnight bag and a hanger with a shirt and a suit on it. After turning around to lock the door, he could sense someone standing behind him. He backed up, almost running into Bobbie. "Wow, you startled me, Bobbie. Give a guy some warning, will you?"

Bobbie didn't respond. Her eye makeup was streaking down her cheeks as if she'd been crying. Her hair looked normal for her, with wads of it going in all directions. She always looked like she'd just gotten up, and she was wearing one of her oversized dresses, the one with different colored cats all over it. And she was loaded with body odor.

"Is there something I can do for you, Bobbie?"

"No, nothing. But it sure looks like you're getting what you deserve, Mr. Tony Calley. Sure, I lost everything I had, but guess what, Mr. Trifecta, you're going to lose everything, too."

"Don't give me any of your shit," he responded as he pushed her aside, heading to his car. "You stink. Instead of worrying about me, why don't you go back inside your cave and take a shower? You smell like a dead rat that's been laying in the sun for three days. And put on some deodorant, you must be due for your monthly cleanup."

"Looks like you're going somewhere, huh? You can't even wait for your wife to get out of town before you shack up with your secretary, Mr. Trifecta. Mary might buy all that bullshit, but I don't. I know who I saw coming to your house all those nights. I met her in your office. I hope Mary takes you to the cleaners, and I'll be the first one in line to speak up for her."

He stopped a few feet from his Mercedes, turning back to look at the neighborhood rhino pest. "What are you talking about? I'm not shacking up with anyone. I'm just dropping some clothes off at the cleaners."

"You and I both know what I'm talking about. Oh yeah, I suppose you're taking that overnight bag to get it cleaned, too? I sure hope she's worth it; I mean, I sure wouldn't trade Mary and Connor for any secretary if I were you. You're a fucking shithead, do you know that?"

"Not as much as you. You got everything wrong, you know that, Porky?" He got in his car and rolled down his window. "Go look in the mirror. You're a three hundred pound pig who never looked sexy in your entire life. No wonder your husband left you. I'd be ashamed to be married to you, too."

He squealed away as she threw a full glass of beer at his car, spreading the orange liquid all across his trunk and back window. "Go to hell, you bastard," she screamed as loud as she could.

"Damn it," Tony hollered as he hit the steering wheel with the flat of his hand, causing the radio to change channels after a finger slid across a control. Bobbie was now a big problem, his only problem. She was the one person in the world who had any kind of proof about him and Brenda Jean. He knew he had to shut her up somehow.

He drove around aimlessly for over twenty minutes, constantly thinking about Brenda Jean, with a little mixture of concern about Bobbie. He still had five minutes to get to the Walmart and find his girlfriend. When he turned onto Esther Street, he could see Walmart ahead on the right. Even from a quarter of a mile away, he spotted Brenda Jean's VW waiting for him. Tony drove up next to the little car with his window facing Brenda Jean, who was sitting in the driver's seat. "Say, you sexy thing you, how would you like to go for a ride with me in my Mercedes?"

It took her less than thirty seconds to throw her stuff in his back seat and climb into his car. A second or two later she was nibbling his right ear, whispering to him how much she loved him.

"Hey, you better cool it, Brenda Jean, or I'll stop the car right now and rape you. Let's save it for later, all right?"

"Oh, okay. Anyway, I'm really looking forward to tonight, Tony. I'm even a little bit nervous. Can you believe it?"

"Sure, I can believe it. It kind of seems like a first date for me, too. You know what it is? I think all the pressure is off both of us because Mary's not around."

"You're probably right. So, you're one hundred percent sure she's gone?"

He looked over at Brenda Jean. "One hundred percent. I went home to get my stuff and I saw her pull out and head east towards the interstate. I even followed her and watched her take the exit heading towards Chattanooga."

"So, what did you do after that?"

"I went home to get my clothes and take a shower, and I ran into some real trouble."

"What do you mean?"

"Do you remember me telling you about our fat neighbor Bobbie, who saw you come over to the house when Mary was gone? She also came to the office to identify you with Mary. Well, when I left the house today carrying that black bag and hang up bag in the back seat, she stopped me as I was leaving, telling me she would be the first to tell everyone about you and me and how terrible I was to Mary."

"So, how can she hurt us?" Brenda Jean asked.

"Listen, after I switch her pills, the insurance company is probably going to be asking questions about Mary and me; I mean, it's a million dollars. I'd bet they'll ask the neighbors, too. No, somehow we've got to get Bobbie to shut her big fat mouth. I don't know how we are going to do that, but we have to or she could spoil everything."

Brenda Jean looked out the passenger window, watching the open land passing by. "It's a good thing we've got till Sunday. I mean, we don't need your neighbor talking to your wife when she gets back." She nodded. "We've still got five days to figure out everything. Right now, all I want to think about is being with you until tomorrow morning."

Tony pulled onto the freeway heading west. In a half hour he came to an exit that looked like it was loaded with restaurants and hotels. He pulled into the parking lot of a very expensive-looking Italian restaurant. "Is this all right, Brenda Jean?"

"It looks wonderful."

After dinner, he checked them into the Jeffers Inn and Suites, getting the presidential suite. Everything was perfect for both of them. They spent an hour enjoying each other, then took a bubble bath in the giant Jacuzzi bath tub. It was like a honeymoon, a honeymoon he never imagined could happen, as she was incredibly beautiful. After their bath, they watched a movie together until the conversation turned to what was going to happen the following week.

Brenda Jean softly rubbed his stomach as she laid her head on his shoulder. "Tony, I can't wait until we can be together every night just like tonight." She turned to look up at him. "But have you thought about what you're going to do about Connor?"

"What do you mean?"

"Oh, we just never talked about it. I mean, what happens after…you know, Mary gets real sick?"

"Well, Connor is my son and he'll always be with me. We can't get married until everything settles down and we let the whole thing cool off. I'll be with you every day, but we have to be careful. That could take a little while, but we'll get through it. When we've given it enough time, then we'll be a family of three."

She put her head back on his shoulder. "Does that mean I'll be his stepmother?"

"It sure does."

Brenda Jean moved up, kissing him on a cheek, then on his lips. "Thank you, Tony." She looked at him, watching him look at the ceiling. "Tony, what's wrong? Is something bothering you?"

"Just Bobbie. I've thought of everything except her." He rubbed his temple with his right hand. "I can't figure out how to take care of her. It keeps coming back to me how much hate she had in her face tonight. She'd do anything to hurt me. Just my stupid luck, she had to be at our house when I left tonight. Yeah, she can kill this whole deal. We've got to think of a way to make sure she doesn't open her big mouth."

"Tony, just let me take care of everything," Brenda Jean said, nodding her head while she bit her upper lip.

"What do you mean, you'll take care of everything?"

"I will. Just cross that off your list of worries, trust me."

"All right, baby doll, but I don't know what you can do. I really don't."

"Tony, can we go over what we're going to do next week when your wife gets back one more time?"

He turned, looking into her beautiful eyes. "Well, she said she'd be back sometime Sunday so Connor could go to school Monday morning. Sunday is also the day she loads up her pill reminder for the week. After she does that, I'm going to switch her thyroid pills with the ones you bought today. Say, I haven't even looked at them. Did you bring them with you?"

"I sure did. I'll grab 'em."

She got up and walked into the living room, and returned with her purse in her hand. Tony watched every move she made as she laid the purse on the bed. She was a remarkably sexy woman as she moved around naked in that giant room.

"You'd better find me those pills fast before I attack you again. I can't believe how much you turn me on."

She smiled as she opened her purse, finding both the pink box of stool softeners she'd bought and the small sandwich bag that was holding one of Mary's thyroid pills. "Here, check them out."

Tony picked up the plastic bag and took out the pill, then opened a blister pack of Greenwalls' laxatives, laying a pill next to Mary's pill. Brenda Jean was right, they looked identical. "Great job, sweetheart. You're amazing, you did it in one day! I thought it would take weeks to find the perfect match." He leaned down, kissing her, allowing all the pills to fall on the floor, then made love to her again.

When they finished, Tony picked up the opened box of stool softeners and the two identical pills off the floor. "Now we've really done it. Which one is which? I guess it doesn't matter, I'll just flush both of them down the toilet."

"Okay. Finish telling me about our plan, Tony."

"Like I said, after Mary loads her pill thing, I'm going to pull all of her thyroid pills out of it and put in these," he said, holding up the pink box Brenda Jean had bought. "So, she's going to take stool softeners all week instead of her regular pills. I don't think it will take more than three or four days before she gets very, very sick. "Then, when she goes into a coma and dies, I'm going to put the pills she originally put in that pill reminder back, so it will look like she didn't take them. I don't even have to touch her prescription bottle, just hide the seven thyroid pills until I put them back. It's foolproof. No one could suspect anything. Then we get the insurance money and wait a little while. Then you, Miss Brenda Jean, will become Mrs. Tony Calley."

"It sounds so easy, Tony. Aren't you worried?"

"Only about two things. First off, I know you told me not to worry about Bobbie, but until she's fixed, I'm going to worry about her. And secondly, Connor…he's going to be crushed when his mother gets sick. I love that boy so much, it's going to be hard. But that's where you come in. You have to become his friend and his shoulder to cry on. Do you think you can do that?"

"No problem, Tony. In fact, if those are your only two concerns, let me take care of both of them for you."

"You sound confident, Brenda Jean. I hope you're right."

"I'm right, you just wait and see."

Chapter 21
Candles and Soft Music

Tony and Brenda Jean spent the next four days moving from hotel to hotel, while acting very professional at work. They were having a great time. Tony didn't want to go home, thinking he might run into Bobbie. After collecting his five thousand dollar check from Parker Hayes, he cashed it at the bank in order to eliminate paying for anything with a credit card. He even bought a new suit with all the trimmings, and took Brenda Jean to a distant mall to shop. Everything was on schedule, but Tony was getting nervous as they approached the weekend. What if Bobbie talked to Mary?

Brenda Jean was feeling the pressure too, wanting to get back to her apartment Friday morning. She was getting tired of staying in different hotel rooms. Tony dropped her off at her car in front of a Publix and went to the office. Thirty minutes later, she called him. "Tony, I've got a monster headache. I woke up with it this morning. I didn't tell you because I thought it would go away, but it's getting worse. If it's okay with you, I'd like to just lay down and turn all the lights out. I can't stand it, it really hurts."

"Have you taken anything for it?"

"Yeah, I had a bottle of Tylenol with codeine in my medicine cabinet. I took one of them and that's why I'm getting sleepy. Maybe all I need is a little sleep. I'm really not complaining, but I haven't gotten much sleep lately. How about if I just lay around my place until you get off? Then I'll park my car wherever you want and we can drive to a hotel somewhere. I'm sure I'll be okay this afternoon. Is that okay with you, sweetheart?"

"Sure. In fact, I'll leave early, say about four. You just recharge your batteries some and I'll call you a few times today. You get some shuteye."

"Tony, you're a doll, I love you."

"I love you too baby. Bye."

161

It was a good break for both of them. Tony loved being with Brenda Jean and loved making love to her. For over three days they'd been together every minute, including work time. It was time for a rest. He leaned back in his chair, taking in a deep breath. It was Friday and O'Donnell might check in, as he should be back from his cruise by now. Ron Burns wasn't supposed to be back until Monday, so Tony had to get all the figures together for O'Donnell, in case he called.

****

Brenda Jean sat in her bathtub, covered with bubbles, thinking about how she was going to take care of Bobbie. She had to move fast. Mary could be back as early as Sunday, based on what Tony said, and there wasn't any guarantee Bobbie hadn't already talked to Mary by telephone. The clock was ticking and it was starting to tick faster. She looked at her toes, watching them go under the bubbly water and then back up. That gave her the idea she was looking for. She jumped out of the tub and grabbed a green fluffy towel off the counter. As she dried herself, she looked in the mirror. "Sure, that might work," she said as she grabbed her bra. Her brain was going a million miles a minute as she developed her plan.

She walked into her closet, looking for a white and red box that was sitting behind a basket of sweaters. Brenda Jean lifted up the box and pulled the lid off. Under a pile of silky scarves, she found what she was looking for, pulling out the old and tangled blonde wig. She put her red hair into a bun and put the wig on, then started to brush the tangles out. Five minutes later it started to look real. She grabbed an eyebrow pencil and created some freckles to go with her new hair. After finding her purse, she put on her biggest pair of dark sunglasses, and suddenly she looked ten years younger and like a totally different woman.

"Oh yeah, you look great," Brenda Jean told the woman in the mirror. She punched in Tony's cell number.

"Hey, baby, how are you feeling?" Tony asked. "I hope you're getting some rest."

"I'm fine, but I miss you, Tony. I'm getting used to being with you all the time. Now I wish I was there and not here. Anyway, I've been thinking...can you tell me what Bobbie's last name is and what her address is?"

"Sure, but why do you want that?"

"I'm thinking about putting a letter in her mailbox trying to convince her that I have a fiancé. I'm hoping that makes her think we aren't lovers and she made a mistake identifying me. I'll let you read it before I deliver it. Do you think that will work?"

"I really doubt it, Brenda Jean. But, anyway, her last name is Williams and she lives at 403 Kingston Hills Road. No offense, but I don't care much for your idea, honey. I wouldn't give her the time of day, let alone anything on paper that she can show Mary. But if you want, go ahead and play with it; just let me see it before you stick it in her mailbox, okay?"

"I will. Thanks, baby. I love you. Bye."

Brenda picked up the paper she'd written Bobbie's information on, then headed to her computer in the second bedroom. She went through a drawer of discs until she found the right one, then stuck it in her computer. Twenty minutes later, she hit the print button.

She studied the letter and smiled. It looked like the real deal. Then she put another disc in her computer, followed by an envelope. Two minutes later, she'd finished what she needed, except for a business card. That was easy to make too, in that she'd had to get a business card disk and kit when she was job hunting. In less than an hour, Brenda Jean had completed the whole package…the package for Bobbie.

She put on the hottest blouse she owned, along with a new pair of designer jeans, then grabbed the makeup kit her mother had given her on her birthday from under her bed. The kit looked like a small suitcase. Brenda Jean was ready. She stood before the bathroom mirror, practicing talking like a twenty year old bimbo.

She jumped into her car, constantly going over in her head what she was going to do when she confronted Bobbie. After finding Kingston Hills Road, she drove by Bobbie's house, parking a block away in front of a three story pillared home with a long driveway. It was perfect. Five minutes later she was looking at the front porch of Mr. and Mrs. Jerry Williams. After taking a deep breath, she walked up the sidewalk to the front door. Brenda Jean straightened out her new blonde hair as she hit the doorbell.

Bobbie answered the door almost immediately. "Hello honey, how can I help you?"

"Are you Bobbie Williams?"

Bobbie looked Brenda Jean up and down. "Yes, that's me."

"Well then, you must be expecting me. My name is Kim Wynrik." She put her hand out.

Bobbie shook hands with the tall blonde. "Who?"

"Kim Wynrik. You did get our letter last month, didn't you?"

"What letter? A letter about what? I don't know what you're talking about."

Brenda pulled the letter out of her makeup kit. "Here's a copy, Mrs. Williams. Today's the day for your appointment." She handed Bobbie the letter with a fancy letterhead.

"Huh?" Bobbie asked as she started reading.

Dear Mrs. Williams:

You have an anonymous friend who purchased our diamond makeover for you, which includes cutting and styling your hair, a relaxing pedicure and manicure, as well as a one hour facial. To top that off, we will be applying a makeup program that will uniquely take advantage of your special features. You will love it. We know that your makeover will be a big change in your life. Your husband or boyfriend will not even recognize you when he sees you. "This is a six hundred dollar value, with no cost to you. Based on our schedule, we will have a makeover specialist in your area on Friday, November 19. We've scheduled your appointment for 10:30 AM, unless you want to change it. However, if you do want it changed, it will have to be moved to next year, as we have totally reserved all makeovers until January. Please respond ASAP if you do not want this free wonderful session or want the appointment changed. If you are happy with the schedule for your makeover, you don't even have to respond, and one of our specialists will see you on the nineteenth of November.

Respectfully,

John Sently,

Vice President, Styles International.

Bobbie handed the letter back to Brenda Jean. "I don't understand. Someone bought this for me?"

Brenda Jean nodded. "That's exactly right, sweetie. You must have a very good friend somewhere. Most of the time when I do a makeover the person I fix up ordered the service. But sometimes it's a gift. Oh, here, I forget to give you my business card." She handed Bobbie her homemade Styles International card. Bobbie looked at it, shaking her head.

"I don't remember ever getting your letter. I guess I must have thought it was junk mail or something."

"That may be, I don't know," Brenda Jean answered. "So, do you want me to make you over this morning? It will take like about three hours for everything, or you can try to get an appointment in January. It's up to you."

"It all sounds too good to be true. Sure, I want a makeover, especially if it's free. And this is the perfect day to get beautiful. My kids don't get home from school until after three. I'd love to be pampered; I've had a tough couple of weeks." Bobbie looked around Brenda Jean with a puzzled look. "Say, where's your car?"

"Oh, Elaine—she's another makeover specialist—she dropped me off because she has an eleven o'clock appointment. She'll be picking me up when she's done. So, let's get going, sweetie. You're going to think you're in heaven when I get done."

Bobbie turned her head as she looked at Brenda Jean. "Are you sure this won't cost me anything?"

"I'm sure, it won't cost you a dime…that is, unless you want to tip me. But that's entirely up to you. Some customers tip me when they're done, and some don't. It's up to you."

"Okay, come on in," Bobbie said as she stepped aside to let Brenda Jean walk by her.

"You have a beautiful home, Bobbie. Like, I really love the colors," Brenda Jean said, looking around, noticing Bobbie studying her. "Oh, forgive me if I don't take off these sunglasses. I just had an eye operation and I need to protect a cornea from any kind of light. My left eye ain't so pretty right now."

"That's okay, I understand. Even with those on, you are a very pretty young lady. I can see why they want you to do the makeovers. I'd love to look like you."

"Maybe we can make you look even better than me, honey."

"That's a nice thought, but I don't think that's possible. So tell me, what we're going to do?"

"Well, just like the letter said," Brenda Jean answered, as she noticed the front door automatically locked after Bobbie closed it. "I'm going to give you a shampoo and a scalp massage first, then I'll trim your hair and give you a facial while you're lying in a warm bubble bath. When I'm done with that, we'll get you a pedicure and a manicure, followed by redoing your makeup. And then, if you like the makeup, I'll give you some free coupons so you can get the same kind of makeup at the drug store."

"Wow, that sounds so wonderful. What do you want me to do first?"

"Well, we need you to have some real peace and quiet while we fix you up. There isn't anyone else here, is there?"

"No, it's just me until my boys get home from school. We've got hours."

"Great. Here's what you need to do. First off, I need, like, some candles to set the mood. Do you have any?"

"I sure do. What else?"

"Oh, I like to have soft music when I do your facial. Do you have a radio?"

"Yep, I've got a clock radio next to my bed."

"Great. Now where is your biggest bathtub?"

"It's upstairs, next to the master bedroom, but it's a mess."

"Don't worry, we'll fix it up. All you have to do is get totally undressed, all but a robe. Then grab me some candles and the radio. So, what do you say? Let's get started…show me the way."

Brenda Jean followed Bobbie up the stairs into the master bedroom. She found the bathroom as her customer got naked. She almost started laughing when she saw Bobbie, who had rolls and rolls of bulging fat that bounced up and down when she opened a drawer in the desk next to the bathroom and pulled out a couple of short white candles. Looking around the master bathroom for some bubble bath, Brenda Jean found a half-full bottle under the sink. She poured almost all of it into the cascading water that was coming out of the faucet. Within minutes, steam was covering the mirror and the tub was filling itself with silky white bubbles.

Bobbie walked into the bathroom, handing Brenda Jean the candles, then plugged the radio into a receptacle next to the door, only three feet from the bath tub.

"Thank you. Now take off your robe and get in the tub. Then you've only got one more job, Mrs. Williams; I need you to just lay back and enjoy. I'm going to give you a shampoo first after I light the candles and put the radio on." Brenda Jean turned on the radio and found a relaxing FM station. "Are you comfortable?"

"Oh yes, this is great. I'm really looking forward to what I look like when you're done. My husband left me and I want him to see me all fixed up."

"Well, I guarantee that when he sees you after this, not only will he not want to leave you, he will be amazed," Brenda Jean said as she put a steaming cloth over Bobbie's eyes. "This should feel real good. Is it too hot?

"No, it's perfect."

"Great, now keep it over your eyes." She picked up the small bottle of shampoo she brought with her and poured it over Bobbie's hair and started to massage it into her scalp. "So, how does that feel?"

"Oh, it's heavenly. I still can't believe someone bought me this. I bet it was Mary Calley."

"Is she a relative?" Brenda Jean asked as she continued to scratch Bobbie's head.

"Oh no, she's a neighbor. We used to be best friends but we got into a fight. Maybe she ordered all this for me trying to make up for our fight. She really is a special person. Sure, I bet it was her."

"Okay now Bobbie, I'm going to rinse out your shampoo so I can put a special conditioner on. I need you to hold that cloth tight over your eyes until I tell you to take it off, okay?"

"Sure," Bobbie answered, holding her eye cover with both hands.

Brenda Jean stood up and grabbed a towel off a hook on the wall next to the linen closet to dry her hands. Then she picked up the clock radio off the counter and dropped it into the tub against Bobbie's left leg, making sure it remained plugged in.

Bobbie's entire body shook as the electricity went through her, and a little bit of smoke started coming out of one of her ears. She kicked her legs, sending water all over the bathroom, until she stopped moving. Brenda Jean leaned down to look at the fat woman, who had stopped breathing. She grabbed a dry washcloth from the linen closet, then wiped down the sink area and the candles, and anything else she might have touched. The shampoo bottle was put back into her makeup box, which was then latched closed. She looked back at her victim, who was very dead. The bathroom looked like the scene of a terrible accident, where a woman reached for her radio while she was taking a bath. Brenda Jean retraced her steps all the way to the front door, wiping away any possible fingerprints. She remembered her business card and found it on a small entry table, then slid it into the closed makeup box. She walked out the front door after wiping the door handle and the doorbell, then put the washcloth in her purse, keeping a souvenir of her adventure.

Brenda Jean slowly and innocently walked back to her car and drove to her apartment, where she immediately changed her clothes. She put her wig, her sunglasses, and all the clothes she took off into which she stuffed into the trunk of her car. Everything had gone so smoothly, she couldn't believe it. She plopped onto her couch, proud of what she had just done, then picked up her cell phone to call Tony, but changed her mind. She might need a phone record of the call for an alibi. She grabbed the house phone and dialed his number.

"Hello," Tony said, as he looked at the number on his cell phone.

"It's me, baby," Brenda Jean answered.

"What number are you calling from?"

"Oh, it's my home phone, my cell is dead. I'm charging it now."

"Well, how's my beautiful secretary doing?"

"I'm okay. I still haven't gotten rid of this headache. I think I'm going to try taking another nap. I went to sleep a little while ago, but the damn dog next door woke me up. Do you want to come over, Tony?"

"I sure wish I could, but I have to stick around here. I'm waiting to hear from O'Donnell."

"All right, I'm going to lay down. Do me a favor and call me before you leave, Tony, so we can work out what we're doing tonight."

"You got it. Have a good nap. I love you, sweet stuff."

CHAPTER 22
The Princess Is Coming Home

"Mr. Calley, you have a call on line two. It's a Bill O'Donnell."

"Hello, Mr. O'Donnell. How was your cruise?"

"Now listen, Tony, I told you once already, I want you to call me Bill. And to tell you the truth, don't ever go on a three week cruise with your wife. It's awful close quarters, if you know what I mean."

"I completely understand, Bill. Anyway, welcome back. How can I help you?"

"I just called to see how much money you made me over the last three weeks."

"I think we did all right. The two hundred grand you wanted in money market accounts didn't make much…let's see." He pulled up the numbers on his laptop. "I only got a return of, let's see, a little over four thousand."

"That's not very good, Tony, although the four grand paid for about a third of our cruise. What happened?"

"The money markets are real tight this month. It looks like…hold on…it looks like that was about the max I could make on any money market account, so it's not that I picked the wrong one; all of them kind of sucked the last couple of weeks."

"How about the two hundred I told you to invest wherever you wanted?"

"Well now, that's a different story. We did a lot better with that…come on computer, let's see…wow…as of this morning, your two hundred grand is worth two hundred and forty two thousand. I was real lucky with some stocks, especially one IPO. How's that?"

"Holy shit, Tony, that's over a twenty percent return in less than a month. You're a magician. I knew I didn't have anything to worry about with your outfit. Great job, young man. Okay Tony, sell the money market accounts right away, but I think I'll hold onto whatever you did with the rest. How about faxing me everything? I want to see how you made me forty two grand in three weeks. Keep it going and you'll find a very big bonus when you're done. Nice going. Now fax it to me. You've got my number."

"I'll give it to my secretary right away. I'm glad we're able to take care of you, Bill."

"You did good, Tony. By the way, is Ron back?"

"No, unfortunately, his father-in-law passed away. He'll be back Monday."

"I'm sorry to hear that. Please pass on my condolences, if you will. It looks like I've got a tough decision to make. I just may want you handling everything for me from here on out. That wouldn't hurt Ron's feelings, would it?"

"Oh no, we're partners. We're both very happy to help you."

"Good. Thanks again. I'll be talking to you; bye, Tony."

"Take care, Bill," Tony said, as he hung up.

How could life get better for Tony Calley? His bookie was paid off. He had the most beautiful girl in the world waiting for him at her apartment. His bitch wife was out of town, and he not only saved a giant account for his company, but he was heading towards a very nice commission check, as well. He had the best and smartest son anyone could have. Yes, life was pretty good, except for one thing...Bobbie Williams and her mouth.

Tony had Rudi send the fax over to O'Donnell, then he looked at his appointments listed on the printout she'd typed up after he told her Brenda Jean was sick. There was only one more customer to see and that was at four o'clock. He told Rudi to call whoever it was and reschedule it for Monday, he was going home. He picked up his cell phone and called Brenda Jean. "Hey sweetie, how's that headache?"

"It's pretty much gone, Tony. I slept for over two hours and I feel a lot better. I'm so anxious to see you. What are we doing tonight?"

"It's almost three and I'm leaving real soon. How fast can you park that little car of yours somewhere where I can pick you up?"

"All I need is about a half hour. Where do you want to meet?"

"Do you know where that new Kroger is on Marriman Street?"

"Sure. I can get there in about twenty minutes."

"Well, park between the Kroger and Penney's near the service road. I'll pick you up there in about an hour, okay?"

"I'll see you there, Tony."

"Great. I love you, Brenda Jean."

They both pulled into the arranged parking lot at the same time. Brenda Jean threw her overnight bag and some clothes in the back seat, next to what he'd picked up at the cleaners. As they pulled out, she was all over Tony, kissing his right neck, then his ear with light, but warm kisses. He was getting excited with every kiss. But his thoughts had turned to where he was going to take her when his cell phone rang.

He looked down at his dashboard screen. It read "Mary," along with her phone number. He didn't punch the answer button. Five seconds after the final ring, Mary's message came over his Bluetooth speaker.

"Tony, where are you? I called your office and they said you left a while ago, now you won't answer your cell phone. I don't even want to guess where you're at. I'll bet you're either in a sports bar so you can watch a race somewhere, or you're meeting someone. I've got it, maybe you're getting a second mortgage on our house…maybe your bookie is after you, who knows? Anyway, we're coming home tomorrow. I can't take my mother for one more day; besides, Connor misses his computer and his books. Why haven't you called us? Maybe my dad is right about you. Anyway, I figure we'll get there around one tomorrow afternoon. I want you to save me some time when I get home, we've got some serious stuff to talk about. I'll see you then. Bye."

"That sure was cold, don't you think?" Brenda Jean asked.

"So, what else is new? But now that changes things," Tony responded. "I need to get by the house early tomorrow to make it look like I was there all week, like messing it up and stuff like that. If I can make her believe I spent the last three or four days at home, that will throw some water on Bobbie's theory that I had an overnight bag when she saw me Wednesday."

"I wish I could help you. Your place needs a woman's touch to know what to mess up."

"Sure, the last thing I need now is Bobbie seeing you there. By the way, what did you do about that letter you were going to put in her mailbox? Did you ever write it?"

"No, you were right. I tried to compose something, but it just didn't come out right. I couldn't make it sound sincere, so I gave up. It looks like you're going to have to convince your wife I'm not your girlfriend, even with Bobbie telling her I am."

"Well, Brenda Jean, let's not worry about that now. Let's find a nice hotel somewhere and then we'll get something to eat, okay?"

"That sounds good to me, Tony." She reached over, hugged his arm, and looked up at him. "This might be our last night together for a long time. Let's have some fun. Where do you want to go?"

"Let's splurge, baby doll. I'm taking you to the Hightower Waldorf Downtown, then we'll go to Reggios, if I can get a reservation. What do you think?"

"Do you think that's safe?"

"Ordinarily I'd say no, but it's a Friday night; all the stuffed shirts I know won't be near downtown on a Friday night. Let's go for it."

"If you think it's okay, it's fine with me."

They checked into the Waldorf, getting a suite on the top floor, where they made love and showered together in one of the largest showers they had ever seen, one with three showerheads. When they finished, they decided to order dinner from room service after failing to get a reservation at Reggios Italian Eatery. Forty minutes later, two steak and lobster dinners were delivered, along with a chilled bottle of champagne. As they were eating, a local channel ran a commercial about the ten o'clock news. "Watch for highlights of the state football playoffs and how our Eastside Tigers pulled out another one, as well as a terrible accident that happened in Rymont today involving a woman accidentally electrocuting herself in her own bathtub. Details at ten on your home for news, channel nine in Nashville."

****

Brenda Jean could tell the news teaser didn't catch Tony's attention, and she looked at the small brown clock radio on her bedside table. It was nine thirty. She had to be sure he was focusing on channel nine in a half hour.

Tony started flipping the channels, finally settling on a basketball game on ESPN.

Twenty minutes later she rolled over, putting her head on his shoulder. "Honey, can we watch channel nine? They're going to have some high school football highlights about Eastside. They had a playoff game tonight and my neighbor's son plays for them. I promised her I'd look for her in the stands if I watched the news tonight. She told me to watch channel nine, as they always cover high school football."

"Now you're a sports fan, too. My God, Brenda Jean, you're perfect. Not many women know anything about football. You continue to amaze me. Sure, here," he answered, switching back to channel nine.

The anchorwoman led off the local news on channel nine exactly at ten o'clock. "Good evening, ladies and gentlemen, welcome to your home for all that's news. This is Valerie Bennett. Before we get to the highlights of Eastside High's playoff game, we'll start with a tragic story. A housewife accidently electrocuted herself today in her bathtub. We go live now to Beth Elaine in Rymont, who is at the scene. Beth?"

"Yes, Valerie, this is a very sad story. A thirty one year old housewife was killed today in Rymont after being electrocuted in her bathtub. Local Rymont police told me that it looks like she was taking a bath and somehow grabbed a radio she had plugged in near her tub. They indicated that she was home alone and was discovered by her two sons after they got off the school bus. The dead woman is identified as Roberta Williams, who lived on Kingston Hills Road here in Rymont."

"That's terrible; just think about those poor boys," Valerie said with a sigh. "Please keep us informed, Beth, if there are any more developments."

Tony and Brenda Jean didn't say a word. They were in shock...well, at least he was. Brenda Jean faked looking stunned as she looked at him with her mouth open. "Did you hear all that, Tony?"

"I sure did. That is incredible. I'm not sure what to say. I guess I should be glad, but I'm not sure if I really am. I mean, that is unbelievable. They did say Roberta Williams on Kingston Hills Road in Rymont, didn't they?"

Brenda Jean nodded. "Isn't that weird? I mean, I was going to put something in her mailbox today, but I changed my mind. No matter what, Tony, this is just plain awful...I mean, her two kids found her dead in that bathtub."

"Do you think I should let Mary know?"

"I wouldn't. Tell her tomorrow."

"You're right. I think what I'll do is get to the house in the morning and then call her before she gets home."

"Tony, do you think your neighbor committed suicide? You told me she was miserable since her husband left her. Do you think she would have done that?"

"I have no idea. I know when I saw her Wednesday night she looked like she'd been crying a lot." He shook his head. "Who knows what goes through the head of someone when their life is as screwed up as hers was? She might have just snapped, I don't know."

"You can't change anything now. What happened happened. So, do you want me to go with you in the morning to get your house ready for your wife?"

"No, it's not worth the chance she might get there early. We've got to get all this shit out of our minds and concentrate on what we're doing next week. But, right now, let's have some more fun," Tony said, as he grabbed Brenda Jean around the waist, pulling her back so he could get on top of her.

After they finished, Brenda Jean leaned on her fist, looking at Tony. "I've never known anyone like you. You really know how to make a woman happy. I can't wait until I can be with you every night and not worry about who knows it."

****

173

The next morning Tony drove Brenda Jean back to her car and headed home, messing everything up from the beds to the laundry. He was proud when he finished. It really looked like he'd lived there while she was gone.

He stopped at the mailbox as he pulled out and grabbed a load of mail, quickly sorting out the junk and leaving a couple of bills in the box as if they were just delivered. As he backed into the street, he got a glimpse of Jerry Williams coming out his front door. Tony pulled into Jerry's driveway, got out of his car, and walked up to his neighbor.

"Jerry, what happened? I just heard this morning." He could tell Jerry had been crying as he wrapped his arms around his neighbor. "Tony, I don't know, I just don't know. Bobbie was taking a bath, and she must have reached for her clock radio. In all the years we've been married, she never put a radio in that bathroom."

"I can't tell you how sorry I am, Jerry. She was like family to Mary and me. Is there anything I can do, buddy?"

"Not that I can think of right now, except maybe Mary helping me with the boys if she gets a chance. They're two really strong kids, but just think what they went through yesterday. My God, they discovered their mother's body in our bathtub. They're a little better this morning, but it was really rough last night. So, if you get a chance, send Mary over to see them, will you? They really love her."

Tony nodded. "I will. I'll send her over as soon as she gets home. She had to go over to help her folks this week; her mother was in a bad car wreck."

"I'm sorry, Tony, but I've been out of the loop. I didn't hear anything about Mary's mother. Is she all right?"

"Oh yeah, she'll be fine. Anyway, Mary and Connor should be back this afternoon." He patted Jerry on the shoulder. "I'll be around all day; just give me a call if you need anything, okay?"

"What am I going to do about the boys? I don't want them living here anymore. The police therapist said they shouldn't stay here after what they saw in our bathroom." Jerry started crying. "What should I do?"

Tony took a deep breath, hugging Jerry as he looked over his shoulder. "Where are the boys now?"

"They're in the basement with Bobbie's folks. They said they'd take the boys for a while, but all they've got is a two bedroom house with a big basement, so that's only a temporary fix. I've been renting a room at a very cheap hotel downtown. What am I supposed to do now?"

"I'll tell you what…after Mary gets back, maybe the three of us can put our heads together and figure out what we need to do."

"Thanks Tony. Listen, I've got to go. The guy from the funeral home is due here any minute. Do you know her body is still in the bathroom? It's awful, just awful! I guess the cops worked all night looking at everything. Please call me when Mary gets back…please. I'm kind of lost."

"I will. Again, I'm so sorry, Jerry. Just remember, we're here to help."

Jerry turned around without answering and walked back towards his front door.

Tony pulled out, found a dumpster behind a Burger King, and put the trash from his house under some empty cardboard boxes. After returning home, he dialed Mary's cell number.

"Mary, where are you?"

"I'm about an hour from home, so why are you asking? Do you have to cover your tracks, is that it?"

"That's cruel. I was only asking because I wanted you to know that Bobbie is dead."

He could hear her slamming on the brakes. "What did you say?"

"I said Bobbie is dead. She died sometime yesterday. She accidentally electrocuted herself in her bathtub."

Mary started sobbing, and it sounded like she was hitting the dashboard. "Oh, my God, Tony, how are the boys?"

"Not too good. They found her when they got home from school yesterday. Jerry is home now. He wants you to try and help the boys when you get here. I told him that you and I would sit down with him and figure out what to do."

Mary stopped crying for a second. "What do you mean?"

"Jerry said since the boys found their dead mother in the bathtub, they can't stay there. I guess the county therapist or whatever said they had to figure out how to live somewhere else, at least for a while."

"I hope you told him we'll take the boys if he wants."

"I offered, but he said Bobbie's parents want them to come live with them. But all they've got is a small place. Like I said, we need to help him make some big decisions."

"Oh, Tony, this is so terrible. My God, the last time I talked to her, I told her off. She was my best friend and I blew her off, and now she's gone. Oh God…." She began to cry again. "Listen, Tony, I've got to go. I'll see you in an hour. I probably need that whole hour to talk to Connor. He's got his big earphones on in the back seat watching a movie, so he doesn't know anything yet. I think I'll stay here for a few minutes and talk to him. Oh, my God, not Bobbie," she said, hanging up on her husband.

Finally, Mary got home. Connor jumped out of the passenger side, running up the steps to find his father. "Daddy, Daddy, where are you?"

Tony opened the front door and spread his arms apart waiting for Connor, who jumped up and landed on his father. He kissed his son on the top of his head.

"I sure missed you, Connor. I'm not used to not seeing you every day." He looked up at his wife walking up the sidewalk. "Hello, Mary, how are you?" he asked as he let Connor down, who headed up to his room.

"Oh, I guess I'm all right. It's just been a long week. Now all this with Bobbie, it's a lot for anyone to handle. I bet you had a good time, though…I mean, having total freedom for a few days." She brushed by her husband after giving him a frigid kiss on his cheek. "Tony, how about getting our stuff out of the car? I'm in a hurry to get over to see Jerry. Oh, I see you didn't do much housecleaning while I was gone." She looked around each room as she headed towards the kitchen. "The least you could have done is picked up after yourself. I mean, I was a slave for my folks all week. I guess it never ends, does it?"

"I'm sorry, princess, I tried. I even tried to do some laundry. I do work fifty to sixty hours a week, you know?"

Mary turned around to look at Tony, who was standing in the doorway of the kitchen. "That's bullshit and you know it. I bet you don't work thirty five hours in an average week. You must count all the time you are gambling."

Tony shook his head. "Wow, you are something else. Here I was, trying my best to keep the house clean and work too, and you still walk in with a giant chip on your shoulder. Do you think I'll ever get any credit from you for anything?"

"I don't know, Tony. I guess I'm just being a bitch. My plate is so full," she said, sitting down on a kitchen chair, starting to cry into her hands. "Just think, Connor is in a new grade, you keep blowing all our money, my mother is really something else right now, and now my best friend killed herself. And that doesn't even take into account that you are probably cheating on me. I'd say my plate is full, wouldn't you?"

Tony sat down next to her. "I think you're wrong about all of that. First off, Connor loves his new class and it's been great for him. I don't keep blowing all our money. Go ahead and check our account, you'll find it to be about the same as when you left. And you don't know if Bobbie killed herself. Jerry said it was just an accident. Plus, I don't know why you keep going back to me being unfaithful."

Mary started walking towards the back door, answering him over her left shoulder. "Let's talk about what Bobbie told me about your visitor when I was helping my mom in the hospital. Do you know you convinced me it wasn't true, but now I'm thinking it was. In fact, I wonder who's been sleeping with you in our bed the last three nights?"

He threw the fruit bowl on the center of the table against the wall, with oranges and bananas splattering out their parts all over the kitchen. "You are a terrible person, do you know that? All you do is listen to your crazy imagination and you think you've got all the answers. Well, you don't have any answers. I've been batching it for most of the week while you've been away feeling sorry for yourself, and I've been doing that batching by myself, I might add. When you think about it, there's a great big world out there full of wives who don't have near what you got." He tried to grab her but she jerked away from him.

"The problem is I don't trust you anymore, Tony. I don't know what to believe. You've become such a liar that I don't even pay much attention to anything you say. I'm going over to see Jerry and the boys." She walked out, slamming the back door behind her. "And don't forget to call your girlfriend and fill her in," she screamed back at him.

E. G. LANDER

CHAPTER 23
I Need To See Your Phone

Mary spent most of Saturday night with Jerry Williams and his family at his parents' house. She tried hard to get the boys to think about anything but their mother's death, but it was a futile effort. The two youngsters held hands most of the evening, with one of them periodically sobbing, causing a chain reaction with their father and their grandparents. It was obvious Bobbie had been the glue that held everyone together in that family.

"Jerry, why don't you let me take the boys home with me?" Mary asked. "Tomorrow is Sunday, and I know Tony would love to take Connor and them to Magiquest. They all love that place so much. What do you think, kids, do you want to see if you can kill the dragon? Connor knows most of the secrets. We'll even have some pizza there. You all really love their pizza, so how about it?"

They didn't get a chance to answer. "Sorry Mary, but we all think it's kind of time for the family to stay together." Jerry answered. "You understand, don't you?"

"Of course I do. But if you all decide you want to let Tommy and Billy go with us to Magiquest, the invite still stands. Just give us a call. I'm gonna head back home to see how my little guy is. I'm so, so sorry for all of you and what just happened."

Mary picked up her purse and walked over to hug the boys. They held onto her hard, not wanting to let her go. She finally pried herself away and bent down to kiss each one of them, then found Jerry to kiss him goodbye. No one said anything…they didn't have to. She left feeling like she was helpless, and she was.

The four mile drive home gave her a little time to catch her breath and start thinking about little Connor. She should have brought him with her to Jerry's parents' house. When she got home, she quietly opened the front door, finding Tony asleep in his recliner and Connor laying on the floor watching the Discovery Channel. He looked up at his mother as she walked in.

"Mom, how are they doing?"

Mary sat down on the couch. "Come here, son."

Connor walked over and sat on her lap. She squeezed him as hard as she could, crying so hard it shook him. He looked up at her, wiping tears off her cheeks. "It's okay, Mommy, Aunt Bobbie is up in heaven, and I'll bet she's happy now. She wasn't very happy down here, was she?"

"No, she wasn't," Mary said, looking down at her prize. "You are something, Connor, you know that?"

"Do you know, I was thinking about her some tonight. I bet she's making God laugh when He hears her crazy giggle, huh?"

"You're probably right, Connor. You're probably right."

"What's going to happen to Timmy and Billy, Mommy?"

"I told Uncle Jerry the boys could come and live with us for a while, but they're going to stay with their grandparents." She ran her fingers through his red hair. "They're kind of lost now, Connor."

He looked up at his mother. "Mommy, will you please, please, please do me a favor? Will you promise me that you'll never die, please?"

"I promise you I'll live a long, long time, so long that you'll be ready to move away one day and have your own family."

"Why would I want to do that? I don't ever want to leave you or Daddy."

She kissed him on his forehead. "That's what you say now, but when you get older your feelings will change, you'll see." She laid her head back as she started to scratch Connor's scalp. He loved that. In less than ten minutes, they were both asleep.

****

Tony woke up before sunrise, noticing Mary holding Connor. He went out into the kitchen to make a cup of coffee. The oven clock said it was six twenty. Should he change her pills now? He knew the pill reminder was in her purse. Could he do it? Just knowing what Bobbie's kids were going through made him rethink. Could he really do that to Connor?

He went outside through the back door and walked around to the front of the house where he picked up the newspaper. The bottom of the front page had a big headline that read, "Local Housewife Electrocuted In Bathtub." Next to the article was a picture of Bobbie. "That must be a picture from twenty years ago," he said, looking at a very pretty and skinny Bobbie Williams. He read the whole story, feeling sorry for the Williams family. It was kind of lucky for Tony the way things had happened, but he still felt bad.

After pulling his cell phone out of his back pocket, he went into the garage and dialed Brenda Jean's number.

"Hello," she whispered, obviously just waking up.

He quietly closed the garage door and whispered back to her. "Baby, it's me."

"What's going on, Tony?"

"I just needed to talk to you. I don't know if I can do it today. I mean, Connor is going through so much because of Bobbie's kids. Maybe we need to wait a day or two before we do anything."

"But Tony, you said it would take four or five days before she would die. Why don't you just make the switch, and then if we change our minds or something else comes up, we can put the right pills back. I'm just afraid if we chicken out now we may never do it."

"I don't know. I think I just want to get through today and do it tomorrow. I want you more than anything and I know I have to do this, but I need one more day to really talk myself into it. Hold on…." He thought he'd heard something. Turning around, he spotted his wife leaning on the garage door frame. He hung up the phone.

"Okay, who were you talking to, Tony, and what did you mean when you said you need one more day to talk yourself into something?"

"Well, uh, it looks like you caught me. I was just making a bet, that's all. I know I promised I wouldn't bet anymore, but this guy I know—his name is Parker—he left a text message on my phone last night. When I got up this morning I saw it, so I called him back."

Mary shook her head. "You're a real piece of work, do you know that? Now you're trying to convince me you call your bookie at what, seven o'clock on a Sunday to make a bet? You must think I'm either very deaf or very stupid. I'll tell you what, let me see your phone, then I'll know who you called." She motioned to him to give her the phone. "Come on, prove what you just said, let me have your phone." She motioned at him again.

He threw his phone as hard as he could against the garage wall, watching it break into about twenty pieces. "There, you crazy woman, there's my phone. See what you can figure out from that." He started heading towards her.

She turned away and walked back into the house and up to their bedroom, where she plopped onto the bed. Tony stormed into the room immediately after. "That's all the proof I need, you fucking asshole. You wouldn't even let me see who you were talking to. We both know you were talking to your girlfriend, who I still think is Brenda Jean. So, I'll ask you one more time; you said to whoever was on the phone that you needed one more day to talk yourself into something…well, what is it? Maybe you want to electrocute me, too? Well, let me tell you something, Mr. Tony the Tiger gambler, you don't need to talk yourself into anything anymore. We are done unless you stop lying to me and tell me the truth."

He stood over her next to the bed. "I did tell you the truth. I was talking to Parker. When you caught me I just snapped, that's all. It's the first time I've talked to Parker in the last two weeks and you're listening...that's just my luck. I told him I was done betting because it was affecting our marriage. He told me he had an inside track on a horse that was running this afternoon. That's when I told him I needed some time to talk myself into betting again, like maybe tomorrow."

"You know, you are getting better at telling your lies...I almost believe you. It looks like it boils down to either you are afraid of getting caught making bets or talking to your mistress. I think you broke your goddamn phone because you were talking to Brenda Jean."

Tony shook his head as he looked out the window. "Mary, I swear on everything...on our love, on my life, on everything I have...that I don't have a girlfriend. I was talking to Parker Hayes, the guy who used to make bets for me."

She stood up. "Who knows? I'll tell you what, Tony, I'll give you one chance to prove that to me. I want you to get me a copy of all of your cell phone calls for the last thirty days, do you hear? Both incoming and outgoing. And if your phone bill shows you are being honest with me, then I'll forgive you for everything. When can you get me that bill?"

"Well, I can't get it on a Sunday, that's for sure. I'll call AT&T tomorrow morning and have a copy sent to your attention by mail; that way I won't even see it or touch it. I have to call them anyway to get a new phone. Will that suffice?"

"That will suffice. Let's see what that says. I'm sick of fighting and I hope I'm wrong. I'd give anything if you stopped gambling and I could be sure you're faithful to me. Now let's see if you can prove it."

"I will and I promise you'll be very proud of me. I've really tried to be so good. I mean, you ought to call the automated line at the bank today, then you'll see nothing has come out of our account in over a week. One more thing, I did work hard to keep the house clean for you, at least the best I could."

It was at that moment that Tony decided he wasn't going to sleep on what to do. He was going to take care of her pill reminder as soon as possible.

Mary laid back down on the bed, pulling her pillow over her head. She was wiped out. Between the drive back, Bobbie's death, and the constant fights with her husband, she'd had enough. She went to sleep five minutes later while Tony was reading the newspaper on the foot of the bed. "Mary," he called out. She didn't answer.

Tony quietly walked down the stairs into the kitchen, looking for her purse. He spotted it on the floor next to a chair. After looking up the stairs to make sure Mary wasn't watching, he pulled her pill reminder out. He turned to look for his wife again, then opened up the pill case. It was empty. She had to fill it up soon. That meant today was his big day. He put her purse back down where he'd found it and walked by the stairs again, glancing up and seeing no one. Tony was starting to get nervous. He never imagined he'd find the guts to do what he was about to do. He walked out into the garage, pulling down his old black tackle box from the top shelf over his workbench. After pushing aside some tools in the box, he found the pink container of women's stool softeners. He gave out a heavy sigh as he looked at it, then put the pills back and lifted the tackle box onto the top shelf again. Everything was ready; but was he?

CHAPTER 24
The Big Switch

Tony kept thinking about Mary. How did all this happen? And how did it happen so fast? He'd gone from being totally in love with his wife to not being able to stand being around her. It was her fault. She was the one who kept bitching about everything. He made a lot of money; so what if he wanted to gamble a little bit? He'd had no interest in any other woman until Mary turned against him. She made him fall in love with Brenda Jean, no one else did. It wasn't his fault, it was hers.

He checked on his wife, making sure she was still asleep, then to be safe, took the portable house phone and got into his car to call Brenda Jean.

"Hello," she answered, short of breath.

"Hey, Brenda Jean, what are you doing? Are you okay?"

"I'm fine. But what phone are you on? I didn't recognize the number."

"Oh, I broke my cell phone. I'm on our house phone. And why are you so out of breath? You don't have another guy with you, do you?"

"No, silly. I was just doing some jumping jacks with this exercise DVD I got at Walgreens. Hold on, let me turn it off. Now I can hear you okay. How'd you get away to call me?"

"I'm in my car in the garage. Mary heard the end of our last call, but I took care of it. Listen, I'm doing the switch tonight. I can't take Mary anymore. I just wanted to tell you I'm a little scared, but I'm going to do what I told you I'd do."

"I know this is probably hard for you, Tony, but think about what our life is going to be like." She caught her breath again. "I mean, we can hold each other every night forever. I can't wait."

"I know, that's why I'm going to do it. I've got to go. I love you, Brenda Jean."

"I love you too, Tony. Bye."

He went into the living room and stretched out on the couch, trying to go to sleep, but he couldn't. He was thinking about the big pill switch. Did he have everything covered? He couldn't stop thinking about the upcoming week. He deleted the call he just made to Brenda Jean from the house phone and laid back, looking at the TV although it wasn't even on. Mary walked in wearing a colorful bathrobe. It reminded him of the stuff Bobbie used to wear.

"Tony, can I talk to you?"

"I don't care, just so you don't start bitching at me. What do you want?"

She sat down on a chair next to the couch. "I just wanted to let you know I checked out our bank account on the phone, and you were right, you didn't take out any money all week. We actually have three hundred dollars more in our account than I thought. I guess I owe you an apology. I'm sorry, it looks like you didn't bet on anything when I was gone."

He looked at his wife, nodding. "I told you. And you just wait until I get you my phone records. You'll see I don't have a girlfriend, either. I mean, there may be some numbers that belong to some customers, but there shouldn't be any number that shows up more than once or twice. And for all I care, you can call every number that shows up to see who I called or called me."

She raised her shoulders as if to say she had no idea what was on that phone bill. "I don't know what to think about that. I still don't know why you destroyed your phone; it still looks like you wanted to hide something. The phone bill will tell us who you had to call from our garage. Anyway, I'm not going to judge you on that until I see the phone calls, so let's try and get along for a while for Connor's sake, okay?"

"So, you're saying I did good not gambling, but you're not going to believe me when I tell you I've been faithful until you see a phone bill? You are something, you know that? Thank you, your majesty, for giving me another chance, after you see the stupid phone bill. Thank you so much. Anyway, I'll go along with you about keeping everything peaceful here for our son. He doesn't need to get involved in our troubles."

She nodded, stood up, and left. They both worked hard trying to act normal around Connor the rest of the day. After dinner, Tony went out to the garage while Mary was doing the dishes. He found his hidden box of stool softeners, pulled six pills out, and put them in his pants pocket. He closed the laxatives and put them back into his tackle box, which went back to its place on the top shelf. After watching a half hour of Kentucky playing Indiana in a basketball game, Tony went out into the kitchen to grab a beer. Mary was going through the flyers from the newspaper, cutting out some coupons.

"I guess we are on a tight budget," he said, closing the refrigerator door. "I never ever thought my wife would become a coupon clipper. What are you going to save with all those coupons, two or three bucks? What's the point?"

Mary didn't look up, she just kept scouring the colorful pages for bargains. "The point is we need to save every penny we can. Times are getting tougher and I'm going to be sure we don't waste any more money. Connor's getting older and we haven't put anything in his college account for months."

"So, whose fault is that?" She didn't answer, so he asked her again. "Are you deaf? Tell me, whose fault is that? I think I'm doing my share. I make over two hundred grand a year. Let me ask you, Little Miss Mary, how much do you make?"

She put her scissors down, glaring at her husband. "I don't have a job that pays anything. My job is to take care of my family and my home. But if I did have a job and it paid me two hundred thousand dollars a year, you could bet—no, there I go using that word again—you could be sure that I'd have more than nine hundred dollars in the bank."

He threw his half full beer can into the garbage next to the back door. "There you go again. Everything is my fault, right? One day I'd like to sit down with you and show you where all of our money goes. Believe it or not, it doesn't go to the track...it goes to stores and restaurants, and beauty parlors, and a new car for my wife every year. Now, you told me this afternoon that we needed to keep everything peaceful because of Connor, but now you're pissing me off again. Why don't you just stay away from me? Then it will be peaceful around here. I am getting so tired of all your bullshit."

Mary wadded up all the papers and coupons from the table, throwing them at him. "That sounds fine to me. I'll stay out of your hair, and you do the same for me. But let me give you some advice; you'd better get those phone bills sent to me this week, because you're not fooling me. And when I get the proof of what you're doing, you are going to be very, very sorry."

He bent over, leaning on the top of the chair next to her. "Now you're threatening me, huh? Do I got that right, you're threatening me?"

"It's not a threat, Tony, it's a promise. I know more than you think I do. You just wait...oh...go fuck yourself. I'm going to go upstairs and take a bath, and there won't be any radio next to the tub. Sorry Charlie."

He didn't answer; he just watched her leave, shaking her head.

Tony plopped down on the chair he was leaning on. He was so mad it was hard to think. He glanced at all the coupons and newspaper flyers on the floor, then noticed her purse was on the counter next to the sink. His heart started beating faster. It felt like it was going to blow a hole in his chest. He stood up, slowly walking to the sink and putting both hands on the front edge of the counter, then robotically turning his head to the right, looking at her purse. The tip of her pill reminder was visible behind her makeup bag. He reached over and grabbed it with two fingers, then slid it into his pants pocket.

Connor came down the stairs. "Hey, Dad, what's happening? I was wondering if you could nuke me a couple of Pizza Rolls?"

Tony let out a big sigh. He was trying to slow down his heart rate. "Sure, how about six? Is that enough?"

"How about eight?" Connor answered as he poured himself a glass of lemonade.

"Eight it is." Tony pulled a paper plate out of the cabinet next to the sink, loaded it with eight pepperoni pizza rolls from an open bag in the freezer, then warmed them for a minute in the microwave.

"Thanks, Pops, you're the best," Connor said, as his dad handed him the snack.

Tony felt the front of his pocket to feel for Mary's medicine box; it was still there. Now was the time. He went into the bathroom, pulled down his pants, and sat on the toilet. He grabbed her pill holder from one pocket and snapped open every lid, finding all slots full except Sunday's two holes. He thought he heard a noise so he leaned over and locked the door. He was shaking so much this little job had become a monster event.

Tony had to be careful not to drop anything. He pulled the six thyroid pills from each of the AM sections of the Monday through Saturday slots and set them on the floor, then replaced them with the pills from his pocket that had come out of his tackle box. Now he only had to hide Mary's thyroid pills that were on the floor and put her pill holder back. He put the six tablets from the floor inside a piece of crumpled toilet paper. After putting the reloaded pill box into the same pocket it came out of, Tony put the toilet paper with her pills in the other pocket.

He stood up, pulled up his pants, and unlocked the door so he could peek around it. It was clear. It looked like there was no one downstairs but him. His knees started to buckle. This was the hardest thing he had ever done, but he was determined to finish it. Tony walked out into the kitchen and put the reminder container exactly where he had first seen it in his wife's purse. It was done. No it isn't, he thought as he put his hand in his pocket, feeling the wadded up toilet paper. His mind was going in fast, hard circles. It was difficult for him to see straight or even think, but he knew he had to hide her pills.

Tony went out into the garage, then stopped. It could be dangerous if he put them in his tackle box. He looked around for a good place to hide them. There was a stack of manuals on his workbench. He put the toilet paper holding Mary's pills about halfway down the stack, under the instructions for his electric drill set.

After he turned to leave the garage, he sensed someone staring at him. He looked over at the doorway and found his wife watching him.

"What the hell are you doing in the garage so late? You got something to hide out here?" Mary asked, biting her lower lip.

Tony was frozen in time for a few seconds. He was still so nervous from what he had just done that he couldn't even talk right. "No, I, uh, I don't have nothing to hide. I just, uh, thought I heard a noise out here so I checked it out. It's getting to the time of year that rats look for warm places to hide, and that's the last thing we need is rats. Why are you so suspicious of everything I do?"

She gave him a small laugh. "You are not a very good actor. I know you too well, Tony, after all these years. You are still hiding something and I know it. Guess what, I'm going to find out what it is, you can count on that."

"Good luck. You're going to need a lot of luck because you're looking for something that does not exist, Mary. By the way, you don't scare me because I've always been a good husband and father. I'm not ashamed of anything I've ever done to you since we got married."

She went upstairs and he went to the couch. He kept thinking about what she may have seen him do in the garage. What if she looked through the pile of user guides on his work bench? He couldn't take that chance. He waited for over an hour and snuck back, moving the tissue holding the pills from the stack of manuals to under the mat in the back seat of his Mercedes.

CHAPTER 25
Good Luck With Your Treasure Hunt

Monday morning Tony overslept, finally waking up at eight. He sat up and rubbed his eyes, then noticed his wife sitting in his office, looking at his computer. "What are you doing on my laptop, Mary?"

She didn't look at him. She was writing down something on a small yellow pad next to the computer. "Oh, I'm just on a little treasure hunt. I'm kind of looking for what you've been doing, that's all."

Tony stood up and headed towards the stairs. "Good luck. By the way, you're not going to find any dirt on me there, I guarantee you that."

She finally looked at her husband. "Who said I was looking for dirt?"

"I don't give a shit what you're looking for, you won't find anything but investing bullshit on that laptop. Even if you do, I don't care. I'm going up to get ready for work. Good luck with your treasure hunt."

Twenty minutes later Tony walked into the kitchen, opened the refrigerator, and took a big gulp out of an orange juice bottle.

"That is so gross," Mary said as she walked around the corner. "Why don't you use a glass like every other human being does?"

He wiped his lips with his hand. "I don't have time. Ron's due back today and I need to get to the office. Are you done with my laptop?"

"I sure am," she said with a satisfied look on her face. "By the way, I bet you didn't even take a shower this morning. You couldn't have with the little time you were upstairs. My goodness, what will your sexy secretary say when she smells a slob for a boss?"

"Go to hell," Tony answered as he grabbed his closed up laptop and went out the front door.

Their world had been shaken to the point of no return. As he was driving to work, he realized he was looking forward to hurting Mary. Just a couple of months ago, he would never have thought it would be possible to do what he was doing. Now, she deserved whatever she got. This was only day one, but by the end of the week it should all be over. He just had

191

to stay cool all week. As he drove by his favorite pawn shop, he realized how much he missed betting on the horses. Yep, it was time to get back on the program.

He looked around for his cell phone before he realized he'd killed it.

When he pulled into the parking lot of Burns and Calley Investments, he noticed Ron's car was already there, parked next to Brenda Jean's yellow VW. He was anxious to see both of them. He walked in the front door just as his secretary was coming out of the woman's restroom. She looked incredible. She was wearing a pink business suit over a red blouse that was buttoned all the way to the top. Even though her outfit covered her up, she was still so beautiful. There was no way she could hide her incredible figure. Her shiny red hair was fixed into a french braid. She looked like a girl anybody would be proud to bring home to meet Mom and Dad.

Their eyes met. He gave her a small smile and a little nod. She knew what that meant. It was day one for her, too. He walked by her, intentionally brushing up against her side while putting one hand on her back, feeling her bra strap through both layers of clothing. He took a deep breath and knocked on Ron's office door.

"Come on in," Ron hollered with his husky voice.

Tony walked in, closing the door behind him. "Hey Ron, it's good to see you. We missed you, Buddy." He sat in the big padded chair in front of Ron's desk.

Burns reached out and shook his partner's hand. "Tony, you can't believe how great it is to get back to work. Do you realize I was gone for over four weeks?"

"I know. But guess what, we took care of things. Everybody here pulled together to keep everything rolling. We really didn't have any issues at all."

Ron sighed and nodded. "Like I said, I'm glad to get back at work. It's kind of crazy, you know, a job can get so tedious you look forward to getting some time off. Well, after four weeks away, your time off gets to be tedious. Anyway, thanks for handling everything for me, I appreciate it."

"How's Vickie Anne, Ron?"

"Oh, I think she's glad to be home, too. She was a basket case for more than a week after D.J. died. Every day she gets a little better, but it's going to take a long time. But we'll be all right down the road. So, tell me, what's been going on? I followed the markets a little bit while I was gone, and it looks like you made some good decisions the last couple of weeks. I can't believe how much you made for O'Donnell. He must think you're the best thing since sliced bread."

Tony interlocked his hands over his knees and gave Ron a smile. "I guess I was kind of lucky with some high tech stocks. It seemed like everything I touched for O'Donnell turned to gold, except for his money market accounts."

Ron looked at his computer screen. "I knew it was dumb to play in those right now. I was praying you made some good calls with the rest, and it sure looks like you did. My God, he's made what, over a twenty percent return in less than a month. I'll bet he's happy. What did he say when he called you Friday?"

"Well, the first thing he said was that he didn't ever want to go on a three week cruise with his wife again. But I cheered him up when I told him about his investments. He's totally hooked, Ron. He'll never leave us now. I don't know who he's going to call Friday; he said he wanted to work with both of us. I told him that would be fine with you."

"Heavens yes. Just as long as we keep making him money and he keeps paying us our commission. We can make a ton off him. Say, one more thing…how's Brenda Jean working out? I noticed she looks a lot more professional now than when I left."

"She's super. Our clients love her, but I was right when I told you she could be a little distracting. That's why I told her to tone down her outfits. She's been great about it." Tony stood up to leave.

"Say, Tony, can you get me my disc of my accounts? I want to call the big fish to let them know I'm back, and I've got some new ideas on getting them a nice return on their money. You know, my normal sell job."

"You got it," Tony said as he left Ron's office.

Brenda Jean was on the phone as he walked up to her desk. She looked up at him with a smile as she continued talking. "I'll tell him, Mr. Fatha. You don't need to worry at all about anything, you know you're my favorite customer. I'll be sure Mr. Calley gets your message the minute he gets done with the client in his office. Now you take care, I'm really looking forward to seeing you the next time you're in the area. You don't need an appointment to just come by and see me. You're so sweet. Bye now."

Tony laughed. "If I was Frank Fatha and a girl like you talked to me like that, I'd come by to see you today; hell, I'd come by and see you every day. That was great." He looked over at the other two girls with his head up. "You ladies must have taught her that. You know, we've got the best bunch of secretaries anywhere."

He could tell that made them feel good as they smiled at each other. He turned back to Brenda Jean. "Brenda Jean, bring a steno pad into my office. I want to go over a lot of stuff you need to type out for Ron. He's backed up and we're going to help him get caught up."

She followed him into his office. After closing the door, he walked up to her and gave her a twenty second kiss. The fires were burning inside both of them.

Brenda Jean sat down in front of him, not being able to wait one more second. "Well, Tony, did you do it?"

He put his index finger in front of his mouth to tell her to lower her voice. "I sure did. This is the first day and I'm not having any second thoughts. Mary was brutal to me this weekend. Neither one of us have any feelings for each other anymore...it's over. Now all you have to do, Brenda Jean, is be patient. I figure by the end of the week everything will be taken care of."

She lifted her shoulders, letting out a big sigh. "I sure hope so. But what if something comes up? Can you stop it?"

"I don't think anything will come up, but let's say it does. I've got her real pills in a safe spot...I mean, the same amount I took out of her pill thing. I can always put them back and she'll get better, but I'm praying I never need to. But remember what I said, right now I'm just your boss, and we have to keep it that way for a while, okay baby?"

"Okay. So what can I do for you, boss man?"

"Well, to start with, I need you to call AT&T and tell them I lost my cell phone. I've got insurance on it. I need a new phone today with the same number. Then you need to go get it when it's ready. But right now, like I told you out there, get ready to write fast, I'm going to give you a ton of info to put in a memo to Ron." He hit a few keys on his keyboard. "Are you ready?"

"Fire away."

He rattled off an update on each one of their accounts, as well as the amount of money they had in escrow, then asked her to get it to Ron as soon as possible, along with the disc Ron had given him when he left. When he was finished, she closed up her memo pad and stood up.

"Oh, Brenda Jean, one more thing; before you do all that, get Parker Hayes on the phone, will you?"

"Yes, sir. But I need to tell you one thing before I leave, Tony."

He looked up at his secretary's serious face. "What is it?"

"Oh, it's not much. I just wanted to tell you I love you with all my heart." She leaned over, giving him an incredibly soft kiss.

"I love you too, sweet stuff," he whispered back to her as she left."Mr. Calley, Parker Hayes is on line three."

"Parker, how are you?"

"Well, this a voice from the past. Where have you been, Tony?"

"I've been around. It hasn't been all that long...I mean, I talked to you about a week ago. You're just used to me calling you every day. Well, guess what, I'm in a betting mood. Do you got anything that's hot?"

"Hot? I've got a lead on a guaranteed long shot at Calder this afternoon that's white hot. It's a maiden race for a two year old that was sired by Instant Hope. But, Tony, he's in with a bunch of losers. I still don't know why he's thirty to one. Let me look; no, now he's twenty eight to one. Hell, the favorite looks like a real dog. Do you want to get in on that?"

"Sure. Put down two thousand to win, will ya? Now let me make sure of something...I'm square with you now, right?"

"You don't owe me a dime, Tony. I'll call your bet in now. The horse's name is Bad Medicine. By the way, it's the fourth race on the card. It should start about three our time."

"Super. And I really like the name, Bad Medicine. That sounds like a very lucky horse for me. Anyway, hopefully I'll see you tomorrow when you bring me a check for about fifty grand."

"I hope you're right, Tony, I really do. Bye."

Tony leaned back in his chair, staring at a framed painting of a hunting dog on the wall in front of him, the one Ron had given him on his birthday. He remembered Ron telling him that it would remind him to sniff around for extra accounts every day. Tony was feeling great about his life now. Everything was going perfectly. How could anything get messed up now? He had planned for everything, he thought. But he was wrong."Mr. Calley, your wife is on line four."

"Thank you, Brenda Jean. Before I pick up, let me ask you, how did she treat you on the phone?"

"Cold, but I'll survive."

"Hello, Mary."

"Tony, I just wanted to see how you were doing. I know I was a real bitch this morning, and even though we've got our problems right now, I need to lighten up, I can see that. Anyway, I'm sorry. Like I said yesterday, we need to try and patch things up the best we can, especially in front of Connor."

"I agree, and I agreed yesterday. But I've got to be honest with you, don't expect everything to get back to the way it was. Too much water has gone under the bridge for that. But I'll try to keep things quiet for Connor's sake."

"That's all I can ask right now. Oh, Tony, we got some insurance papers in the mail this morning from Bo Foster. I didn't get a chance to study them much, but as soon as I get back from the grocery store, I'll

195

check it out. Maybe he's trying to sell us something, but they kind of look official. Anyway, what do you want for dinner tonight?"

He could feel sweat rolling down his temples. My God, did Bo's letter have anything to do with the increase on her policy, the one he'd signed for her? "Oh, I don't care, fix us anything. I guess it's better than eating out every night or my cooking. Just surprise me. I've got to go, Mary, bye."

He hit the intercom button on his phone. "Brenda Jean, I need to see you."

She walked in almost instantly.

Tony shook his head. "Close the door."

"What's wrong, sweetheart?"

"Listen to this one. Just when I thought I had covered all the bases, Mary called me to let me know we got some insurance papers in the mail from Bo Foster."

"You don't think they're…?"

"Of course I do, Brenda Jean. I bet they're the new life policies on her. What the hell do you think we should do?"

"Tony, let's not panic. Maybe they don't say anything about any changes or her approving anything. Damn it, why did they have to come today? I mean, she was out of town all last week. That's just our luck…if it would have been delivered Saturday and not today, we'd be all right. Do you think she'll figure anything out?"

"I don't know, but I can't stand waiting until tonight to see those papers. She just told me that she was going to the grocery store. I think I'll run home, and is she's not there, I'll see if I can find the mail and check it out. You hold down the fort until I get back, and don't forget to get my new phone."

"I can get it in a half hour. I'll take care of it. By the way, I'm done with all of Mr. Burns's stuff. He has everything now."

"You're something. When everything is over with, I might have a wife who is also my secretary. You're too good to stay home."

"We'll see. You better get going. Oh, take my cell phone." She pulled the pink and white phone out of her pocket, handing it to him. "How about giving me a call me on the office line when you start back?"

"Okay. I've got to go," he said, quickly leaving the office.

All the way home he was wondering how he would explain the new life insurance policies. Mary was no dummy, she would figure it out when she saw the changes. Now it looked like everything could come unraveled in a hurry. His shirt was sticking to him as little sweat beads were racing down his chest. He realized he should have told Bo to keep everything confidential and send all the paperwork to the office.

He pulled up in front of his neighbor's house, leaning to see if Mary's car was in the garage or on their driveway. He couldn't tell if she was still there. He picked up speed and drove by his house, daring to take a quick glance to the left. She wasn't home.

He unlocked the back door, sticking his head around the corner. On the kitchen table was the stack of mail. Next to that stack was the letter from Bo. His hand was shaking as he picked it up. His shoulders lifted up as he started to read the letter, then he let out a long sigh. The letter read: "Tony, enclosed is a copy of our most popular homeowner's policy, per our conversation in your office the other day. I would love to bundle your life, home owners, and auto coverage together and save you a lot of money. Please give me a call at your convenience to discuss this. Take care, Bo."

"Thank God," Tony said, as he put all the papers back where he'd found them. He backed out of his driveway and headed back to his office, knowing that he had just avoided a catastrophe. After grabbing Brenda Jean's cell phone off the seat, he called her.

"Brenda Jean, don't say anything, just listen. It's okay. It was just a letter from Bo, along with a sample homeowner's policy."

Tony pulled into the parking lot of his office, wondering if Mary was feeling any side effects from taking a laxative this morning and not her thyroid pill. It was only the first morning and she had sounded normal on the phone. He opened his car door, noticing that Brenda Jean's car was gone. When he pulled the office door open, he could see the VW reflecting off a window. He turned around to see her walking towards him, carrying a white and red AT&T bag.

"I got your new phone, Tony. They couldn't program all your stuff onto it because they needed your old phone to do that. If you make me a list of the names you want me to put on it, I'll take care of it from my Rolodex and from your Blackberry."

"Sure, Brenda Jean, go ahead. Just do me a favor and get it done as soon as you can. I'm lost without my phone." Tony had just settled back in his office when Brenda Jean called him."Mr. Calley, Parker Hayes is on line one."

Tony looked at his watch. It was three twenty. Parker must have the results of how well Bad Medicine had done at Calder. "Hello, Parker. So, what happened?"

"Well, old buddy, you can't win 'em all."

"No shit, Parker, I suppose you're going to tell me he lost by a nose. That won't make me feel any better."

"I know, Tony. I said you can't win them all, but you can win some of them, and guess what? Bad Medicine became good medicine for you. You hit it, Tony."

Tony wanted to scream, but he held back. "Wow, what did he pay?"

"He came off at twenty five to one. I now owe you forty five thousand. Do you want it tomorrow or do you want to start a tab?"

"I'm an investment specialist. So, what do you think? Of course I want it tomorrow, at least most of it. I'll tell you what, just bring me thirty thousand. Let's leave fifteen grand on your books for a while. I trust you with it. Besides, it will be nice betting without worrying about what I owe you. Thanks, Parker, I've got to go. I'll see you tomorrow." He hung up the phone, spreading his arms wide apart, and nodded. "Yes," he said quietly, then repeated it.

****

When Tony got home, he could smell something Mexican cooking. He walked into the kitchen, spotting Mary stirring something in a big silver pan. "So what smells so good, Mrs. Calley?" he asked as he put his coat on the stair railing post.

She turned around, giving her husband a small fake smile. "I decided to make some homemade chili. Connor asked for it. It will be ready in about a half hour. Do you want anything else with it?"

"Grilled cheese sandwiches sound good." He looked up the stairs. "Where is Connor, anyway?"

"He's over at Hunter's. I told him to be back by six thirty."

"Okay. I'm going upstairs to take a shower. I didn't have time this morning and I feel kind of grubby."

Mary turned back to her chili. "Uh huh."

He looked back at her as he picked up his coat. She seemed very normal. Bitchy, but normal, he thought, wondering when she would start showing the effects of the pill switch. He wanted to ask her how she felt, but that might tip her off. Tony finished his shower then put on an old grey sweatshirt and a pair of shorts. He ate his chili and cheese sandwiches with his wife and son, talking mostly to Connor. Mary acted like she didn't want anything to do with him, either. After dinner, he watched a basketball game with Connor in the living room before he nodded off. Tony woke up around three Tuesday morning, still laid out in his recliner with the TV off. He went to the bathroom and laid back down on the couch, cursing how uncomfortable it was, then dozed off again. The next thing he knew, Connor kissed him on the cheek, then went out the front door to jump on the bus.

Tony walked into the kitchen as Mary gulped down a glass of water, then she picked up a bottle of Advil from the counter and put it back on the medicine shelf. "You got a headache, Mary?"

She sighed. "Yeah, I woke up with it around six. It's a real bad one. I usually don't get headaches first thing in the morning, but this one got me right away. But I'll be all right. You just go ahead and get ready for work. I wouldn't want to keep either your bookie or your secretary waiting."

"Man, you never give up, do you, Mary? All I was doing was wondering how you felt, and all you care about is blasting me with your imaginary thoughts again. The hell with you. Just leave me alone."

He stayed mad all day Tuesday. Even Brenda Jean avoided him. It was easy to read Tony, and the office staff knew to be careful when he was in one of those moods. Even Parker Hayes knew Tony was upset when he got there.

"What's wrong, Tony? You should be happy. It's not every day I bring you a check for thirty grand," he said, handing him the payoff from Bad Medicine.

"I know, I'm just going through some bad times with my wife. You know, it's so damn hard to concentrate on anything when your old lady is a bitch. Do you have any idea what I mean, Parker?"

"Fuck yes. I divorced the wicked witch of the north two years ago. Let me tell you something, Tony, if your wife gets her thrills out of kicking your ass, it's time to say adios. Listen, I got a lead on a sure thing at the Sarasota Kennel Club tonight. Do you want a piece of that? Remember, you got some money on the books."

"No, that's all right. I'll give you a call tomorrow or the next day. But, anyway, thanks for the tip on Bad Medicine, and thanks for the marital advice. I'll be talking to you." Tony shook Parker's hand and watched him leave. The next morning began day three. After he woke up, he was anxious to see how Mary was doing, since it was a little after seven and she wasn't even downstairs. He walked up the stairs wondering what he would find. After waking Connor, Tony went into the master bedroom and found Mary still sleeping. When he nudged her, she opened her eyes and raised her eyebrows.

"Tony, what time is it?"

He looked at the alarm clock next to the bed. "It's seven fifteen, and Connor's got to catch his bus in thirty minutes."

She sat up, rubbing her eyes. "Tony, can you do me a big favor?"

"I'll try, Mary, what is it?"

"Can you take care of Connor this morning? I laid out his clothes in his bathroom. Just ask him what he wants for breakfast and do the best you can. His lunch is packed and it's in the refrigerator. Please, do this for me. I'm so tired. I was up all night going to the bathroom. Something gave me diarrhea. I need to get some more sleep, okay?"

"Sure, I'll take care of everything. You just lay back down and get some rest." After feeding Connor and getting him onto the bus, Tony went back upstairs to take a shower and get dressed, leaving Mary asleep in their bed. Glancing at her as he left, he knew it was just a matter of a day or two now.

Brenda Jean knocked on his office door within minutes of his arrival at the office. "Come on in."

She closed the door behind her and sat in her usual chair. Once again, she was dressed more like a librarian than a model, but she couldn't hide the model under those clothes. "Tony, I worried about you all night. You were tied up in knots yesterday, I could tell. Are you all right, baby?"

"I'm sorry, Brenda Jean. This whole thing is starting to get to me. When Mary got sick the first time, she skipped four pills. Today is the third day. I guess I'm getting a little scared, that's all."

She shook her head. "Tony, you can call this off if you want, I'd understand. The only thing is, I can't wait forever. I can't imagine all the feelings inside of you right now. Like you said, we've just got to be patient. But if you want to stop this, I won't nag you forever…I'll still love you."

Tony thought for a few moments. "No, we're two-thirds of the way home, I'll finish it. I'm not happy living with her, and I know you'll be well worth the wait."

"I was hoping you would say that. By the way, what is happening with her now?"

"She woke up this morning, but I couldn't get her to stay awake. But now I'm starting to worry about Connor. What is he going to do if he comes home from school tonight and he can't wake her up?"

"We've just got to keep our fingers crossed, Tony. Let's see what happens tonight."

"You're right. The only thing is today's going to drag by."

She stood up to leave, then turned back. "Is there anything you want me to do to help you?"

"Oh yeah, I need you to cash a check for me." He opened up his wallet, pulled out the Bad Medicine check, endorsed it, and handed it to her. "I'll tell you what, instead of cashing it, just put it into my checking account. You still got the number?"

She looked down at the check, nodding. "I'll bring you the deposit slip when I get back. Tony, do you think since she wants to sleep so much, you can come by my apartment for lunch?"

"I'd love to. You have no idea how much I'd love to do that. But we're so close, I think we better wait for a couple of days until this is all over. But it won't be long, I promise."

She left his office without saying another word. They both knew it was almost over. Tony called home at four, knowing Connor should be home. Mary answered the phone. "Hello, Tony. I see you got a new phone?"

"Yeah. I had insurance on it. They replaced it instantly and it only cost me fifty bucks. So, how'd your day go?"

"I must have a sleeping disease. I didn't get up until almost one this afternoon, and to tell you the truth, I could go back to sleep right now. I must need to take some vitamins, who knows?"

"Is Connor home?"

"Yeah, he's upstairs. He seemed a little upset about something, but he wouldn't tell me about it."

"Maybe I can get it out of him when I get home, Mary. What's for dinner?"

She yawned. "I don't know. I'm too tired to worry about it right now. I'm going to lay down for a little nap. Why don't you bring home some pizzas?"

"Okay, I'll see you in a couple of hours. I've got a late appointment, so I won't be home until around six, but I'll bring home dinner."

She yawned again. "Thanks, Tony, I'll see...."

"Hello. Hello, Mary. Are you there?" There was nothing but silence on the other end of the phone.

He punched in his intercom. "Brenda Jean, can you come in here for a minute?"

She walked in, carrying her tan steno book. "Yes sir?" she asked as she closed the door.

"Brenda Jean, I want you to do me a favor. Go home now. I'll meet you there in about fifteen minutes."

"I thought you said we should wait?"

"I can't wait anymore, baby doll. I need you now. Besides, I just told Mary I was working late, and then she went to sleep while she was on the phone. She's out again. You would have been so proud of me. I was actually very sweet to her. So, I'll see you in a couple of minutes at your place, okay?"

"You bet. I'll be waiting for you."

When he got to her apartment, she really was waiting for him. She answered the door wearing only a bright red see through nightgown. They made love for almost an hour until she wore him out. He dragged himself into her shower and let the water pour over him as he leaned against the tiled wall. For ten minutes he didn't move, letting the cascading water bounce off his head. Brenda Jean opened the shower door with a dry washcloth in her hand. She stood next to him, grabbed some shower gel off the little shelf in the corner, lathered up the washcloth, then gently washed every inch of her lover. He was squeaky clean when she was done. Then he did the same thing to her.

When Tony got home, Mary was sitting on a kitchen chair, mumbling. She saw him walk in the front door carrying the pizzas and tried to get up, but she couldn't stand up. He put their dinner on the table. "Hey, Mary, what's happening?"

She started talking, but slurred her words. What he could get out of her was that she'd called Dr. Hunnington, telling him she didn't feel very good. The doctor asked her if she was taking her thyroid pills and she said she was, and he told her to go the hospital if she started feeling worse, that she might just have a twenty four hour virus.

"Mary, do you want me to help you get upstairs to bed, or do you just want to take a nap in the living room?"

She looked up at her husband, her eyes slightly rolling. "I think I'll just go upstairs for a little while, but I don't need any help." She stood up, balancing herself with a hand on the kitchen table, then lunged at the stairway post and began pulling herself up. She walked up the steps, constantly leaning against the stair rail. Within a minute she was at the top, then she disappeared to the left, heading towards their bedroom.

Connor came downstairs after Tony called him, telling him dinner was ready. He sat down next to his father and pulled one of the pizza boxes toward him. "This must be yours, Dad, it's got veggies on it." After opening the other box and finding a double pepperoni pizza, Connor grabbed a piece, putting half of it in his mouth. "Dad," he asked between bites. "Is Mom all right? I just saw her go to bed. She acted like she was drunk. Is she okay?"

Tony took a long drink out of a Coke. "No, but she's not real sick. She called her doctor today and he told her to just rest, that she's probably got the twenty four hour flu. We need to leave her alone tonight, and she'll be fine. Don't worry about it, son, I'll watch her. I think all she needs is plenty of sleep and some liquids. So, tell me about your day?"

"Well, I've had better days, Dad. Everything was fine until fifth period. My teacher bragged some about how quickly I'd passed everyone in math. She made a big deal about it. I could have died. It wasn't like anyone picked on me because of what she said, it's just that I don't like everyone looking at me."

Tony grabbed another piece of pizza and folded it in half. "Connor, I wouldn't let anyone bother me. Who cares who looks at you? You're not wanting special treatment or anything. I think the more the kids get to know you, the easier it will be to hear stuff like that. They'll probably just start expecting you to do good."

"You're right, Dad. I just don't like anyone acting like I'm different, you know what I mean?"

"I sure do. Now finish your pizza and pick out some clothes for tomorrow while I make your lunch. With your mother being sick, we need to pick up the slack, right?"

They both finished their chores quickly. Tony cleaned up the kitchen and made a bagged lunch for Connor loaded with snacks. Then he went upstairs to check on Connor, who had his entire outfit, including shoes, laid out on the chair next to his bed. "Nice job, son. Now do me a favor and go brush your teeth and put on your pajamas. I know it's early, but I want you to be ready for bed exactly at nine, okay? That means lights and TV off."

Connor nodded as he walked towards his bathroom. Tony went into his bedroom to check on Mary. She was snoring on top of the covers, fully clothed. He reached down and pushed on her shoulder.

"Huh, what dooooo yoooooo...?" That was all she said. Tony undressed her, leaving her in her bra and panties, covered her up, and left.

He stopped in his son's room. "Connor, I doubt if your mother will be up in the morning. You better set your alarm for six thirty and I'll set mine, too. Good night, Buddy." He leaned in, kissing Connor on his cheek.

Tony went back downstairs, debating on using the couch or his recliner for his bed. He decided on the recliner. He went into the kitchen, grabbed a Coke and his cell phone that was sitting on the table, then detoured into the living room to pick up the blanket and pillow that was behind the couch. Once he hit his recliner, he called Brenda Jean and talked to her for over two hours. He made her promise to call him at six thirty in the morning, and if he didn't answer to keep calling until he picked up. The next morning was day four. What was going to happen? That was answered the second Tony opened his eyes. He could smell bacon frying. What was going on? He found Mary in the kitchen turning those wonderful smelling strips in a black pan. He cleared his throat as he walked in.

"Good morning, Tony," she said without turning around. "How did you sleep?"

"I slept fine. I'm surprised you're up, Mary. You were a basket case last night. What happened?"

She turned around, holding the pan full of bacon, and put it on a plate on the table. "I don't know. I'm still not myself. I can hardly swallow and

I'm real dizzy—I mean real dizzy—but I wanted to be sure you guys got something in your stomach before you left."

Tony scratched his head, trying to figure out what was going on. It was day four. What had caused her miraculous recovery? He kept watching her as she moved around the kitchen, making their breakfast. She pulled two glasses out of the cabinet next to the sink, dropped both of them, and grabbed the counter to keep from falling.

Tony jumped to keep her upright, then looked at her. Her eyes were a funny color and they were rolling around in their sockets, like small boats bouncing on a rough stretch of water. She must have gathered every ounce of energy she could find to fix them something to eat.

She passed out in his arms. He carried her upstairs and put her back into their bed, once again undressing her. She waved an arm like she wanted to say something, but she couldn't. He covered her up with the top sheet, then something started smelling terrible. He lifted up the sheet and noticed her panties were full, giving out a smell that could stop the traffic in front of their house. Sure, it was the pills, the stool softeners…they were really working. What should he do now? He didn't have the stomach to clean her up. He decided to fix her when he got home after work. When he got downstairs, Connor picked up a piece of bacon, chewed it up, and poured some cereal in a bowl. "I heard Mom talking to you, Dad. Is she better?"

"I think so, Connor. At least she got up to make breakfast, but I just took her upstairs because she was still so weak." He poured a glass of orange juice and sat next to Connor.

"Dad, don't you think you should call her doctor or take her to the hospital or something?"

"She talked to her doctor and he told her just to rest and come see him tomorrow if she's not any better. So, that's what I'm going to do. Don't worry, Connor, I'll come home a couple of times today to check on her, but I really think all she needs is some sleep and lots of fluids."

Connor got on the bus while Tony cleaned up the kitchen, making it look like Mary did it all. He took a glass of apple juice and a glass of cranberry juice up to her and put them on her bedside table. Now the whole bedroom smelled like a sewer. He finished getting ready for work and headed out. The drive to his office seemed like it took forever, and his head felt like it was going to explode. He pulled into the parking lot of a closed Wendy's just to think. This was it. This was his last chance to either save her or let her die. What was he going to do? He kept thinking about Mary, about Connor, and about Brenda Jean. What did he really want for the rest of his life? He kept seeing Brenda Jean in his head.

Finally, he made up his mind. He started the Mercedes and turned left towards his office.

CHAPTER 26
Daddy, Please Come Home

Tony got to the office just as Ron Burns pulled in. They walked towards the front door together. "Hey, Tony, what's going on?"

Tony shook his head. "Not much, except Mary's kind of sick."

"Oh yeah, what's she got?"

"Her doctor said it was probably a twenty four hour bug. I'll probably have to run home a couple of times today and check on her."

Ron unlocked the door and opened it for his partner. "I don't blame you. Listen, if you need to spend some time with her today, do it. I can take all your clients if you want. Heaven knows I owe you for all the time I was in Duluth."

"Thanks anyway, but it's Thursday. I've got that conference call set up for the Killian family, like every other Thursday. I can't miss that. Bob and Linda Killian have been like family to me; no, I won't disappoint them, I'll just sneak out for a few minutes a couple of times today to see how Mary's doing."

As Ron was turning on the lights, he turned back to look at Tony. "Oh, do you think Mary will be better by Sunday? Vickie Anne wanted me to ask you to come over Sunday for dinner. She really misses Mary."

"I'll let you know Saturday. I'd bet on her being better by then. You know, she said just last night that she was going to call Vickie Anne sometime this week to see if she could go shopping with her after she feels better."

"Well, Tony, just let me know if you need any help today. And please go home if Mary needs you. Nothing is more important than taking care of her."

Tony veered off, reaching his office. A minute later, Brenda Jean called him on the intercom. "Mr. Calley, can I talk to you?"

"Sure, Brenda Jean, come on in."

She walked in and stood next to his desk. "Tony, I had—"

He motioned for her to close the door, which she did.

Tony leaned back in his chair. "Now, what were you saying?"

She sat down, but not in her normal chair. She sat on the small sofa near the door. "Tony, I had some bad dreams last night, and I'm scared."

"Sweet stuff, don't be scared. Dreams don't mean anything."

She shook her head. "I've always believed dreams do mean something. And this one was so clear I can't get it off my mind."

Tony leaned forward. "What was your dream about?"

"I dreamt that your wife crawled out of her grave and came after us. It was so real. I mean, she was really scary looking. After I woke up I couldn't sleep a minute after that. I kept seeing her squeezing a rope around your neck." She put her hands together, showing him how Mary squeezed the life out his throat.

Tony gave her a tiny giggle. "Brenda Jean, it's just a dream. She's not coming out of her grave, I promise. She's going to die today or tomorrow and she'll be gone forever. Oh yeah, I'll be a grieving husband for a while, but she'll be just a memory real fast."

"Do you promise, Tony?"

"I promise, Brenda Jean. Don't worry about it again. Let me worry about Mary, and let me take care of you."

"I know you will, Tony, but I'm frightened." She had a look of terror covering her face. "Maybe we should call this off while we still can."

"Brenda Jean, I can't stop it now. This is day four. It's probably her next to last day. If I take her to the hospital now, who knows what they'd do? They'd probably fix her. No, we've got to finish this thing, we're so close."

"Okay, Tony, but I hope I don't have any more dreams like last night."

"You won't. Now, get over here and give me a kiss. We've got a big weekend ahead."

She wiped the tears off her cheeks, then gave him the kiss he asked for. It seemed to make her feel better; she even found a smile before she left his office.

Tony called Mary a couple of hours later, but there was no answer. He went home for lunch and found his wife completely out. He tried to wake her, but she just laid there. He put his ear near her mouth, feeling her breath. That was the only sign of life coming from his wife. Then he went back to work.

At three forty, his intercom button lit up. "Mr. Calley, your son is on line two."

"Thank you, Rudi."

"Daddy, something is wrong with Mommy."

"What do you mean?"

"She won't wake up. I even screamed right in her ear and she didn't move. She won't wake up. Daddy, please come home, please."

"I'll be right there, Connor. Can you tell, is she breathing all right?"

"Yeah, she's breathing. I learned in science to put a mirror on a person's mouth to see if they're breathing, so I did that and I could see her breath on the mirror. Please hurry, come home."

"Don't get scared, Connor, it will be all right. I'll be right there."

Tony was shaking. It was almost over. Would she be gone by the time he got home? He slowly walked out to his car and sat in the front seat for a few minutes. He was in no hurry. He pulled out into the traffic and grabbed the slow lane. It took him over twenty minutes to get home, a trip that normally took less than ten.

When he turned onto his street, an ambulance was pulling into his driveway with its red lights flashing. "Oh my God, someone must have called 911," Tony said, as he hit the steering wheel with his hand. He stopped his car behind the ambulance; it was now time for his planned show to start. "Oh, my God," he screamed. "Oh, my God, what is going on?"

An EMT grabbed him. "Are you the husband?"

"What do you mean, the husband? What's wrong? Where's Mary?"

"She's in bad shape. We're checking her out now. You are Tony Calley, right?"

"Of course I'm Tony Calley. Where's my son, where's Connor?"

Connor came running out the front door. He grabbed his father around the waist. "Daddy, oh Daddy, I had to call 911. I put the mirror on Mommy's mouth and I didn't see any breaths. Is she dead, Daddy? Don't tell me she's dead."

"I don't know. I'll find out." He let go of his son and walked into his house. Another EMT stopped him, but Tony pushed him aside. "Listen, that's my wife you're working on. Someone has got to tell me what's going on."

A woman coming down the stairs said, "Damn, that's an awful smell." She spotted Tony and stopped to talk to him. "You must be Mr. Calley?"

"Yeah, what's going on? Oh my God, what's going on? My son told me Mary wasn't breathing. Don't tell me she's dead; I've got to see her!"

The female EMT grabbed his arm. "Your wife is still alive, but she's sick, very sick. We're trying to piece this all together. You can't go up there right now. Listen, Mr. Calley, you have to help us. What medications is she taking?

"She takes a water pill and an aspirin twice a day, and she takes her thyroid pill every morning. That's all, as far as I know. So, please tell me, what is wrong with her?"

"Mr. Calley, your wife appears to be in a coma. That's all we know for now. We'll be transporting her to the hospital as soon as we can." She lifted the metal cover that was over some paperwork. "I need you to sign some papers so we can go." She showed him where to sign and he did. "Now, Mr. Calley, where can I find her medicine bottles?"

"I don't give a damn about any medicine bottles, I want to see my wife…where the hell is she?"

"She's up in the bed in the master bedroom, but they're still working on her. I can't let you go up there right now."

Tony pulled her hand away from its grip on his arm. "Fuck you, I want to see my wife."

"Billy, grab him," the female EMT hollered. Two large men kept Tony from going upstairs. They each grabbed an arm, walking him to the kitchen where they put him down on a chair. "I'm sorry, Mr. Calley," the female EMT said. "I know you're worried, but you can't help her by getting in our way. You can see her when they bring her down, and you and your son can go to the hospital with us. That's the best I can do. Now, again, where are her pills?"

"Up there," Tony said, pointing to the medicine shelf in the cabinet next to the sink.

She opened the cabinet, pushed aside a bottle of aspirin, and grabbed the two brown prescription bottles, putting them into her coat pocket. Tony didn't say a word. It was a day early for all this to happen, and he didn't want them to find Mary's pill reminder. He looked over at her purse that was sitting on the big chopping board next to the sink. "I need to get a drink of water," he said. He grabbed a glass out of the cupboard, filled it with water, and drank it as he lifted her pill counter out of her purse and put it in his pocket. No one saw a thing.

Tony turned to see his wife coming down the stairs on a gurney. Her head had a large elastic band around it and she had a neck brace below a hard, clear face mask. There was a small tube coming out of the mask that went to a blue tank lying next to her. Her hands were together on her stomach under a belt that looked like it was too tight. He walked over and rubbed her forehead when the EMTs stopped for a second to load a lot of equipment on the foot of the gurney.

"Mary, I'm here. Don't worry, sweetheart, I'm here." He started to cry. Then he wiped his eyes with his arms. "Why? Oh God, why? Please, Jesus, help us." He spotted Connor running towards him.

"Daddy, is Mommy dead? Please, Daddy, don't let her die." Connor put his arms on top of his mother's stomach, then looked up at his father. "Please don't let her die."

Tony caught his breath. "Connor, she's not going to die. We'll stay with her. They said we can go with her in the ambulance to the hospital." He sobbed, looking up at the ceiling with tears rolling down his cheeks. It was a performance worthy of an academy award. Tony and Connor jumped into the ambulance after Mary was rolled in. Tony kept his arm around his son, as the boy's head bounced up and down, as though he was in some kind of trance. "Don't worry, son, God won't take her away. She's so special, she can't leave us. We need her. Oh God, Mary," he moaned, as he put his head into his hands.

The ride to the hospital was bumpy as the ambulance wove in and out of traffic. When they finally got to the emergency entrance, they pulled the gurney carrying Mary out of the ambulance and ran it into two big swinging doors that opened the second the gurney touched them. A nurse grabbed Tony and Connor as they tried to follow Mary down the hall. "I'm sorry, sir, you all can't go any further. Just go out into the waiting area over there." She pointed to a brown door with a big glass window in it.

"Don't tell me I can't follow her, she's my wife."

"That's exactly what I'm telling you. You need to wait in the waiting area. I'll come out as soon as I can and give you an update."

Tony didn't say a word. He'd already been manhandled by the ambulance guys, he didn't want to push his luck any more. He grabbed Connor's hand and went where he was told, looking for a pair of soft chairs to sit on, but he never got a chance to use them. A woman walked up to him with a clipboard. "Are you a relative to the lady that was just brought in?"

"Yeah, that's my wife. Her name is Mary Calley."

"Okay, Mr. Calley, please follow me." She looked down at Connor. "Is he your son, Mr. Calley?"

"Yes, I am," Connor said. "I'm Connor."

"Well, Connor, you can come, too. And I don't want you to worry about your mother, we'll take good care of her."

The three of them walked down the hall to a set of doors under a big sign that said Registration. She pointed to the door that had a big three on it. The Calley boys walked in and sat on two chairs in front of the metal desk. The same woman that had brought them there reappeared and sat at the desk. She punched something on her computer keyboard, then turned to Tony, getting information about Mary and their insurance coverage.

They went back to the waiting area after they finished the registration process. Connor continually watched the door, waiting for someone to come tell them how his mother was doing. Twenty minutes later, the nurse they'd met when they got there walked up to them. "Mr. Calley, I'm Nurse Jeffers. We're sending your wife up for some tests. It's going to be a while before you can see her."

Tony stood up. "What tests? What's wrong with her?"

"At this point, we're not sure why she went into a coma. That's why we're doing the tests. I know we're going to do a brain scan, and we'll have to do a ton of blood tests. It could take a couple of hours."

"Is she going to be all right?" Connor asked.

"We don't know. She's a very sick lady, but she has one thing going for her. She's in great shape. Her blood pressure is good, her oxygen level is good, and her pulse is fine. We'll figure this out, just give us an hour or two. Oh, by the way, we've already talked to Dr. Wheeldon, and he's on the way. He's a brain disorder specialist, one of the best."

Tony put his arm around Connor. "A brain specialist? What does that mean? Did she hurt her head or something?"

"She's in a coma, Mr. Calley. At her age, especially with her being in such shape, we think she's got some kind of malfunction inside of her. We can't rule out anything. That's why we're doing these tests, to find out what caused this. When we figure that out, we'll attack the problem and hopefully fix it. Anyway, I'll keep you informed when I hear anything."

"Thank you. Connor and I will be right here."

They sat in the chairs they had picked out that were very close to the TV that was hanging from the ceiling. Tony looked around, finding no one else interested in the program on the TV. He found the up and down channel buttons on the side of the TV and found Connor the Discovery Channel, which was airing a special on Egyptian Pyramids.

Tony looked down at his shoes after he stretched his legs out. Out of the corner of his right eye he could see the tip of Mary's pill box. He looked at Connor, who was totally into the pyramid show, then pushed the pink plastic holder further down his pocket. He had to hide that damn thing until he could switch the thyroid pills back into it, but his car wasn't even there. There was only one answer.

He walked outside, constantly watching Connor through the windows, then called Brenda Jean.

"Hello, Tony."

"Brenda Jean, I'm at Mercy Arms Hospital in the emergency room."

"Are you okay, darling?"

"I'm fine. Listen, Connor called 911 before I could get home. An ambulance brought Mary over here about an hour ago. She's in a coma."

"Is she going to make it?"

"I don't know, they're doing some tests on her now."

"How's Connor doing?"

"He's okay for now. He thinks they're going to fix her. Anyway, I need you to do me a favor. How long will it take for you to get here?"

"Oh, maybe fifteen minutes. I don't have anything going on. Do you want me to come by? You don't want your son to see me, do you?"

"No, I don't want you to come in. Just park in the emergency room parking lot and look inside until you see me. I want to give you Mary's pill holder. I'll come out when I spot you. We don't need anyone else seeing it. You know why, right?"

"I guess because she's only taken four stool softeners and there's still two in the case."

"That's one reason; the other is I haven't had a chance to put her real pills back in that thing to show why she doesn't have any of that medicine in her system."

"I'll see you in a couple of minutes, sweetheart."

Twenty minutes later, she drove up to the emergency entrance and parked around the corner from the waiting room. After walking down the sidewalk, she spotted Tony looking out the window. He said something to Connor and walked out the door, motioning to Brenda Jean to move further down the sidewalk, out of Connor's view.

He grabbed her hand, pulling her into an empty doorway that had a "Not An Entrance" sign taped to the door, and gave her a quick kiss.

"I've got to go back inside, Brenda Jean. I told Connor that I had to go to the bathroom. I'll call you when I know anything. You just put that pill thing in a safe spot."

She smiled and headed back to her car.

Tony went back to the waiting area, where Connor was still zeroing in on ancient Egypt.

Two hours later, Nurse Jeffers walked up to the Calleys. "We figured out why your wife went into a coma. The doctor will be out to see you in a couple of minutes and he'll explain it to you. All I can tell you now is that she has a chemical deficiency. He'll fill you in."

"Is she going to be all right?" Tony asked.

"We don't know much yet except what caused her to go into a coma. These things are very fragile, I mean brain issues. But she's in good hands, especially with Dr. Wheeldon involved. Anyway, you can ask him about anything when you see him." She shook Tony's hand. "Good luck, Mr. Calley."Nothing was going as planned for Tony. They'd probably filled Mary with the same medicine that had brought her around last month, and she'd probably be back to normal in a couple of hours. He was getting nervous. Where was this Dr. Wheeldon?

Ten minutes later, a nurse walked into the waiting room with a piece of paper in her left hand. "Mr. Calley?" Tony stood up.

"That's me. Right here."

"Mr. Calley, please follow me."

He motioned to Connor to get up and go with him. She led them through a second set of doors to a small room with a "Consultation" sign above the door. When they walked in, a very tall doctor stood up.

"Mr. Calley?"

"Yes, and this is my son Connor."

The lanky doctor shook both their hands. "I'm Doctor Wheeldon, please sit down," he said, pointing to two brown and yellow padded chairs next to the desk loaded with his papers. He looked over at Connor. "You look scared, Connor. Don't worry, we're working hard to fix your mother. Do you know she's one of the strongest patients I've ever had? She's a real fighter, and I don't blame her, looking at you. You're worth fighting for, and you look like you're brave, too."

Connor cleared his throat. "I just want her to get better."

"Me, too," Wheeldon said. "Now, let me tell you where we're at, Mr. Calley. As you know, your wife had a problem about a month ago with her thyroid gland. I don't know if you remember what they told you about her condition and I know it's a long word, but she has a very volatile case of hypothyroidism. That's a fancy word for a thyroid gland that doesn't produce enough hormones for her body." He looked down at a paper on the desk. "They gave her an IV of a drug called levothyroxine, which is the same thing she supposedly takes every day. Anyway, according to what I'm looking at, the IV brought her around real quick, but it says here that she had stopped taking her prescription, is that true?"

Tony nodded. "That's exactly right. Is that the same thing that happened today?"

"Kind of. Her blood test shows that she has not taken her thyroid medicine for quite a while. Do you know anything about that?"

"No, I sure don't. After what happened before, I've been nagging her about taking her medicine every day. She told me last time she stopped taking them because it made her monthly easier. I even bought her a pill reminder box from the drug store. In fact, I watched her load it last Sunday."

"Me, too," Connor said.

"Can you get me that pill reminder?" Howard asked.

"Sure, it's probably in her purse and that's at home. I can get it tonight."

Wheeldon took a business card out of his smock pocket and handed it to Tony. "Give me a call in the morning after you find the reminder box, will you? Anyway, as I told you it was kind of the same thing as last month. Because her thyroid is messed up, she needs to take a pill every day, just like some diabetics need insulin every day. Well, her system was so deficient of what her thyroid is supposed to produce, it sent a bad signal to her brain."

Tony raised his shoulders up and released a long sigh. "What does that mean?"

"It means Mary is in a stage three hypothyroid coma. I don't want to alarm you, especially with your son here, but there are only four stages. Stage four is death. You see, your brain is made up of electrical signals, and if a chemical that one of your organs produces is absent, the electrical signal for that function shuts down. It's kind of like the water in your car battery; if the water cells are dry, you can't get an electrical charge." The doctor gave Tony a puzzled look. "Mr. Calley, do you have any idea why your wife didn't take her medicine? Did she say anything to you about it?"

"No, all I know is that she started acting funny yesterday, like she was seasick or something. But she never said anything to me about not wanting to take her medicine. My God, after what happened last month, I would have reacted fast if she said she missed even one pill."

"I've got to tell you that her thyroid counts were almost ten when she got here. That means she's been off the medicine for at least four or five days. You said she filled up her pill reminder Sunday and this is Thursday. I'd say she probably hasn't taken one pill since Sunday. That makes it very unlikely she will be wake up soon. Her body has to kind of fix itself."

Tony gave him a puzzled look. "But you said she is what, in stage three? Why can't you just give her a jolt of the same medicine they gave her last month? Wouldn't that fix her?"

"Mr. Calley, we're talking about two separate things. Yes, we gave her a ton of levothyroxine and her thyroid levels went back down to normal. But her thyroid level was so high because she obviously didn't take her medicine. For whatever reason, the electrical signal I was telling you about lost its charge. So now what we have is this…a very strong young lady with a fixed thyroid condition, who is now missing that electrical signal in her brain relating to that thyroid. And I have to be honest with you, a brain injury like this is very unpredictable. I've seen stage three comas where a patient comes out of them in twenty four hours, others where they stay in a fetal position for years; and unfortunately, I've seen some that caused death."

Connor grabbed his father's hand. "Daddy, did he say Mommy was going to die?"

"No, that's not what he meant," Tony answered.

The doctor shook his head. "What I'm trying to say, Mr. Calley, is that we don't know what's going to happen. All we can do is pray and watch her. Only God knows everything about the human brain. I'm supposed to be a specialist, but I'll bet I only know ten percent of what goes on the brain. It's a giant incredible work of art. It sounds silly, but the brain has a mind of its own, and us mere mortals can only hope it works right. Sometimes it fixes itself and sometimes it blows a gasket. Right now, Mary's brain is in a very fragile state, so she'll be in intensive care for a while so we can watch her. She's heading there now."

"Doctor Wheeldon, I have one more question. I don't know much about comas...I always thought that when you're in a coma, you're like sleeping. Is that what Mary is doing?"

"We can't be sure. That's because no one that's ever been in a coma has told us what it was like...kind of like not being able to remember dreams. We did some brain activity tests on your wife. She does have some things going on in her head, but not very many. We have no way to measure exactly what she's going through. I can only tell you that she can't react to anything external, like feeling anything when we give her a shot or move her. No, she's not feeling any pain. Now, can she think? Who knows?"

"How soon can I see my mom?" Connor asked, looking up at the doctor.

"In about an hour. We should be done with everything by then."

Wheeldon stacked the papers he was looking at into an orange file folder. He turned and rubbed the top of Connor's head. "Now, you all just leave everything to me. I wouldn't be surprised if your mother just wakes up in a day or too. I'd bet on her, especially with how healthy she is, other than the brain damage. Oh, we had to give her an IV because her system was so empty, like she probably had a bad case of diarrhea or hadn't eaten for quite a while. Was she on some kind of crash diet or something?"

"No, she's been eating with us. I don't know if she was dieting, Doc."

Wheeldon had a quizzical look on his face. He shook Tony's hand and patted him on the shoulder. "We'll do the best we can for Mary. The next twelve hours are critical. Oh, do you need me to show you how to get out of here?"

"No, I remember the way. Thanks anyway. Let's go, son." He grabbed Connor's hand. "Let's see if we can find intensive care, okay?"

CHAPTER 27
The Nurse Looked Over At Room 5

They found an elevator and hit the button to the fourth floor. After they got off the elevator they discovered the doors were locked to the intensive care unit. Two tan windowless doors with metal plates running from top to bottom were adjacent to the area. Tony tried to push the doors open, but they were locked. He stood there for a minute until a nurse came by and punched in some numbers on a small black keyboard about eight feet away from the entrance to intensive care. When the doors opened, Tony approached her.

"Excuse me, nurse. Can you help us?"

She turned to look at him. "I'll try. What can I do for you?"

"My wife is supposed to be coming up here tonight. Me and my son," he pointed to Connor, "we want to see her. She went into a coma today."

"I'm so sorry. What's her name? I'll check and see if she's here."

"Calley, Mary Calley."

"Let me check. I'll be right back."

Connor went to stand near his dad, who put an arm around the little guy. A minute or two later the same nurse came out. "She's not here yet, but she's supposed to get here any minute."

"Will she go by us to get in there?" Tony asked.

"No, she'll be coming up on an elevator inside intensive care. Come over here, I'll show you something."

Tony and Connor watched her as she pointed to the keypad she used to open the doors. "Do you see this? This is how you call the nurse's station inside. Just push on this little bar under the numbers and someone will talk to you. Look." She put a finger on the bar and pressed it once. "Hello, can I help you?"

"It's just me, Betty, I'm showing someone how to call us." She looked back at Tony. "Now, when your wife gets here, it will take us about an hour to get her set up, so I suggest you wait for at least an hour, then push the button to see if you can go in and see her. If you can, the doors will open and if you can't, then we'll tell you about how long it will be before you can come in."

After the nurse left, they waited exactly an hour. Tony looked at his watch and walked to the number pad to push on the bar.

"Can I help you?"

"Yes, we're here to see Mary Calley. I'm her husband and I've got my son with me. Can we come in?"

The big doors opened, exposing a circular desk area with four nurses looking at charts and computer screens. They were surrounded by about ten private rooms, loaded with red and blue lights emitting from various machines. Other than those lights, it was so dark and quiet, it was almost scary.

Tony leaned over to the first nurse he saw. "We're here to see Mary Calley."

The nurse looked at a clipboard she was carrying. "She's in room number five. You both can go in to see her." She pointed the way. "But remember, there's a no noise rule here."

****

When they walked into Mary's room, she was totally covered up except for her face and her arms. A white sheet was pulled up under her chin. Her head was held by a big elastic brace, and there was a plastic wire coming out of her skull under a mummy-looking white wrap that covered the top of her head. Both of her arms were laying still, loaded with wires and tubes, while one finger had a grey pincher on it that looked like a clothes pin.

Tony and Connor moved up to her carefully, like they were afraid to wake her up.

Tony kissed Mary on the cheek and started rubbing her forehead as Connor kissed her. "Mommy. Oh, Mommy. Please don't die." Connor started to sob.

Don't cry, baby. Mommy's going to be just fine.

Tony put his arm around Connor. "It's okay, Buddy, they're going to fix her."

"But Daddy, she's just laying here. Why can't they wake her up?"

"You heard Dr. Wheeldon. When her brain fixes itself, she'll open those beautiful green eyes and smile at us."

I can't believe this. I can hear them, but I can't open my eyes or even feel them. Why the hell don't they give me something to wake me up? Is this a dream or what? I want to hold my son. What's wrong with the doctors and nurses in this place, don't they have the medicine I need?

A nurse walked into the room to check the drip on the IV bottle. "Hello, my name is Nurse Ellen. You must be Mary's relatives, huh?"

No shit, Sherlock. She sounds like a real Einstein.

"Yes, I'm her husband Tony and this young man is our son, Connor."

She looked over at both of them. "Nice to meet you. So, what happened to your wife?"

Tony shrugged. "She stopped taking her thyroid pills for some reason, and the next thing we know she's in a coma."

That's a lie. I took my pills every day. Just look at my pill reminder.

Nurse Ellen patted Mary on the arm. "Wow, that can be very dangerous…I mean, not taking levothyroxine if you've got a bad thyroid. It looks like you may have caught it in time; you know that can be fatal."

What are you talking about? I might die because I didn't take my pills that I really took? What the hell is going on?

"Yeah, Dr. Wheeldon told us that," Tony replied. "Is it okay if we stay a while?"

"Of course. Our visiting hours end at ten, but tonight's my overnighter. As long as you are very quiet, we can bend the rules a little bit."

"Nurse Ellen, does she know we're here? Can she hear anything?"

"I'd say her brain right now is almost a hundred percent closed down. Her chart says she has a small amount of brain activity, but it's very unlikely she knows anything happening around her." She pinched Connor's cheek as she left. "Don't worry, we'll take real good care of your mom."

Tony pulled a chair over in front of him so he could stretch his legs out. They both got up every few minutes just to look at Mary. An hour later, Connor went to sleep. Tony looked at his wife and then his son. He pulled out his cell phone and punched in Brenda Jean's number.

"Brenda Jean," he whispered. "I can't talk long and I have to be quiet. I'm in Mary's room in intensive care. I can't go outside to talk to you because I've got Connor with me. No, no one can hear; Connor's asleep and I'm the only one in here except for the sleeping bitch. Listen, I've been thinking, darling. Do me a favor and take the last stool softener out of the pill reminder, the one for Friday, and flush it down the toilet. That could screw up everything if someone finds out she's been taking laxatives for four days, okay? I love you too, baby. What? No one knows; they say her brain is all messed up and people have died from it, or she might just wake up one day. I know, sweetheart, but we don't have any choice, we just have to wait and see what happens. I don't know, she'll probably die, just like we planned. I miss you, too. Listen, I'll call you when we head home. Oh, maybe in a couple of hours. Sure, after Connor goes to sleep. I'll see you then. Bye."

You scumbag. You fucking asshole. I can't believe it, you're trying to kill me for that whore. I can't wait until I wake up and get out of here. I'm going to take care of you, you son of a bitch.

Tony went to sleep for a few minutes until Nurse Ellen came in. She had a wide happy smile and a bubbly personality to match her red hair. He woke up, rubbing his eyes.

"I'm sorry if I woke you, Mr. Calley. You look beat. I'm sure today was a long and trying day for you."

"Yeah. You know, you don't realize how much you love someone until they get sick."

"I hear that every day working up here."

Nurse, don't believe that asshole. He doesn't love me. He's got his little whore to love.

"I'll bet you do. Well, do you think there will be any change with Mary tonight? I better think about taking our little boy home, he needs to sleep in his own bed."

"Mr. Calley, there's no way anyone can predict with a coma when anything might change. It's after midnight. Why don't you take off and we'll call you if anything changes?"

Tony stood up, stretching his arms away from his body. "I'm kind of tired too, but I know I probably won't sleep, thinking about Mary all night."

Hey, asshole, you aren't going to sleep because little miss Brenda Jean's going to be screwing you all night in our bed. Just go, Tony, I don't want you here.

Tony woke up Connor and they both walked over to Mary again.

Connor rubbed her cheek, then kissed her forehead. "Good night, Mommy, I love you. Daddy said he'd bring me back after school tomorrow. I'll see you then. Please get better fast." His tears landed on her nose so he wiped them off.

I love you, too, sweetheart. And I know you can't hear me, but I'm not really sleeping. I can hear you. I am going to wake up real soon, and you and me are going away. Sleep tight, my little angel, come see me tomorrow.

Tony kissed Mary on the cheek, trying to avoid the tube that was coming out of her nose. "Good night, darling, I love you."

Fuck you. I hate you.

****

220

Tony and Connor drove home, with Connor sleeping in the back seat. Tony carried his son up to bed, letting him sleep in the clothes he was wearing. The minute he closed Connor's door, he called Brenda Jean.

"Brenda Jean, we're home now and I can talk. How soon can you get here?"

"How does five minutes sound? I've been driving around your neighborhood for over an hour. Where do you want me to park?"

"I parked my car leaving you enough room to drive right into the garage. Just give me a minute to turn off the lights in the garage door opener, then I'll open it and you can come in."

A couple of minutes later she pulled her yellow VW into his garage, and he immediately hit the button next to the door and closed it. She got out of her car, carrying a small leather overnight case. The minute she saw him she dropped the bag and jumped on him. They kissed for over a minute.

"Did you bring her pill kit?"

"I sure did. It's right here," she answered, pulling it out of her purse. "I need to take care of that first." He walked out the side door of the garage and opened his Mercedes. He lifted the floor mat in the back seat to grab Mary's thyroid pills, but there weren't any pills there. He started to sweat. What could have happened to them? He didn't even have her original prescription bottle, the EMT had taken that. Now how could he convince anyone he didn't have anything to do with her not taking her pills? And what was he going to tell Brenda Jean?

He walked around the car and opened up the back door on the other side, once again lifting the floor mat. They there were. Those sweet pills, all wrapped up in a tissue. Life was good, they were there.

Tony put the precious tissue in his pants pocket and walked back into the house. Brenda Jean was already there, pulling a beer out of the refrigerator.

"I've got the pills; where's the pill holder?" Tony asked.

She picked it up off the counter next to the sink. "Here it is, Tony," she answered, handing it to him. His hand was shaking as he put one of Mary's thyroid pills in each AM section for Monday through Friday. After snapping the plastic lid down on the pill box, he softly threw it on the kitchen table. "Now we're set, Brenda Jean. It's perfect. Now everyone will say she didn't take her pills on purpose. It wasn't a suicide, it was just a woman trying to outfox her doctor. Now all we have to do is hope she never wakes up; or even better, she dies."

Brenda Jean walked over to her lover, putting her arms around his neck. "Maybe I'll just sneak up there and pull some plugs if she's stubborn about staying alive. What do you really think, Tony? Do you think she'll pull out of her coma or what?"

"I don't know. But one thing the doctor told me sounded pretty good. He said she was in a stage three coma and it could be fatal. If she gets any worse, she's a goner."

"Tony, do you remember that girl in Florida they made all that fuss about?"

"What do you mean?"

"Well, she was in a coma for years and years, and her husband wanted to pull her plug but her parents didn't. Do you remember that?"

He turned his head slightly, giving her a puzzled look. "I think so; what are you getting at?"

"I mean, what if Mary just keeps staying alive in a coma? What do we do then?"

"We just have to think of another way to end it. Trust me, baby, she's not going to be alive very long. Plus, you and I are destined to be together. I mean, we were worried about Bobbie, and look what happened to her. We didn't know where we'd get pink pills that look like her thyroid pills, and you found them the first day you started looking for them. Now, we weren't sure if the pill reminder plan would work, and it sure has. Like I said, it's our destiny to be together. All we have to do is wait for her to die."

She kissed him again, this kiss begging him to take her upstairs. There was something about all the intrigue that made her want him. She put her half full beer down on the table and grabbed his hand, pulling him up the stairs, locking the bedroom door. Five minutes later they were both naked, holding each other under Mary's favorite sheets.

"Boy, am I glad I called that cleanup service, Brenda Jean. You wouldn't have believed how much of a mess was in here when I got home. And the smell…holy shit, I can't believe they cleaned everything up in what, four hours? I'm glad you thought of that, baby."

There was a knock on the door. Tony put an index finger to his lips, asking Brenda Jean to be quiet. Then there was another knock.

"Daddy, can I please come in? I can't sleep, I'm scared. I can't stop thinking about Mommy. Can I sleep with you?"

Tony leaned over and whispered to his mistress. "I'll let him in, and when he goes to sleep I'll move him back to his room. Pick up your clothes and go through the bathroom. There's a door just past the shower that goes to the landing area above the stairs. You can go downstairs from there. I'll come get you when he's back in his room."

"Okay, Tony, just give me a minute." She kissed him, gathered up all her stuff, and headed towards the bathroom.

"Hold on, Connor, I'm in the bathroom. I'll be right there."

Tony walked to the bathroom and flushed the toilet, then unlocked his door to let his son in.

"Why did you lock the door, Daddy?"

"I sure didn't mean to. I guess when I closed it, it must have locked itself. Now you just climb up and jump in my bed. You can stay with me all night if you want to."

Connor plopped down on Tony's king-sized bed, then crawled up to get under the covers. He rolled over to get close to where his mother normally slept. "I'm so tired, Daddy, but I keep wondering about how Mommy is doing. You're not going to stay up, are you?"

"No, I'm beat too, Connor." He turned the bedside lamp off and put his arm around his boy. "Good night, son, I'll see you in the morning."

"Boy, something smells good. Did you shave or something, Daddy? I like whatever it is, it sure smells good."

Tony knew Connor was talking about Brenda Jean's perfume. "I smelled something too when I pulled the covers back. I think your mother must be using a new fabric softener. Who knows? Now you get to sleep, that bus will be here in six hours."

Thirty minutes later Connor was snoring. Tony carried him back to his own bed, then went downstairs and found Brenda Jean sleeping on the couch. He nudged her and she jumped, as if she was startled. "Brenda Jean, you can come back upstairs. Connor's asleep in his bed now."

"Tony, I'd love to spend the night holding you, but I really want to go home. I'm afraid Connor will want to get back in your room, and I couldn't sleep worrying about that…and no offense, but I can hardly stay awake."

"Sure, go ahead and go home. I need to catch some shuteye anyway, and if you were next to me all night, I don't think I could sleep at all. I'll open the garage door and you can back out."

She kissed him. "I knew you'd understand. Are you going to the office tomorrow?"

"No, I can't. I've got to do my 'oh, my God, my wife is sick' role-playing. But I'll call you when I can. Connor will be in school so I can leave Mary's room a lot and then we can talk."

She followed him to the garage and got in her car as he hit the button to open the big door. After blowing him a kiss, she backed out and turned her headlights on, vanishing into the night.

Chapter 28
When Is This Going to End?

Connor was cranky when Tony tried to wake him up for school the next morning. He wasn't used to getting just a couple of hours of sleep. Tony had to help him get dressed, then washed his son's face with a cold washcloth. It didn't help, Connor was a zombie. He begged his father to let him stay home and sleep, but Tony couldn't do that. He had to go see his wife and look like he cared, and he sure didn't want to be tied down to Connor. As Connor was heading out the front door to catch the bus, Tony put a breakfast bar in his hand. "Now, Connor, you try to eat that on the way to school. I'm sorry I couldn't make you any breakfast; I barely was able to even make your lunch. I did put it in your backpack. I'm tired too. Maybe we can go to bed a little earlier tonight."

"That's okay, Dad. I'll sleep some on the bus...you know, like a power nap. I'll be fine. Are you going to see Mommy today?"

"I am. Now you get out there, your bus is waiting." He kissed his son on the cheek and patted his little butt as he went out the door. "Damn, that's a good kid," he said as he waved at the driver.

Tony got to the hospital an hour later. He walked into the intensive care unit just as Dr. Wheeldon was leaving. "Hello, Dr. Wheeldon, how's Mary doing?"

"There's no change yet, and that's good. We've been watching her closely. This is day two, and normally on day two we start seeing a little swelling of the brain. But she's not losing any fluid yet. Like I told you yesterday, she's a fighter. She almost seems visibly determined to beat this thing. I sure hope she does."

"Me too. Oh, here's her pill box, Doc." He pulled the pill reminder out of his pocket and handed it to the doctor.

Wheeldon opened up the lids for each day, seeing a pink thyroid pill in every day's slot. "That's what I thought I'd see. You know what this means, Mr. Calley?"

"I guess it means she didn't take all her pills. Do you know that Sunday Connor and I saw her fill up each day's pills, her thyroid and her other two pills? Now it looks like she took the water pill and the aspirin, but didn't take her thyroid pills."

"Yes, but it also means she hasn't taken one for what, five days? She's lucky to be alive. I was hoping it was more like three days...five is tough. At least her thyroid numbers are fine now, but I'm still very concerned about her brain."

Tony looked down at his feet. "Doc, have you had a lot of patients who went into a coma who were taking the same medication as Mary?"

"More than you could imagine. I thinks it's an ego thing. Her medicine makes her periods very painful, and a lot of woman think they somehow look fatter when they take that medicine. Don't ask me why, but they do. They think they can get along without it for a day or two, but they can't. Pretty soon, a day or two turns into four or five days. That's when some women overreact to their monthly cycle, like Mary did."

"You mean by not taking the right medicine?"

"Oh, I've seen a lot of weird stuff. Mary is not the first woman I've treated who ignored prescriptions and took stool softeners when they felt fat and bloated on their period. Her digestive track was almost empty. She must have taken a lot of laxatives. Was she a big eater?"

"No, not really. I sure didn't know about her taking any laxatives. She usually eats her share. But one thing, she sure had a mess in her panties yesterday."

"Well, that doesn't matter now. All that matters is that we fix her brain. And I can assure you, Mr. Calley, we are going to do everything we can to do just that," he said as he patted Tony on the shoulder and headed towards a computer screen on the counter in front of the nurse's station.

Tony walked into his wife's room and bent over to kiss her on her forehead as he sensed a nurse coming in behind him. "Good morning, darling, I sure hope you can hear me somehow. I just want you to know I love you more than you'll ever know." He started to swell up with fake tears, playing his part very well.

****

Oh, it's show time again. What, is someone there with you, dirtbag? I hope you go straight to hell. You can bet—now that's a good word—you can bet on me taking care of you and your asshole whore when I wake up. That almost makes this whole thing worth it, you piece of shit.

"Good morning, Mr. Calley," the nurse said as she washed Mary's face with a white towel. "She's looking very beautiful this morning, don't you think?"

"Mary always looks beautiful. And she always has a smile on her face. She's an incredible woman. I thank God every day she's my wife," he replied as he sat down in the chair next to his wife's head.

I wish I could move, so I could puke all over that asshole. I've never heard so much bullshit coming out of one man's mouth. What a loser. Oh, nurse, don't listen to him, he's a prick, a fucking prick. And don't let any young, good-looking nurses near him. He'll try to fuck em, just like he's fucking his secretary. I mean, he wins the prize as the biggest asshole on earth.

The nurse left and Tony kicked off his shoes, letting his feet rest on the bottom bar of Mary's bed. He laid back and went to sleep. An hour later, he woke up when a male nurse nudged him as he walked by to roll Mary onto her side so another nurse could finish giving her a bath. Ten minutes later, Tony was alone with his wife. He pulled his cell phone out of his pocket, speed dialing Brenda Jean.

"Hey, princess," Tony whispered. "I'm in her room again, so I have to be careful and I can't talk very loud. Yeah, I gave it to Wheeldon. He opened it up and said he wasn't surprised they were all still there. He even said he'd seen the same thing before with other women, kind of an ego thing. Yeah, he noticed that. He even said it wasn't unusual for a woman to take laxatives during her monthly. This is all coming together better than I could have hoped for, except of course that we needed a fifth day to end it. If Connor wouldn't have gotten scared and called 911, it'd be over by now."

Oh, what a shame, you couldn't kill me off. You know what? I don't think either one of you have the brains to do anything right. I'm sure messing you up, aren't I? Well, guess what, shitheads, maybe I can figure a way to kill both of you off after I wake up. That would be a beautiful thing. Looks like I got plenty of time to figure it out, you mother-fucking bastards.

"I know, I'm sorry, Brenda Jean, but it just worked out that way. I'm pooped too. Say, is everything okay at the office? Oh, he did. Well, tell him thanks for me. I think I'll have to be away at least a couple more days. I don't want to look like a non-caring husband. Sure. I'll give him some Benadryl around nine; plus he'll still be tired from last night. I'd guess around ten, but I'll call you. Listen, it looks like a nurse is heading this way. Love you, bye."

I don't even want to listen to this anymore. Why don't you take your cell phone outside or out to the hall, or somewhere else, or shove it up your ass? Nurse, if you're there, please get this man out of my room, will you?

The nurse pulled an almost empty IV bottle off a metal hook and replaced it with a full one. Tony watched her do everything. It looked like it would be easy to turn off an IV drip, he thought, as he watched her twist a little control button on the plastic tube. Maybe that was his last resort; it sure didn't look hard to do.

An elderly black man dressed in all white entered the room, leaned over, and twisted some bars next to the wheels on her bed. "Excuse me, sir, but I have to take Mrs. Calley for a little ride down to get a scan. She should be back in about an hour."

****

Tony watched her leave, then decided to go get some breakfast. He found his car in the hospital garage and drove out to a pancake house less than a mile away. As he was getting out of his car, his cell phone rang.

"What, you win fifty g's and you forget about me, huh?"

"No, I've been busy with my wife in the hospital. She's in a coma, Parker."

"You're shitting me."

"No, it's the truth. She didn't take her medicine right and her brain's all fucked up now."

"I'm sorry, Tony. I shouldn't be bothering you. Can I call you when things get better?"

"That's all right. I can't do anything to help Mary right now. Maybe a bet or two will help me handle all this. What you got?"

"Well, I've got the inside tip of inside tips. It seems a bunch of jockeys are getting together tonight to let a fifty to one long shot win the sixth race at Flamingo. The horse's name is Sleepless. What a name for you right now, huh? Do you want some action?"

"Are you sure he's fifty to one?"

"I just checked it, but I've got a feeling he'll drop fast with the bets I've already taken. I don't want to bother you with what's going on in your life, but maybe it will cheer you up if you win another big one. So, what do you say, what do you want to do?"

"Put a thousand on Sleepless to win. I'm ready for another fifty grand, I just hope the odds hold."

"I'll do it, Tony. Say, I'll say a prayer for your old lady tonight, and another one for Sleepless. I'll call you tonight after the race."

"Thank you, Parker, I'll see you later."

Tony got out of his car, chuckling. How could life get any better? There was only one thing left that could improve anything, and that was Mary going past stage three.

He took his time eating his breakfast as he stayed on his phone talking to his lover, then drove back to the hospital, concentrating on his acting job. It was so boring, pretending like he gave a shit about Mary, but he had to do it.

****

After he entered her room, a nurse came in and checked the plastic bag under the bed that was almost full of urine. She switched the bag with an empty one.

"It looks like there's nothing wrong with her bladder," Tony said with a small chuckle as he sat down.

"You're right about that," the nurse said. "As far as I can tell, there's nothing wrong with her anywhere except her coma, but I hear her brain waves are getting better."

Getting a little scared, huh, Tony? Maybe I'll pull through this after all. That will ruin your plans, won't it? Nurse, damn it, wake me up. Wake me up, damn it...when is this going to end?"

"What does that mean, the brain waves are getting better?" Tony asked.

"I'll let Dr. Atlas tell you about it. He can explain it better than I can. They said the last scan showed some improvement, that's all I know. Do you want to talk to him? He's right out at the nurse's station."

"Who's Dr. Atlas?"

"He works with Dr. Wheeldon, who's in surgery the rest of the day, so Dr. Atlas is filling in for him. I'll try and get him back to talk to you."

Tony sat down in his chair. "This is not good," he whispered, looking out the window. A man in a lab coat entered the room and went to Mary's side, put a finger on her temple, then turned to look at Tony. "Hello, you must be Mr. Calley. My name is Dr. Atlas. I'm Dr. Wheeldon's partner. He asked me to do a scan on Mary today and take a look at the results." He looked down at a clipboard he had carried into Mary's room. "According to the scan, your wife has improved a lot in the last twelve hours. Her brain firings are twice what they were last night. That's a great sign."

"That sounds wonderful, but what are brain firings?"

"That's what the brain does...it fires off and receives signals from your body. Brain firings are those specific signals. It looks like we might get a better idea what firings she's lacking and address them. It's kind of tricky right now. We are much more optimistic than yesterday, Mr. Calley. She's been upgraded to having a stage two coma. That means she is more likely to come out of it than she is to remain comatose for a long time or die."

Tony smiled, trying to produce some tears. "That sounds super. I can't wait for her to open her eyes and look at me. It looks like God is answering my prayers. Thank you so much." Once again, he was on a stage, and he was playing out his role masterfully.

Uh huh, now you're fucked, aren't you, Tony? I'll tell you what I'll do for you, my darling husband; when I wake up, I'll be the sweetest little wife in the world, just wait and see. Then I'm going to do to you and your whore what you couldn't do to me. I'm going to pull off the world's most perfect crime. You'll see. And when I do, I hope they bury the two of you in the same smelly coffin.

"You're welcome, Mr. Calley," Dr. Atlas said, then he left Tony alone with his bride.

Tony pulled his vibrating cell phone out of his pants pocket and saw Brenda Jean's number. He rose from his seat and moved close to the window behind his wife, trying to get as far as possible from the nurses out at their station. "Hey, darling," he whispered. "What are you doing calling me here? Oh, I don't care. Just tell the girls to cover for you, tell them you got a headache. No, I can't. I'd love to but I've got to be the doting husband right now." He sneaked a peek out at the nurses, none of whom were looking his way. "Besides, you're kind of wearing me out. I mean, I can't go see you at lunch and then take care of you at night at my place. That's real funny, Brenda Jean. I'm not getting old, let's just say I've got a lot going on right now. Listen, Mary's folks are coming tonight, so they can probably help watch him some this weekend. I miss you too. Say, why don't you come up here? Bring some papers and tell the nurses you've got some papers I need to sign. They'll let you in. Then I'll take you to the parking lot, and who knows what will happen in my car? Okay, I'll be here. Love you too, bye."

So your hot little secretary wears you out, huh? That's why you didn't want me, you couldn't handle taking care of business at home after you screwed her during the day. I should have figured it out. That's all right, I already know what I'm going to do. I'm going to spend the rest of this fucking coma figuring out how to kill both of you while you're in bed together. I wish I could tell you that to your face, you dirtbag.

CHAPTER 29
I Think She'll Wake Up

An hour later, Brenda Jean waltzed into Mary's hospital room carrying a large tan envelope. She glanced down at Mary after spotting Tony asleep in a corner chair next to the window, then cleared her throat loud enough to wake her lover. Tony shook his head, rubbing the back of his neck. "Hello, Brenda Jean," he said, glancing around her to be sure no nurse was close enough to hear him. "Man, was I ever sleeping sound, even with these terrible chairs that mess up my back."

Brenda Jean looked at Mary again. "Tony, can we talk? Are you sure she can't hear us?"

"She's in a coma. She doesn't know what's going on. Don't worry about that. Just be careful what you say when there's a nurse or a doctor in here, that's all."

"Okay, baby. What's the latest with her?"

The latest is that I know all about the two of you, and I'm getting better. Of course, you don't know that, right, bimbo? I'll just lay here and listen to you two lovebirds for a while, while I go over my plan again. Go ahead and say whatever you want. You're a dead woman, anyway.

"Well, she's been upgraded to having a stage two coma. The doctors say that's encouraging. But don't give up, they also told me she could slip back into stage three just as easy. We just have to wait and see what happens. I swear to God I've thought about turning off her IV or unplugging her respirator at least twenty times."

"Just say the word, Tony, and I'll do it. I'm not afraid of yanking the thing out and watching her die, then plugging it back in at the end. I'm getting sick of all of this, baby doll."

"You can't pull the plug. They got a monitor in the nurse's station on everyone in here. The second the machines stop, they'll come running. I've already seen them sprint to the old lady's room next door. No, that won't work. You've got to look at it from the bright side…at least she can't follow us. That way we can do whatever we want outside the hospital."

"I know, Tony, but it's kind of like she's still out there watching us. I mean, I have to sneak around waiting for Connor to go to sleep just to see you at night. I love being with you, but it's a pain in the ass being so careful all the time."

"I know, darling. Listen, I just got a great idea. There's a hotel across the street from the emergency room entrance. Why don't I get a room there for a couple of days? That way I can slip out of here and meet you anytime. How about that? Then you don't have to sneak around, especially with her folks coming."

She walked up next to him, lightly scratching the back of his neck, constantly watching for anyone looking their way. "I'd really like that. All you would have to do is call me an hour or so before we meet and I'd be there ready for you. Can you get a room now?"

"I sure can. I'll head over there in a minute. Why don't you just watch for me coming out of the parking garage, then follow me to the hotel? That will be fun."

Who cares, shithead? Just go. I get sick just hearing your voice. Go screw your secretary. I know everything now, so who cares. Get the hell out of here.

Tony turned to the nurse who was pulling some sheets out of the drawer next to the bathroom, and noticed her name badge pinned onto her front pocket. "So, Nurse Little, she looks a little better today, huh?"

"Oh yeah, your wife is getting stronger every day. I think she'll wake up real soon, because she's a fighter. You must be proud of her."

"You've got that right. I've put my trust in God. He knows she's special and He'll take care of her."

"I think that's a safe bet. It's been a long time since I've seen anyone improve so fast from a brain injury like your wife had. Maybe there is divine intervention going on."

"If anyone deserves God's help, it's her. She's an angel. I think I'll go get something to eat. You just take care of my princess, okay?"

They can take care of me a lot better than you can. I wish I could wake up, walk over, and stab you in your cheating heart a hundred times.

"I will; enjoy your lunch."

****

Tony walked out of his wife's room, located his car in the parking lot, then drove to the Parkside Hills Motel, with Brenda Jean following him. He got a room for three days, providing them their little safe hideaway. It was perfect. He could slip away from his sleeping wife whenever he wanted and enjoy Brenda Jean, and on this Friday afternoon he really enjoyed his young secretary.

When he got back to his wife's hospital room, she was gone. He stuck his head out the door, looking both ways. There was no sign of her. He walked up to the nurse's station, finding Nurse Little. "Excuse me, do you know where my wife went? Her room is empty…it doesn't even have a bed in it."

"Oh hi, Mr. Calley. Mary's down getting another scan. While you were gone, Dr. Atlas came by and said her eyes looked a lot clearer, and he wanted another look inside of her head. I would expect she'll be back in about an hour."

"Wow, she's changing by the minute. Every time I ask someone how she's doing they say she's improving. Maybe my prayers are being answered after all."

Nurse Little turned back to her computer screen. "The longer I'm a nurse, the more I realize that prayers are always the best medicine, that's for sure."

Tony looked at his watch. It was almost two thirty. "Oh my God, I've got to get home and meet my son when he gets off the bus. I'll be back as soon as I can."

"That should be fine, Mr. Calley."

He pulled into his driveway just as bus number 1949 stopped in front of their house and opened the door to let Connor get off. Tony walked out to meet his son, grabbing his backpack as he hugged him. "Hey, Connor, how was school?"

"It was fine, Dad, except I couldn't concentrate, thinking about Mom. How's she doing today?"

"Well, she's still sleeping, but guess what? The doctors say she's getting better every day, and they expect her to pull out of her coma pretty soon."

"That's great. Can we go see her now?"

"Sure. Just put your stuff on the porch and jump in the car, and we'll go over to the hospital."

****

When they got to intensive care, Mary was back in her room. Connor laid next to her, watching her breathe. "Mommy, I missed you today. Daddy said you're getting better. I can't wait until we bring you home. Our house isn't the same without you. I'm so scared."

Don't you worry, Connor, I'll be home real soon. Then I've got some things I need to tell you about your dad. He's a real asshole, and he doesn't care about either one of us. His world revolves around his girlfriend and his gambling, not us. That's why you have to trust Mommy when I tell you that you and me will be going away, but at least we'll be together.

Tony sat down in his normal chair. "Connor, she can't hear you. She can't feel anything, either. You can pinch her as hard as you want and she wouldn't even know it. Nobody knows what's going on inside of her, but one thing's for sure, she doesn't know you're here."

That's bullshit. Don't listen to him, Connor. I know you're here, it's just that you don't know I can hear you or that I'm talking to you right now. You say whatever you want, darling.

An hour later, Nurse Ellen came in and met little Connor. "Mr. Calley, how about if I take Connor for a little walk and show him the kid's room?"

Tony looked up at the aging nurse. "What's a kid's room?"

"That's a special place for little ones to go while they're here. It's a wonderful room full of toys and TVs. He'll love it. I'll take him down there if it's all right. There's always someone from the hospital that works there supervising the kids until around seven." She turned to Connor. "What do you say, do you want to go there?"

"Sure, as long as it's okay with Dad." He looked at Tony, who nodded. "Do they have a phone there so I can check in every once in a while to see how Mom's doing?"

"They sure do; let's go." The nurse grabbed Connor's hand and headed to the play room.

Thirty minutes later, Nurse Ellen brought Connor back. He crawled up on his mother's bed again, laying his head on her shoulder, and went right to sleep. A couple of minutes later, Tony snoozed off, too.

He woke up to someone tapping his arm. He looked up to see Mary's father staring down at him.

"Hey, Dad, I'm glad you got here."

"Don't call me Dad, I'm not your dad."

Give him hell, Daddy.

"Now, Paul, you promised to be nice," Mary's mother said. "We have to be civil to each other now, for Mary's sake."

Paul turned to the right, looking at his sleeping daughter. "Lacey, I know I promised, but how in the hell can I be so forgiving after hearing what my daughter said about him?"

Tony stood up. "Listen, Paul, Mary's had this crazy idea that I'm having an affair and that I'm gambling away all of our money for months now. Is that what she told you about me?"

Mary's father looked back at his son-in-law. "That's about it in a nut shell. And I believe my daughter, not you. I don't need no proof, all I need is for Mary to wake up and explain all of it to us in front of you. Now we came here to see her, not you."

I love you, Daddy. I knew you wouldn't listen to his bullshit. Don't hurt him, let me take care of him. After I get out of here you're going to be so proud of me, just wait and see.

Lacey grabbed her husband by his left arm, pulling him away from Tony. She shook her head, looking at Mary, then back to Tony. "We don't know what the truth is, Paul. All we know is what she said last week. Tony, I've always known you to be a great husband, so I don't know what to think. But, that doesn't mean much to me anymore. All I care about is Mary. You two boys are going to have to get along for her sake."

Tony sat back down, trying not to look at Paul, but it was pointless. Paul walked over and stuck out his hand, and Tony grabbed it. Lacey's little lecture worked.

"Okay, Tony, for Lacey and Mary's sake, I'm sorry. I won't give you anymore grief. Just do me a favor…whatever you've done to hurt my little Mary, don't ever do it again, okay?" Paul asked.

"I have never intentionally hurt my princess, so you don't have to worry."

Oh my God, am I hearing what I think I'm hearing? Daddy, don't believe him. He has turned out to be the worst husband in the world. If you only knew what he's done, you'd probably beat the shit out him right here in this hospital room. But I've almost finished my plan, so I can take care of him and his red-headed bitch. Guess what, Daddy…I'm gonna kill both of them. You hear me, I'm gonna kill them!

Connor woke up and saw his grandparents. He jumped out of Mary's bed and into their arms. "I'm so glad to see you," he said, squeezing them as hard as he could.

"So, Tony, what are the doctors saying now?" Lacey asked.

Tony opened his eyes as wide as he could, licking the bottom of his lower lip with his tongue. "It's looking good. They all say that she's one hell of a fighter and her brain is getting better every hour. She came in here with a stage three coma—"

"What's that? Paul asked.

"That's almost the worst one. That means she could be in a coma for a long time or it could kill her. But they already upgraded her coma to a stage two. That means she could wake up soon, but no one can ever be sure with a coma. Anyway, all we can do is just wait to see what happens. I'm glad you're here. How long can you all stay?"

Lacey stopped rubbing Mary's forehead to look back at Tony. "We're staying until our little girl wakes up, I don't care how long that

E. G. LANDER

takes. Plus, we figured you'd need us to help with Connor so you could come up here."

"Oh, thank you, I was worried about that. Now, you all just stay at the house and we'll take turns coming up to see Mary. We'll get through this together."

You just want them to babysit so you can meet Brenda Jean at your hotel. I'd give anything to be able to tell them what you're up to, you shithead.

****

Mary was continually getting better. It looked like she got more color in her face every time Tony saw her. His mind was still swirling with thoughts about unplugging the respirator or shutting down her IV's, but it was too dangerous. Mary had another scan on Sunday and they moved her coma classification to level one. The doctors and the nurses all kept saying she could wake up at any time. It was like she was purposely keeping her husband in agony. Mary's mother had taken over the house. She did the laundry, cooked all the meals, and constantly cleaned something every spare minute she had. It looked like she'd given Paul the assignment to entertain Connor. When they were home together, they played every video game Connor owned. Paul took his grandson to the movies Saturday and Sunday, and along with Lacey, took him to see his mother twice each day. Tony was given a reprieve. When he was supposed to be at the hospital he was with Brenda Jean. When Connor wanted to see his mother, his grandparents took him. Tony did not see Paul or Lacey much all weekend. That was the way they all probably preferred it, anyway.

Everything changed Monday morning. Tony had decided to stop by his office to check on a few things when his cell phone rang.

CHAPTER 30

I Can't Believe It Finally Happened

Tony's mother-in-law was on the phone. "Tony, you won't believe it…Mary just woke up. She's been asleep what, five days? Now, she's awake and she's asking for you."

"What? Oh my God, that's incredible. I can't believe it finally happened. How did you find that out?"

"I called the nurse's station just now to see how she was doing. I talked to a Nurse Rennau. She was very nice. She said there was a lot of activity going on in Mary's room, but she'd call me right back. Less than a minute later she did call back and told me that Mary is awake. Isn't it wonderful? Paul and I are heading over there; we'll see you there."

Tony made a U-turn as he got to his office parking lot, just as Brenda Jean arrived. He stopped and waved at her to stop. She pulled up next to his Mercedes so they could talk eyeball to eyeball. "Brenda Jean, I just got a call from Mary's mother. It seems our beloved little coma victim just woke up. Not only is she awake, but she's asking for me."

His secretary was stunned. "Tony, you said switching her pills would put her into a coma and probably kill her. Now, less than a week later, she's not only alive but she's asking for you. This nightmare never ends. It's like Groundhog Day, everything is starting over. Now we have to sneak to see each other again. I don't think I can take it anymore."

"Now listen to me, Brenda Jean. Just because she's awake doesn't mean I'm not going to get rid of her. I'll think of something, I promise. I don't like this whole mess any more than you do. I'll fix everything, I promise I will. Just give me some time to think on it."

Brenda Jean lowered her head into her chest. "Tony, you're my whole world, but you better take care of this fast, and I mean real fast. I've been patiently waiting for you for over a month. I can't go on much longer like this."

"I don't blame you, sweetheart, but all you have to do is trust me and give me a little more time. I'll think of something, you'll see. Now, I've got to go to the hospital. I'll call you when I can."

He pulled out, not giving her a chance to respond or even say goodbye. His world had gone from one of great promise to one of disgust, all because Connor had to call 911 on day four. Now Brenda Jean was right, it was Groundhog Day. Everything was like it was before Mary got sick. He had to come up with a plan to take care of his wife. He couldn't lose Brenda Jean now.

When Tony walked into Mary's hospital room, a nurse was removing her respirator. Mary was sitting up, giving out a winning glow. She had come back and she knew it. She saw Tony walk in and she extended her arms, inviting a hug. He complied.

"Mary, oh Mary, I was so worried. You did it, you won. I'm so proud of you." He hugged her hard, but felt some coolness coming back at him.

Paul and Lacey were standing next to their daughter on the other side of the bed. Lacey held out her hand to Tony, squeezing his hand as tears flowed down her cheeks. Everyone was excited about what had just happened, at least on the outside. Tony had to go back to his acting job, but he was crushed on the inside.

Dr. Wheeldon walked in. "I just got a call from the nurses. Oh my God, look at this, why it's little Mary. You look so beautiful. No one could ever guess you've been asleep for five days. How do you feel?" he asked, looking into her eyes with his silver flashlight.

"I'm kind of dizzy, more like disoriented. Who are you?"

"My name is Dr. Wheeldon. I've been taking care of you, along with Dr. Atlas, since last Thursday when you went to sleep. You've been in a coma since then. I'm still amazed at you, young lady."

Mary laid back, letting out a big sigh. "Why's that, Doctor?"

Wheeldon put his stethoscope on her neck. "We almost lost you, but you fought every inch of the way. It was like you decided to come back no matter what happened. You have the guts and the strength of ten men. Yep, you're my hero. You don't even need a respirator anymore."

Mary shook her head. "I don't know what you're talking about. The last thing I remember is hearing Connor calling me from inside a hall a long way away. I'm not a hero. I guess I just decided not to die, that's all."

The doctor picked up her wrist and looked at his watch. "Do you know why you went into a coma, Mary?"

She looked at her parents, then at Tony. She didn't respond.

"I asked you if you know why you went to sleep last Thursday," Wheeldon repeated.

She shook her head. "No, I don't remember; is that bad?"

"No, that's normal. You went into a coma because you didn't take your thyroid medication for four or five days. You're lucky to be alive. Do you remember anything about that?"

"No, I sure don't. Why would I not take my pills?"

Wheeldon patted her on the arm. "You're not the first patient I've had who didn't like her thyroid meds. But you've got to listen to me, they keep you alive; you can't play around with them. Most woman who skip them do it during their periods because they have a lot worse cramps when they're on that medicine, and they bloat more. But you can't skip them again, Mary. Like I said before, we almost lost you; next time you might not be so lucky."

Tony rubbed her forehead. "Princess, I prayed and prayed you'd come back to me, and you did. I'm so lucky. Thank you for being so brave. I love you so much."

She looked up at her husband with wide open eyes. "I love you too, Tony."

Tony bent down and kissed her on the cheek while she patted his back.

"When do you think my little girl can go home?" Paul asked.

Dr. Wheeldon raised his shoulders, looking at Mary. "We're not out of the woods yet. She just woke up. We have to watch her for another day or two here in intensive care, and do some tests to make sure she's really okay. When we get done with that, we'll put her into a regular room for a few days, and if everything is fine, she can go home. So I'd say she'll be here a minimum of four to five more days."

Mary raised her hand only about a foot over her sheet. "Doctor, a couple of things…I've got a terrible headache, and when do you think I'll start feeling normal? I kind of feel like I've got a bad case of vertigo right now."

"Both things are quite normal after a short coma. We'll give you something for the headache, but as far as the disorientation goes, that will just take some time. The sooner we get you on your feet, the sooner you'll feel better. Your body is not supposed to be immobile for a week…you've got some catching up to do. I'll leave all your instructions with the nurses. It looks to me like you'll be very close to normal in a few days."

"So Doctor, what do you want us to do now?" Lacey asked.

"I think all of you should just be patient. Believe it or not, she's probably still going to sleep more than normal. That doesn't mean she's back in a coma. Mary looks like she's going to be fine. I don't know if she will ever recover all of her memory. She probably won't remember everything so I wouldn't push her too fast, but she needs to hear about her life. At least she recognizes all of you and she mentioned Connor. That's a good start. Just do two things right now…comfort her and let her open up about what she can remember. The nurses will take care of everything else, like getting her on her feet and stuff like that."

"Doc, I saw you all removed the respirator already. Is she going to still have an IV?" Paul asked.

"We talked about removing the respirator a lot this morning even before she woke up. Now that she's awake, she doesn't really need it anymore. As far as an IV goes, she still needs nutrition from that for another day or two. We don't want to go too fast. We'll slip in some soft food tonight, but I don't want her to shock her intestines too soon with a lot of solid food. Plus, an IV gives us a good port to give her any meds she needs." He looked around the room. "Does anyone else have any more questions?"

"Doctor Wheeldon, when will you know if she has any brain damage from all this?" Tony asked.

"That's a hard question to answer. You see, normally there is some damage. I mean, there were parts of her brain that were basically shut off for five days. Don't get alarmed if she is not exactly herself. And to tell you the truth, no one knows if she will ever be the same as she was before last week. The key is ninety days out; when she gets there, she will be what she will be. That doesn't mean she'll be stupid or anything, it means she may be different than you all are used to." He looked around the room. "Any other questions?"

Their silence gave him his answer. He patted Mary on the shoulder. "You are something. I'm so proud of you." He waved at the family and left.

Mary stared at her husband for two minutes. He could tell she was working hard, trying to remember something. Finally, she spoke up. "Tony, I want to see Connor. Will you please go get him? I know he's in school, but would you bring him to me anyway?"

Tony bent down again, kissing Mary on her lips. "Of course I will. I'll be back in about an hour." He looked at Paul and Lacey. "I'll see you all later."

He called Brenda Jean on the way to pick up Connor. "Yeah, she's awake. I don't think she can remember much. That's good for us, because she's not sure if she did or didn't take her thyroid pills. I was a little concerned when the doctor asked her if she knew why she went into a coma, then told her she didn't take her medicine. I had my fingers crossed, hoping she wouldn't convince anyone she did take her pills."

"Do you think her memory will ever come back?"

"I doubt it; who knows?"

"So, when will she come home?"

DAMN IT WAKE ME UP

"It sounds like she'll be there for most of the week."

"Well, that's about the only good news you've told me in a long time. I thought maybe when she woke up she'd be going home right away. But what are we going to do after that? I mean, after she comes home?"

"I'll tell you what we can do, both of us. We can start now trying to figure out how we're going to finish the job. We can't do a pill switch again, that's for sure. But there's got to be something else out there we can find to get rid of her, so start thinking about it, will you?"

"I'm on it, boss man."

"Okay, Brenda Jean, I've got to go pick up Connor. Mary wants to see him right away. I'll call you later. I'm not sure if I can meet you at the hotel tonight, I'll let you know. Oh, sweet stuff, one more thing. I love you."

"Back at you, Tony. Bye."

Tony got Connor and brought him to the hospital. Mary lit up the second she saw him. It was like there was no one else in her room but Connor. She hugged him hard for over a minute, while looking over her shoulder at Tony. "Thanks, Tony, for bringing him to me. That means a lot."

The next four days everyone worked with Mary, trying to get her back to normal. The only thing they couldn't fix was her memory. Paul and Lacey had someone overnight some photo albums of Mary's life, from her birth to her wedding. They spent hours showing her the pictures. She acted like she only remembered pieces of her life, but there were a lot of holes she couldn't fill in. She too was a great actor. While all that was going on, Tony was balancing his acting job of keeping both women happy. Somehow he managed to see Brenda Jean every day, and no one suspected anything.

On Friday they finally took Mary home, stalling Tony and Brenda Jean's affair, except when they resorted to some lovemaking in his office after everyone else had gone home. Tony couldn't help but think about his secretary almost all the time, but he had to be extra careful with Paul and Lacey hanging on his every word. It was as if they wanted to catch him. Both of them wouldn't let go of what Mary had told them before she got back from Athens.

Mary acted like she didn't have a care in the world. She was sweet to Tony, sweeter than she had been in years. She didn't say anything to him about either Brenda Jean or his gambling. If she had a problem with either, he couldn't tell. The following Tuesday Paul and Lacey went home. Both Tony and Mary were glad to see them go, as it was getting tense with them around for so long. That afternoon Tony took his wife to see Dr. Wheeldon, who suggested that she take up a hobby so she could concentrate on something. The three of them decided aerobics would be the answer, both to strengthen her body and her mind. The Calleys spent the rest of that afternoon checking on aerobic gyms in the area. Tony knew he couldn't take her there every week, so she started driving again. By Friday she was driving to her daily aerobics sessions at Midtown Woman's Club. She loved it. It also gave her time to be alone and think about her future and how she was going to kill her husband and his whore secretary. Just as Tony had been a wonderful actor throughout the whole ordeal, she was even a better one. She hadn't lost her memory. She hadn't forgotten what she'd heard in the hospital, but she wasn't going to let anyone know that, including her parents. She had a score to settle. All of the times she acted forgetful, she was faking it. And she was so proud of herself...even Dr. Wheeldon was fooled by her acting skills.

As the days went by, she started planning all the details she had worked up while she lay in that hospital bed. The first step was to learn how to get and use a gun, and to buy a wig somewhere.

One afternoon, following an aerobics class, she drove to the mall and bought a blonde wig. She put it on in the car and looked at herself in the rear view mirror. "Why didn't I do this earlier? I look good in this. Yeah, this will work," she mumbled.

Next to the mall was a gun shop. She kept the wig on and walked into the tobacco smelling store wearing her exercise outfit, which consisted of a tight pair of pink jogging pants under some red bikini-like shorts. She was hot and she knew it, wearing her big brown sunglasses and a baseball cap with a pony tail that stuck out the hole in the back. Everyone in the store noticed her, but no one could possibly recognize her with that getup on.

She walked up to the counter, using the fake southern-drawl accent she'd been practicing. "Hey, cutie, how do I go about buying a gun?"

The fat balding man behind the counter put his unlit cigar into an ashtray, then smiled at the colorful lady wanting a weapon. "Now honey, what do you need a gun for? I bet you got an old man who is always there to protect you. I mean, you must be used to guys hitting on you, the way you look."

She smiled at the fat man. "Now aren't you sweet? I don't need one of them there guns to protect me from men bothering me. I need a gun so I can rob a bank."

The clerk and three or four men within listening range all laughed. She started to laugh with them. The fat man bent over, leaning his elbows on the counter. "Now, you know I'm not supposed to sell a gun to anyone who talks about robbing a bank."

"I know, honey. I just thought I'd mess with you a little bit. You all look like you're bored, so I thought I'd just liven up the place. You know little old me ain't going to rob a bank. The truth is, I live in an apartment building that's had a lot of break-ins lately, and I sure don't want anyone getting into my itty bitty place and hurtin' me. So how do I get a gun?"

"I can help you, little darling. All you have to do is pick out the gun you want to buy, then fill out some paperwork, and it's yours."

"I always thought there was some kind of background check and a waiting period to get a gun; is that true?"

"Not in this state…we take the second amendment seriously here. Now, what kind of gun do you want?"

"Oh, I want a gun that will fit in this purse and one that doesn't knock me down when I shoot it. And I wouldn't mind getting one that has a— what's the word?—a silencer for it, too. I hate loud bangs. I know I'll probably never use a gun, but if I do, I don't want to get a heart attack when it goes off."

"Well, I got just the number for you." He unlocked a glass case, pulling out a black gun with a silver handle. "This here is what is called a .45. It's the gun you see on police shows a lot. It has a little kick, so when a little thing like you fires it, you probably should hold it with two hands." He pointed the gun towards the back wall, showing her how to hold it.

"That looks a little big for me. Do you got anything a little smaller with a silencer?"

"Here, try this one. It still packs a big wallop, but it's not as hard to handle as that .45. And do you see the threads on the end of the barrel? That's to screw the silencer on." He pulled out a silver rod and screwed it on the end of the tan pistol. "See, this is how it goes on."

"That's perfect, I'll take it. How much do I owe you?"

"Let's see, the pistol is one ninety and the silencer is one twenty. That's three hundred and ten dollars plus tax. How do you want to pay for it?"

"Here," she said, pulling out three one hundred dollar bills from her purse, followed by a twenty.

"Okay, now I got some papers for you to fill out and sign." He handed her two self-copying sheets, a white one over a pink one.

She pulled a pen out of her purse and finished the paperwork, all with fictitious information, and he asked her for an ID. She went through her purse looking for her driver's license. "Oh, I must have left my driver's license at home. Do you want me to go home and get it? I'm kind of short on time right now."

"Nah, sweetheart, don't worry about it. I trust you. I just needed to verify who you are, but it's no big deal. Do you want any ammo for your pistol?"

"Not right now. I'm late for my judo class. I'll get some later."

He put her gun and silencer into a bag and gave her the change. "It's been a pleasure doing business with you, young lady. You come back, you hear?"

"I definitely will. I like you. Bye," she said, waving at him and the other men watching her every move.

Now the first step was done. That gun dealer would probably never forget the blonde lady who flirted with him. Mary was still working out the next couple of steps in her brain, the brain everyone thought was damaged. She drove home and took off all her clothes and put them in a garbage bag, along with the wig and sunglasses, then put them in an empty suitcase in the attic. She had plans to use them again. Walking down the attic stairs, she realized it was getting close to dumb-down time again. The asshole was coming home from work in less than an hour.

CHAPTER 31
It's Housekeeping

It had been over three weeks since Mary got home from the hospital. Whenever she looked at her husband she cringed inside. Every little thing he did annoyed her. His fake smiles drove her crazy. Just washing his clothes almost made her gag. She picked up his dirty underwear to put in the washer with two fingers, then washed her hands. The lipstick on his work shirts didn't bother her any more. To her, he was a nobody.

There was no saving this marriage. She was able to avoid any issue around Connor with her sideshow of forgetfulness. Her projected dumbness also kept her out of making love to Tony, although he never really wanted her affections anyway. It was fun for her. He would say something at the dinner table and she would act like she didn't understand what he was talking about. Anything she wanted to avoid became possible with her acting skills.

That was the way she wanted it. She wanted to lay low and listen for the right time to follow through with her grand plan. She had tons of freedom because she was supposed to be going to aerobics. Mary could tell Tony she was going there any day of the week and he didn't care. It was like he wanted her to do anything instead of bothering him or spying on him. Those were the times she could get things done, like going to a gun shop over twenty miles away to buy the ammo she needed for her pistol, or taking up shooting lessons. The men at the shooting gallery knew her as Jo Bruce, the name she used every time she saw them, wearing her hat, sunglasses, and wig.

Once she learned how to use her gun and the silencer, she had completed step two in the program.

Tony had no idea Mary knew about anything that was discussed in her hospital room. She purposely left her pill minder on the kitchen counter. She would take the thyroid pill out of the plastic container, flush it down the toilet, then take a pill out of the original bottle that was hidden in her closet. Never again would she wonder if it was safe to take any medicine. No one ever mentioned gambling or Brenda Jean. Mary didn't care what he did now anyway, his time was drawing near.

One day on her way to aerobics, Mary stopped to get gas at a convenience store. After filling her tank, she went inside to get a cup of coffee and a doughnut. When she returned to her car, Brenda Jean pulled up in her VW in the next lane. As Mary started to open her car door, Brenda Jean reached over to pick up the gas hose. Their eyes met. Both of them had no choice but to acknowledge the meeting.

"Hello, Mrs. Calley, how are you?"

"I'm fine. Uh, do I know you, Missy?"

"I'm your husband's secretary, Mrs. Calley. My name is Brenda Jean."

"I thought I recognized you. Now I remember. You're the one whose boyfriend lives where, in Atlanta?"

Brenda Jean started to fill up her tank with gas. "No, he lives in Knoxville, and he's my fiancé."

"Oh, that's right. So, when is the wedding, Jean?" Mary asked, looking around the corner of the gas dispenser. "We haven't decided yet. We're looking at May sometime."

"That's nice. Well, I've got to go. I think I've got to go get some groceries for dinner. Say, one day it would be nice to have you over for dinner. We've got a nine-year-old I think you'd love to meet."

Brenda Jean put the gas hose back and pulled out her receipt. "I've already met Connor. He's a great kid."

"Oh...I don't remember that. Well, anyway, it was nice meeting you. I've got to go, goodbye, uh...Belinda."

"It's Brenda Jean, Mrs. Calley. I'll see you later."

Mary pulled away, chuckling inside. She knew she just gave the two lovebirds a lot to talk about. The trap was set even wider; now they really would let their guard down. They were getting ripe for the picking. This whole game was really getting to be fun. She was now ready for step three.

Step three was Mary's getting the final items for the plan. She found a post office in Nashville and rented a post office box, again using a fictitious name. On her way home, she stopped at a hotel near the interstate, casually walked into their customer's computer office, and Googled "handcuffs." She found a store in downtown Nashville that sold authentic police handcuffs, then wrote down their address. She Googled again, punching in "Devices to Track a Car's Location." There were dozens of companies online advertising mini-locators and GPS tracking devices, many of which would send a unit out for a next day delivery. She picked one, writing all the info on the same paper as the handcuffs source.

The next day Mary drove to the store that sold the handcuffs and bought two pairs, paying for them with cash. Then she bought a money order at a 7-Eleven for the amount of the GPS device and the overnight freight charge. She put the money order into an envelope with a small typed letter asking the company to send it to her post office box, along with the name she used to rent the box. Step three was now complete.

Step four was getting the opportunity to finish her plan. Somehow she had to create a story that convinced Tony and his mistress it would be safe for them to meet. Mary also knew that it was possible they wouldn't take the bait on her first attempt, but her so-called "air head" acting should give her as many chances as she needed. After she got the tracking device from her post office box, she realized how easy it was to install on Tony's Mercedes. All she had to do was put two AA batteries in it and attach it under his car to anything metallic, as it had a magnet on the bottom. She planted it one night after he went to sleep. After that was done, she was ready to set the trap.

The next day was Friday and Tony got home from work early. "Mary, I've got a monster headache. I'm going to lay down on the couch for a while."

"Oh, I'm sorry, sweety. Do you want some Tums?"

He shook his head, trying not to giggle. "No thanks; some aspirin might help, though."

"Okay, I'll get you some. What do you want to drink with them?"

"I don't care, just something cold," he responded as he took off his coat and tie and laid them on a nearby chair, then reached for the remote.

Mary went into the kitchen and poured him a half of a glass of lemonade, then filled up the rest of the glass with pickle juice and maple syrup, along with some ice cubes. She handed him his drink, anxious to see his reaction.

Tony threw three aspirins in his mouth, chugged almost half of his wife's homemade cocktail, then spit it out. "What the hell are you doing to me, Mary, trying to poison me?"

"Of course not. I fixed your drink like you always tell me too, with some surprises."

"Well, do me a favor, don't surprise me anymore. That tasted like shit. Where's Connor?"

"Oh, he's over at Hunter's house. He's spending the night there."

"Good. Then it'll be quiet here. What do you have planned for dinner?"

Mary sat down on the chair next to the couch with her hands on her knees. "I made you a homemade pizza. You know, the kind that comes in a box with dough and sauce. I haven't put it in the oven yet; I didn't expect you so early."

He ran his fingers through his hair. "I know, I should have called you. I'm starving. I didn't eat anything all day...oh, except for one glazed doughnut first thing this morning. That's probably why I have a headache. Why don't you put your pizza in the oven? You know, better yet, how about showing it to me before you cook it?"

"Sure, I'll go get it." She brought the circular pan filled with her homemade pizza out to her husband. It looked strange.

"That looks great, except for one thing...it doesn't have any sauce. You know, tomato sauce, the red stuff."

"Oh, that explains it. I thought that little can was gravy, and I knew you didn't want gravy on your pizza. But it kind of does look good with cheese on top of the dough, don't you think?"

Tony looked at her concoction, shaking his head. "Yeah, I like the cheese, but it really needs some kind of tomato sauce, Mary."

"Oops, sorry, I'll get the can out of the garbage. I never opened it. It'll be just fine, you'll see. I hope you don't think I'm stupid; it's just that it's been a while since I made a pizza."

"I can't wait to try it," he said, as he surfed channels on the TV. "So, how was your day, Mary?" he asked her as she was walking back to the kitchen.

"I'll be right there." Five minutes later she came back out to see her husband. "Boring as usual, except for the bug problem."

"What bug problem?"

She looked down at her feet, then to her left, like she was looking for something. "We've got a family of roaches living here now. I started to notice them all over. There was a couple under the sink and one in the downstairs bathroom, I've been chasing them all day with a flyswatter. I got tired, so I called a guy in the yellow pages. He's coming out in the morning, and he said he was going to set off some bombs in the house. The only thing we got to do is make sure there's no food left out."

"What time is he coming?"

"He'll be here at ten, if that's all right?"

"That sounds fine to me. But with this headache I'm going to be long gone when he gets here. At least I don't have to get up at dawn or anything. How long do we have to leave the house because of the roach bombs?"

"He said we couldn't come back until Sunday night, so I was wondering…how about the three of us going to see my parents for the weekend?" she asked, crossing her fingers behind her back.

"I don't know, they seem so cold and distant towards me lately. How about you go to see them, and I'll get a hotel room in town somewhere? Oh, and you can take Connor with you to keep you company."

"Are you sure you don't want to go with us? I don't know if I can get there without getting lost." She knew she was taking a chance asking him that.

He took in a deep breath, then let it out. "Why don't I just set your GPS in your car for your parent's address, and then all you and Connor have to do is follow the screen."

"You'd do that for me?"

"Sure, I wouldn't want you to get lost."

"Great. I'll go up and pack for me and Connor. I told him I'd pick him up sometime tomorrow; now I can surprise him when he gets in the car. Oh, why don't you pack your own bag? You know what you want."

Mary continued talking as she went up the stairs. "Now, let's see, Connor needs two pairs of socks and underwear and…." She snuck back down into the kitchen. Tony was talking on the phone. She hid behind the door going out to where he was, hearing him say that it would be a fun weekend and that he was going to show whoever he was talking to a great time. The trap was set. The mice were venturing out to play.

The next morning Tony left about nine thirty. Mary put her and Connor's clothes in her car, then went upstairs, pulled down the attic steps, and grabbed her preloaded duffel bag out from under some old suitcases. It was ready to go, with her gun, the silencer, some ammo, the handcuffs, and the receiver for the GPS tracking device, along with her hat and giant sunglasses, a complete set of clothes, and a camera. She put the bag in her back seat, then pulled three insect bombs she had bought at Lowes out from her trunk. She ignited them in the kitchen, the living room, and the laundry room. Finally, she jumped in her car and turned on the tracking device.

Mary called Hunter's mom, telling her she'd be there between one and two.

"Sure, you can pick him up anytime you want. He's such a great kid, we'd like to keep him. Just come get him whenever you want."

She wondered how long it would take Tony to meet Brenda Jean. Mary had set it up beautifully. He knew she approved of him getting a hotel room, and she'd be in Athens all weekend. It couldn't get much easier for Tony than that.

Mary pulled out of the garage and parked her car in front of a Wendy's about two miles away. She put on her new wig and her sunglasses. They were enormous, covering a lot of her face. She picked up the duffel bag, entered the lady's restroom at Wendy's, and changed her clothes. Once again, she had figured all the angles. No one could possibly ever recognize her. Who said she was brainless, or dumb?

She started to follow the GPS signal from the black device stuck under Tony's car. He was eight miles away, but he wasn't moving. When she got to within one mile, she pulled over and parked. Mary knew that one mile ahead was the mall, and there were no hotels anywhere close to the mall. She listened to the radio and periodically looking at the receiver. He still hadn't moved. Maybe he got into Brenda Jean's car at the mall. That would foul up everything, as his car was the only one she could track.

An hour later he was moving again, getting further and further away. She started up the Mustang, chasing the location shown on the device. She hit the gas pedal, starting to gain on him. Before long, he was only three miles away and was slowing down. Mary wondered if they had found their hotel for the weekend.

Tony stopped a half mile ahead. As she entered a curve, she saw a tall sign for a Holiday Inn and knew that must be their hotel. She was hoping Brenda Jean was with him, as she felt her heart starting to beat faster and faster. Then she saw them. Tony was walking out of the registration office and Brenda Jean was in the front seat of his Mercedes. They backed up, then turned around the corner, coming to a stop halfway down the parking lot in front of their room. There were two other vehicles parked next to the hotel on that side…an old black Cadillac about eight rooms closer to the office, and an oversized pickup truck ten to twelve spots further down the hotel from Tony's Mercedes.

Mary drove past the hotel, watching Tony unlock the door of a room directly in front of his car. She stopped a block away to try to get her heart under control. The moment she'd been waiting for was almost here, and it couldn't be more perfect. The hotel was basically empty…after all, it was one o'clock on a Saturday afternoon. She knew exactly what room they were in, it should be easy. But she could hardly breathe. Mary started to doubt if she could do it. Her hands were shaking uncontrollably, but she had to do it. It had to happen. She pulled the handcuffs out of her duffel bag, put them in the back pocket of her blue jeans, then double checked to be sure she had the key for them in her front pocket. After grabbing her gun, she screwed on the silencer and checked the magazine, making sure it was full. The last thing she needed was her camera, which she forced into the open front pocket of her jeans.

Mary drove by their room, trying to talk herself into following her plan, then drove around to the back of the hotel. She parked for a minute, looking at her gun sitting on the passenger seat. She knew she had to finish this. What was the worst thing that could happen? She'd get caught. So who could blame her for killing them? They were in a hotel room cheating on her. "You can do this; you can, you can do this," she said, taking in some deep breaths. She put the gun halfway under the waist of her jeans, just like she had practiced. Her oversized shirt hid it from view. After parking behind the big truck, she was hidden from both the highway and from Tony's car. Mary was ready. The handcuffs were in place, as was the key. The gun was where it should be, her sunglasses were perfect, and her blonde wig hair stuck out from under her hat. It had to be done now, everything was coming together.

She walked up to the door in front of Tony's Mercedes and knocked on it lightly. "Housekeeping," she said, in her charming southern accent, standing at the side in case one of them looked through the peephole.

"We don't need anything, we just checked in," Tony said without opening the door.

"It's housekeeping," Mary said again.

"Okay, okay, I'm coming," Tony hollered.

Mary could hear someone slide the chain lock to the side, then start to turn the door knob. Her chest felt like it was going to explode. She had to do this right. She pulled the gun out of her pants and held it against her chest. Tony opened the door and Mary put her gun in his face; he backed away. She motioned for him to move even farther back, then shut the door. Brenda Jean pulled the bed sheet up under her chin with her mouth open. She was in a frightened shock.

Tony raised his hands up. He was completely naked, as the towel he must have been wearing was on the floor next to the door. "Who are you and what do you want?"

"You don't know?" Mary said again in her southern drawl.

"No, I don't know. If you want money, I'll give you all I have, just don't shoot that thing." He took a step toward Mary. She cocked her gun, then he moved back again.

"I'm not going to hurt either one of you as long as you cooperate."

"Okay, what do you want?"

"Get back in bed with her now." He didn't move. "I said now." Mary raised her accented voice. He jumped into the bed next to his mistress.

Mary pulled out her camera. "All I want is some pictures." She pulled off her hat and pulled off the wig, causing her hair to fall to her shoulders. Then she removed the giant sunglasses.

"Oh, my God, it's Mary. Look, Brenda Jean, what the hell…? Mary, what are you doing? Now, listen honey, just give me that gun. We can talk about all this. You can't be serious. You don't even know how to use a gun. You want a picture, go ahead and take it, but give me that gun."

"Listen to me, scumbag. I've been taking shooting lessons for over a month. Nothing would make me happier than you trying to stop me so I could shoot you. But I have no intentions of hurting either one of you if you just do as I say. Brenda Jean, you better keep your mouth closed. I don't want to hear a sound out of either one of you until I get my pictures and leave, do you understand?"

Brenda Jean nodded.

"Okay, it must be clear to both of you why I want pictures. I know you've been screwing each other for months now, and I really don't give a damn. But I want to be able to take care of Connor right, so I'm going after everything we own—I mean everything—and these pictures should convince any judge what kind of shitheads you both are. Now take these, Brenda Jean," Mary said, throwing a pair of handcuffs on the bed next to her. "Tony, you turn around and let her put them on you. That's right, Brenda Jean, make sure they are good and tight. Good. Now you turn over so I can put them on you, too."

Tears were rolling down Brenda Jean's face. She was terrified, but she did as she was told, turning her naked body face down with her hands behind her back. Mary walked to the side of the bed and put the cuffs on her, making sure they were snug. "Okay, you all did good. Now Tony, I want you to get on top of her. Brenda Jean, you turn over so he can do his thing. You all are going to make me some x-rated pictures. No, don't worry about any sheets or blankets, these are going to be nude pictures of you all doing it, you got it? That's right. Now put it in like the stud you think you are. I'm going to get some close-ups."

They followed orders, then Mary walked up to them with a camera in one hand and her gun pointing at them in her other hand. "Now, smile, let's get some good shots."

She pointed the camera at the two lovebirds, snapping a picture with her left hand, then put her pistol about a foot away from her husband's temple and pulled the trigger. Blood oozed out of his head instantly. He was dead. Before Brenda Jean could scream, Mary shot her in the front of her neck. It worked out exactly as planned…even better. No one raised their voice or screamed. The silencer totally muted the rounds that went into the two assholes. Blood and brains were already streaming all over the white sheets underneath the two bodies.

Mary got the handcuff key and took the cuffs off, putting them back in her front pants pocket. She went into the bathroom and grabbed a white towel off a silver shelf over the toilet. She pushed her dead husband off his lover, and watched him roll off the bed onto the floor. After finding his billfold, she took all his money and put it with her camera and the gun into Brenda Jean's purse, then wiped the billfold clean before she threw it on her husband. She noticed it landed open with his men's club card showing.

Mary surveyed the entire room, thinking about what she may have touched. The only thing she thought she'd touched was the door when she closed it and his billfold. She put her hair back in a bun, put on her wig, hat, and sunglasses, then grabbed Brenda Jean's purse and walked to the door, rubbing down the entire back of it before she turned the door knob with the towel. She stepped out of the room onto the walkway, glancing both ways but not seeing anyone, then wiped the outside door knob clean and put the towel into the red purse. After putting the Do Not Disturb sign over the outside knob, Mary closed the door and went to the side of Tony's Mercedes, leaned down to remove the tracking device, then walked down the sidewalk to her Mustang that was still hidden behind the pickup.

The plan that was created in Mary's mind while she was in a coma had worked out perfectly. After all, she had rehearsed it thousands of times laying in that hospital bed. Every detail was planned down to the second. Now, no one would find Tony and his mistress until around noon the next day, and everyone would think it was a robbery. "Damn it, why didn't I tell them I wasn't really dumb and I heard everything that was said in intensive care? That would have been the icing on the cake," she lamented as she turned onto the highway in front of Holiday Inn.

CHAPTER 32
But Where's Daddy?

Mary drove back towards town, stopped at a Burger King, and parked near the back door. She walked in, carrying the duffel bag that contained her change of clothes and Brenda Jean's purse. She found the women's bathroom without anyone seeing her, changed back into her normal clothes, and put the colorful, oversized outfit, along with her wig and sunglasses, back into the duffel bag.

Ten minutes later she pulled onto Hunter's parents' driveway, walked up the sidewalk, and rang the doorbell. Almost instantly Connor came out, carrying a laundry bag full of clothes and Nerf guns he'd taken with him the night before.

Mary opened the screen door, peeking inside. "Thanks, Cindy, take care."

Cindy came out of the kitchen wiping her hands on a blue and white kitchen towel. "You bet, Mary; tell Connor we'll miss him. He was great, as usual. He always amazes us. You must be awful proud of him."

"You bet I am. Thanks again." She walked back to her car, opened the trunk, and filled it with Connor's overnight bag and the two suitcases and duffel bag from the back seat. Within three minutes, they were driving up the entry ramp to the interstate, heading towards Athens, Tennessee.

Connor put on his headphones, looking out the window. "Why are we going this way, Mommy?"

"I thought I'd surprise you. We're going to see your grandparents in Athens. The bug stuff is in our house, so we have to stay somewhere else. That's when I decided we'd go see MeeMaw and PeePaw."

"But where's Daddy? Isn't he coming too?"

"No, he's got too much work to do. He told me to tell you he loves you, but he can't come with us." She glanced at him through the side of her right eye to see his reaction. There was none.

The speed limit on the interstate was seventy miles an hour. Mary knew she had to make up some time to give her a foolproof alibi. She pushed on all cylinders of the Mustang, going over ninety. If she didn't have to stop, she'd get to her parent's house in less than two hours, making it impossible for her to have been at the Holiday Inn when they were shot.

She weaved in and out of traffic, speeding along for nearly an hour, when she spotted some flashing lights in her rear view mirror. "Shit, this ain't going to help at all," she said quietly as she slowed down. She looked at the clock. She left the hotel at one twenty, and now it was two twenty. Three fifteen was in the cards, but not with a state trooper slowing her down.

She reached to open the glove box to get her registration as she slowed down to sixty miles an hour, and the trooper flew by her. He wasn't after her; she was saved again. All the elements of her plan were falling into place. She pushed down hard on the gas pedal, and within two minutes she was back up to ninety five. They got to her parents' house at exactly two fifty. That was one hour and thirty-five minutes. She was even ahead of schedule.

Lacey and Paul were sitting on their front porch when Mary and Connor pulled up. They spread their arms to welcome their daughter and grandson as they stood up. The four of them walked up the sidewalk to the front porch in twos, with their arms wrapped around each together. Paul looked down at his daughter. "So, what brings you back over here? You're not having more problems with that husband of yours, are you?"

"Heavens no. We got a bug problem at the house, so I set some of those bomb-like things off and the cans said we had to leave for a couple of days. You know, so we either had to stay at some hotel or come by to see you. I think Tony had a lot of work to do so he's staying over there…I think. I'm not sure; I think that's what he said, I'm a little mixed up." She was acting even with her parents. "But we have to go home tomorrow night. Tony said he didn't mind if we came over without him."

"Of course he didn't mind. Now he can have total freedom all weekend. He's really something, you know that?" Paul asked.

She smiled and raised her shoulders. "Daddy, let's just have a fun weekend. Let's not worry about anyone but us. How about taking Connor fishing tomorrow…what do you say?"

Lacey stopped, then looked at her grandson. "How does that sound? You feel like going over to Lake Shrogram in the morning, sweetheart?"

"You bet. Are we going to take out Grandpa's boat?"

"What about that, honey?" Lacey asked as she turned back, looking at her husband.

"Sounds like a good plan to me."

That night the four of them played Monopoly on the family room floor next to the fireplace. Mary kept messing up, acting like she was confused. She kept shaking the dice and they would go anywhere; one time they even went into the fire. A little after ten, Paul and Lacey went to bed. Connor started playing with his 3D Nintendo, while Mary went out to her car and carried in the two suitcases and her duffel bag. She pulled out her Holiday Inn clothes, noticing a few spots of blood on her blouse, then put them back in the bag. Looking downstairs, she noticed Connor.

"Connor, honey, you get ready for bed. Go brush your teeth and get your pajamas on…they're in the blue suitcase."

"But Mom, it's Saturday. I don't want to go to bed this early."

"I didn't say anything about going to bed, I said get ready for bed. Now listen to me, do as I say, then you can play your video games in the room you normally sleep in when you're here. I don't care if you stay up until twelve, I just don't want you downstairs, keeping your grandparents awake, okay?"

"Okay."

Mary emptied the two suitcases into an empty chest of drawers next to the bed in her old bedroom. Lacey always insisted that Tony and Mary sleep in the same bedroom Mary grew up in whenever they came over.

She grabbed the duffel bag and took it downstairs, then found a pair of scissors in the junk drawer in the kitchen. She plopped down on a chair next to the fire, along with the bag full of souvenirs from her exciting Holiday Inn adventure. Mary spent the next two hours cutting the hat and clothes from the bag, as well as the bag itself, into strips, continually adding them to the flames in the fireplace. She pried open the disposable camera and pulled out the film, cutting it up as well. That left her with a gun, a purse that was still full, an empty camera, and two pairs of handcuffs. Almost everything in Brenda Jean's purse could be burned, including her billfold. Mary took all of her money and added it to the money from Tony's billfold, putting it all her pants pocket. She walked upstairs with a set of keys, a gun with a silencer on it, two pairs of handcuffs, and an unusable camera in the red purse. All the other evidence was destroyed, including the white towel.

The next morning Mary asked her parents if they could take care of Connor after he woke up, because she wanted to get her car washed. She had worried all night that there might be some blood in the Mustang somewhere. She took a bucket, a bottle of dish soap, and a sponge with her to the coin operated car wash on Twelve Oaks Boulevard in South Athens, carefully scrubbing every inch of her car, inside and out. Now all she had left to worry about was the purse and what was in it. Disposing of it was also part of her grand plan.

When she got back to her parents' house, her dad was connecting his boat to his truck. The boat normally sat on a trailer behind the house, but it looked like it was almost ready to go to the lake. Mary watched Paul hoist a handful of fishing poles over the side of the boat.

"Looks like you're about ready to go somewhere, huh Daddy?" He shook his head slightly, then answered her. "Nothing's better than taking my grandson and my baby girl fishing, if you know what I mean."

"I do. I remember when you took me when I was little. I know you loved it."

"Now, Mary, we've gone fishing a lot with you and Tony and Connor, don't you remember?"

She walked into the garage without answering, heading for the kitchen door, when she noticed a small stack of red bricks against the wall. She turned and looked at Paul, who was putting a quart of oil into the motor on the boat. Mary bent down and picked up a brick, put it under her sweatshirt, and held it there while she walked up the stairs to her room. She put it into Brenda Jean's purse with the rest of the unburnable items.

An hour later they got into Grandpa's truck. Mary was carrying the red purse. They slid the boat down the ramp at the lake and Paul pulled the trailer out, leaving his boat at the dock with Lacey holding the rope that was connected to the boat. Mary helped Connor get into the boat and get his life jacket on. Then she jumped in next to him.

Lacey watched Mary get into the boat. "Mary, where'd you get that purse? I've never seen that one before."

"Oh, this old thing? I've had it for years. When I left yesterday I saw it and thought it might come in handy, because it's so big and I thought we might go fishing. It's got my suntan lotion in case we go to the beach, and a change of clothes if I get wet. Remember the last time we went fishing, how we all decided to jump in the water because it was so hot? Now I'm prepared."

Lacey didn't respond. She had no idea what her daughter was talking about.

Paul took them out to the middle of Lake Shrogram and turned his motor off. The lake was way too deep for an anchor. Then he repeated his normal fishing story.

"Connor, do you know this is the exact spot I caught that twelve pound trout? Yep, right here. I'm the only one who knows how to find the right spot. Look over there," he said, pointing to the north. "Do you see that long shadow on the lake from that monster pine tree? Well, when that shadow points directly at us and the one over there to the south points this way, all you have to do is go exactly to the middle of the lake and figure out where they would intersect, and that's where the big fish holes are."

"We know, Grandpa, an old Indian told you that, right? The one whose brother died trying to swim across the lake to his lover. And that's why the middle is three miles deep, because he drowned and all the Indians' tears filled it up."

"You remembered. Great job, Connor."

"I don't know how deep it is, but it's really cold, dark water," Mary said, as she made mini waves with her hands over the side of the boat. She looked back, watching her father straighten out the fishing poles while Lacey was looking through his tackle box. Connor was playing with his Nintendo, waiting for the fishing to start. The time was perfect. Mary leaned over, putting her chest on the side of the boat as if she was looking into the depths of the grand old lake. With her right hand, she reached down and grabbed the purse, quietly putting it over the side of the boat, helping it start to sink to a three mile deep grave. Now, everything was taken care of, everything was covered up.

Mary felt like a five hundred pound weight was pulled off her back. It looked like she'd gotten away with what she wanted to do all along, commit the perfect crime and get rid of her husband and his whore. She started fishing with her parents and her son, and she no longer had any worries. They ended up catching five bluegills and two bass. "Not a bad day's work, I'd say," Paul said as he lifted the stringer of fish up and put them in the boat so they could get back before dark. Mary laid back on the little seat on the front of the boat with her arms stretched out and lowered into the cool, dark water. Then her cell phone rang.

"Where's my purse?" Mary asked, looking around and under the aluminum seats. "Has anyone seen my purse? My phone is ringing."

"Your cell phone isn't in your purse, Mommy, it's right here." Connor handed her the phone that was sitting next to her.

She looked to see who was calling, but didn't recognize the number. "Hello."

"Mary, this is Ron Burns."

"Well, hello stranger, how are you?"

"Not so good, Mary." He sighed. "I'm so sorry I have to tell you this."

"Tell me what?"

"We just found out that Tony is dead. He was murdered."

"What? What? Daddy," she screamed. "Daddy, I can't...." She handed her father the phone and grabbed Connor, sobbing.

"This is Mary's father. What's going on?"

"This is Ron Burns. I'm Tony Calley's partner. Sir, Tony is dead. The police found him this afternoon in a very bloody hotel room."

"Oh my God, what happened?"

"They said on the news he was with a woman and they were both shot. It looks like a robbery. The cops think it happened sometime last night. Are you at Tony's place?"

"No, Mary and Connor are with us over in Athens. Oh my God, can I call you back? Is the number on my phone your cell number?"

"Yes it is, call me anytime. I'm real sorry for the bad news, especially for Mary and Connor. When you can talk to Mary, tell her me and my wife are praying for her and that we love her."

Paul set the phone down and went to the front of the boat. Mary was shaking. He put his arms around her, patting her head, whispering to her what he knew. "Lacey, you drive the boat back, will you? I want to stay here with my little girl."

Lacey turned and sat in front of the motor. She looked bewildered, as did Connor. All they heard were pieces of a conversation. What had happened? She shook her head and pulled on the starter rope.

Ten minutes later, they were back on shore. Mary got out of the boat and fell to the ground, hollering for Connor. She put her arms around her little guy and whispered to him as calmly as she could what the phone call was about.

Connor started screaming. "Daddy, no, Daddy, no, Daddy, no!"

Paul told Lacey what he'd learned from his conversation with Ron Burns. She didn't know which way to go, to her baby daughter or to her beautiful grandson. Paul got on the ground, putting an arm around Mary, so Lacey went to Connor, but she couldn't stop him from screaming. It was a terrible scene on the shoreline of Lake Shrogram, near the boat ramp.

"Give me the phone. Give me the phone, oh my God, this can't be happening," Mary said, extending her arm towards her mother.

Lacey picked up the phone that was only about four feet from Mary and handed it to her. She was shaking as she hit the call back button. "Ron, oh Ron, please tell me this is a bad dream. Tony can't be dead, he can't."

"I'm sorry, Mary, but he is. He died sometime last night."

She screamed again. A minute later, she tried again. "What happened, was he in an accident?"

"I hate to be the one to tell you this, Mary, but he was shot in the head by someone who robbed him."

"What do you mean?"

"You're going to have to hear this from someone, so I guess I need to be the one to tell you. He was at a hotel with his secretary last night, and that's where he died."

"You mean Brenda Jean?"

"Yes. The police say they were robbed and then someone shot them."

"Is she dead, too?"

"Yes, she is."

"Oh, my God. Oh my God, Ron. When did this happen? I just saw him yesterday morning."

"The guy on the news said they think it was sometime last night. I guess it was awfully bloody in that hotel room. I heard they're asking anyone who was at that hotel yesterday to call the cops."

"Holy shit, I can't believe this. Now I've got to bury my husband who was at a hotel with his secretary. You know, part of me is embarrassed, really embarrassed. But Ron, I want him back; no matter what he was doing or who he was doing it with, I want him back...." She started sobbing again, throwing the phone across the grass. Once again, she deserved an academy award. She was great. She knew that and she didn't care about anyone else.

Lacey walked over and picked up the phone. "Hello?"

"Hello, is this Mary's mom?"

"Yeah, I'm Lacey. You must be Ron. Well, Ron, what do you think we should do now?"

"I think you all need to come back. I'll be here to help, but Mary's got a lot on her plate now. Yeah, she needs to come home."

"You're right. Let me talk to my husband, I'm sure we'll be on the road in about an hour. We should get to Mary's house around nine." They took two vehicles back to Rymont. Paul drove the Mustang with Mary and Connor in the back seat. It was a quiet ride, as Mary held on to a crying Connor the entire drive. When Paul finally got to the Calley residence, there were five television news vans parked along the street, along with two blue police cruisers. He put his arm around his daughter and his grandson on their way to the back door by the kitchen.

Lacey parked Paul's truck on the street in front of the neighbors, as there was no room left on the driveway or on the street in front of the house. As she walked to the front door, she was besieged by reporters screaming questions at her.

The four of them met in the kitchen. The whole house spelled like insecticides. "Man, that was something," Paul said. "What the hell is that smell?"

Mary wiped her eyes with her sleeve. "We got roaches. Remember, I told you we came over to see you because we couldn't stay here. We set off some bug bombs yesterday morning. I think it was yesterday…I can't remember. Yeah, yesterday. Anyway, we set them off and left."

"Let me get those picked up," Paul said to Mary. He found all three of the empty insecticide containers, then threw them in the trash can just as there was a knock on the front door. He looked around the corner, seeing a bright silver badge reflecting the porch light. Two policemen were waiting for someone to respond. Paul opened the door.

"Who are you?" The burly-chested cop with a handle-bar mustache asked.

"I'm Mary Calley's father. What can I do for you?"

"We need to ask Mrs. Calley a few questions. Is she home?"

"Listen, she just found out her husband got killed. Can't you give her a little time before you talk to her?"

"I'm sorry, but we're working hard on this case; every minute counts. For all we know, the killer or killers are already out of the state. Please ask her if she can answer just a couple of questions. We'll be gentle, I promise."

Paul pushed open the front door. "Here, come on in. I'll get her."

The two policeman walked in, closing the door behind them.

A minute later, Mary came out to the family room. She was a wreck. Her makeup had rolled down her face with her tears. Her eyes were bloodshot and her hair looked like it had never been brushed. "Hello," she said to the cops without looking at them.

"Mrs. Calley, do you feel up to answering a couple of questions? We know it's not a great time for this, but we don't want to lose a single minute of our investigation into who killed your husband."

"Okay…uh, do you want to sit down?" Mary asked as she sat on her couch, followed by her father. One cop sat on the end of the couch and the other sat on a nearby chair. The one on the couch was obviously in charge. He pulled a little black notebook out his front shirt pocket, along with a pen. He flipped the cover over on the notebook, then looked at Mary. "Mrs. Calley, first of all, we want to say how sorry we are for your loss. And we know how tragic this is for you, especially with all the circumstances involved. But like I told your dad, we want to solve this while the trail is still hot, if you know what I mean."

"What do you mean, a trail?"

He looked at her, then at Paul, then back to her. "Mrs. Calley, someone killed your husband last night and we want to find who that was. That's why we're here, to see if you can help us before the killer gets too far away."

"Uh, okay, I'm sorry, I just didn't understand what a trail meant." He looked around the family room.

"Okay, before I start, what's that smell?"

"They had to set off some bug bombs to kill some roaches," Paul said.

"Uh huh. Now Mrs. Calley, I have to ask you some touchy questions…I hope you understand? After all, this is not a simple case. First off, did you have any idea your husband was meeting his secretary at a hotel?"

"Of course not," she answered, wiping the tip of her nose with a very wet tissue.

"Did you know they were having an affair?"

"Not really, but I knew something might be going on. We've been married a long time so I knew Tony real well. Something was happening in his life; I didn't know what it was, but I could sense a change. Oh, I don't know, it's all so hard to understand…uh…I don't know. Everything is so blurry since I got out of the hospital. When was that, Dad?"

"That was about a month ago, honey." He turned to look at the cop. "Mary has a little problem remembering everything. She was in a coma for about a week and she suffered a little brain damage."

"Oh, okay," the policeman said. "Mrs. Calley, just for our records, where were you last night?"

"I was with my mom and dad in…now, ah, that was…yeah, in Athens. We had to go somewhere because of the roach bombs, so I took my son over to see them." She nodded. "We spent the night over there."

"About what time did you leave to go to Athens?"

"I left to go get Connor right after I set the bombs off. I think it was about ten or so." She wiped the corner of her eye with that tissue. "I had to fill up with gas, so I'd say I got him before…uh…eleven, and we got to Mom and Dad's around one thirty or a little before that. I'm not sure; yeah, it was about one thirty our time, or two thirty their time. They're only about two or three hours away, but they're in another time zone."

"And why didn't your husband go with you?"

"To tell you the truth, he doesn't like my folks very much and they don't like him either. So, he told me he had a lot of work to do and he wanted to go to the post office and just get some stamps for some work stuff." She started crying again.

The cop turned to Paul. "Sir, what's your name?"

"Paul Joseph Hudson."

"And what's your address, Mr. Hudson?"

"10220 Bekinstone Lane, Athens, Tennessee."

"And can you verify what your daughter just said, that she spent the night at your house last night and she got there around two thirty your time?"

"I can. So can my wife."

He flipped a page in his notebook, looking at Mary. "Just a few more questions, Mrs. Calley, do you mind?"

"No, I sure don't, I don't."

"Okay, do you know if anyone else you know might have known he was going to spend last night in a hotel?"

"No."

"Do you have any idea how much cash he had on him yesterday?"

"No, I never know that. But he always has a lot, why?"

"We found his wallet and it was empty, and the girl he was with didn't even have an ID. They took all his money and all of her information. We didn't even know who the woman was until we found her cell phone in your husband's car. First we thought she might have been a prostitute until we dug enough to find out she worked for him."

"Can I ask you a question?" Mary asked.

"Sure, go ahead."

"Did he suffer? I mean, I couldn't stand it if he suffered."

"No, he didn't suffer. He was shot once at point blank range. He didn't feel a thing."

The policemen stood up, extending their hands to both Mary and her father. They all shook hands. The policeman who didn't say a word during the interview finally asked her a question. "Mrs. Calley, if you can think of anything else, please call at this number, will you?" He handed her a business card.

"Thank you officers, let me help you out," Paul said.

The bigger cop stopped before they opened the front door, looking at Paul. "Has she been like this the whole time since she got of the hospital?"

"Oh, she has good days and bad days. I'd say this is an average day. The doctors say it's likely that the way she is now is how she'll be forever."

"So, why did she go into a coma?"

"She has a bad thyroid and she missed taking her pills for a week and it almost killed her. We're okay with how she is now; at least she's happy most of the time, but she's taking Tony's death very hard." He patted the policeman on the back as he opened the door. "Say, can you do us all a big favor? Is there any way you can get all these reporters away from here? They're making my wife and Mary very nervous."

The burly cop spoke up. "I'm sorry, but I can't do that. It's their first amendment right. Now, I can give them trespassing warnings if you want, that's about all, but I don't think that will scare them off. I'll tell you what I will do, I'll tell them that no one will be coming out anymore tonight. Maybe then they'll leave. Goodnight." He tipped his hat towards Paul.

The crowd in front of the house didn't go home. The double murder at the Holiday Inn was the biggest thing that had ever happened in Rymont, Tennessee. The news folks and the police weren't about to let all this fun go away that easily.

CHAPTER 33
That's the End of That Story

The next morning when Paul walked out to the front sidewalk to grab the newspaper, he noticed that there was only one television news van still sitting on the street in front of the house. As soon as he picked up the paper, a very skinny middle aged man jumped out of the van and trotted as fast as he could, trying to button his shirt and catch up to Paul.

"Excuse me, sir, can I ask you some questions?" Paul had made it almost all the way to the front door. He turned around and looked at the pleading reporter, who was out of breath, bent over with his hands on his knees. "Were you talking to me?"

"Come on, give me a break, will you? I don't want to bug you, but this is a big story, and I sure could use a quote or two, please? Or even better yet, how about if we have a five minute interview on tape? My camera man is…." He looked around, seeing no one. "Where the hell is George?"

"Listen, it's not my place to say anything. This is about my daughter and her family. I will tell you that she's in shock and she really needs to be left alone. I'm sure you understand. If you want to do anything to help, please pray for her, okay? Thank you." Paul gave the poor guy a half smile and opened the front door.

"Did Mrs. Calley know about her husband's affair with his secretary?"

Paul looked back again. "I don't have any more comments. Please leave us alone. I've told you all I can, goodbye." He shut the door behind him, finding Lacey looking out around the curtains on the front window.

"What did he want, Paul?"

"Oh, he wanted to know if Mary knew about Tony's affair. I told him I didn't have anything to say. I can see why this story is so big here. I mean, a top financial advisor was killed with his secretary in a hotel room, while his wife and son were over in Athens. It sounds like a great novel or an incredible movie. Anyway, did you make some coffee?"

"It's about done, Paul. Why don't you come out in the kitchen and we'll look at the paper together?"

Paul pulled the paper out of the plastic bag and spread it open as he walked towards the sweet smell of brewing coffee. The entire front page was about the murders. The enlarged headline read "Local Businessman Killed In Hotel With Secretary." Just below the headline were three pictures side by side...a picture of Tony, one of Brenda Jean, and one of the bloody hotel room. He sat down at the kitchen table and laid the paper out so he could share the article with Lacey. They sipped on their coffee as they read the entire story, shaking their heads a number of times. "That son of a bitch, he got what he deserved," Paul said, just before he finished reading.

Lacey looked at her husband. "That's not right. Just think what Mary and Connor are going through. I know he was an asshole...I mean, he was in a hotel with his secretary while his wife was out of town. Her mind's not right because of the coma, but you could tell yesterday her heart was broken, despite Tony having an affair. No, I think it's awful, just because of her and Connor. That little boy doesn't have a daddy now. His world is turned upside down, that's for sure. I could care less about Tony. It might be a while before our beautiful daughter understands everything, honey. I feel so sorry for her."

"What do you all mean, understands everything?" Mary asked as she came around the corner.

Lacey looked at her husband, then at her little girl. "I mean, who would have guessed Tony was cheating on you? It's hard to figure. Every time I saw him with you, it looked like you were head over heels in love."

"That's what I thought, too, Mom. They sure fooled me."

Paul looked up from the paper. "What do you mean?"

"I mean, they both made a big deal about Brenda Jean having a fiancé in Knoxville and getting married sometime soon. I guess that was just a cover up. I really wish he never would have hired her when...what was her name? Whatever...when his other secretary left." Mary remembered to throw in some show time tidbits. "Why would he do this to me, Mom?" she asked, putting her arms around Lacey. "Poor Connor, poor Connor. You all have to help me with him."

"We will," her mother responded, patting her on the back.

For the next two days Mary and Connor and his grandparents stayed inside the house. They only opened the front door to let friends in. There were TV vans parked in front of the house awaiting any news they could get, but there were less of them every day. Finally, when they woke up on the third day after the murders, no one was around. That was the day they had to go to the funeral parlor. Mary held Connor's hand as they moved up the green carpeted stairs of the Wilson and Bayone Funeral Home. When they walked in the door, they noticed a black sign with adjustable white letters in a standing frame that had Tony's name on it. Everything was being prepared for the visitation that night. They were offered an opportunity to look at Tony's body. "We really did a good job with him," the man in the black suit said.

Everyone was silent for a few seconds. Finally, Mary spoke up. "Daddy, why don't you go look at him first? Then you tell us if it's okay. After all, he got shot."

"If that's what you want, honey," Paul said, and he was led into another room. The casket was open and Paul walked over to look at his son-in-law. Tony looked somewhat normal, except he was much whiter than usual.

The man in the black suit stood next to Paul. "This was a tricky one. I mean, with the autopsy and all, and the bullet holes. Did you know a bullet went all the way through his skull? It was really a mess. We had to do a lot of patch work on him. But he's presentable, wouldn't you say?"

Even as much as Paul hated Tony and wasn't sorry to see him dead, the parlor guy seemed so cold. "I think you all did great. I'll tell my daughter everything's okay. Say, who picked out the casket?"

"That's just a loaner. Mrs. Calley told us yesterday her husband wanted to be cremated. As soon as she signs the paperwork, we'll get it set up."

Paul was surprised. There had been no discussion about cremation since Tony died. But he didn't care. He just wanted to get the whole thing over with. Lacey, Mary, and Connor finally saw Tony. Mary gave them another award-winning performance, sobbing when she first walked up to his coffin.

They got through the day and into the evening, finally getting to the visitation. Mary was getting very tired with all the friends and relatives that came by to see her. One lady with pinkish hair walked over to Mary as she stood in the corner looking at the names on the flower arrangements. "Mrs. Calley, I am so sorry for your loss," she said, shaking Mary's hand.

Mary looked into her eyes. The lady really was in pain as she tried to find a small smile, but couldn't. She lowered her head, trying to find any words to give to Mary.

"Thank you for coming," Mary said. "I'm sorry, but do I know you?"

"No, this is the first time we've ever met. But I'm so sorry. You see, I'm Patty Sanders; Brenda Jean Sanders was my daughter. I didn't know if

I'd come over here tonight, but I decided we both had our world destroyed last weekend and we kind of needed each other, but I also thought you might be mad at me."

"Why would you say that? It's not your fault. It just happened. I'm sorry for you, too. It's all so incredible, but thanks for coming, I really do appreciate it."

The woman walked away and headed out the door. She turned around, glancing back at Mary, who nodded at her. They both were okay with each other.

The next day, at the funeral, Mary had to do it all over again. She couldn't wait until it was over. At least there wasn't a procession to the cemetery, with her husband being cremated after the service. An overweight man wearing a pinstriped suit walked up to her outside the funeral parlor as everyone was leaving. His face was loaded with long deep wrinkles that made him look much older than he really was. He put his hand out to Mary. "Mrs. Calley, my name is Captain Summers. I'm from the Rymont Police Department. I was wondering if I could come by and see you tomorrow or the next day? I have a few loose ends to tie up about your husband's murder. Would that be okay?"

"Of course; now what's your name again?" she asked.

"It's Summers, Captain Kevin Summers."

"Do you know where I…I mean, where we live?"

"Yeah, I've got your address. How about if I come over there about two tomorrow afternoon?"

"That should be fine."

He shook her hand again. "I'll see you then." He turned and walked away. That night Mary started thinking about what that police captain wanted. Had she forgotten something? Maybe there were some outside video cameras at the hotel. But why would it take so long for the cops to find anything? She really had to play dumb for Captain Summers. It was time to practice again.

She walked out to the front porch, sitting on the swing next to her mother. "Hey, Mom, what time is it?"

Lacey looked at her watch. "It's ten after eight."

Mary thought for a minute. "Is that AM or PM?"

Paul put down the paper he was reading and looked at his daughter. "Huh? What do you mean?"

Mary looked up at the street light. "I was just wondering if we were going to be late getting to Grandma's funeral, that's all."

Paul and Lacey both shook their heads. They didn't say anything.

Connor came out and sat on his grandfather's lap. Mary smiled at her son, motioning for him to sit next to her. She pushed her mother over so hard she fell off the swing.

"Are you all right, Mom?"

Lacey grabbed the chain holding the swing and pulled herself up. "Yeah, I'm okay, Mary. Why did you push me so hard?"

"I'm sorry, Mom. That was an accident. I forgot how strong you are."

Connor finally sat next to his mother. "Hi Mommy."

"Hey, little guy. I didn't see you come home. How was school today?"

He looked up at his mother. "Mom, I didn't have no school today, remember?"

"Oh, uh, okay. Mommy's sorry, she's just a little mixed up."

Paul glanced over his paper at Lacey. "She's really having a tough night, huh? Maybe the pressure of the funeral made her thought process even worse."

Lacey brushed herself off. "I don't know, but I'm going inside, and I think you should join me, honey."

****

They went inside to sit in front of the fireplace. "What are we going to do, Paul? Do you really think she's going to be like this the rest of her life?"

"I don't know, but we've got to give her some time. Remember what the doctors told us after her coma? We got to accept some changes. Lacey, I really want to go home, but I think she's going to need our help for a while. I mean, what if she puts something stupid in the microwave and burns the house down? What should we do?"

"Why don't we leave notes around stuff? Like being sure she turns the oven off after she cooks something, or a note in the bathrooms not to have any electrical item near the bathtub, stuff like that. We can probably get everything dangerous on notes for the whole house, and maybe then we can go home on Sunday. What do you think?"

"Okay, I'll start doing that tomorrow, honey."

****

The next morning Mary woke up to the wonderful smell of bacon frying. She put on her robe and slid her feet into her slippers, then walked into the bathroom. "Today's a big day. I need to be real forgetful for that cop," she whispered as she looked in the mirror. "Wow, you look rough. Let's take a long shower, okay?"

After getting cleaned up and dressed, Mary got downstairs and found the rest of her family sitting around a kitchen table full of fried eggs, bacon, sausage, pancakes, toast, and homemade biscuits, along with milk and orange juice. "Wow, Mom, you got enough here to feed the whole county. What made you decide to cook so much?"

"Oh, I don't know; I got started and couldn't quit."

"That's wonderful, Mom. Only thing is, who's going to clean this mess up when we're done eating?"

"We'll do it," Paul said. "Mary, I need to let you know I'm going to put some notes up all over the place reminding you of some things so you don't hurt yourself, if that's okay with you."

Mary put a forkful of eggs into her mouth, then patted her chest. "Uh, I don't care, if that's what you want to do, but I was hoping you'd do me a big favor today."

"Sure, honey, what is it?"

"I wanted you to get all of Tony's stuff together and take it to the cleaners so we can drive it over to Goodwill." She poured herself a cup of coffee, awaiting his answer.

"Honey, I'll be glad to take his things to Goodwill, but we don't need to take it all to the cleaners first."

"No, Daddy, I want everything looking new. I even want to get all his shoes shined before we give them away, too."

Paul rolled his eyes. "Sure, honey, I'll start on that tomorrow. I want to get all those reminders up for you first."

Lacey and Paul spent the rest of the morning putting up stick-on notes. The house looked like a yellow parade went through it. At two fifteen, the front doorbell rang. Connor pulled open the door, and found Captain Summers standing there with his hat under his arm, carrying a small briefcase. "Hello, young man, is your mother here?"

"I'll get her."

Mary came to the door and greeted the captain. "Can I help you?"

"Mrs. Calley, I met you yesterday, don't you remember? I'm Captain Summers." He handed her a business card. "I'm sorry, Captain...," she looked down at his card, "Captain Summer. I met a lot of people yesterday. My husband's funeral was yesterday."

Summers scratched his half-bald head. "Can I come in?"

"Sure, be my guest," Mary answered, gesturing for him to sit down on the couch.

Paul and Lacey walked into the living room, trying to figure out why a cop was there. "So, what can we do for you?" Paul asked Summers, as he sat next to him on the couch.

"I wanted to ask Mrs. Calley some questions about her husband. We still have a live case going on, and I'm sure you all want us to find his killer."

"To tell you the truth, I really don't care what you do, or if you find the killer. Tony was an asshole. I guess it would be right to find out who killed him and his secretary, but speaking for myself, I don't give a shit. He was a terrible son-in-law."

"Paul, don't be so vengeful," Lacey added. "And don't let Connor hear any of that." She looked around. "Where is he, anyway?"

"I think he went up to his room," Mary answered. "Okay, Corporal Summer, what can I help you with?"

"It's Captain Summers, not Corporal Summer, Mrs. Calley…it's Captain Summers. Can we talk in private?"

Paul shook his head. "No way. Just take a look around. Do you see all the stick-on notes? That's because we have to help Mary with everything. If you were a good cop, you already would have known my daughter came out of a coma last month with some issues. No, me and her mother need to be right here with her."

Summers took in a big breath while he raised his shoulders. "All right, I still have some questions for her, but you can stay."

He looked at Mary before he pulled a legal pad out of his briefcase. "First off, Mary, how well did you know your husband's secretary?"

"Not very well. I met her a couple of times. She seemed real nice, but I mostly stayed away from Tony's office."

"And why was that?"

She looked puzzled. "I just got my own world and it's not in an office."

"Uh huh, okay. What kind of a car do you drive?"

"A Mustang."

"Can I take a peek at it?"

"What the hell does this have to do with anything?" Paul asked.

"That's okay, Daddy, he can look at it." She turned back to Summers. "I'll show you." She took him through the kitchen and opened the garage door. He stepped down into the garage and walked around her car, looking closely at the door handles, even rubbing his fingers against them.

"Thank you, Mrs. Calley, that's good enough. I've seen all I need to see. Mrs. Calley, can we go back inside?" he said, wiping his hands on a white handkerchief. "Let's go back inside."

They re-entered the living room, finding the same seats they'd left a few minutes earlier. "Mrs. Calley, do you own a gun?"

"A gun? Sure, I got a gun. Oh, I mean my son's got a gun…he's got a lot of guns. They're called Nerf guns; he collects them."

"No, I mean do you own a real gun yourself?"

"What would I need a gun for, Corporal? No, I don't have a gun."

He shook his head, giving up correcting her about his name and rank. "Okay, Mrs. Calley, so that means you never took any shooting lessons, huh?"

"How do I do that?"

Summers lowered his head, sighing. "I understand Mr. Calley was cremated the same day as the visitation. Was that what he wanted?"

Mary looked puzzled. "Yeah, uh, he always said that, didn't he, Mom?"

Lacey looked at Mary, then to the captain. "Yeah, that's right."

"Mrs. Calley, I would like to take your picture. Do you mind?"

"I don't ever mind that. I like picture-taking. Do you want my parents in the picture, too?"

"No, just you. Do me a favor and hold all your hair back so I just get a picture of your face."

She did as he asked and he took her picture with a disposable camera he'd taken out of his briefcase. "Do you like to take pictures, Mrs. Calley?"

"I guess. But I'm not too good with a camera. They kind of confuse me."

"Oh, I meant to ask you something. When you drive over to Athens, how fast do you usually go?"

"I don't know. Oh, about fifty-five I guess. I try to be as careful as I can, especially with my son in the car."

Paul stood up. "What is going on? All you are doing is mixing her up. Are you going to tell me what you're doing?"

"I'm just doing my job, that's all. We've got a few missing links in this case and I was hoping Mary could help me figure some of them out."

"So why would you want to look at her car and take a picture of her, or ask her about guns, or driving to Athens? It almost sounds like you think she did it."

"I'm not saying anyone did it. It's just that when a man gets shot in a hotel with his mistress, one would think to ask his wife some questions."

"Well, you asked your questions. Now go, will you? You can see Mary is under the weather a little bit. Why don't you leave her alone? Hell, she was in Athens for hours and hours before Tony got killed. That should be enough."

"You're right, that's enough. I think I will go." He shook Mary's hand. "I'm sorry if I inconvenienced you in any way, Mrs. Calley. I was just doing my job."

"That's okay, Mr. Summer. You didn't bother me."

The captain put his hat under his arm, grabbed his briefcase, then let himself out.

Mary and her parents sat quietly in the living room for ten minutes after the intruder left, thinking what was said, hoping that the hotel killings were now finally history and no one else would bother Mary.

On Sunday, Paul and Lacey left as planned. All of Tony's stuff was out of the house. Paul evened cleaned out the garage and the attic, removing any sign that Tony Calley had ever lived there. After they left, Mary put her arm around her son and walked him back into their house.

The next morning, two men came to see Mary, an hour apart. They both made a big difference in her life. At ten thirty Bo Foster from Foster and James Insurance brought her some forms to sign, authorizing the payment to her of two million dollars. She was shocked, having no idea that Tony had doubled their coverage. At least he'd done something right for her, without trying to. She had no doubt he'd changed the policy because he planned on killing her, but now she was the beneficiary, not him. It made her giggle a lit bit inside. She gave him a copy of the death certificate, and he told her she would have her check in two weeks. It was a wonderful surprise, but she didn't want to show her excitement. But after he left, she watched him through the curtains as his car drove out of sight, then she spread her arms out, screaming, "Yes!"

At eleven thirty, Captain Summers knocked on the door. She had just gone through a shocker with Bo. So, now, what did he want? What was next?

"Good morning, Mrs. Calley."

"Hello."

"Mrs. Calley, I wanted to come by and see you today. I'm sorry I bothered you before. I did some thinking last night and I can't imagine everything you've gone through. First you were in a coma, and I've been thinking maybe that was caused by someone else. I guess you almost died. Then your husband is having an affair, gets killed with his secretary, with the story filling up all the news channels and papers. That had to be terrible for you. Your poor little boy lost his dad, and you've lost a lot of your memory. Anyway, I just wanted to let you know that as long as I'm around, no one from my department is ever going to bug you again, about any of this. The way I look at it, you've had your share and it's time to leave you alone. As far as I'm concerned, that's the end of that story."

"Thank you, Captain Summers," Mary said, watching him heading towards his car.

He turned totally around, noticing she'd called him by his right rank and name for the first time. He gave her a little smile and a wink, then shook his head as he got into his police car. She walked back to her porch, deciding it was time for her to act only half-dumb.

E. G. LANDER

The End

ABOUT THE AUTHOR

E.G. Lander grew up in northern Minnesota on a fishing resort owned by his family, deep in the heart of a Chippewa Indian reservation. There wasn't a television, a radio, or even a telephone for miles. E.G.'s father entertained his guests by hosting hour-long storytelling events. That's when he decided that one day he would become a teller of stories too, and write...after college and a 35 year career with Walgreens. So that's exactly what he did- he began his second career- the writing one.

Lander's first work was an 87,000 word murder/mystery with a family saga backdrop called *What's in the Rear View Mirror?* (Published by World Castle Publishers). It became a number 1 best seller in October 2014.

E.G. then completed his next manuscript, a 32,000 word project entitled *An Email From God,* a true story of how God performed miracles in his life after his beloved wife Nancy died. This is being published by Sarah Books.

The next novel was *The Incredible Bucky Berrot,* the story of an unbelievable little hero in the hidden woods of western Australia. This 67,000 word fantasy is designed for readers of all ages, with lessons for everyone. It's co-authored with E.G.'s ten-year-old grandson Connor, giving a child's view of the Berrot world. This was published by Sarah Books, and it too became a #1 best seller in February 2015.

Then came *Damn It, Wake Me Up,* set in Nashville, Tennessee. It's the 118,000 word story of an All-American family that becomes unraveled when the husband (Tony) gambles away everything they have. Tony and his girlfriend decide to kill his wife for the life insurance and manipulate her medicine, leaving her in a coma. What happens to her is amazing and leads to incredible developments that sends everything spiraling towards total destruction. This was also published by World Castle Publishing and became a #1 best seller in April 2015.

E.G. lives in a small community on a river in Tennessee with his two grandbabies, Connor and Kaylee. He shares everything with them, even his stories, starting with his days on that resort in Minnesota.